About the Author

Cathy Williams can remember reading Mills & Boon Modern books as a teenager, and now that she is writing them she remains an avid fan. For her, there is nothing like creating romantic stories and engaging plots, and each and every book is a new adventure. Cathy lives in London, and her three daughters—Charlotte, Olivia and Emma—have always been, and continue to be, the greatest inspirations in her life.

Louise Fuller was a tomboy who hated pink and always wanted to be the prince—not the princess! Now she enjoys creating heroines who aren't pretty pushovers but are strong, believable women. Before writing for Mills & Boon she studied literature and philosophy at university and then worked as a reporter on her local newspaper. She lives in Tunbridge Wells with her impossibly handsome husband, Patrick, and their six children

Jennifer Hayward has been a fan of romance since filching her sister's novels to escape her teenage angst. Her career in journalism and PR—including years of working alongside powerful, charismatic CEOs and travelling the world—has provided her with perfect fodder for the fast-paced, sexy stories she likes to write—always with a touch of humour. A native of Canada's east coast, Jennifer lives in Toronto with her Viking husband and young Viking-in-training.

The Love Islands

COLLECTION

March 2019

April 2019

May 2019

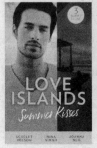

June 2019

July 2019

August 2019

Love Islands: Passionate Nights

CATHY WILLIAMS

LOUISE FULLER

JENNIFER HAYWARD

MILLS & BOON

First published in Great Britain 2019
by Mills & Boon, an imprint of HarperCollins*Publishers*
1 London Bridge Street, London, SE1 9GF

Love Islands: Passionate Nights © 2019 Harlequin Books S.A.

The Wedding Night Debt © 2015 Cathy Williams
A Deal Sealed by Passion © 2016 Louise Fuller
Carrying the King's Pride © 2016 Jennifer Drogell

ISBN: 978-0-263-27548-3

MIX
Paper from
responsible sources

FSC
www.fsc.org

FSC® C007454

This book is produced from independently certified FSC™ paper to ensure responsible forest management.

For more information visit: www.harpercollins.co.uk/green

Printed and bound in Spain
by CPI, Barcelona

THE WEDDING
NIGHT DEBT

CATHY WILLIAMS

To my three wonderful and inspiring daughters

CHAPTER ONE

DIVORCE. IT WAS something that happened to other people: people who didn't take care of their marriages; who
didn't understand that they were to be nurtured, looked
after, handled as delicately as you would handle a piece
of priceless porcelain.

At any rate, that had always been Lucy's way of thinking, and she wondered how it was that she was standing
here now, in one of the grandest houses in London, waiting
for her husband to return home so that she could broach
the subject of divorcing him.

She looked at her diamond-encrusted watch and her
stomach knotted in anxiety. Dio was due back in half an
hour. She couldn't remember where he had spent the past
week and a half. New York? Paris? They had places in
both. Or maybe he had been in their Mustique villa. Maybe
he had gone there with another woman. Who knew? She
certainly didn't.

Self-pity threatened to engulf her and she stemmed the
tide with ease of practice born of habit.

She'd been married for nearly a year and a half, plenty
of time to get accustomed to the way her youthful dreams
had crumbled to ashes.

When she glanced up, she could see herself reflected in
the huge, hand-made contemporary mirror which domi-

nated the ultra-modern drawing room. Five foot ten, slender as a reed, long blonde hair that dropped to her shoulders, vanilla-blonde and poker-straight. When she was sixteen, she had been spotted by an agency and her father had tried to shove her into a career in modelling, because why waste a pretty face? After all, women weren't cut out for anything more challenging, not really... But she had resisted—not that it had done her any good at all, in the end, because what good had been her degree when she had ended up...here? In this vast house, wandering in and out of rooms like a wraith, playing the perfect hostess? As if perfect hostessing was any kind of career for someone who had a degree in maths.

She barely recognised the woman she had turned out to be. On a warm evening in the middle of July, she was languishing in silk culottes with a matching silk vest top, just a few discreet bits of fairly priceless jewellery and high heels. She had turned into a Stepford Wife, except without the adoring husband rolling in at five-thirty every evening and asking what was for dinner. That might have been a distinct improvement on what she actually had, which was...nothing.

Or, *had* been nothing. She allowed herself a little smile because things weren't quite as sterile as they had been. Her situation had changed in the past two months and she hugged that secret pleasure to herself.

It made up for all the time she had spent dressed up like an expensive doll, administering their various properties, smiling politely when she needed to smile politely and hosting dinner parties for the great and the good. Or at any rate, the very, very rich.

And now...a divorce would set her free.

Provided Dio didn't kick up a fuss. Although she told her

self that there was no reason for him to, she could still feel a prickle of nervous perspiration break out over her body.

When it came to the concrete jungle, Dio Ruiz was the pack leader. He was an alpha male who played by his own rules. He was the sexiest man on earth and also the most intimidating.

But he wasn't going to intimidate *her*. She had spent the past few days telling herself that, ever since she had decided which turning she would take at the crossroads—the turning that would put as much distance between herself and her husband as possible.

The only slight fly in the ointment was the fact that this would be the last thing he would be expecting and Dio didn't do well when it came to flies in the ointment, not to mention the unexpected.

She heard the slam of the front door and her stomach lurched sickeningly but she only turned around when she sensed him at the door, his powerful, restless personality permeating the room even before she looked at him.

Even now, after everything, hating him as much as she hated him, his physical beauty still managed to take her breath away.

At twenty-two, when she had first laid eyes on him, he had been the most sinfully stunning guy she had ever seen and nothing had changed on that front. He was still the most sinfully stunning guy she had ever seen. Raven-black hair framed arrogantly perfect features. His pale, silver-grey eyes, so unusual against his bronzed skin, were dramatically fringed with thick, dark lashes. His mouth was firm and sensuous. Every little bit of him relayed the message that he was not a guy to be messed with.

'What are you doing here? I thought you were in Paris…' Lounging in the doorway, Dio began tugging at his tie, strolling into the room at the same time.

Surprise, surprise. It wasn't often he found himself anywhere with his wife that hadn't been meticulously planned in advance. Their meetings were formal, staged, never, ever spontaneous. When they were both in London, their lives were hectic, a whirlwind of social events. They each had their separate quarters, readied themselves in their own private cocoons and met in the vast hall, both dressed to the nines and ready to present the united image that couldn't have been further from the truth.

Occasionally, she might accompany him to Paris, New York or Hong Kong, always the perfect accessory.

Smart, well-bred…and most of all stunningly beautiful.

Tie off, he tossed it onto the white leather sofa and circled her, frowning, before coming to rest directly in front of her, where he began undoing the top two buttons of his shirt.

'So…' he drawled. 'To what do I owe this unexpected pleasure?'

Her nostrils flared as she breathed him in. He had a scent that was peculiarly unique to him. Clean, woody and intensely masculine.

'Am I interrupting your plans for the evening?' She averted her eyes from the sliver of tanned chest just visible where he had unbuttoned the shirt.

'My plans involved reading through some fairly dull legal due diligence on a company I'm taking over. What plans did you think you might be interrupting?'

'No idea.' She shrugged her narrow shoulders. 'I don't know what you get up to in my absence, do I?'

'Would you like me to fill you in?'

'I don't care one way or another, although it might have been a little embarrassing if you'd come home with a woman on your arm.' She gave a brittle laugh, hating herself for how she sounded—hard, cold, dismissive.

It hadn't started out like this. In fact, she had actually been stupid enough, at the very beginning, to think that he was actually interested in her, actually attracted to her.

They had gone out on a few dates. She had made him laugh, telling him about some of her university friends and their escapades. She had listened, enthralled, about the places he had seen. The fact that her father had actually approved of the relationship had been a green light because her father had made a career out of disapproving of every single boy she had ever brought home, all three of them. In fact, he had made a career out of being critical and disapproving of everything she had ever done, and every choice she had ever made, so the fact that he had been accepting, *encouraging*, even, of Dio had been a refreshing change.

If she hadn't been so wet behind the ears, she might have asked herself why that was, but instead, heady with the joy of falling in love, she had chosen to overlook his sudden benevolence.

When Dio had proposed after a whirlwind romance she had been over the moon. The intense but chaste courtship had thrilled her, as had the fact that he hadn't wanted to wait. No long engagement for him! He had been eager to slip the ring on her finger and his eagerness had made her feel loved, wanted, desired.

Sometimes, she wondered whether she would have stupidly continued feeling loved, wanted and desired if she hadn't overheard that conversation on their wedding night. She'd been floating on a cloud, barely able to contain her excitement at the thought of their honeymoon in the Maldives and their wedding night, the big night when she would lose her virginity, because until then he had been the perfect gentleman.

He'd been nowhere to be seen and she had eventually

floated away from the marquee in her father's garden, from
the music and the people dancing and getting drunk, and
had drifted off towards the kitchen and past her father's
office, where she had immediately recognised the deep
timbre of his voice.

A marriage of convenience…a company takeover…
He had got her father's company, which had been losing
money by the bucket load, and she had been an accessor
thrown in for good measure. Or maybe, when she had
bitterly thought about it later, her father had insisted on
the marriage because if she was married to Dio he would
remain duty-bound to the family company. No doing the
dirty once the signatures had been written on the dotted
line! No dumping her father in the proverbial because he
was no longer an asset!

She would be her father's safety net and Dio—as her father had spitefully told her when she had later confronted
him with what she had overheard—would get the sort of
class that his vast sums of money would never have been
able to afford him.

Lucy, in the space of a couple of hours, had grown up.
She was a married woman and her marriage was over before she had even embarked on it.

Except, she couldn't get out of it, her father had told her
not that easily. Did she want to see the family company go
under? There'd been some uncomfortable stuff with some
of the company profits…a little borrowed here and there…
he might go to prison if it all came out. Did she want that…
to see her father behind bars? It would hit the news. Did
she want that? Fingers pointed? People smirking?

She had acquiesced to her sham of a marriage although,
frankly, her father might have escaped a prison sentence
but only by handing the prison sentence over to her.

The one thing she had resolved, however, was to b

married in name only. No sex. No cosy time together. If Dio thought that he had bought her body and soul, she had been determined to prove him wrong. When she thought of the way she had fallen for his charm, had thought he'd actually been interested in inexperienced little *her*, she had burned with shame.

So she had quietly put her dreams into a box, shut the lid and thrown away the key…and here she was now.

'Is there a problem with the Paris apartment?' Dio asked politely. 'Can I get you a drink? Something to celebrate the one-off occasion of us being in the same room alone without prior arrangement? I can't think of the last time that happened, can you?' But, at a push, he would have said before they'd got married, when she had been studiously courting him, even though at the time he had thought it to be the other way around.

He had set his sights on Robert Bishop and his company a long, long time ago. He had covertly kept tabs on it, had seen the way it had slid further and further into a morass of debt and, like any predator worth his salt, he had bided his time.

Revenge was always a dish best eaten cold.

He just hadn't banked on the daughter. One glimpse of Lucy and her innocent, ethereal beauty and he had altered his plans on the spot. He had wanted her. She had touched something in him with her innocence and, cynic that he was, he had fallen hook, line and sinker.

He hadn't banked on that complication, had thought that she would hop into bed with him, allowing him to get her out of his system before he concluded business with her father. But, after a few weeks of playing a courting game that wasn't his thing at all, he had concluded that he wanted more than just a slice of her.

Only thing was…nearly a year and a half later and their

marriage was as dry as dust. He still hadn't touched that glorious body, leaving him with the certainty that, whilst he had thought he had the upper hand, she and her conniving father had actually played him for a fool. Instead of swinging the wrecking ball to the company and setting the police on Robert Bishop—who had been embezzling for years—he had ended up saving the company because he had wanted Lucy. He had wanted her at his side and in his bed and, if saving the company came as part of the deal, then so be it. Course, he had saved it and made money from it, ensuring that Robert Bishop was firmly locked out with just enough pocket money to teach him the joys of frugality, but still…

He had been unwittingly charmed by her open, shy, disingenuous personality. When she had looked at him with those big, grave brown eyes, her face propped in the palm of her hand, her expression enraptured, he had felt as though he had found the secret of eternal life and it had gone to his head like a drug.

She'd led him on. God knew if her slime of a father had kick-started the idea but that didn't matter.

What mattered was that they had got what they wanted while he had certainly missed out on what *he* had banked on getting.

She was shaking her head at the offer of a drink and he ignored her, fetching himself a glass of whisky and a glass of wine for her.

'Relax,' he said, pressing the glass on her and then retreating to the bay window where he sipped his drink and watched her in absolute silence. She had made it crystal clear on their wedding night that theirs was not a real marriage. No sex, no chit-chat, no getting to know one another. So he'd taken over her father's company but that didn't mean that she came as part of the package deal and, if he thought he'd been short-changed, then that was too bad.

He hadn't asked how she knew, what her father had said or what she had been told. He'd been duped and that was the end of the story.

The thought of having any kind of soul-searching conversation about the quality of their marriage had never crossed Dio's mind. He had made no effort to talk things through. And no one could ever accuse her of not being the 'perfect wife'. She certainly looked the part. Willowy, blonde, with a devastating *prettiness* that conveyed an air of peculiar innocence underneath the polished exterior. It was a quality that no model or socialite could replicate. She looked like someone waiting for life to *happen* and people fell for it. She was the greatest business asset a man could have. The woman, Dio had often thought, had missed her career as an Oscar-winning actress.

'So, if you're not in Paris, it's because something's wrong with the apartment. You should know by now that I don't get involved with the nitty-gritty details of my houses. That's *your* job.'

Lucy stiffened. *Her* job. That said it all. Just what every young girl dreamed of…a marriage completely lacking in romance which could be described as a *job*.

'There's nothing wrong with the Paris apartment. I just decided that…' she took a deep breath and gulped down some wine '… I decided that we needed to have a talk…'

'Really? What about? Don't tell me that you're angling for a pay rise, Lucy? Your bank account is more than healthy. Or have you seen something you'd really like? House in Italy? Apartment in Florence? Buy it.' He shrugged and finished the remainder of his whisky. 'As long as it's somewhere that can be used for business purposes, then I don't have a problem.'

'Why would I want to buy a house, Dio?'

'What, then? Jewellery? A painting? What?'

His air of bored indifference set her teeth on edge. This was worse than normal. Usually, they could manage to be polite for the five minutes they were forced to spend in one another's company—cooped up in a taxi, maybe, or else waiting for his driver to take them to some opening or other; or else back in one of their grand houses, removing coats and jackets before disappearing to opposite ends of the house.

'I don't want to buy *anything*.' Restively she began walking, stopping to look absently at some of the expensive artefacts in the room. As with all their houses, this one was the last word in what money could buy. The paintings were breath-taking, the furniture was all hand-made, the rugs were priceless silk.

No expense was ever spared and it was her *job* to ensure that all these high-end properties with their priceless furnishings ran like clockwork. Some were used by him, if he happened to be in the country at the time; occasionally they both found themselves in one at the same time. Often he arranged for clients to have use of them and then she had to oversee all the arrangements to make sure that his client left satisfied, having experienced the last word in luxury.

'In that case,' Dio drawled, 'why don't you get to the point and say what you have to say? I'm having a night in because I need to get through some work.'

'And of course, if you'd known that I would be waiting here like a spare part,' Lucy retorted, 'you would have made sure you didn't bother returning.'

Dio shrugged, allowing her to draw her own conclusions.

'I feel...' Lucy breathed in deeply '...that circumstances

between us have changed since…since dad died six months ago…'

He stilled and dropped his empty glass on the side table next to him, although his silver-grey eyes remained on her face. As far as he was concerned, the world was a more pleasant place without Robert Bishop in it. Certainly a more honest one. Whether his wife would agree with him, he didn't know. She had been composed at the funeral, her eyes hidden behind over-sized sunglasses and, since then, life had carried on as normal.

'Explain.'

'I don't want to be shackled to you any more, and there's no longer any need.' She did her best to get her thoughts in order but the cool intensity of his gaze was off-putting.

'You also happen to be shackled to a lifestyle that most women would find enviable.'

'Then you should let me go and you should find one of those women,' she retorted, her cheeks burning. 'You'd be happier. I'm sure you would because you must know that I'm…not happy, Dio. Or maybe,' she added in a lowered voice, 'you do know and you just don't care.' She sat and crossed her legs but she couldn't meet his eyes. He still did things to her, could still make her feel squirmy inside, even though she had done her best over time to kill that weak feeling. It was inappropriate to be attracted to a man who had used you, who had married you because you happened to be a social asset. That didn't make sense. Yes, when he had pretended to be interested in her, she could understand how she had been hot for him, so hot that she had spent her nights dreaming about him and her days fantasising about him. But not when she had found out the truth, and certainly not now, after all this time of cold war.

'Are you telling me that you want out?'

'Can you blame me?' She answered a question with a

question and finally met those cool, pale grey eyes. 'We don't have a marriage, Dio. Not a real one. I don't even understand why you married me in the first place, why you took an interest in me at all.' Except, of course, she did. Robert Bishop had been happy enough to tell her. Dio had wanted more than just his company; he had wanted social elevation, although why he should care she had no idea.

It was something she had never asked her husband. It was humiliating to think that someone had married you because you could open a few doors for them. She had been a bonus to the main deal because she had looked right and had had the right accent.

'You could have bought my father out without marrying me,' she continued, braving the iciness of his eyes. 'I know my father tried to shove me down your throat because he thought that, if you married me, he wouldn't end up in prison like a common criminal. But you could have had your pick of women who would have flung themselves in your path to be your wife.'

'How would you have felt if your dear daddy had ended up in jail?'

'No one wants to see any relative of theirs in prison.'

It was an odd choice of words but Dio let it go. He was shocked at the way this evening was turning out but he was hiding it well.

Had she really thought that she could play games with him, reel him in, get the ring on her, only to turn her back on his bed on their wedding night? And then, as soon as her father died, turn her back on him a second time?

'No, a relative in prison tends to blight family gatherings, doesn't it?' He rose to pour himself another drink because, frankly, he needed one. 'Tell me something, Lucy, what did you think of your father's…how shall I put it?… *creative use* of the company's pension pot?'

'He never told me in detail…what he had done,' she mumbled uncomfortably. Indeed, she had known nothing of her father's financial straits until that overheard conversation, after which he had been more than willing to fill her in.

Lucy thought that Dio might have been better off asking her what she had thought of her father. Robert Bishop had been a man who had had no trouble belittling her, a man who had wanted a son but had been stuck with a daughter, a chauvinist who had never accepted that women could be equal in all walks of life. Her poor, pretty, fragile mother had had a miserable existence before she had died at the tender age of thirty-eight. Robert Bishop had been a swaggering bully who had done his own thing and expected his wife to stay put and suck it up. He had womanised openly, had drunk far too much and, behind closed doors, had had fun jeering at Agatha Bishop, who had put up with it with quiet stoicism because divorce was not something her family did. Cancer had taken her before she'd been able to put that right.

Lucy had spent her life avoiding her father—which had been easy enough, because she had been farmed out to a boarding school at the age of thirteen—but she had never stopped hating him for what he put her mother through.

Which wasn't to say that she would have wanted to see him in prison and, more than that, she knew her mother would have been mortified. There was no way she would have sullied her mother's reputation, not if she could have helped it. She would rather have died than to have seen her mother's friends sniggering behind their backs that Agatha Bishop had ended up with a crook.

Looking at her, Dio wondered what was going through that beautiful head of hers. There was a remoteness there that had always managed to feed into his curiosity. No woman had ever been able to do that and it got on his nerves.

'Well, I'll fill in the gaps, shall I?' he said roughly. 'Your father spent years stealing from the pension fund until there was nothing left to steal. I assume he had a drinking problem?'

Lucy nodded. At boarding school and then university she had not had much time to observe just how much of a drinking problem he had had but it had been enough, she knew, to have sent his car spinning off the motorway at three in the morning.

'The man was an alcoholic. A functioning alcoholic, bearing in mind he was crafty enough to get his greedy hands on other people's money, but the fact of the matter was that he nicked what didn't belong to him to the point that his entire company was destined to sink in the quicksand if I hadn't come along and rescued it.'

'Why did you?' she asked curiously. She assumed that he must have come from a working class background, if what her father had implied was true, but certainly, by the time he had crash-landed into her life, he was a self-made millionaire several times over. So why bother with her father's company?

Dio flushed darkly. Such a long and involved story and one he had no intention of telling her.

'It had potential,' he drawled, his beautiful mouth curving into a smile that could still make her heart beat a little faster. 'It had tentacles in all the right areas, and my intuition paid off. It's made me more money than I know what to do with. And then,' he continued softly, 'how many failing companies come with the added bonus of...*you?* Have you looked in the mirror recently, my darling wife? What red-blooded male could have resisted you? And your father was all too happy to close the deal and throw you in for good measure...'

He saw the way her face reddened and the way her eyes suddenly looked as though they were tearing up. For a split second, he almost regretted saying what he had said. *Almost*.

'Except,' he carried on in that same unhurried voice, 'I didn't get you, did I? You went out with me; you smiled shyly as you hung onto my every word; you let me get so close, close enough for me to need a cold shower every time I returned to my house, because you had turned retreating with a girlish blush into an art form... And then, on our wedding night, you informed me that you weren't going to be part of any deal that I had arranged. You led me on...'

'I...I...never meant to do that...' But she could see very clearly how the situation must have looked to a man like Dio.

'Now, I wonder why I find that so hard to believe?' he murmured, noticing with some surprise that he had finished his second drink. Regretfully, he decided against a third. 'You and your father concocted a little plan to make sure I was hooked into playing ball.'

'That's not true!' Bright patches of colour appeared on her cheeks.

'And then, once I had played ball, you were free to drop the act. So now you're talking about divorce. Your father's no longer in danger of the long arm of justice and you want out.' He tilted his head to one side as another thought crept in. For the first time, he wondered what she got up to in his many absences.

He could have put a tail on her but he had chosen not to. He had simply not been able to imagine his frozen ice-maiden doing anything behind his back. Except she hadn't always been that ice maiden, had she? There was more to her than that cool detachment. He had seen that for himself before she had said 'I do'... So *had* she been getting up to anything behind his back?

Was it a simple case of her wanting to divorce him, having given a sufficiently adequate period of mourning for her dear old daddy? Or was there some other reason lurking in the background...?

And, just like that, rage slammed into him with the force of a sledgehammer.

Had she been seeing some man behind his back? He couldn't credit it but, once the nasty thought took hold, he found he couldn't jettison it.

'I want out because we both deserve something better than what we have.'

'How considerate of you to take my feelings into account.' Dio raised his eyebrows in a phoney show of gravity that made her grit her teeth. 'I never realised you had such a thoughtful, pious streak in you.'

First thing in the morning, he would have her followed, see for himself where this was all coming from. He certainly had no intention of asking her whether there was some guy in the background. In this sort of situation, nothing could beat the element of surprise.

'There's no need to be sarcastic, Dio.'

'Who's being sarcastic? Here's what I'm thinking, though...' He allowed a few seconds, during which time he pretended to give what was coming next some careful thought. 'You want out—but you do realise that you will leave with nothing?'

'What are you talking about?'

'I had a very watertight pre-nup made up before we married, which you duly signed, although I'm not entirely sure whether you read it thoroughly or not. My guess is that you were so eager to get me on board that signing anything would have just been a formality. Am I right?'

Lucy vaguely remembered signing something extremely long and complicated and very boring. She decided that she wouldn't take issue with his accusation that she'd been eager to get him on board; with his accusation that she had been in cahoots with her father to lure him into buying the company with her in the starring role of sacrificial lamb. She wasn't going to get involved in any sort of argument with him because he would emerge the winner. He had the sharpest brain of any person she had ever known in her life.

She would get out, never see him again. For a fleeting second, something wrenching and painful tugged inside her and she shoved the feeling away.

'As a rich man,' he said, 'I thought it best to protect myself. Here's what you signed up to. I got the company. Lock, stock and smoking barrel. Just recompense for rescuing it from imminent collapse and saving your father's frankly unworthy skin. I'm not sure if you know just how much he skimmed off the pension funds, how much I had to inject back in so that your employees didn't find themselves of pensionable age with nothing but a begging bowl for company? Enough for me to tell you that it was millions.' He breathed an exaggerated sigh and looked at her from under sinfully thick lashes. It had always amazed him that such a stupendously pretty face, so stunningly guileless, could house someone so cunning. It took all sorts to make the world.

Lucy hung her head because shame was never far away when her father's name was mentioned. She looked at her perfectly manicured nails and thought how wonderful it would feel never to wear nail polish ever again. She might have a burning-of-the-nail-polish ceremony.

She distractedly half-smiled and Dio, looking at her, frowned. So…what was the joke? he wondered.

More to the point, what was the little secret? Because that had been a secretive smile.

'As long as you are my wife,' he informed her, banking down the simmering rage bubbling up inside him, 'you get whatever you want. There are no limits placed on the amount of money you can spend.'

'You mean provided you approve of the purchases?'

'Have you ever heard me disapprove of anything you've ever bought?'

'All I buy are clothes, jewellery and accessories,' Lucy returned. 'And only because I need them to…play the part I have to play.'

'Your choice.' He shrugged. 'You could have bought a fleet of cars as far as I was concerned.'

She made a face and his frown deepened. He considered the possibility of giving her a divorce and dismissed the idea, although the reasons for that instant dismissal were a bit vague. Was he that possessive a man that he would hold on to a woman who wanted to escape? He had wanted revenge. And it might have come in a different shape from the one he had planned, but it had still come. He had still ended up with Robert Bishop's company, hadn't he? So what was the point of hanging on to Lucy and an empty marriage?

But then, she wasn't just any woman, was she? She just happened to be his wife. The wife who had promised a lot more than she had ended up delivering. What man liked being short-changed?

'You leave me,' he told her in a hard voice, 'and you leave with the clothes on your back.'

Lucy blanched. She loathed the trappings of wealth but wasn't it a fact that that was all she had ever known? How would she live? What sort of job had years of being pampered prepared her for? She had never had the opportunity to do the teacher training course she had wanted to do. She had, instead, jumped into a marriage that had turned her into a clone of someone she didn't like very much.

'I don't care,' she said in a low voice and Dio raised his eyebrows in a question.

'Of course you do,' he told her. 'You wouldn't know where to begin when it came to finding a job.'

'You can't say that.'

'Of course I can. You've grown up in the lap of luxury and, when most other girls would have branched out into the big, bad world, you married me and continued your life of luxury. Tell me, what has prepared you for that ugly, grim thing called reality?'

He would turf her out without a penny. She could see that in his eyes. He had never cared a jot about her and he didn't care about her now. He had wanted the company and she had been a useful tool to acquire along with the bricks and mortar.

She just recently might have dipped her toe in that grim thing he was talking about called reality, but he was right. A life of creature comforts hadn't prepared her for striking out with nothing. It would take ages for her to find her feet in the world of work, and how would she survive in the meantime? When he told her that she would leave with nothing but the clothes on her back, she was inclined to believe him. The clothes on her back wouldn't include the expensive jewellery in the various safes and vaults.

'I can see that you know where I'm coming from...' He leaned forward, arms resting loosely on his thighs. 'If you want out, then you have two options. You go with nothing, or...'

Lucy looked at him warily. 'Or...what?'

CHAPTER TWO

DIO SMILED SLOWLY and relaxed back.

Sooner or later, this weird impasse between them would have had to find a resolution; he had known that. Always one to dominate the situations around him, he had allowed it to continue for far longer than acceptable.

Why?

Had he thought that she would have thawed slowly? She'd certainly shown no signs of doing anything of the sort as the months had progressed. In fact, they had achieved the unthinkable—a functioning, working relationship devoid of sex, a business arrangement that was hugely successful. She complemented him in ways he could never have imagined. She had been the perfect foil for his hard-nosed, aggressive, seize-and-conquer approach to business and, frankly, life in general. He hadn't been born with a silver spoon in his mouth, he had had to haul himself up by his boot straps, and the challenges of the journey to success had made him brutally tough.

He was the king of the concrete jungle and he was sharp enough to know that pretenders to the throne were never far behind. He was feared and respected in equal measure and his wife's ingrained elegance counterbalanced his more high-voltage, thrusting personality beautifully.

Together they worked.

Maybe that was why he had not broached the subject of all those underlying problems between them. He was a practical man and maybe he had chosen not to rock the boat because they had a successful partnership.

Or maybe he had just been downright lazy. Or—and this was a less welcome thought—vain enough to imagine that the woman he still stupidly fancied would end up coming to him of her own accord.

The one thing he hadn't expected was talk of a divorce.

He poured himself another drink and returned to the chair, in no great hurry to break the silence stretching between them.

'When we got married,' Dio said slowly, 'it didn't occur to me that I would end up with a wife who slept in a separate wing of the house when we happened to be under the same roof. It has to be said that that's not every man's dream of a happy marriage.'

'I didn't think you had dreams of happy marriages, Dio. I never got the impression that you were the sort of guy who had fantasies of coming home to the wife and the two-point-two kids and the dog and the big back garden.'

'Why would you say that?'

Lucy shrugged. 'Just an impression I got.' But that hadn't stopped her from falling for him. She had got lost in those amazing eyes, had been seduced by that deep, dark drawl and had been willing to ignore what her head had been telling her because her heart had been talking a lot louder.

'I may not have spent my life gearing up for a walk down the aisle but that doesn't mean that I wanted to end up with a woman who didn't share my bed.'

Lucy reddened. 'Well, both of us has ended up disappointed with what we got,' she said calmly.

Dio waved his hand dismissively. 'There's no point trying to analyse our marriage,' he said. 'That's a pointless exercise. I was going to talk to you about options...' He sipped his drink and looked at her thoughtfully. 'And I'm going to give you a very good one. You want a divorce? Fine. I can't stop you heading for the nearest lawyer and getting divorce papers drawn up. Course, like I said, that would involve you leaving with nothing. A daunting prospect for someone who has spent the last year and a half never having to think about money.'

'Money isn't the be all and end all of everything.'

'Do you know what? It's been my experience that the people who are fond of saying things like that are the people who have money at their disposal. People who have no money are usually inclined to take a more pragmatic approach.' Having grown up with nothing, Dio knew very well that money actually was the be all and end all of everything. It gave you freedom like nothing else could. Freedom to do exactly what you wanted to do and to be accountable to no one.

'I'm saying that it doesn't always bring happiness.' She thought of her own unhappy, lavish childhood. From the outside, they had looked like a happy, privileged family. Behind closed doors, it had been just the opposite. No amount of money had been able to whitewash that.

'But a lack of it can bring, well, frustration? Misery? Despair? Imagine yourself leaving all of this so that you can take up residence in a one-bedroom flat where you'll live a life battling rising damp and mould on the walls.'

Lucy gave an exaggerated sigh. 'Aren't you being a bit dramatic, Dio?'

'London is an expensive place. Naturally, you would have some money at your disposal, but nothing like enough to find anywhere halfway decent to live.'

'Then I'd move out of London.'

'Into the countryside? You've lived in London all your life. You're accustomed to having the theatre and the opera and all those art exhibitions you enjoy going to on tap... But don't worry. You can still enjoy all of that but, sadly, there's no such thing as a free lunch. You want your divorce? You can have it. But only after you've given me what I expected to get when I married you.'

It took a few seconds for Lucy's brain to make the right connections and catch up with what he was telling her but, even so, she heard herself ask, falteringly, 'What are you talking about?'

Dio raised his eyebrows and smiled slowly. 'Don't tell me that someone with a maths degree can't figure out what two and two makes? I want my honeymoon, Lucy.'

'I...I don't know what you mean...' Lucy stammered, unable to tear her eyes away from the harsh lines of his beautiful face.

'Of course you do! I didn't think I was signing up for a sexless marriage when I slipped that wedding band on your finger. You want out now? Well, you can have out just as soon as we put an end to the unfinished business between us.'

'That's blackmail!' She sprang to her feet and began restively pacing the room. Her nerves were all over the place. She had looked forward to that wretched honeymoon night so much...and now here he was, offering it to her, but at a price.

'That's the offer on the table. We sleep together, be man and wife in more than just name only, and you get to leave with an allowance generous enough to ensure that you spend the rest of your life in comfort.'

'Why would you want that? You're not even attracted to me!'

'Come a little closer and I can easily prove you wrong on that point.'

Heart thudding, Lucy kept a healthy distance, but she was looking at him again, noting the dark intent in his eyes. The desire she had shoved away, out of sight, began to uncurl inside her.

She'd been foolish enough to think that he had been interested in her, attracted to her, and had discovered that it had all been a lie. He had strung her along because he had decided that she would be a useful addition to his life.

There was no way that she would sleep with him as some sort of devil's bargain. She had watched the car crash of her parents' marriage and had vowed that she would only give her body to a man who truly loved her, that she would only marry for the right reasons. Her parents had had a marriage of convenience, the natural joining of two wealthy families, and just look at where they had ended up. The minute she had realised that her marriage to Dio had not been what she had imagined was the minute she'd made her decision to withhold the better part of herself from him, to remain true to her principles.

She watched, horrified, as he slowly rose from his chair and strolled towards where she was standing by the window. With each step, her nerves shredded a little bit more.

'A matter of weeks...' he murmured, delicately tracing his finger along her cheek and feeling her quiver as he touched her.

She was the only woman in the world he had never been able to read.

There had been times during their marriage when he had surprised her looking at him, had seen something in her eyes that had made him wonder whether his dear wife was slightly less immune to him than she liked to portray, but he had never explored the possibility. There was such a thing as pride, especially to a man like him.

He was willing to explore the possibility now because he knew that, if she left and he never got to touch her, she would become unfinished business and that would be a less than satisfactory outcome.

'Weeks...?' Transfixed by the feel of his skin against hers, Lucy remained rooted to the spot. Her breasts ached and she could feel her nipples tightening, sensitive against her lacy bra. Liquid was pooling between her legs and, although she remained perfectly still, she wanted to squirm and rub her legs together to relieve herself of the ache between them.

'That's right.' Plenty long enough to get her out of his system. She was his and he intended to have her, all of her, before he allowed her her freedom.

At which point, he would close the door on a part of his past that had gnawed away at him for as long as he could remember.

His erection was hard enough to be painful and he stepped a bit closer, close enough for her to feel it against her belly. He knew that she had from the slight shudder that ran through her body. Her eyes were wide, her mouth parted.

An invitation. One that he wasn't going to resist. He hadn't been this physically close to his wife since he had tied the knot with her and he wasn't about to waste the opportunity.

Lucy knew he was going to kiss her. She placed her hand flat on his chest, a pathetic attempt to push him away before he could get too close, but she didn't push him away. Instead, as his mouth found hers, treacherous fingers curled into his shirt and she sighed, losing herself in the headiness of feeling his tongue probing into her mouth, his tongue moving, exploring, with hers, sparking a series of explosive reactions in her body.

Like a match set to tinder, she felt her whole body combusting. Their brief courtship had been so very chaste. This wasn't chaste. This was unrestrained hunger and his hunger matched her own.

She felt him slip his hand underneath the silk top to cup her breast and, when he began to rub her nipple through the lacy bra, she wanted to pass out.

Or else rip off his shirt so that she could spread trembling, eager fingers against his broad, hard chest.

He pulled back. It took her a couple of seconds to recognise his withdrawal and then horror at what she had allowed to happen filtered through her consciousness and washed over her like a bucket of freezing cold water.

'What the heck do you think you're doing?'

Dio smiled. 'Giving you proof positive that we could have a couple of weeks of very pleasant carnal adventures...' Keen eyes noted the hectic flush in her cheeks and the way she had now prudishly folded her arms across her chest, as if she could deny the very heated, very satisfactory, response she had just given him.

He hadn't been mistaken when it came to those little looks he had surprised her giving him after all.

'I have no intention of...of sleeping with you for money!'

Dio's lips thinned. 'Why not? You married me for money. At least sleeping with me would introduce the element of fun.'

'I did not marry you for money!'

'I have no intention of going down this road again. I've given you your options. You can decide which one to go for.' He spun round on his heels, heading for the door.

'Dio!'

He stilled and then took his time turning to face her.

'Why?'

'Why what?'

'Why does it matter whether you sleep with me or not? I mean surely there have been…women in your life over the past year or so more than willing to jump into bed with you… Why does it matter whether I do or not?'

Dio didn't answer immediately. He knew what she thought, that he spent his leisure time between the sheets with other women. There had been no need for her to vocalise it. He had seen it in her face on the few occasions when he had happened to be in conversation with another woman, an attractive woman. He had seen the flash of resentment and scorn which had been very quickly masked and he had seen no reason to put her straight.

He didn't think that there was any need to put her straight now. Not only had he not slept with any other woman since his marriage, but he had not been tempted. There wasn't a human being on earth who wasn't driven to want what was out of reach and his wife had been steadfastly out of reach for the past eighteen months. During that period, he had not found his eyes straying to any of the women who had covertly made passes at him over the months, happy to overlook the fact that there was a wedding ring on his finger.

'I just can't,' Lucy breathed into the silence. 'I…I'm happy to leave with a small loan, until I find my feet.'

'Find your feet doing what?' Dio asked curiously.

'I…I have one or two things up my sleeve…'

Dio's eyes narrowed as hers shifted away. He was picking up the whiff of a secret and he wondered, again, what was going on behind his back. What *had* been going on behind his back? Had the mouse been playing while the cat had been away?

'What things?'

'Oh, nothing,' she said evasively. 'It's just that…I think we'd both be happier if we brought this marriage to an end, and if I could borrow some money from you…'

'Lucy, you would need a great deal of money to begin to have any life at all in London.'

'Money which you are not at all prepared to lend me, even though you have my word that you would be repaid.'

'Unless you're planning a big job in the corporate world or have a rich backer,' he said dryly, 'then I can guarantee that any loan I make to you would not be paid back. At least, not while I have my own teeth and hair.'

'How do you think it would look if your wife was caught with a begging bowl, looking for scraps from strangers?'

'Now who's being dramatic?' When he had met her all those months ago, she had been blushing and shy but he had had glimpses of the humour and sharp intelligence behind the shyness. Over the past year and a half, as she had been called on to play the role of perfect wife and accomplished hostess, her self-confidence had grown in leaps and bounds.

He also knew that, whatever she felt for him, she wasn't intimidated by him. Maybe that, too, was down to the strange configuration of their lives together. How could you be intimidated by someone you weren't that interested in pleasing in the first place?

'You will, naturally, walk away with slightly more than the clothes on your back,' Dio admitted. 'However, you would still find it a challenge to have a lifestyle that in any way could be labelled comfortable. Unless, of course, there's a rich patron in the background. Is there?'

Asking the question was a sign of weakness but Dio couldn't help himself.

She shrugged. 'I'm not into rich men,' she told him

'I've always known that and having been married to you has confirmed all my suspicions.'

'How's that?' Frankly, he had never heard anything so hypocritical in his life before, but he decided to let it pass.

'Like you said, there's no such thing as a free lunch. I know you say that it's the most important thing in life...'

'I can't remember saying that.'

'More or less. You said it *more or less*. And I know you think that I wouldn't be able to last a week unless I have more money than I can shake a stick at but—'

'But you're suddenly overcome with a desperate urge to prove me wrong...' His gaze dropped to her full mouth. Something about the arrangement of her features had always turned him on. She wasn't overtly sexy, just as she wasn't overtly beautiful, but there was a whisper of something other-worldly about her that kept tugging his eyes back to her time and time again.

She had screwed up his clear-cut plans to buy her father's company at a fire sale price before chucking him to his fate, which would undoubtedly have involved wolves tearing him to pieces. He had been charmed by that other-worldly *something*, had allowed it somehow to get to him, and he had tempered all his plans to accommodate the feeling.

She had, over time, become the itch he couldn't scratch. He might have had her signed up to a water-tight pre-nup but, even so, he would never have seen her hit the streets without any financial wherewithal.

In this instance, though, he was determined to have that itch scratched and, if it meant holding her to ransom, then he was pretty happy to go down that road.

Especially now that he knew that the attraction was returned in full.

'I'm just trying to tell you that there's no rich anyone

in the background.' Did he imagine that she fooled around the way he did? 'And there never will be anyone rich in my life again.'

'How virtuous. Is it because of those free lunches now coming for free? Do you honestly think that hitching your life to a pauper would be fertile ground for happily united bliss? If so then you really need to drag your head out of the clouds and get back down to Planet Earth.' He abandoned the decision to go back to work, not that he would have been able to concentrate. 'I don't know about you but I'm hungry. If we're going to continue this conversation, then I need to eat.'

'You were about to leave,' Lucy reminded him.

'That was before I became intrigued with your radical new outlook on life.'

He began heading towards the kitchen and she followed helplessly in his wake.

This felt like a proper conversation and it was unsettling. There were no crowds of people around jostling for his attention. No important clients demanding polite small talk. And they weren't exchanging pleasantries before heading off in opposite directions in any one of their grand houses.

She knew the layout of the kitchen well. On those occasions when they had entertained at home, she had had to supervise caterers and familiarise them with the ins and outs of the vast kitchen. When he was out of the country, as he often was, this was where she had her meals on her own, with the little telly on, or else the radio.

However, it was a bit different to see him here, in it.

For a few seconds, he stared around him, a man at sea trying to get his bearings.

'Okay. Suggestions?' He finally turned to her.

'Suggestions about what?'

'Thoughts on what I can eat.'

'What were you planning to eat if you hadn't found me here?' Lucy asked jerkily, moving from doorway to kitchen table and then sitting awkwardly on one of the chairs while he continued to look at her in a way that made her blood sizzle, because she just had to see that mouth of his to recall his very passionate kiss. Her lips still felt stung and swollen.

'I have two top chefs on speed dial,' he drawled, amused when her mouth fell open. 'They're usually good at solving the "what to eat?" dilemma for me. Not that it's a dilemma that occurs very often. If I'm on my own, I eat out. Saves hassle.'

'Go ahead and order what you want from your two top chefs,' Lucy told him. 'Never mind me. I...er...'

'Ate already?'

'I'm not hungry.'

'And I don't believe you. Don't tell me,' he said, 'that you feel uncomfortable being in a kitchen with me and breaking bread? We're a married couple, after all.'

'I don't feel uncomfortable,' Lucy lied. 'Not in the slightest!'

'Then where are your suggestions?'

'Do you even know where to find anything in this kitchen?' she asked impatiently.

Dio appeared to give that question a bit of thought then he shook his head. 'I admit the contents of the cupboards are something of a mystery, although I do know that there's some very fine white wine in the fridge...'

'Are you asking me to cook something for you?'

'If you're offering, then who am I to refuse?' He made for a chair and sat down. 'It doesn't offend your feminist instincts to cook for me, does it? Because, if it does, then

I'm more than happy to try and hunt down one or two in-gredients and put my cooking skills to the test.'

'You don't have cooking skills.' From some past re-membered conversation, when she had still had faith in him, she recalled one of his throwaway remarks that had made her laugh.

'You're right. So I don't.'

This wasn't how Lucy had imagined the evening going. She had more figured on dealing with shock at her an-nouncement followed by anger because she knew that, even if he heartily wanted to get rid of her, he would have been furious that she had pre-empted him. Then she had imagined disappearing off to bed, leaving him to mull over her decision, at which point she would have been di-rected to a lawyer who would take over the handling of the nitty-gritty.

Instead she felt trapped in the eye of a hurricane...

She knew where everything was and she was a reason-ably good cook. It was something she quite enjoyed doing when she was on her own, freed from the pressure of hav-ing to entertain. She expertly found the things she needed for a simple pasta meal and it would have been relaxing if she hadn't been so acutely aware of his eyes following her every movement.

'Need a hand?' he asked as she clanged a saucepan onto the stove and she turned to him with a snappy, dis-believing frown.

'What can you do?'

'I feel I could be quite good at chopping things.' He rose smoothly to join her by the kitchen counter, invading her space and making her skin tingle with sexual awareness.

Stupid, she thought crossly. But he had thrown down that gauntlet, brought sex into the equation, and now it was on her mind. And she didn't want it to be. She had spent the past months telling herself that she hated him and hating him had made it easy for her to ignore the way he made her feel. It had been easy to ignore the slight tremble whenever he got too close, the tingling of her breasts and the squirmy feeling she got in the pit of her stomach.

He'd never been attracted to her, she had thought. He'd just seen her as part of a deal. He'd used her.

But now…

He wanted her; she had felt it in his kiss, had felt his erection pressing against her like a shaft of steel. Just thinking about it brought her out in a fine film of perspiration.

She shoved an onion and some tomatoes at him and told him where to find a chopping board and a knife.

'Most women would love the kind of lifestyle you have,' Dio murmured as he began doing something and nothing with the tomatoes.

'You mean flitting from grand house to grand house, making sure everything is ticking over, because Lord help us if an important client spots some dust on a skirting board?'

'Since when have you been so sarcastic?'

'I'm not being sarcastic.'

'Don't stop. I find it intriguing.'

'You told me that most women would envy what I have and I told you that they wouldn't.'

'You'd be surprised what women would put up with if the price was right.'

'I'm not one of those women.' She edged away, because he was just a little too close for comfort, and began busying herself by the stove, flinging things into the saucepan, all the ingredients for a tomato-and-aubergine dish, which was a stalwart in her repertoire because it was quick and easy.

Dio thought that maybe he should have tried to find out what sort of woman she was before remembering that he knew exactly what sort of woman she was. The sort who had conspired with her father to get him where they had both wanted him—married to her and thereby providing protection for her father from the due processes of law.

If she wanted to toss out hints that there were hidden depths there somewhere, though, then he was happy enough to go along for the ride. Why not? Right now he was actually enjoying himself, against all odds.

And the bottom line was that he wanted her body. He wanted that itch to be scratched and then he would be quite happy to dispose of her.

If holding her to ransom was going to prove a problem then what was the big deal in getting her into his bed using other methods?

'So, we're back to the money not being the be all and end all,' he murmured encouragingly. 'Smells good, whatever you're making.'

'I like cooking when I'm on my own,' she said with a flush of pleasure.

'You cook even though you know you could have anything you wanted to eat delivered to your doorstep?' Dio asked with astonishment and Lucy laughed.

He remembered that laugh from way back when. Soft and infectious, with a little catch that made it seem as though she felt guilty laughing at all. He had found that laugh strangely seductive, fool that he had been.

'So…' he drawled once they were sitting at the kitchen table with bowls of steaming hot pasta in front of them. 'Shall we raise our glasses to this rare event? I don't believe I've sat in this kitchen and had a meal with you since we got married.'

Lucy nervously sipped some of the wine. The situation

was slipping away from her. How many women had he sat and drank with in the time during which they had been supposedly happily married? She hadn't slept with him but that didn't mean that she wasn't aware that he had a healthy libido. One look at that dark, handsome face was enough to cement the impression.

She had never, not once, asked him about what he did behind her back on all those many trips when he was abroad, but she could feel the questions eating away at her, as though they had suddenly been released from a locked box. She hated it. And she hated the way that fleeting moment of being the object of his flirting attention had got to her, overriding all the reasons she had formulated in her head for breaking away from him. She didn't want to give house room to any squirmy feelings. He had turned on the charm when they had first met and she knew from experience that it didn't mean anything.

'That's because this isn't really a marriage, is it?' she said politely. 'So why would we sit in a kitchen and have a meal together? That's what real married couples do.'

Dio's mouth tightened. 'And of course you would know a lot about what real married couples do, considering you entered this contract with no intention of being half of a real married couple.'

'I don't think it's going to get either of us anywhere if we keep harping back to the past. I think we should both now look to the future.'

'The future being divorce.'

'I'm not going to get into bed with you for money, Dio,' Lucy told him flatly. For a whisper of a second, she had a vivid image of what it would be like to make love to him—but then, it wouldn't be love, would it? And what was the point of sex without love?

'So you're choosing the poverty option.' He pushed his

bowl to one side and relaxed back in the chair, angling his big body so that he could extend his legs to the side.

'If I have to. I can make do. I...'

'You...what?' His ears pricked up as he detected the hesitancy in her voice.

'I have plans,' Lucy said evasively. And she wasn't going to share them with him, wasn't going to let her fledgling ambitions be put to the test by him.

'What plans?'

'Nothing very big. Or important. I just obviously need to think about the direction my life is going in.' She stood up and briskly began clearing the table. She made sure not to catch his eye.

Dio watched her jerky movements as she busied herself around the kitchen, tidying, wiping the counters, doing everything she could to make sure the conversation was terminated.

So she wanted out and she had plans.

To Dio's way of thinking, that could only mean one thing. A man. Maybe not a rich one, but a man. Lurking in the background. Waiting to get her into bed if he hadn't already done so.

The fake marriage was going to be replaced by a relationship she had probably been cultivating behind his back for months. Maybe—and the red mist descended when he considered this option—she had been cultivating this relationship from way back when. Maybe it had been right there on the back burner, set to one side while she'd married him and had done what she had to do for the sake of her father.

It might have come as a shock that she would face walking away empty handed but clearly, whatever her so-called plans were, they were powerful enough to override common sense.

Faced with this, Dio understood that first and foremost he would find out what those plans were.

Simple.

He could either follow her himself or he could employ someone to do it. He preferred the former option. Why allow someone else to do something you were perfectly capable of handling yourself?

The past year or so of their sterile non-relationship faded under the impetus of an urgent need that obliterated everything else.

'I'm going to be in New York for the next few days,' Dio said abruptly, standing up and moving towards the kitchen door where he stood for a few seconds, hand on the door knob, his dark face cool and unreadable. 'While you're still wearing a wedding ring on your finger, I could insist that you accompany me, because I will be attending some high level social events. But, under these very *special* circumstances, you'll be pleased to hear that I won't.'

'New—New York?' Lucy faltered. 'I can't remember New York being in the diary until next month…'

'Change of plan.' Dio shrugged. He stared at her, working out what he planned to do the following day and how. 'You can stay here and spend the time thinking about the proposition I've put to you.'

'I've already thought about it. I don't need to do any more thinking.'

Over his dead body. 'Then,' he said smoothly, 'you can stay here and spend the time contemplating the consequences…'

CHAPTER THREE

LUCY HAD HAD better nights.

Spend her time contemplating the consequences? The cool, dismissive way he had said that, looking at her as if he had complete authority over her decisions, had set her teeth on edge.

Their sham of a marriage had worked well for him. She knew that. Her father had told her that Dio wanted someone classy to be by his side and she had fitted the bill. Whilst he had been alive, he had never ceased reminding her that it was her duty to play the part because, if she didn't, then it would be within her husband's power to reveal the extent of the misappropriated money—and if he went down, her father had told her, then so too would the memory of her mother. The dirty linen that would be washed in public would bring everyone down. That was how it worked.

That had been Lucy's Achilles' heel so she had played her part and she had played it to perfection.

The day after their wedding, Dio had taken himself off to the other side of the world on business and, during the week that he had been away, she had obeyed instructions and had overhauled her image with the aid of a top-notch personal shopper.

Like a puppet, she had allowed herself to be manoeuvred into being the sort of woman who entertained. He had returned and there and then the parameters of their personal life had been laid down.

He had said nothing about her physical withdrawal. The closeness that had been there before her father's revelation had disappeared, replaced by a cool remoteness that had only served to prove just how right she had been in reading the situation.

He had used her.

What he had wanted was what he had got. He had wanted someone to whom the social graces came as second nature. He mixed in the rarefied circles of the elite and she could more than hold her own in those circles because she had grown up in them.

As far as she knew, the sort of woman he was attracted to was probably completely the opposite to her.

He was probably attracted to dark-haired, voluptuous sirens who didn't hang around the house in silk culottes and matching silk vests. He probably liked them swearing, cursing and being able to drink him under the table, but none of *them* would have done as a society wife. So he had tacked her on as a useful appendage.

And now he wanted her.

With divorce on the horizon, he wanted to lay claim to her because, as far as he was concerned, she was his possession, someone he had bought along with the company that had come with her.

He'd even set a time line on whatever physical relationship he intended to conduct!

Did it get any more insulting?

He knew that he'd be bored with her within a month!

She burned with shame when she thought about that.

She hated him and yet her sleep was disturbed by a series of images of them together. She dreamt of him making love to her, touching her in places she had never been touched before and whispering things in her ear that had her squirming in a restless half-sleep.

She awoke the following morning to an empty house. Dio had disappeared off to New York.

She'd used these little snippets of freedom to her benefit and now, as she got dressed, she felt that she should be a little more excited than she was.

It irritated her to know that, thanks to Dio, the glorious day stretching ahead of her was already marred with images of his dark, commanding face and the careless arrogance of what he had told her the evening before.

She made a couple of calls and then she headed out.

Dio, in the middle of a conference call, was notified of her departure within seconds of her leaving the house.

His personal driver—who had zero experience in sleuthing but could handle a car like a pro and could be trusted with his life—phoned the message through and Dio immediately terminated his conference call.

'When she stops, call me,' he instructed. 'I'm not interested in whether she's leaving the house. I'm interested in where she ends up.'

Suddenly restless, he pushed himself away from his desk and walked towards the floor-to-ceiling glass panes that overlooked the busy hub of the city.

He'd had a night to think about what she had told him and he was no nearer to getting his head around it.

So, she wanted out.

She was the single one woman who had eluded him despite the ring on her finger. To take a protesting bride to his bed would have been unthinkable. There was no way he would ever have been driven to that, however bitter he might have been about the warped terms of their marriage.

And he could see now that pride had entered the equation, paralysing his natural instinct to charm her into the place he wanted her to be.

With the situation radically changed, it was time for him to be proactive.

And he was going to enjoy it. He was going to enjoy having her beg for him, which he fully intended she would do, despite all her protests to the contrary.

And, if he discovered that there was a man on the scene, that she had been seeing someone behind his back...

He shoved his hands in his pockets and clenched his jaw, refusing to give in to the swirl of fury that filled every pore and fibre of his being at the thought of her possible infidelity.

When he had embarked on Robert Bishop's company buyout, this was not at all what he had envisaged.

He had envisaged a clean, fatal cut delivered with the precision of a surgical knife, which was no less than the man deserved.

Never one to waste time brooding, Dio allowed his mind to play back the series of events that had finally led to the revenge he had planned so very carefully.

Some of what he had known, he had seen with his own eyes, growing up. His father fighting depression, stuck in a nowhere job where the pay was crap. His mother working long hours cleaning other people's houses so that there would be sufficient money for little treats for him.

The greater part of the story, however, had come from his mother's own lips, years after his father's life had been claimed by the ravages of cancer. Only then had he discovered the wrong that had been done to his father. A poor immigrant with a brilliant mind, he had met Robert Bishop as an undergraduate. Robert Bishop, from all accounts, had been wasting his time partying whilst pretending to do a business degree. Born into money, but with the family fortunes already showing signs of poor health, he had known that although he had an assured job with the family business he needed more if he was to sustain the lifestyle to which he had become accustomed.

Meeting Mario Ruiz had been a stroke of luck as far as Robert Bishop had been concerned. He had met the genius who would later invent something small but highly significant that would allow him to send his ailing family engineering concern into the stratosphere.

And as for Mario Ruiz?

Dio made no attempt to kill the toxic acid that always erupted in his veins when he thought of how his father had been conned.

Mario Ruiz had innocently signed up to a deal that had not been worth the paper it was written on. He had found his invention misappropriated and, when he had raised the issue, had found himself at the mercy of a man who'd wanted to get rid of him as fast as he could.

He had seen nothing of all the giddy financial rewards that should have been his due.

It had been such an incredible story that Dio might well have doubted the full extent of its authenticity had it not been for the reams of paperwork later uncovered after his mother had died, barely months after his father had been buried.

Ruining Robert Bishop had been there, driving him forward, for many years…except complete and total revenge had been marred by the fresh-faced, seductive prettiness of Lucy Bishop. He had wavered. Allowed concessions to be made. Only to find himself the revenge half-baked: he had got the company but not the man, and he had got the girl but not in the way he had imagined he would.

Well, he just couldn't wait to see how this particular story was going to play out. Not on her terms, he resolved.

He picked up the call from his driver practically before his mobile buzzed and listened with a slight frown of puzzlement as he was given his wife's location.

Striding out of his office, he said in passing to his secretary that he would be uncontactable for the next couple of hours.

He wasn't surprised to see the look of open-mouthed astonishment on his secretary's face because, when it came to work, he was *always* contactable.

'Make up whatever excuses you like for my cancelled meetings, be as inventive as the mood takes you.' He grinned, pausing by the door. 'You can look at it as your little window of living dangerously...'

'I live dangerously every time I walk through that office door,' his austere, highly efficient, middle-aged secretary tartly responded. 'You have no idea what you're like to work for!'

Dio knew the streets of London almost as comprehensively as his driver did but he still had to rely on his satnav to get him to the address he had been given.

Somewhere in East London. He had no idea how Jackson had managed to follow Lucy. Presumably, he had just taken whatever form of public transport she had taken and, because he was not their regular evening driver, she would not have recognised him.

It was a blessing that he had handed the grunt work over to his driver because he had just assumed that his wife would drive to wherever she wanted to go, or else take a taxi.

Anything but the tube and the bus.

He couldn't imagine that her father would ever have

allowed her to hop on the number twenty-seven. Robert Bishop had excelled in being a snob.

He wondered whether this was all part of her sudden dislike of all things money and then he wondered how long the novelty of pretending not to care about life's little luxuries would last.

It was all well and good to talk about pious self-denial from the luxury of your eight-bedroomed mansion in the best postcode in London.

His lips curled derisively as he edged along through the traffic. She had been the apple of her father's eye and that certainly didn't go hand in hand with pious self-denial.

He cleared the traffic in central London, but found that he was still having to crawl through the stop-start tedium of traffic lights and pedestrian crossings, and it was after eleven by the time he pulled up in front of a disreputable building nestled amongst a parade of shops.

There was a betting shop, an Indian takeaway, a laundrette, several other small shops and, tacked on towards the end of the row, a three-storeyed old building with a blue door. Dio was tempted to phone his driver and ask him whether he had texted the wrong address.

He didn't.

Instead, he got out of his car and spent a few moments looking at the house in front of him. The paint on the door was peeling. The windows were all shut, despite the fact that it was another warm, sunny day.

His mind was finding it hard to co-operate. For once, he was having difficulty trying to draw conclusions from what his eyes were seeing.

He could hear the buzzing of the doorbell reverberating inside the house as he kept his hand pressed on the buzzer and then the sound of footsteps. The door opened a crack, chain still on.

'Dio!' Lucy blinked and wondered briefly if she might be hallucinating. Her husband had been on her mind so much as she had headed off but the physical reactions of her body told her that the man standing imperiously in front of her was no hallucination.

From behind her, Mark called out in his sing-song Welsh accent, 'Who's there, Lucy?'

'No one!' They were the first words that sprang into her head but, as her eyes tangled with Dio's, she recognised that she had said the wrong thing.

'No one...?' Dio's voice was soft, silky and lethally cool. The chain was still on the door and he laid his hand flat on it, just in case she got the crazy idea of trying to shut the door in his face.

'What are you doing here? You said that you were going to New York.'

'Who's the man, Lucy?'

'Did you follow me?'

'Just answer the question because, if you don't, I'll break the door down and find out myself.'

'You shouldn't be here! I...I...' She felt Mark behind her, inquisitively trying to peer through the narrow sliver to see who was standing at the door, and with a sigh of resignation she slowly slid the chain back with trembling fingers.

Dio congratulated himself on an impressive show of self-control as he walked into the hallway of the house which, in contrast to the outside, was brightly painted in shades of yellow. He clenched his fists at his sides, eyes sliding from Lucy to the man standing next to her.

'Who,' he asked in a dangerously low voice, 'the hell are you, and what are you doing with my wife?'

The man in front of him was at least three inches shorter and slightly built. Dio thought that he would be able to flatten him with a tap of his finger, and that was exactly what he wanted to do, but he'd be damned if he was going to start a brawl in a house.

Growing up on the wrong side of the tracks, however, had trained him well when it came to holding his own with his fists.

'Lucy, shall I leave you two to talk?'

'Dio, this is Mark.' She recognised the glitter of menace in her husband's eyes and decided that, yes, the best thing Mark could do would be to evaporate. Shame he wouldn't be able to take her with him, but perhaps the time had come to lay her cards on the table and tell Dio what was going on. Before he started punching poor Mark, who was fidgeting and glancing at her worriedly.

She felt sick as she looked, with dizzy compulsion, at the tight, angry lines of her husband's face.

'I'd shake your hand,' Dio rasped, 'but I might find myself giving in to the urge to rip it off, so I suggest you take my wife's advice and clear off, and don't return unless I give you permission.'

'Dio, please…' she pleaded, putting herself between her husband and Mark. 'You've got the wrong end of the stick.'

'I could beat him to a pulp,' Dio remarked neutrally to her, 'without even bloodying my knuckles.'

'And you'd be proud of that, would you?'

'Maybe not proud, but eminently satisfied. So…' He pinned coldly furious silver eyes on the guy behind her. 'You clear off right now or climb out from your hiding place behind my wife and get what's coming to you!'

With a restraining hand on Dio's arm, Lucy turned to Mark and told him gently that she'd call him as soon as possible.

Dio fought the urge to deal with the situation in the most straightforward way known to mankind.

But what would be the point? He wasn't a thug, despite his background.

His head was cluttered with images of the fair-haired man, the fair-haired wimp who had hidden behind his wife, making love to Lucy.

The heat of the situation was such that it was only when the front door clicked shut behind the loser that Dio noticed what he should have noticed the very second he had looked at Lucy.

Gone were the expensive trappings: the jewellery, the watch he had given to her for her birthday present, the designer clothes...

He stared at her, utterly bemused. Her hair was scraped back into a ponytail and she was dressed in a white tee-shirt, a pair of faded jeans and trainers. She looked impossibly young and so damned sexy that his whole body jerked into instant response.

Lucy felt the shift in the atmosphere between them, although she couldn't work out at first where it was coming from. The tension was still there but threaded through that was a sizzling electrical charge that made her heart begin to beat faster.

'Are you going to listen to what I have to say?' She hugged her arms around her because she was certain that he would be able to see the hard tightening of her nipples against the tee-shirt.

'Are you going to spin me fairy stories?'

'I've never done that and I'm not going to start now.'

'I'll let that ride. Are you having an affair with that man?'

'No!'

Dio took a couple of steps towards her, sick to his stomach at the games going on in his head. 'You're my wife!'

Lucy's eyes shifted away from his. Her breathing was

laboured and shallow and she was horrified to realise that, despite the icy, forbidding threat in his eyes, she was still horribly turned on. It seemed that something had been unlocked inside her and now she couldn't ram it back into a safe place, out of harm's way.

Dio held up his hand, as though interrupting a flow of conversation, although she hadn't uttered a word.

'And don't feed me garbage about being my wife in name only, because I sure as hell won't be buying it! You're my wife and I had better not find out that you've been fooling around behind my back!'

'What difference would it make?' she flung at him, her eyes simmering with heated rebellion. 'You fool around behind mine!'

'In what world do you think I'd fool around behind your back?' Dio roared, little caring what he said and not bothering to filter his words.

The silence stretched between them for an eternity. Lucy had heard what he had said but had she heard correctly? Had he really not slept with anyone in all the time they had been married? A wave of pure, undiluted relief washed over her and she acknowledged that resentment at her situation, at least in part, had been fuelled by the thought that he had been playing around with other women, having the sex she had denied him.

She would have liked to question him a bit more, tried to ascertain whether he was, indeed, telling the truth; if he was, more than anything else she would have loved to have ask him *why*.

'Now...' His thunderous voice crashed through her thoughts, catapulting her right back to the reality of him standing in front of her, having discovered the secret she had held to herself for the past couple of months. 'Who the hell was that man?'

'If you'd just stop shouting, Dio, I'll tell you everything.' Lucy eyed him warily.

'I'm waiting—and you'd better tell me something I want to hear.'

'Or else what?'

'You really don't want to know.'

'Oh, just stop acting like a Neanderthal and follow me…'

'Neanderthal? You haven't see me at my best!'

They stared at one another. Hell, she looked so damned hot! He should have obeyed his primitive instincts and laid down laws of ownership from the get-go. He should have had a bodyguard walk three inches behind her at all times. If he'd done that, he wouldn't be standing here now with his brain spiralling into freefall!

'Just come with me.' Lucy turned on her heels and disappeared towards a room at the back, just beyond the staircase that led upwards, and he followed her.

'There!' She stepped aside and allowed him to brush past her, then looked at him as he, in turn, looked around him. Looked at the little desks, the low bookshelves crammed with books, the white board and the walls covered with posters.

'Not getting it,' Dio said, after he had turned full circle.

'It's a classroom!' Lucy controlled the desire to yell because he was just so pig-headed, just so consumed by the business of making money, that he couldn't think outside the box.

'Why are you seeing some man in a classroom?'

'I'm not *seeing some man in a classroom*!'

'Are you going to try and convince me that the loser I got rid of was a figment of my imagination?'

'Of course I'm not going to do that, Dio! Okay, so

maybe I've been meeting Mark here over the past couple of months...'

'This has been going on for months?' He raked his fingers through his hair, but his blood pressure was at least getting back to normal, because she wasn't having an affair. He didn't know why he knew that but he did.

Which didn't mean that he wasn't interested in finding out just what *had* been going on...

'Oh, please, just sit down.'

'I'm all ears to hear what my wife's been getting up to when I've been out of the country.'

He dwarfed the chair and, even though he was now safely sitting down, he still seemed to emanate enough power to make her feel a bit giddy and unsteady on her feet.

'Did you plan this?' Lucy suddenly asked, arms still folded. 'I mean, when you told me that you were going to New York, did you lie, knowing that you intended to follow me?'

'A man has to do what a man has to do.' Dio shrugged, not bothering to deny the accusation. 'Although, if we're going to be completely accurate, *I* didn't follow you. Jackson, my driver, did. When he alerted me to your location, I drove here to find out what was going on.'

'That's as good as following me yourself!'

'It's better because I gather you took the tube and the bus to get here. It might have been difficult getting onto the same bus as you without you recognising me.'

'But why? Why now?'

'Why do you think, Lucy?'

'You never seemed to care one way or another what I got up to in your absences.'

'I never expected my wife to be running around with some man when I wasn't looking. I didn't think that I had to have you watched twenty-four-seven.'

'You don't. Didn't.' She flushed, recognising the measure of trust he had placed in her. She had met many women, wives of similarly wealthy men, whose every movement was monitored by bodyguards, who had little or no freedom. She had once mentioned that to Dio and he had dismissed that as the behaviour of paranoid, arrogant men who were so pumped up with their own self-importance that they figured the rest of the world wanted what they had.

It cut her to the quick now that he might think that his trust had been misplaced.

She hated him, she told herself stoutly, but she wasn't the sort of girl who would ever have fooled around.

Suddenly it seemed very, very important for her to make him believe that.

'I would never have done anything behind your back, Dio,' she said evenly. 'And I haven't. Mark and I are work mates.'

'Come again?'

'I follow a local website,' she told him. 'All sorts of things get posted. Advertisements for used furniture, rooms to let, book clubs looking for members. Mark posted a request for anyone interested in teaching maths to some of the underprivileged kids around here. I answered the ad.'

Dio stared at her, astounded at what he was hearing.

'I remember telling you once that I wanted to go into teaching.'

'I wanted to be a fireman when I was eight. The phase didn't last.'

'It's not the same thing!'

'Strange that you wanted to teach yet ended up marrying me and putting paid to your career helping the underprivileged.'

'I didn't think I had a choice!' Lucy answered hotly.

'We all have choices.'

'When it comes to…to…family, sometimes our choices are limited.'

Dio wryly read the subtext to that. There had been no way that she was going to leave Daddy to pay the price for his own stupidity and greed. Better that she put her own dreams and ambitions on hold. And of course, saving Daddy *had*, after all, come with a hefty financial sweetener…

'And, now your choices are wide open, you decided that you'd follow your heart's dream…'

'There's no need to be cynical, Dio. Don't *you* have any dreams you've ever wanted to follow?'

'Right now my imagination is working full-time on getting the honeymoon you failed to deliver…' And that was precisely how he intended to harness his roaming mind. He had fallen hard for what he had thought was her disingenuous innocence. If she thought that he was mug enough to repeat his mistake, by buying into the concept of the poor little rich wife whose only dream was to help the poor and the needy, then she was in for a surprise.

'You're not even interested in hearing about this place, are you?' she asked in a disappointed voice. 'When I told you that I wanted a divorce, you weren't even interested in asking me why.'

'Would you like me to ask you now?' Dio looked at her with raised eyebrows and Lucy drew in a couple of steadying breaths because he could be just so unbearable when he put his mind to it. He believed the worst of her and there was no way that he was going to revise his opinions, whatever she told him.

It didn't matter that *he* had married *her* for all the wrong reasons! He played by his own rules.

'Is all of this going to pay enough to keep the wolf from the door?' He spread his arms wide to encompass the little room but he kept his eyes fixed on her face. She looked as though she wanted to cry.

'It doesn't pay anything at all. It's all purely voluntary work.'

'Ah… And what's your relationship with the man who scarpered when I threatened to beat him up?'

'He didn't scarper.'

'Not the answer I want.'

'You're so arrogant, Dio!'

'I'm interested in finding out whether my wife has a crush on some man she met on the Internet!'

His voice was calm and only mildly curious but Lucy could sense the undercurrent of steel running through it. She shivered because, just for the briefest of seconds, she wondered what it would be like for that possessiveness in his voice to indicate jealousy.

She wondered what it would feel like to have this sin-fully good-looking, charismatic and utterly arrogant man… *jealous*.

She shakily dismissed that insane curiosity before it even had time to take root.

'I don't have a crush on Mark,' she told him quietly. 'Al-though, he's just the sort of guy I might have a crush on.'

'What do you mean by that?' Dio was outraged that they were sitting here having this conversation.

'I mean he's a really nice guy. He's kind, he's consider-ate, he's thoughtful and the kids adore him.'

'Sounds like a barrel of laughs.'

'He can be,' Lucy retorted sharply. 'He can actually be very funny. He makes me laugh,' she added wistfully and Dio took a deep, steadying breath.

'And I don't?'

'We haven't laughed together since…'

Suddenly restless, he stood up and began pacing the room and, this time, he actually took in what he was seeing, all the evidence of classes in progress. He flicked through one of the exercise books lying on a desk and recognised his wife's handwriting. Ticks, corrections, encouraging smiley faces…

'So, no crush on the hapless teacher,' Dio eventually drawled. 'And is that reciprocated?'

For a moment, Lucy considered throwing caution to the winds and telling him that *the hapless teacher* was crazy about her. Something dark inside her wanted to see if she could make him jealous, even though she already knew that answer to that one.

'Mark isn't interested in women,' she said baldly. 'Not in that way. He's very happy with his partner who works for a legal firm in Kent. We're just good friends.'

Dio felt a bolt of pure satisfaction and he allowed himself to relax. It had been inconceivable that she had been fooling around behind his back. It was also inconceivable that he would allow her to walk away from him without him first sampling the body that had preyed on his mind ever since he had first laid eyes on her.

Whether she knew it or not, she was his weakness, and he was determined finally to put paid to that. The momentary threat of another man had shown him what he had casually assumed. He had allowed his pride to call the shots, to subdue a more primal instinct to assert himself under a civilised, remote veneer that just wasn't his style. No more. She was his and he wanted her, never more so than now, when she was stripped of the make-up and the designer clothes, when her raw beauty was on show. Her teacher friend might be gay but it still bothered Dio that the man had even seen her like this, in all her natural glory.

Her talk about some mythical man who was kind and caring, waiting out there for her, had also got on his nerves.

His eyes slid lazily to her face and he watched her for a few seconds in silence until he could see the tide of pink creep into her cheeks. When she began to fidget, he allowed his eyes to drift a little lower, slowly taking in the jeans, the tee-shirt and the jut of her pert little breasts underneath.

'So...' he murmured, finding a slightly more comfortable position. 'At least my woman hasn't been screwing around behind my back...'

'Since when am I *your woman*?'

'I like you like this.'

'What are you talking about?'

'Unadorned. It's sexy.'

Lucy went redder. She felt tell-tale moisture seep through her panties, felt an ache down there that throbbed and spread under the unhurried intensity of his gaze.

'I told you, I'm not interested...' But she could hear a wobble in her voice and the shadow of a smile that tugged his lips was telling. She straightened and gave herself a stern mental talking to. 'I'm going to build a life for myself, Dio. A real life—no pretending, no having to talk to people I don't want to talk to, no dressing up in clothes I don't like wearing!'

'Laudable.' He cocked his head to one side. 'So your plan is to continue your voluntary work here?'

'Like I said, it isn't all about money!'

'But you never qualified as a teacher, did you?'

'I will as soon as I can and the work I do here will be invaluable experience.'

'The place is falling down,' Dio pointed out. 'You might want to devote your talent for teaching here but, frankly, I doubt this building will stay the course. You may not have noticed, but there's a bad case of rising damp going on and I'd bet that the plumbing goes back to the Dark Ages.'

'Mark is doing an excellent job of trying to raise funds.'

'Really?'

Lucy didn't say anything for a while and Dio nodded slowly, reading what she was reluctant to tell him.

In hard times, it was always difficult to get well-meaning individuals to part with their cash and certainly, if they were providing a service to the needy, then the parents of those needy children would just not have the cash to give anyway.

The building was collapsing around them and neither of them would be able to stall the inevitable.

'I never knew you were so…engaged in wanting to do good for the community,' he murmured truthfully. 'And I'm willing to lend a hand here.'

'What are you talking about?' Lucy dragged her mind away from a brief picture of how her father would have reacted to what she was doing. With horror. He had always been an inveterate snob of the very worst kind. Women were not cut out for careers and certainly not careers that involved them dealing with people lower down the pecking order! A nice job working for a posh auction house might have met with his approval but teaching maths to school kids from a deprived background? Never in a month of Sundays.

To think of the kids not having this facility was heart breaking. She hadn't been there long, but she knew that Mark had poured his life and soul into trying to make something of the place. And the kids, a trickle which was steadily growing, would be the ones who fared worst.

'You want to walk away from our marriage with nothing rather than face getting into bed with me.' Dio didn't bother to gift wrap what he had to say and he didn't bother to point out that that kiss they had shared was proof positive that she wasn't immune to what he had to offer. 'I can't help that—but you want this building bought…? Repaired…? Turned into a functioning high-spec space…? No expense spared…? How does that sound to you, Lucy? You see…' He relaxed, met her bemused gaze coolly and steadily. 'I want you and I'm not above using any trick in the book to get what I want…'

CHAPTER FOUR

Lucy was appalled.

'What kind of thing is that for you to say?' she demanded shakily. 'You'd stoop so low?'

Dio inclined his beautiful head to one side and shrugged elegantly. 'I don't look at it that way.'

'No? And what way *do* you look at it?'

'I look at it as a form of persuasion.'

'I can't believe I'm hearing this.'

'You're my wife,' he said in the sort of voice that implied he was stating the glaringly obvious and irrefutable. 'When you started concocting your little plan to walk out of my life, you must surely have known that I wouldn't lie down on the ground waving a white flag and wishing you every success. Since when did I turn into that kind of person?'

Lucy shifted uncomfortably and then began fiddling with a pile of exercise books on the desk at which she had sat. Teacher in the front with wayward pupil facing her. Except Dio was far too intimidating to be any old wayward pupil.

'Well?' he prodded coolly.

'I just think it's out of order for you to jeopardise the welfare of lots of deprived children who happen to be benefitting from what is on offer here!'

'I'm not jeopardising anyone's welfare. You are.' He

glanced at his watch. He had been optimistic about getting back to the office at some point during the day and had thus dressed in his suit but, the way things were going, the office felt out of reach at the moment and, strangely enough, that didn't bother him.

He was far too invigorated by what was taking place.

'Is this taking longer than you expected?' Lucy asked with saccharin sweetness that wouldn't have fooled an idiot and he grinned.

Her stomach seemed to swoop and swirl inside her, as though she had been suddenly dropped from a great height without the aid of a parachute. That grin; it transformed the harsh, forbidding contours of his lean face. It reminded her of her youthful folly in letting it get under her skin until she had been walking on clouds, hanging onto his every word, waiting for the next meeting with barely bated breath.

And just like that it dawned on her why the thought of making love to him was so terrifying.

Yes, she hated him for the way he had manipulated her into marrying him for all the wrong reasons. Yes, she hated the way he had showcased her, like a business asset to be produced at will and then dispatched when no longer needed.

But what really scared her was the fact that he could still do things to her, make her feel things that were only appropriate in the domain of a real, functioning marriage.

When she thought of having him touch her, make love to her, she knew that somehow she would end up being vulnerable. He still got to her and she was scared stiff that, the closer he approached, the more ensnared she would become.

Like it or not, she was not nearly as detached as she had presented herself over time.

And that lazy grin was enough to remind her of that unwelcome reality.

'For my dear wife, I would be willing to put business on hold indefinitely.'

Lucy shot him a glance of scathing disbelief and Dio laughed, a rich, sexy, velvety sound that shot right past her defences.

'Or at least for a couple of hours, while we try to work out our little differences. Show me around.' He stood up and flexed his muscles. 'I can't carry on sitting in this chair for much longer. It's far too small. My joints are beginning to seize up. I need to stretch my legs, so give me the guided tour. If I'm going to revive this dump, I might as well start assessing what needs to be done.'

Lucy's full mouth compressed. Was he deliberately trying to goad a response out of her? Or was he just supremely confident of getting his own way, whatever she said to the contrary?

'You're not going to *revive this dump* and you're not interested in what I do here, anyway!'

Dio looked at her long and hard, hands thrust into his trouser pockets.

'I'm going to disagree on both counts,' he told her softly.

Lucy's eyes fluttered and she looked away hurriedly. The dark, naked intent in his gaze was unsettling. She decided that showing him around the school, what little there was of it, was a better option than standing here and having to brave the full frontal force of his personality.

She gave a jerky shrug and directed him to the exercise books on her desk. This was the main classroom, where she and Mark did their best to accommodate the children, whose abilities varied wildly, as did their ages.

She warmed to her subject.

Dio saw what had been missing all these months. She

had presented a beautiful, well-educated, cultured mask to the outside world but the animation had gone. It was here now as she talked about all the wonderful things the school was capable of providing; how much the considerate, funny and thoughtful Mark had managed to do with minimum help and almost no funding. Her eyes glowed and her cheeks pinked. She gestured and he found himself riveted by the fluid grace of her hands as she spoke.

There were several rooms on the ground floor. The building was like the Tardis, much bigger inside than it appeared from the outside.

'Volunteer teachers come whenever they can,' she told him, leading the way into another small room. 'Mark has managed to get a rota going and several subjects are now covered by experts.' She looked at Dio and her voice softened. 'You wouldn't believe the conditions some of the kids who come to us live in,' she explained. 'The fact that they're brought to us in the first place shows a great deal of parental support but there are stories of almost no food, noise pollution from neighbours, overcrowding in small flats...the list goes on.'

Dio nodded and let his eyes drift over that full mouth, the slim column of her neck, her narrow shoulders. Vanilla-blonde strands of hair were escaping the confines of the ponytail and the way they wisped around her face made her look incredibly young, barely a teenager.

'How safe is it?' he asked suddenly.

'Huh?'

'What are the safety procedures around here? Is there just the pair of you working here? And have you been working at night?'

'Are you telling me that you're concerned for my welfare?' Lucy's voice was mocking.

'Always.'

She felt the steady thud of her heart banging against her rib cage. His face was so serious that she was momentarily deprived of the power of speech and, when she did rediscover her vocal cords, she could hear a thread of jumpiness in her voice as she explained that neither of them worked nights and the place was always busy with people coming and going during the handful of hours in which they did work.

'Be that as it may,' Dio continued, 'now that I know where you spend your time, and what you get up to when I'm not around, you're going to have two of my guards close at hand whenever you come here—and, Lucy, that's not negotiable.'

'You used to say that you didn't agree with men who felt that they had to surround their wives with bodyguards!'

'You wouldn't require a bodyguard if you spent your time doing your nails and shopping…which was what I thought you got up to in your spare time.'

'What sort of impression is that going to give?' Lucy cried, feeling the wings of her freedom being clipped and resenting it even as she warmed with forbidden pleasure at the thought of him wanting to protect her.

To protect his investment. She brought herself back down to earth with a sobering bump. An investment he was keen to look after now that he wanted to take full advantage of it before he consigned it to the rubbish bin.

'I've never cared about what other people think. So, how many classrooms are there in this place and what's upstairs…?'

'I can't have great big, bulky men lurking around. They'll scare off the kids.'

'I doubt that in this neighbourhood.'

'Stop being provocative, Dio!'

'If you think I'm being provocative, then how would

you describe yourself?' He strolled towards her and she found herself nailed to the spot, mesmerised by the casual grace of his movements.

'I'm just…just trying to tell you that I don't want to… to…stand out when I come here.' Perspiration beaded her upper lips as he curled a strand of wayward hair around his finger. 'What are you doing, Dio?'

'I'm talking to you. You can't object if your soon-to-be ex-husband takes a little interest in the safety and wellbeing of his wife, can you?'

'That's not what I meant.'

'No?' He looked perplexed. 'Then what did you mean?'

'You…I…' Her sluggish brain could not complete the remainder of her thoughts. Her body felt heavy and lethargic. Right now, she yearned for him to touch her in other places; she absolutely yearned for him to take her to all those places he frequently took her to in her dreams.

She had to exert every ounce of willpower to drag herself physically out of his mesmerising radius, stepping back and sucking in a lungful of restorative air.

'It won't work having great big guys standing on either side of me. Plus, when I come here, no one knows who I am.'

'You're not recognised?' Dio frowned and she allowed herself a little smile.

'Why would anyone recognise me? I dress like this, in jeans, tee-shirts and jumpers, and I scrape my hair back and I don't wear tons of make-up and expensive jewellery.'

He heard the derision in her voice and was struck, once again, at hidden depths swirling just out of sight.

It confused him and that was a sensation he was not accustomed to dealing with. Least of all in a woman whose motivations had left him in no doubt as to the sort of person she was. Not one with hidden depths, for starters.

He raked his fingers through his hair and shook his head impatiently, clearing it of the sudden fog of doubt that had descended.

Did she enjoy the novelty of pretending to do good undercover? Was that it?

'Now, you were asking about the other rooms downstairs.' She briskly took him on the tour he had requested. More rooms with more low bookshelves and a scattering of stationery. She could have equipped the entire school with computers had she so desired simply by flogging one of the items of jewellery locked away in the safe in her bedroom. But she had chosen not to and he presumed that that was because she wanted, as she had told him, to keep her identity under wraps. To keep the extent of her wealth under wraps.

And yet how did that make sense?

She had been a Bishop, through and through. Surely the last thing she should have wanted would be...*this*.

He looked around at the shabby walls which someone had optimistically painted a cheerful yellow, similar to the walls in the hallway. Nothing could conceal the wear and tear of the fabric of the building, however, and the fact that it was practically falling down.

'Mark should be back shortly.' She ended the downstairs tour in a room that was very similar to the others he had been shown. 'If you're really interested, you can ask him whatever questions you like.'

'Think I'll pass on that one.' He leaned against the wall and looked at his wife whose face had become smudged with pencil at some point during their tour. 'I wouldn't want to have to administer smelling salts because he has a fainting fit seeing me still here.'

'Very funny,' Lucy muttered, making sure to keep a healthy distance.

'I have some questions to ask *you*, though. Is there any-where around here we can go for lunch?'

'Lunch?' she parroted, because lunch, just the two of them, was not something they had done since getting married.

'Unless you've travelled with sandwiches and a flask of hot coffee…? In your anxious attempts not to stand out…?' He could have told her that she stood out just looking the way she did.

'There's a café just round the corner.'

'Café?'

'It's not much but they make nice enough sandwiches and serve very big mugs of tea.'

'I'll give that one a miss. Any other suggestions?'

Lucy eyed him coolly and folded her arms. 'You're in my territory now, Dio.'

'*Your* territory? Don't make me laugh.'

'I don't care what you think but I feel I belong here a lot more than I belong in any of those soulless big houses, where I've had to make sure the fridges are stocked with champagne and caviar and the curtains are cleaned on a regular basis just in case…'

Dio's lips thinned. 'If you're trying to annoy me, then congratulations, Lucy—you're going about it the right way.'

'I'm not trying to annoy you but I meant what I said. If you want to continue this conversation and ask whatever questions you want to ask, including questions about the divorce I've asked you for, then you can jolly well eat in the café Mark and I eat in whenever we're here! I can't believe you're such a snob.'

'I'm not a snob,' Dio heard himself reply in an even, well-measured voice. 'But maybe I've seen enough of those greasy spoon cafés to last a lifetime. Maybe I come from enough of a deprived background to know that getting out of it was the best thing I ever did. I certainly have no desire to pretend that it holds any charm for me now.'

Lucy's mouth fell open.

This was the first time Dio had ever mentioned his background. She had known, of course, that he had made his own way up in the world, thanks to her father's passing, derogatory remarks. But to hear him say anything, anything at all, was astounding.

Dio flushed darkly and turned away. 'I'll talk to you when you return home this evening.'

'No!' Seeing him begin walking towards the door galvanised Lucy into action and she placed a detaining hand on his arm.

Just like that, heat from his body seared through her, and she almost yanked her hand back as if it had been physically burnt.

'We…we should talk now,' she stammered, stepping back. 'I know you must have been shocked at what I've asked and I never thought that you would…well, that you would see what I've been up to here…but, now that you have, well, I don't mind having lunch with you somewhere a little smarter.'

Dio sighed and shook his head before fixing fabulous, silver eyes on her flushed face. 'Take me to the café. It's no big deal.'

She locked up behind her and they walked side by side to the café where she and Mark were regulars.

She was desperate to ask him about his past. Suddenly it was as though locked doors had been opened and curiosity was bursting out of her.

He'd grown up without money but had he been happy? As she knew only too well from personal experience, a moneyed background was no guarantee of happiness.

She sneaked a glance at his averted profile and concluded that he wasn't in the mood for a soul-searching chit chat on his childhood experiences.

And it surprised her that she was so keen to hear all about them.

'It's not much,' she reminded him as they pulled up in front of a café that was still relatively empty and smelled heavily of fried food.

'Understatement of the year.' Dio looked down at her and noticed the way the sun glinted off her blonde hair; noticed the thick lushness of her lashes and the earthy promise of her full lips. His breathing became a little shallower. 'But I won't forget the virtues of the brimming cups of tea and the big sandwiches…'

They knew her!

Dio was stunned. Two of the people working behind the counter had kids who had started drifting in to do maths lessons and there was a brief chat about progress.

'And this…' she turned to Dio and glanced away quickly '…is a friend. Someone thinking of investing in the building, really turning it into somewhere smarter and better equipped…' She felt him bristle next to her. She'd always removed her wedding ring before coming here; it was just too priceless to take chances. She sneaked a sideways glance and caught the look of annoyance in his eyes and she returned that look of simmering annoyance with a special look of her own, one that was earnest and serious. 'He's very interested in helping the kids in this area really reach their full potential at school.'

'Because…' Dio said instantly, with the sort of charming smile that would knock anyone off balance, which it seemed to be doing to Anita, whose mouth had dropped open the second she had clocked him. 'Because I happen to have grown up not a million miles from here,' he said smoothly. 'On an estate not unlike the one we passed and, take it from me, the only way to escape is through education.'

Anita was nodding vigorously. John was agreeing in a manly fashion. Lucy was feeling as though she had been cleverly outmanoeuvred.

'This lovely young woman and I…are in discussions at the moment. It could all hinge on her acceptance of my proposal: no more rising damp, all the rooms brought up to the highest specification. Naturally, I would buy the building outright, and the cherry on the cake would be the equipment I would install. I find that computers are part and parcel of life nowadays. How else can children access vital information? Like I said, though, Lucy and I are in talks at the moment…'

As soon as they were seated, with mugs of steaming tea and two extra-large doorstop sandwiches filled to bursting in front of them, Lucy leaned forward, glaring.

'Thanks for that, Dio!'

'Any time. What else are friends and potential investors for? Why didn't you introduce me as your husband?'

'Because there would have been loads of questions to field,' Lucy said defensively. 'They would want to know who I really was…'

'To have snagged me?'

'You have a ridiculous ego.' She sipped some tea and looked at him over the rim of the mug. 'Were you lying when you said what you said?'

Dio knew exactly what she was talking about. Why had he suddenly imparted information about his past? He had always kept the details of his background to himself. Growing up on a tough estate, where the laws of the jungle were very different from the jungle laws of the business world, he had learnt the wisdom of silence. It was a habit that was deeply ingrained.

'Be more specific,' he drawled. 'Nice sandwich, by the way.'

'Did you grow up near here?'

'We *are* breaking into new and unexplored territory, aren't we?' he murmured, his fabulous eyes roving over the stunning prettiness of her heart-shaped face. It amazed him that he had never seen that body. His success with women had started at a very young age and was legendary and yet, with her, *his wife*, he had yet to discover what lay underneath the tee-shirt and the jeans.

Bitterness refused to dampen the sudden thrust of his erection and it occurred to him that he had spent an awful lot of time fantasising about the untouchable ice-maiden who had conned him into marriage.

Not for much longer. That was a very satisfying thought.

'Unexpected announcements, revelations all round, time together without high society peering over our shoulders… Where does it end, I wonder? Oh, yes, I know. In bed.'

Lucy flushed. Those amazing pale eyes sent her nervous system into freefall and as soon as he mentioned the word 'bed' she couldn't stop the tide of graphic images that pelted into her head at breakneck speed.

The principles she had held so dear became gossamer-thin under the impact of those images.

But for her, sex and love were entwined. They were!

'You were out of order implying to John and Anita that you were willing to sink money in the place if I agreed to your demands.'

'Was I?' Dio shot her a perplexed frown. 'I thought that I was only being honest. Nice people, by the way. They seem to have bought into the usefulness of having the after-school tutoring scheme there, but then I guess they would, considering they both have children who attend. Must be tough.'

Lucy was beginning to feel as though she had been stuck in a washing machine with the speed turned to full.

'What must be tough?' She knew what was tough. Tough was the way her carefully laid plans had unravelled at the speed of light in the space of twenty-four short hours. She had suspected that talk of divorce wouldn't fall on completely fertile ground, because her husband was nothing if not proud, but she had not banked on the route he had taken which had now landed them both up here.

With talk of sex shimmering between them.

'Tough being a working parent, trying to make ends meet while still attempting to find the spare time to sit and do homework with kids. I guess that's the situation with your two…friends.'

'They're going to repeat what you told them to Mark.'

'Oh dear. And would that be a problem?'

'You always have to get your own way, don't you?' Lucy looked at him resentfully and then immediately diverted her eyes, because he was just too sexy and too good-looking to stare at for very long. Especially now that the dynamics between them had changed, subtly but dramatically.

'Always,' Dio confirmed readily. 'What do you think your caring, sharing friend will think when he discovers that you're the person standing between the success and failure of his little baby…? Because, from what you've told me, this has been more than just a flash in the pan, try-it-on-for-size experiment for him.'

Lucy bristled. 'Are you implying that that's what it's been for me?' she demanded, sinking her teeth into her sandwich and chewing angrily on it.

'I never noticed just how cute you are when you're

angry,' Dio murmured. 'But then, anger didn't score high on the list of required emotions in our marriage, did it?'

It surprised him just how much he was enjoying himself. Was it the bizarre novelty of the situation? He didn't know and he wasn't going to waste time with pointless questions. He was in very little doubt that as soon as he had had her, as soon as he had slept with her, he would regain healthy perspective on just the kind of woman she was, at which point he would bid farewell to his manipulative wife. But in the meantime…

Lucy lowered her eyes, reminded of just how hollow and empty their marriage had been, and then further reminded of all the high hopes and girlish dreams that had driven her to marry him in the first place.

'I find working with these kids fulfilling,' she told him, ignoring his barb. 'Much, much more fulfilling than making stupid small talk to people I don't like and barely know. Much more fulfilling than going to the opening of an art gallery or a society wedding.'

Privately, Dio couldn't have agreed more. One of the more odious things he had to do in his steady, inexorable rise to the very top of the pecking order was attend events he couldn't give a damn about. But it came with the job and he was too much of a realist to think otherwise.

Funnily enough, it had never occurred to him that his well-bred wife would ever have found that side of life a bore. In fact, he would have thought that that might have been one of the many things she enjoyed about the position into which she had cleverly manoeuvred herself.

Now he looked at her with a frown, trying to work out the little inconsistencies he was beginning to spot underneath the polished veneer he had always associated with her.

'It's going to be all round the neighbourhood that a big

shot investor has taken an interest in our little local after-school club.'

'Not just any old big shot investor, though.'

'What am I supposed to say?' she demanded, pushing her plate to one side, making sure to keep her voice low and calm because people were beginning to filter into the café now and curious looks were being directed at them.

'You could tell them that you didn't care for the terms your big shot investor demanded.'

'You should never have followed me!'

'You know you want me…'

'I beg your pardon!'

'Shocking, isn't it?' He leant back in the chair and was amused when she leaned forward, all the better to make sure that their conversation wasn't overheard. 'You don't want to face up to it, but let's cut to the chase. You're hot for me.'

'I am not!'

'Would you like to put that to the test?' He cast his eyes round the small café and the curious faces. 'Why doesn't the hot shot investor apply a little physical pressure…? Hmm…? How about I reach across this table and kiss you? Remember that kiss? How about we have a repeat performance right here? Right now? Then we could take a vote… find out how many people agree with me that you're attracted to me…'

'You took me by surprise when you kissed me!' Patches of red had appeared on her cheeks. She knew that she didn't look like the calm, composed teacher everyone around here expected her to be. She looked just like she felt. Hassled, overwhelmed, confused.

Excited…

'So this time you'll be prepared. We can both gauge just how much you can withstand what's simmering between us.'

'There's nothing simmering between us!' Desperation threaded her voice.

'Of course there is.' Dio dismissed her in a hard, inflexible voice. 'And it's been there all the way through our sexless marriage.'

'Shh!'

He ignored her frantic interruption. 'I've seen the way you've looked at me when you thought you weren't being observed. You may have connived your way into marriage, and then pulled back once you'd got me hooked, but you still can't quite help what you feel, can you?'

Lucy rested her head in her hand and wondered if she could just wish herself some place else.

'Tell me…did you find it offensive to think of me in terms of being your lover?'

She looked at him, horrified. 'How can you say that? What are you talking about?'

'We couldn't have come from more opposite sides of the tracks,' Dio said drily. 'Did you imagine you might catch a working class infection if you got too close to me?'

'I'm not like that! We didn't have a proper marriage and I wasn't going to…to…'

He waved aside her half-baked, stammering explanation with an air of sudden boredom. 'Not really interested in going down this road,' he drawled. 'The only thing I want is *you*, my beloved wife. I want to feel your naked body writhing under me. I want to hear you scream out my name and beg me to bring you to orgasm.'

'That'll never happen!'

'Oh, it will. You just need to give the whole thing a little bit of thought and stop pretending that it'll be any great hardship for you. It won't be.'

'And you know this because…?' She was aiming for snappy and sarcastic; she got reedy and plaintive.

'Because I know women. Trust me. It won't be a hardship. And just think of the rewards… Fat alimony allowance…your little school shiny and well-equipped…grateful parents and happy little children… Could there be a better start to your wonderful bid for freedom…?' He leaned forward so that they were both now resting their elbows on the table, their faces close together, locked in their own private world. 'In fact, I have a splendid idea. Let's take our honeymoon, Lucy. Two weeks. After that, I have to be in Hong Kong to close a deal on a company buyout. I'll head there and you can… Well, you can begin your life of independence. How does that sound…?'

CHAPTER FIVE

PREY TO WARRING EMOTIONS, Lucy was left to consider her options for three days while Dio disappeared to Paris for an emergency meeting with the directors of one of his companies over there.

By her calculation, that left eleven days of honeymoon time before he vanished across the Atlantic to Hong Kong.

She knew that she had been cleverly but subtly outmanoeuvred.

For a start, the story of the brand new school spread like a raging wild fire. He had played the 'hot shot investor' to perfection. Now, as far as everyone in the neighbourhood was concerned, ordering computers, stationery and getting the builders in was just a little formality because everything was signed, sealed and delivered bar the shouting.

If the whole pipe dream collapsed, Lucy knew that she would have to dig deep to find an excuse that would work. The blame would fall squarely on her shoulders.

The day after she and Dio had lunched in the café, Mark had arrived at work clutching brochures for computers and printers. He had made noises about getting the national press involved to cover a 'feel good' story because 'the world was a dark place and it was just so damn heart-warming to find that there were still one or two heroes left in it'…

Lucy had nearly died on the spot. In what world could Dio Ruiz be classed as a hero?

No one had actually asked what the mysterious conditions were that had been imposed on her, for which she was very grateful, because she had no idea what she would have said.

They had been dependent on various money-raising ventures and government help to cover the scant lease on the building; now two members of the local council descended, beaming, to tell her that there were plans afoot to buy the place outright. They delivered a rousing speech on how much it would benefit the community to have the place brought up to scratch and in permanent active use.

They dangled the carrot of helping to subsidise three full-time members of staff who could perhaps assist in teaching non-English-speaking students, of which there were countless in the borough.

And, twice daily, Dio had called her on her mobile, ostensibly to find out how she was—given their new relationship, which involved conversation—but really, she knew, to apply pressure.

Two weeks…

And then, after that, freedom was hers for the taking.

Was he right? Would sleeping with him be such a hardship? They were married and, when she had married him, she had been hot for him, had counted the hours, the minutes and the seconds till they could climb into bed together. Her virginity was something precious to be handed over to him and she hadn't been able to wait to do it.

She was still a virgin but she was now considerably more cynical than she had once been. And how precious was it, really? So once upon a time she had had a dream of only marrying for love and losing her virginity to a guy she wanted to spend her life with. She had woken up. Big deal.

And she was *still* hot for him. It pained her to admit it, especially since he had gloatingly pointed it out to her and, worse, had proved it by kissing her, feeling her melt under his hands.

What was the point in denying reality? She'd been damned good at facing reality so far; she had not once shied away from the fact that she was trapped in a marriage and forced to play the part of the socialite she probably should have but never had been.

On day three she picked up her mobile to hear his dark, velvety voice down the line and, as usual, she felt the slow, thick stir of her heightened senses.

Once more or less able to withstand the drugging effect of his personality, Lucy had now discovered that her defences had been penetrated on all fronts. Even when he was on the opposite side of the world, she just had to hear his voice and every nerve inside her body quivered in response.

Overnight it seemed as though all the walls she had painstakingly built between them had been knocked down in a single stroke.

'What are you up to?'

Lucy sat down. Was she really interested in launching into a conversation about the porridge she had just eaten?

'Marie has handed in her notice. I knew she was going to at some point. She's far too ambitious to be cleaning. She's got a placement at a college. So I'm afraid you're going to have to find someone else to do the cleaning in the Paris apartment.'

'*I'm* going to have to find someone else?'

'Well, I won't be around, will I?' Lucy pointed out bluntly. She projected to when she would shut the door of their grand, three-storey mansion in London for good and she felt her heart squeeze inside her.

Sitting in the first class lounge at JFK airport, Dio frowned. By the time he returned to London, he wanted an answer from her, and the only answer he was prepared to accept was the one he wanted to hear.

That was what he wanted to chat about now. He certainly didn't want to have a tedious conversation about their apartment in Paris and finding a cleaner to replace the one who had quit. He didn't want her to start the process of withdrawing from the marriage. No way. Nor had he contemplated the prospect of not getting what he wanted from her.

It occurred to him that there really was only one topic of conversation he was willing to hear.

'I'll cross the bridge of hiring a new cleaner when the time comes.'

'Well, it'll come in the space of two weeks, which is when Marie will be leaving.'

'What are you wearing? It's early over there…are you still in your pyjamas? Does it strike you as a little bizarre that we've never seen each other in the confines of a bedroom, wearing pyjamas?'

Lucy went bright red and cleared her throat. 'I don't know what my clothes have to do with anything…' She automatically pulled her dressing gown tighter around her slender body and was suddenly conscious of her bra-less breasts and the skimpiness of her underwear.

'I'm making small talk. If we're to spend the next two weeks together—'

'Eleven days,' Lucy interrupted.

Dio relaxed and half-smiled to himself. He had made sure to phone her regularly while he had been away. Over the marriage, they had managed to establish a relationship in which she had been allowed to retreat. That retreat was not going to continue.

And now, without her having to say it, he could hear the capitulation in her voice. It generated the kick of an intense, slow burn of excitement.

'If we're to spend the next eleven days together, then we need to be able to converse.'

'We know how to converse, Dio. We've done a great deal of that over the course of our marriage.'

'Superficial conversation,' Dio inserted smoothly. 'No longer appropriate, given the fact that our relationship has changed.'

'Our relationship hasn't changed.'

'No? I could swear you just told me how long we're going to be spending on our long-overdue honeymoon...'

Lucy licked her lips nervously. The dressing gown had slipped open and, looking down, she could see the smooth lines of her stomach and her pert, pointed breasts.

She had made her mind up about his ultimatum and she hadn't even really been aware of doing so.

Soon that flat stomach and those breasts would be laid bare for him to see and touch.

A little shiver raced through her. She slipped her finger beneath her lacy briefs and felt her own wetness. It shocked her. It was as if her body was already reacting to the knowledge that someone else would be touching it—that *Dio* would be touching it.

'Okay,' she said as loftily as she could manage. 'So, you win, Dio. I hope it makes you feel proud.'

'Right now, pride is the very least of the things I'm feeling.' His voice lowered, sending a ripple of forbidden excitement through her.

Out of all the reasons she had privately given herself for yielding to his demands, she now acknowledged the only reason that really truly counted for anything.

It had nothing to do with the school, duty towards her students or, least of all, money.

She had yielded because she fancied him and because she knew, as he did, that to walk away from a dry marriage would be to wonder for ever what it might have been like to sleep with him.

Her head might not want to get into bed with Dio but her body certainly did and this was her window.

The fact that there were a lot of up sides and bonuses attached to her decision was just an added incentive.

'I'd tell you what I'm feeling,' he said roughly, 'but I'm sitting in the lounge at JFK and I wouldn't want anyone to start noticing the hefty bulge in my trousers...'

'Dio! That's...that's...'

'I know. Unfortunate, considering I'm going to have to wait a few more hours before I can be satisfied.'

'That's not what I meant!'

'No?'

'No,' Lucy told him firmly. To add emphasis to her denial, she very firmly tightened the dressing gown so that she could cover up her treacherously over-heated, semi-naked body. 'I...I'm happy to discuss the details of...er... our arrangement.'

'Speak English,' Dio said drily.

'I'll do this honeymoon business with you but only because I don't have a choice.'

'That's not very enthusiastic,' Dio admonished, hanging onto his temper. If he could put his feelings to one side, if he could forget her duplicitous take on their marriage, then he was damned if he was going to let her get away with dragging her feet and somehow blaming him for the fact that she wanted to sleep with him.

'Everyone expects you to descend and start flinging money at the school.'

'I find it doesn't do to mould your life according to other people's expectations.'

'How do I know that once this so-called honeymoon of ours is over you'll do what you say…?'

'You don't.' Dio was affronted. He had always been a man of his word, which was saying something, in a world where very few men were. He might not have been born with a silver spoon in his mouth but he knew one thing for sure: in his business practices, and in fact in his whole approach to life, he was a damned sight more ethical than a lot of his counterparts whose climb up the ladder had been a great deal less precarious than his had been!

'You'll have to rely on that little thing called trust.'

Lucy didn't say anything and Dio felt the significance of her silence like a disapproving slap on the face.

Rich, coming from the ice-maiden who had strung him along.

'I'm not a man who breaks his word,' he said coolly. 'I know many who do.'

Lucy thought of her father, who had cheated so many people out of their pensions, and she flushed guiltily. Were Dio's thoughts running along the same lines? He might have married her for all the wrong reasons but then he had never claimed to love her, had he? Even when they had been dating, he had never talked about love.

And something deep inside her knew that, if he had given his word, then he wasn't going to break it.

'Shall I book somewhere?' she asked stiffly. 'I expect you want to use one of the houses…'

'I think you can climb out of "personal assistant" mode on this occasion,' Dio said softly. 'It somehow ruins the… sizzle.'

His husky voice was doing all sorts of peculiar things to her body and she squirmed on the chair, idly glancing round at all the top-notch, expensive equipment in the very expensive kitchen.

'I surely need to book flights for us?' Lucy intended to do her very best not to let either of them forget that their weird honeymoon was built on stuff that was very prosaic.

This wasn't going to be one of those romantic affairs where they would spend their time whispering sweet nothings and staring longingly at one another over candlelit dinners before racing to their room so that they could rip the clothes off one another.

This was more getting something elemental out of their systems.

'Don't give it a thought,' Dio said briskly. 'I'll get my secretary to do the necessary.'

'But where will we be going? And when, exactly?'

'I'm at JFK now. When I return to London, I'll have a quick turnaround. Be prepared to be out of the country this time tomorrow.'

'What? I can't just leave here at a moment's notice.'

'Of course you can. My secretary will take care of everything. You just need to get ready for me...'

'Get ready for you?'

Dio laughed at the outrage in her voice. He was so hard for her right now, he was finding it difficult to move.

Small, high breasts... He had glimpsed the shadow of her cleavage in some of the more daring dresses she had worn to social events over the course of the marriage. He wondered what colour her nipples were. She was a natural blonde and he imagined that they were rosy pink, kissable nipples. He wondered what she would taste like when he buried himself between her thighs.

He wondered who else she had shared her body with before she had met him.

It was a grimly unappealing thought and he ditched it before it had time to take root.

'Use your imagination,' he drawled. 'Get into the head set...'

'Yes, sir...' Lucy muttered under her breath and she heard his soft laughter down the end of the line. Sexy laughter. The laughter of a man who'd got exactly what he wanted. She fidgeted a little more and forced herself to focus. 'And what should I pack?'

'Don't. I'll make sure that there are clothes waiting for you at the other end.'

'I don't want to be dressed up like a Barbie doll,' she told him quickly. 'That's not part of this arrangement.'

'I shall see you very soon, Lucy...'

'But you still haven't told me where we'll be going!'

'I know. Isn't it exciting? I, for one, can't wait.'

And he disconnected. Lucy was left holding a dead phone and feeling panicked because now there was no going back.

She tried to think of life after the next ten days but she found her mind getting stuck with images of Dio in bed with her. After she had discovered the truth behind their sham of a marriage, she had told herself that that was why he had not tried to get her into bed before they had tied the knot.

She had thought that he was being a gentleman, respecting her wish to wait until they were married before having sex. She had been too embarrassed to tell him that she was still a virgin, and anyway the subject had not arisen.

Instead, he had been stringing her along. She had stopped day dreaming about him but the day dreams were rearing their heads once again and she couldn't stop them.

How was she supposed to travel to some unknown destination? They could be going to the Arctic, the Caribbean or a city somewhere. Had he even decided or was he going to let his assistant choose where they went?

And what was it going to be like when he returned to the house?

The knowledge that they would be cooped up together for the better part of a fortnight would lie between them like a lead weight...

Wouldn't it?

She was a bundle of nerves as evening drew round. For the first time in as long as she could remember, she didn't dress up for his arrival. Usually, she never dropped the role unless she was on her own. Usually he saw her formally attired, even when she was in casual clothing.

But things were different and she had defiantly chosen to wear a pair of jeans and a faded old tee-shirt from her university days. Nor was she plastered with make-up and she hadn't curled her hair. Instead, she was a make-up-free zone and her hair hung heavily just past her shoulders, neatly tucked behind her ears.

She was in the same place as she had been when she had confronted him with talk of divorce, standing in the drawing room. And she was just as jumpy.

And yet, staring through the window into the, for London, relatively large garden with its row of perfectly shaped and manicured shrubs, she didn't hear him until he spoke.

'I wondered if you would wait up for me.' Dio strolled into the drawing room, dumping his jacket, which he had hooked over his shoulder. It had been a tiresome flight, even in first class, but he felt bright eyed and bushy-tailed now as he flicked his eyes over her.

He'd half-expected her to go into a self-righteous melt-down between speaking to her on the phone and showing up at the house. She was very good at adopting the role of blameless victim. He guessed that the lure of money was irresistible, however. She might play at her volunteer work and make big plans to teach but teaching didn't pay nearly enough for her to afford the sort of lifestyle to which she had always been accustomed.

Cynicism curled his lips when he thought that.

'Drink?'

A feeling of déjà vu swept over Lucy as she helplessly followed him into the kitchen, although this time she had eaten, and she expected he would have as well, so there would be no pretend domesticity preparing a meal.

'I thought we could chat about plans for tomorrow,' she began valiantly. 'I need to know what time we will be leaving. I...I've packed a couple of things...' He looked drop-dead gorgeous and she could feel the electricity in the air between them, sparking like a live, exposed wire. It made the hairs on the back of her neck stand on end.

And the way he was looking at her, his pale eyes skewering her, brought her out in a nervous wash of perspiration.

She wanted crisply to remind him that their arrangement was for the honeymoon period, which technically would only start when they reached wherever they were heading, and so for tonight they would retreat to their separate quarters as per normal. However, her tongue seemed to have become glued to the roof of her mouth.

'Have you been thinking about me?' Dio asked lazily. 'Because I've been thinking about you.' And marvelling that it had taken them this long to get where they were now, but then again the whole question of the penniless divorce had driven the situation.

He walked slowly towards her and she gave a little nervous squeak. 'I thought we were going to...er...well, when we were away...'

'Why stand on ceremony? The honeymoon's been cut

a little short by my unexpected meeting in New York any-way, so fair's fair, wouldn't you say? I don't want to be short-changed on time. If I'm to pay for two weeks, then I want my two weeks, or as good as…'

The last thing Lucy was expecting was to be swept off her feet. Literally. The breath whooshed out of her body as she was carried out of the kitchen. She felt the thud as he nudged the door open with his foot and then she was bouncing against him, heart racing as he took her up the stairs.

To his bedroom, which she had been into many times before. It was a marvel of masculinity. The colours were deep and rich, the furniture bold and dark with clean lines. Even with her eyes squeezed tightly shut, she could visual-ise it. Once, when he had gone away, leaving the house a lot earlier to catch a transatlantic flight, she had gone into the bedroom to air it before the cleaner came and had remained frozen to the spot at the sight of the rumpled bed, still bear-ing the impression of where he had been lying. She could remember tentatively touching it and then springing back because it had still held the lingering warmth of his body.

It had shaken her more than she had thought possible.

He dumped her on the bed and then stood back, arms folded, for once lost as to what his next move might be.

He had been fired up with confidence downstairs, when he had hoisted her into his arms like a true caveman and brought her to his bedroom. But now…

She looked unimaginably beautiful and unimaginably fragile, her eyes wide and apprehensive, making him feel like a great, hulking thief who had snatched her from her bed and carried her off to his cave so that he could have his wicked way.

Dio raked his fingers through his hair and moved to the window where he stood for a few seconds, looking outside, before snapping the wooden shutters closed, blocking out the street light.

Lucy stared at him from under her lashes. Her heart was still pounding and the blood was still rushing through her veins, hot and fierce. She wanted him so badly right now that she felt like she might die of longing, yet he was just standing there, looking at her with brooding stillness.

Maybe he had come to his senses, she thought.

Maybe he had realised that you couldn't just bargain with someone's fate the way he had with hers. Maybe he had seen the light and come to the conclusion that to blackmail someone into sleeping with you just wasn't on.

And if that was the case then why wasn't she feeling happier? Why wasn't she sitting up and making a case for having her divorce without a bunch of stupid stipulations? Why wasn't she striking while the iron was hot, trying to locate Mr Decent who must surely be there hiding behind Mr Caveman?

She wasn't feeling happier because she wanted him, simple as that.

Maybe if he had never mentioned sleeping with her, had never looked at her with those amazing, lazy, sexy eyes, she would have walked away from their marriage with her head held high and all her principles burning a hole inside her.

But he had opened a door and she wanted that door to remain open. She wanted to enter the unexplored room and see what was there...

She stirred on the bed then pushed herself backwards so that she was propped against the pillows, which she arranged under her, her vibrant blonde hair tangled around her flushed face.

Dio was her husband yet she felt as tongue-tied as a teenager on her first date with the cutest boy in class.

'Why are you just standing there?' she challenged, dry mouthed. 'Isn't this what you wanted? To carry me up here so that you could get *what you paid for*?'

Dio flushed darkly and scowled. Was that how he had sounded? Like a thug?

'Nearly a year and a half with no sex, Lucy. Are you telling me that I got a fair deal when I married you?' His voice was harsher than he had intended and he saw her flinch.

'Maybe neither of us got much of a fair deal.'

Personally, Dio thought the deal she had ended up with had been a hell of a lot better than his.

'You haven't answered my question.'

'You brought me up to your room for sex and here I am. You're getting what you paid for!' Brave words, but the way she cleared her throat alerted Dio to the fact that she might be talking the talk, but that was where it probably ended.

It seemed just one more thing that wasn't fitting into the neat slot he had shoved her into for the past year and a half.

A cold, opportunistic woman would surely not have been able to replicate the nervous wariness he could see beneath the brave statement of intent?

Her fingers wouldn't be digging into her arms to stop them from trembling…

'I find that I'm not as much into self-sacrificing martyrs as I had imagined,' Dio said, pushing himself away from the window ledge against which he had been leaning.

'Even the ones you forked out good money to buy?'

'You were never that cynical, Lucy.' He had a vivid image of her laughing at him with genuine, girlish innocence, the sort of girlish innocence that had made him lose his mind. She might not have been quite as innocent as she had pretended but she certainly hadn't been as sharp-tongued as she was now.

'I grew up,' she said with painful honesty.

'You can run along,' he told her, reaching to the top button of his shirt. 'I've had a long flight. I'm tired. I'm going to have a shower and hit the sack.'

She didn't want him to.

She could play the passive victim and scuttle off but she wasn't going to do that. She felt as though she had spent the past year or so playing the passive victim—had spent practically *her whole life* playing the passive victim—and now would be her only window in which to take control of a situation.

'What if I decide that I don't want to run along?' she asked with considerable daring.

Dio stilled, hand still poised to remove his shirt. Her chin was mutinously jutting out and he smiled, reluctantly amused by the expression on her face: stubborn, holding her breath, eyes squeezed tightly shut..

'What are you saying?'

'You know what I'm saying.'

'I like things to be spelt out in black and white. No room for error then…'

'I've wondered, okay?'

'Wondered what?' He was standing right by the bed now, looking down at her with a smile of male satisfaction.

'What it would be like…you know…? With you…'

'Even though you've spent many months being an ice-queen?'

'I've been very friendly with all your clients.'

'Maybe I've been longing for a few of those smiles to be directed my way,' Dio murmured. He slowly began unbuttoning his shirt, watching her watching him as his brown chest was exposed inch by inch.

Lucy was riveted. How long had she wanted this? How had this insane desire been so successfully hidden under layers of resentment and simmering anger, with a large dose of self-pity thrown in for good measure?

She watched as he tugged the shirt out from the waistband of his trousers, drew in a deep breath and held it as he shrugged off the shirt altogether, tossing it casually on the ground.

'So, you're curious...' He felt as though he was suddenly walking on clouds. It was an extremely uplifting sensation. In fact, when it came to the feel-good factor, this was as good as it got. Her eyes were huge and, yes, curious. He was bulging in his trousers, thick and hard and desperate for a release, which he was going to take his time getting to.

Drugged by the sensational vision of him half-naked... her bronzed god of a soon-to-be ex-husband... Lucy was deprived of speech. She nodded and didn't even bother trying to tear her eyes away from his glorious body.

'I confess I'm curious too,' Dio admitted, basking in her undiluted fascination with his body. 'So it's time for you to return the favour...'

'Huh?' Lucy blinked.

'One good turn deserves another,' Dio said drily. 'Or, in this case, one semi-striptease deserves another.'

'You want me to...?'

'We're man and wife.' He gestured broadly. 'A little bit of nudity should be as nothing between us.'

'I hate it when you do that,' she complained. He grinned and that grin erased all the forbidding, harsh lines of his beautiful face; made him seem almost boyish.

'Do what?'

'Oh, don't play the innocent with me.' But she smiled shyly and sat up. Her fingers were shaking; her hands were shaking. He had no idea that she had never done anything like this in her life before. Okay, at university there had been some good-natured fumbling with the two boys she had dated for six months and three months respectively. But they'd been boys and he was...

Dio...

Nerves ripped into her with a vengeance, but she had committed to this path, *wanted* this path, and she wasn't going to give in to cold feet now.

But that didn't mean that she wasn't shaking like a leaf as she dragged the tee-shirt over her head and flung it to the ground where it joined his shirt.

He had folded his arms and was staring, just as though she really was performing a proper striptease for his benefit only.

Which, she supposed, she was, in a way.

She closed her eyes, reached behind, unclasped her bra and, still with her eyes shut, flung the bra onto the little growing heap of discarded clothes.

'You can open your eyes,' Dio drawled. He was surprised he could talk at all because the sight of her was enough to take his breath away.

He loved the way she was sprawled there on his bed, her head averted. He could see the tiny pulse beating in her neck and, God, he wanted to fall on her, take her, sate himself with her body.

She was beyond captivating.

Pale, slender, her small breasts pert and pointed, her nipples as pink as he had imagined, but bigger. Perfect, circular discs that sent his blood pressure soaring.

Lucy opened her eyes and slid a hesitating, self-conscious sideways glance at him. She had no idea where she had found the courage to do what she had done, but she had had to do it, and one look at the naked hunger and desire in his eyes was enough to restore every scrap of her wavering self-confidence. She glanced at his trousers, then back to his face, and he laughed.

'So my beautiful ice-maiden thaws...' He slowly un-looped his belt from his trousers and then pulled down his zipper. He was utterly confident when it came to his own nudity and he really liked the way she was still looking at him. He pulled down the trousers and his boxers in one easy movement, and her eyelids fluttered as she took in the impressive girth of his erection.

'Your turn now...and then you can touch...' He loosely held himself and noted her quick, sharp intake of breath. Just one more of those little hot reactions and he knew that he wouldn't be responsible for what happened next.

Their eyes held and she wriggled her jeans down until she was left only in her panties. She couldn't stop looking at his big hand holding himself.

'Let me feel you first,' Dio said raggedly. He reached down and slipped his hand to cup the moist mound between her legs, then he pushed his finger in before sliding it along the slippery slit until he felt the throbbing nub of her clitoris.

Lucy gave a long, low groan and parted her legs.

There was no room in her head to contemplate her absolute lack of experience.

He would find out soon enough...

CHAPTER SIX

DIO STRADDLED HER and for a few seconds he just looked down at her. His fingers were wet from where he had touched her and felt her excited arousal.

She still seemed unable to meet his eyes in the shadowy darkness of the room and he gently tilted her face so that she was forced to look at him. He wanted to take her fast and hard...he was so aroused that he could scarcely breathe...but he could sense her nerves and, with a sigh, he lay down alongside her then hitched himself up on one elbow.

'Tell me you're not in the grip of second-thought syndrome,' he murmured, stalling her attempts to cover herself with his duvet.

Lucy's burst of self-confidence was fading fast. Her husband was the most beautiful man she had ever laid eyes on and, having spent far too long fantasising about him, she was even more bowled over at his beauty in the flesh. No fantasy could do him justice. He was a man in the very peak of his prime. No part of his impressive body was untoned. His stomach was washboard-flat, his shoulders broad and muscled. His sheer perfection not only made her teeth chatter with nerves but also made her very, very much aware of her lack of experience.

He would have slept with countless women. You could

tell that just from the way he was so comfortable in his own skin. He was a man who didn't mind women feasting their eyes on him, who probably enjoyed it.

She didn't imagine that *his* teeth were chattering with nerves at the thought of hopping into the sack with her.

She had to fight off the urge to leap off the bed and make a sprint for her clothes on the ground.

'No, of course I'm not,' she said, dry-mouthed. If he'd been short-tempered or impatient at her sudden shyness, she might have found sufficient anger to rally her mental forces and shrug off her attack of nerves. But his voice was low and curiously gentle and it reached something deep inside her that she hadn't revealed in the long months of their marriage.

Something vulnerable and hesitant. Gone was the hard veneer she had manufactured to protect herself.

'Then why the sudden reticence?' He traced the circle of her breast, running his finger in a spiralling motion until he was outlining her luscious pink nipple. He watched it stiffen and lowered his head to flick his tongue over the toughened nub.

Lucy took a dragging breath and stifled a groan.

'I…I just never thought that we would find ourselves in this situation,' she confessed, expecting the barriers that had existed between them to shoot back into place but, when he replied, his voice was pensive.

'Nor did I, not that I didn't want it.'

'I'm afraid,' she laughed nervously. 'The package without clothes might not be exactly what you'd expected.'

'What makes you say that?'

'I'm not the most voluptuous woman on the planet,' she said lightly. 'Too flat-chested. When I was at school, and all the other girls were developing breasts and hips, I just developed height and everything else stayed the same. I barely need to wear a bra. Men like women with big boobs. I know that.'

'You know that, do you?' He teased her throbbing nipple with his tongue and felt her melt under his touch.

'Yes. I do. Why else do you think those men's mags have always been so popular?'

'I can't say I've ever given it a passing thought. I've never read those things. What's the point of looking at a picture of a woman when you could be lying in bed with one?' Dio told her truthfully. He hadn't actually banked on doing a whole lot of talking in this arrangement. He had wanted the body she had deprived him of. And since when had sex involved long, soul-searching conversations?

Certainly they never had with him.

In fact, before Lucy, women had been pleasant interludes in a hectic, stressful work life. He had never become emotionally attached—had never encouraged any woman to think that he was, had never given any of that a passing thought. Meaningful conversations had been thin on the ground.

Against all odds, considering she should have been the last woman on earth he would want to have any sort of relationship with, Lucy had been the one woman to lodge underneath his skin. He had never delved deep into asking himself why that was. He had assumed that it was because she was also the one woman who hadn't made bedding him a priority.

Which—and why wouldn't this have been a natural conclusion?—was why he wanted her; why he had been unable to treat the marriage as the sham it had turned out to be and carry on playing the field. It had irritated the hell out of him that she had not given a damn one way or another whether he fooled around or not during their marriage and that, in turn, had been a source of slow-burning anger and dissatisfaction.

Now that she was within reach and he could see that burr under his skin finally being dislodged, he thought that conversation was the least he could do.

If she wanted to talk, then why not?

He couldn't, however, understand the self-denigration. Where had *that* come from? She had led a pampered, privileged life, the only child of wealthy parents. True, her father had been no better than a common criminal, but that didn't nullify all the advantages she had had.

She was, literally, the golden girl. Seeing her in action over the past year or more had really shown him just how easy she found those social graces; just how at home she was moving in the circles which he had been denied, thanks to her father.

He couldn't care less because he had made it to the top but he couldn't seriously credit that the self-confidence she had always oozed was anything but bone-deep.

He wondered where she was going with this and reluctantly was curious to find out.

He kissed the corner of her mouth and she squirmed and manoeuvred her body so that they were facing one another.

'Have you any idea how tough this is for me?' Dio asked her roughly and Lucy blushed.

'What?'

'Feeling your sexy little body pressed up against me. No, I take that back. I think you have a very good idea of how tough this is for me because you can feel my desire against your skin. That says it all.'

'You're…you're very big,' Lucy whispered, and Dio grinned.

'I'll take that as a compliment.'

'I mean…have you ever found that a problem?'

Dio frowned. 'What are you talking about? Why would I have found that a problem? A woman's body is engineered to accommodate a man of my size.'

'There's something I feel you ought to know,' she whispered, heart beating fast. 'I'm not as experienced as you probably think I am.'

'I never thought you were the sort of woman to sleep around.'

'I'm not. In fact, actually, I haven't slept around at all,' she admitted awkwardly and Dio edged back from her.

'Are you telling me that you've never made love to a man before?'

'It's not that big a deal,' she returned defiantly.

Dio remained silent for so long that she wondered whether he was trying to concoct an excuse to withdraw from the situation which he had been so keen to engineer.

'How come?'

'I don't feel comfortable having this conversation. I just thought that…that it was something you should know before…well…' She laughed nervously. 'When you're disappointed, then you'll understand why.'

Dio sat up.

His wife was a virgin. Incomprehensible. How had she managed to withstand the advances from men, looking the way that she did? *Why* had she? He raked his fingers through his hair then swung his legs over the side of the bed.

Lucy took advantage of the moment to yank the duvet over her.

This was a nightmare. What on earth had possessed her? Dio was a man of experience, a guy who had married her as something convenient that came as part of the package deal. He wasn't into virgins and he certainly wouldn't be into holding her hand while she lost her virginity.

She must have been mad.

Mortification swept over her in a hot wave.

Typically, he hadn't bothered to get dressed. While she had felt an urgent need to cover herself, he was as comfortable having this hideous conversation in the buff as he would have been in one of his hand-made Italian suits. He had moved to sit in the chair by the mahogany desk by the bay window.

'How come?' he repeated. 'And please don't tell me again that you don't feel comfortable having this conversation.'

'It just never happened for me.' Bright patches of colour delineated her cheekbones.

There was no way she intended pouring her heart out with some little-girl story of how unhappy her childhood had been; how she had witnessed her mother's miserable stoicism in the face of her father's selfishness and philandering. She wasn't going to drone on in a self-pitying manner about her lofty determination only to have sex with the man she truly loved which, frankly, would have been a confession too far—especially considering the man she had thought she loved had turned out to be just the kind of man she should never have got mixed up with in the first place.

'No testosterone-filled boys creeping through the windows of your prim and proper boarding school to have their wicked way with the innocent virgins?'

His lightly teasing tone was so unlike him that she felt herself begin to relax.

'None of that. There was always the house mistress on red-hot alert, waiting with a rolling pin for any daring intruders.'

She lowered her eyes but could still feel him staring

thoughtfully at her and she didn't like that. It made her feel exposed.

'And I suppose daddy was just as protective with his little girl?' His voice was hard-edged.

Lucy shrugged. Yes, he'd seen off potential boyfriends all right, not that there had been many of them, but only because he had been such a crashing snob that no one had fitted the bill.

In retrospect, taking into account his dire financial situation, none of them had had the necessary bank balances to provide a rescue package anyway. Dio had certainly fitted the bill and he had not been on her father's ridiculous social-climbing radar.

Watching her, Dio saw a shadow cross her face, gone as quickly as it had come, and he was struck by a sudden intense curiosity to find out what lay behind that shadow.

'I would completely understand if you'd rather call it a day right now.' She laughed a little unsteadily. 'It was a stupid idea, anyway. You can't just *have a honeymoon* and pretend that all the stuff that's happened between us never took place.'

'You'd be surprised,' Dio murmured.

He stood up and strolled over to the bed. She was a virgin. The thought rocked him, brought out a fierce possessiveness which he never knew he had. All those nervous little looks and shy glances now made sense. He'd never have guessed, but then he hadn't been looking, had he? He had accepted the cover version of her, the cool, elegant woman born into wealth and comfortable with it.

He hadn't thought to look any deeper. She had deceived him, as far as he was concerned, that that was the end of the story. He had closed the door and it had been a lot easier to keep it closed.

'I'm surprised,' he murmured, 'to think that you have

never made love to a man before…shocked, even…but not turned off. I have no idea where you got that notion from, my dearest wife.'

His voice was low and husky, his grey eyes glittering with intent.

'But can I ask you one thing?' He returned to the bed, depressing the mattress with his weight, and very slowly pulled down the duvet which she had dragged up to her neck in a vain attempt at modesty. 'Why choose the husband you're keen to divorce? Seems an unusual option.'

Lucy felt that if he listened hard enough he would be able to hear the steady, nervous thump of her heart.

Now, wasn't *that* a question?

'I fancy you.'

'And fancying me is enough to paper over the fact that you don't like me?'

Lucy felt that she could say the same about him, but men were different from women, weren't they? Women looked for love and men sought sex. That was why Dio had never been tempted in the past to hitch his wagon to any of the many women he had slept with. There had been no broken engagements or heart-rending tales of thwarted love. When they had been dating, during that brief window when she had actually believed that he was interested in her for herself, he had laughed when she had asked him whether he had ever been in love.

Dio might have used her, and certainly did not feel anything for her, not even affection—but he would still have no problem getting into bed with her because, as far as he was concerned, that was part of the marriage contract which he had been denied and, besides, he didn't think she was half bad-looking.

It was slowly dawning on her that she might hate him for stringing her along—might hate that core of coldness inside him that had allowed him to be the kind of man who could do that—but there was still something deep in the very heart of her that wasn't quite as immune to him as she would have liked to be.

She would rather have chewed her own arm off than ever admit that to him.

'Why not?' she asked.

Dio frowned. Their marriage had been little more than a business transaction and he wasn't sure why he now found her attitude unsettling.

'I was young when I married you, Dio. I'm only twenty-four now. Before you came along, I was totally wrapped up doing my maths degree and it didn't leave a whole lot of time for men.'

'You mean I was the first guy you really ever fancied...'

'You're a good-looking man.'

To his ears, that sounded like agreement, which made him wonder why she had retreated to her ivory tower the second the ring was on her finger.

'Then why wait until now?'

'Because maybe I've discovered that I'm more like you than I wanted to admit, even to myself.' She breathed with the panicked sensation of someone treading on thin ice.

So much safer when she had been able to keep her distance and set aside all the uncomfortable thoughts now besieging her.

'Now that we're going to be getting a divorce—'

'That's a matter that's still up for debate...'

'I know the conditions and I accept them,' Lucy told him bluntly. And then she added for good measure, for just that little bit of protection, 'And you're right—I can't see a way forward if I leave this marriage with nothing. I've never known what it was like to be broke.'

'Because Daddy protected you even when he was going under and all but waving a white flag…'

'Whatever.' She took a deep breath and did her utmost to disconnect from the contempt she felt for a man who had betrayed her mother and herself for pretty much all of his life. 'Now we're going to part company for ever in a couple of weeks' time, why deny the fact that I find you an attractive man? It makes sense to sleep with you, Dio. Like you said to me, it won't be a hardship.'

Pretty much everything she said got on Dio's nerves even though there was not a single thing he didn't agree with, not a single thing that shouldn't have eased his conscience.

'And what if I told you that you could have the money you want without the sex?' he heard himself ask.

Lucy looked at him, surprised.

'You mean that?'

'What if I told you that I did?' For a man who didn't deal in hypotheses, he discovered that he was a dab hand at dishing them out. He had seen nothing wrong with going after what he wanted, *what he was owed*, and likewise he had seen nothing wrong in using whatever tools were at his disposal to get there. After all, he owed nothing to a woman who had been his wife in name only for reasons that had suited her at the time. Why should he care about a woman who had turned out to be no better than a gold-digger?

Annoyingly, it now irked him to think that she was only going to hop into bed with him because he had dangled that money carrot in front of her. So she fancied him. Big deal. From the age of thirteen he had known what it was like to be fancied by the opposite sex. But did she fancy him enough to sleep with him if she didn't think that it made financial sense?

He loathed the direction his thoughts were taking but seemed unable to stop the flow now that it had begun.

'Are you? Because, if you're just speculating, then I don't want to be having this conversation. You're free to walk away cash in hand, Lucy, and you don't have to sleep with me as part of the deal.' He flung himself onto his back and stared up at the ceiling. If this was what it felt like to be the good guy, then he could say in all honesty that he'd felt better.

'Really?'

'Feel free to show your true colours, my beloved wife,' Dio said acidly, still staring up at the ceiling but conscious of her naked, sexy body next to his with every treacherous pore of his being.

'I meant what I said when I told you that I want to sleep with you—money doesn't have anything to do with it.'

Dio inclined his head to look at her. He couldn't credit the soar of triumph that greeted her unsteady admission.

'Is that the sound of you telling me that you're using me…?' He shifted so that he was lying on his side and lost himself in a shameless observation of her beautiful body, even though it was costing him not to touch that beautiful body. Yet.

'And what would you say if I told you that I was?'

'I'll live with it,' he murmured. 'Now, lie back. I don't think I've ever had so much talk before sex in my life before.'

Lucy's eyelids fluttered and she obeyed, sprawling with feline satisfaction, arching slightly so that her small breasts were pushed up.

With an unsteady groan, Dio planted a trail of kisses along her neck, then lower across her collarbone. He found heaven when he finally took one nipple into his mouth. It was sweet and succulent and he suckled on it, feeling it tighten in his mouth and hearing her moan as he swirled his tongue across the sensitive surface before drawing it long and deep into his mouth once again.

Gently he cupped her other breast, massaging it, and then rolling his fingers over her nipple, a warm-up for his mouth.

It was pure agony taking his time but he refused to let himself forget that she was a virgin. His virgin. His virgin bride. The thought of that fired him up on all fronts and appealed to the very essence of his masculinity.

He took his time as he straddled her, pushing her legs wide open to accommodate him, and gently stilling her instinct to snap them shut.

He was so aroused that he could scarcely breathe. If he began telling her what he wanted to do with her, he knew that he would find it impossible not to come.

This was a first for her and in some ways it was a first for him as well. The slight tremble which he knew she was trying hard to contain gentled his natural raw instincts.

Her other nipple was waiting for him and he took it gently into his mouth and teased and licked and sucked until she was writhing underneath him, arching up, her fingers curled into his hair so that she could push him down against her breast.

Her nipple was taut and glistening as he finally drew away. Hands flat on either side of her, he continued to trace a path along her rib cage, over her stomach, pausing to circle her belly button and then lower still…

Lucy's eyes flew open as his mouth moved to caress her inner thigh.

'Dio…'

He looked up and smiled. 'Dio…what…?'

'I…I…'

'Relax. Trust me. You're going to enjoy me kissing you

down there.' The scent of her filled his nostrils. 'And don't close your eyes,' he commanded. 'I want to know that you're watching me when I begin licking you...'

Lucy moaned as her imagination took wonderful flight. She was so wet for him, wanted him so much. She marvelled that she had spent so many months primly keeping her distance, little knowing that he had the power to melt every bone in her body until she was as pliant as a rag doll.

She watched as he settled between her legs, hands against the soft flesh of her inner thigh preventing her from closing her legs, making sure that she was open for him.

Delicately he slid his tongue between the soft folds, finding the throbbing bud of her roused clitoris with ease and tickling it.

The pleasure was exquisite.

She wanted to keep her eyes open so that she could see his dark head moving with purpose between her legs but she couldn't. She tilted her head up and arched her back, an instinctive response to what he was doing.

When he plunged his finger into her, whilst keeping up the insistent pressure of his tongue on her clitoris, Lucy could no longer hold herself back.

The waves of pleasure were too much, far too much. She didn't want this...she wanted him in her... But with a long, shuddering groan she gave in to the ripples that increased into an unstoppable riptide of her orgasm.

She came against his mouth, rising up, crying out, moving wildly as his tongue continued its ruthless plunder.

Her own lack of experience stared her in the face as she gradually came back down to earth.

'I'm sorry.' She turned away as he moved up to tilt her chin gently so that they were looking at one another.

'Only tell me you're sorry if you didn't enjoy it.'

'You know I did,' she whispered. 'But I...I should have

been able to hold off. I shouldn't have come…not like that…not when I want you in me…'

'I wanted to bring you to an orgasm, Lucy. This is just the foreplay…'

'It's pretty mind-blowing,' Lucy returned shakily.

'You're so beautiful and wet that I'll be able to slide into you, and I'll be gentle. I don't want to hurt you.'

Lucy found it remarkable that this powerful, ruthless man, accustomed to getting his own way at all costs, could be so tender between the sheets.

Yet, wasn't that the hallmark of the expert lover? That was what she told herself because it was bad enough that he was climbing out of the box into which she had securely placed him. She just didn't need yet another side of him to hit her in the face and overturn yet more preconceptions.

He said that she should trust him and that he didn't want to hurt her but some little voice inside cautioned her that it was within his power to deliver a great deal of hurt.

He already had! Surely the proof of the pudding was in the eating? He had married her so that he could so-cially elevate himself. Her father had been cruelly clear on that count. He had turned her into the cynical woman she was now! It would be wise to remember those things. She knew that the most important thing in the world was self-preservation.

She wanted a divorce, wanted to rid herself of a marriage that was a joke, and tellingly he hadn't argued against that. He wanted her but, once he got that out of his system, he would be more than ready to ditch her and move on with his life, find himself some woman he actually had feelings for and wanted to settled down and have children with.

That woman would never be her.

But, Lord, it was hard to marshal her thoughts when her whole system was in crazy free fall!

She felt him nudge against her and, just like that, a slow burn began. She wrapped her arms around him, loving the hardness of his body.

'Tell me what to do,' she whispered. Those were words that Dio had never heard from any woman and they were curiously thrilling.

'Do nothing but what feels good for you, and lose yourself, Lucy. It's what making love is all about.'

That sounded like a pretty scary concept to her but she nodded obediently and then stopped thinking altogether as he began to kiss her, slowly, taking his time.

She could taste herself as their tongues meshed. She reached down to hold him; he was massive, a hard shaft of steel that sent her senses spinning.

But she wasn't scared. She knew that he was going to be gentle.

And she wasn't filled with regret either. So what if this didn't make sense? So what if he had offered her the way out she had asked for without the blackmail? He had told her that she could walk away and that she wouldn't walk away penniless and she believed him.

But walking away would have opened the door to, if not regret, then a life of wondering what this husband of hers would have been like in bed, what it might have been like to have touched him.

No. She was doing the right thing.

He cupped her breast and played with it, idly stroking her roused nipple while he remained kissing her until she felt like she was drowning.

Then slowly, oh, so slowly, his hand smoothed over her stomach to cup the mound between her legs. Only then did he caress her down there, but so lightly that she had all the time in the world for her body to crank back into full gear, until she was throbbing and aching for more.

She wanted to push his hand in deeper, but instead she twisted so that she could taste him.

She'd never done anything like this before. She took him into her mouth and heard his sharp intake of breath as she began to lavish attention on the rigid shaft. She ran her tongue exploratively along it, sucked it, filling her mouth; cupped him between his legs and felt him expand under her attentions.

This time, he was the one spiralling out of control, but he pulled back before she could do what he had done to her and bring him to an orgasm with her mouth only.

Their bodies were slick with perspiration.

'Don't be nervous,' he whispered as he settled between her legs.

'I'm not nervous.' She felt the thickness of his erection and shivered with a mixture of wild excitement and apprehension.

'No?'

Lucy heard the amused disbelief in his voice and some of her apprehension drained away. 'Okay. Maybe a little.' Though he was someone whose very being posed a threat—who could be daunting and intimidating; whose presence she had contrived to avoid as much as possible from the very instant she had overheard that conversation on her wedding night—she trusted him wholly and completely with her body.

'You're so wet,' he murmured unsteadily, barely able to control his shaking hands as he blindly reached for protection in the little drawer by the bed, fumbling like an amateur. He nudged into her, feeling her tightness expand to hold him and fighting against a natural urge to ram himself in her right up to the hilt. 'You're going to enjoy everything I do...'

'I already have,' Lucy confessed honestly. She sensed

him taking his time and knew that it must be difficult for him. She didn't think that her husband was at all accustomed to taking his time with anything if he wanted it badly enough. It just wasn't in his nature. But he was taking his time now, gently probing deeper, but making sure to ease out before continuing to penetrate her in little stages.

'I like that.' He whispered things in her ear, sexy things he wanted to do with her, that had her blushing to her hairline. With each nudge, her nerves dissipated until she was desperate to feel all of him in her, desperate for the surge of his formidable strength inside her.

With the intuition of experience, Dio felt the change in her and offered a prayer of thanks because holding back was sheer torture.

He thrust deeper and more firmly inside. Rearing up on both hands, unable to hold back any more as he gazed down at her small, perfectly formed breasts, Dio moved with assurance, building up a rhythm until each thrust took her closer and closer over the edge.

Lucy had never thought that sex could feel so good. He'd been right. He had fitted into her as perfectly as a hand fitted into a glove; had fitted into her as though their bodies had been crafted to slot together. And now...

Her fingers dug into the small of his back as he continued to thrust, deeper and deeper, until she felt as though they were fusing into one. It was indescribable.

She hurtled over the edge in a wave of pure ecstasy. There was no room in her head for thought or analysis. Pure sensation took over. Every part of her body was on fire, soaring high, swooping thrillingly, until at last the crashing waves of pleasure became ripples and finally subsided, leaving her limp and utterly sated.

She clung shamelessly to him as he withdrew. Her mind

was still in a whirl. She couldn't think straight; her body was tingling and burning and as weak as a kitten.

'Enjoyed?' Dio didn't immediately feel his usual compulsion to vacate the bed the second love-making had come to an end but, then again, he told himself that it wasn't every day he made love to a virgin who also happened to be his lawfully wedded wife.

'It was lovely.'

'Lovely?' He gave a low growl of laughter and swept her damp hair away from her forehead. 'I prefer sensational...' And she had come to him without any pressure at all. Triumph made him heady with renewed desire.

'So, I guess that now we've...made love...' She shifted to disentangle herself from his embrace and he tightened his grip.

It had been easy not to think when she had been caught up in the wonder of making love but now reality began to drip in.

This was her first time and, yes, sensational was definitely the word to describe the experience. But for him this was all routine stuff. He had already given her a time limit of a fortnight, after which he anticipated getting bored, but perhaps she should establish a bit of cool and restraint herself. She'd acted like a limpet and the last thing she wanted was for him to get the idea that this strange situation was one that was out of her control.

Out of control were her physical responses. But that was where it ended.

She wasn't the foolish romantic she'd once been. She'd toughened up.

'Yes?'

The low timbre of his voice was a drag on her senses. 'Would you say we've put this thing between us to rest?' She chuckled lightly.

'What do *you* think?' Dio murmured. He'd been prepared to do the decent thing and let her escape with the money she wanted but things had changed since that bout of decency. He curved his hand possessively between her thighs and felt the slick moisture between her legs.

'You had your chance to fly away, my dearest wife, and you decided not to. Well, fair's fair, wouldn't you say? Ten days of happily wedded bliss and then we part company. Like I've said to you, Lucy, it won't be a hardship for either of us...'

CHAPTER SEVEN

LUCY GAZED DOWN as the plane dipped below the clouds and a vision of glittering blue water dazzled brightly up at her.

Originally, Dio said, he had thought about taking her on safari but had decided that a week and half making love in the sun was a far better idea.

'Why let some lions and elephants interrupt our journey of discovery?' he had drawled, catching her eye and holding it. 'Activity holidays are all well and fine but the only activity I want to do with you involves a bed and not much else…'

Heady stuff, she had thought with a strange pang.

The journey of discovery had not been the one she had contemplated in those giddy days before they had tied the knot. This journey of discovery would be a physical journey, and the only thing they would be discovering would be each other's bodies, but she had been utterly unable to resist.

After that first session of making love, they had made love again and again. Ingrained habit had propelled her out of his bed in the early hours of the morning but he had pulled her back to him and told her that he wanted to wake up next to her in the morning.

She had stayed and they had made love again in the morning, taking their time.

She found it almost impossible to keep her hands off him but she had uneasily given herself permission.

This was an arrangement of sorts, just as their marriage had been.

He could disconnect and so could she. It might not be in her nature but the option of walking away felt as impossible as climbing Mount Everest barefoot.

So the honeymoon that had never happened was arranged without delay. Given that he would then disappear off to the other side of the world to return to his high-octane life of big deals and even bigger money, time was of the essence for him, she guessed.

He had his catching up to do before she was dispatched without a backward glance.

They would be going to his place in the Caribbean. It was one of the few houses which Lucy had not had to personally see to as it hadn't been used since they had married. It was not on the map when it came to entertaining clients. Townhouses and apartments in city centres always received a lot more use.

'Excited?' Dio snapped shut his computer and devoted his attention to his wife, now that the plane was about to land.

He had worked for the duration of the journey even though he had felt her next to him, her floral scent filling his nostrils and driving him to the insanity of joining the Mile High Club.

The sex was going to be explosive. In fact, he couldn't wait to get her into bed again. If he had his way, they wouldn't make it as far as the private beach that surrounded his villa.

That said, he had no intention of losing perspective on this little episode, and keeping a firm hand on the situation was imperative. Raw physical instincts were all well and good provided they obeyed the order he had always imposed on himself. Work first.

'I've never been to the Caribbean before,' Lucy admitted.

'Never?' Dio was astounded.

'In fact, we didn't do a great deal of travelling at all.' Because, she could have added, that would have been a little too much family time for her father to deal with. For them all to deal with, come to it.

'You surprise me,' Dio murmured. 'I would have thought that you and your family would have been fully signed-up members of the playground of the rich club...'

Lucy shrugged and said lightly. 'Life is full of surprises.'

'As I'm discovering,' Dio breathed.

'So...' She dragged the conversation back to its starting point. 'When you asked me whether I was excited... I am. To see the island and to experience island life.' She had twisted to look at him and as their eyes met she felt a sliver of intense excitement race through her body.

'Is that all that's exciting you?'

Lucy reddened. Her mind shot back to the intimacy of their caresses, the way he had made her body come alive, and she licked her lips nervously. He was probably accustomed to women praising him to the skies but, since she wasn't one of his doting fans, she refused to do that.

'Tell me about your house,' she said a little breathlessly.

'What would you like to know?' Dio drawled, breaking off eye contact. 'It was a celebration purchase when I made my first million in profit. Since then, I've collected a few more properties along the way, as you know only too well.'

Because I look after them like an employee, Lucy thought. It was a timely reminder of their respective roles and the game they were playing and she was thankful for it.

'And you're right.' She dropped her voice to a husky whisper. 'The island and your house aren't the only things I'm looking forward to...'

Dio laughed appreciatively under his breath. This was more like it. The language of desire was a language he understood.

He was barely aware of disembarking. His head was caught up in all sorts of pleasant images of what he intended doing with her the very second they reached his villa. He had made sure that the place was aired, cleaned and supplied with sufficient food and drink to keep them going for the duration if they decided not to venture out. He had a person out there fully employed, even though their only job was to make sure an empty villa was looked after and unused gardens were kept under restraint.

All in all, he looked forward to smooth sailing and satisfying those physical needs he had foolishly underestimated over the past months.

His remarkably non-existent libido in the company of other women, including women who had done their utmost to distract him, should have sounded a warning bell that he still fancied the hell out of his opportunistic wife.

Life, as she had so succinctly pointed out, was certainly full of surprises—and, though never a man to enjoy the unexpected, he intended to enjoy this particular surprise to the full.

And then...divorce.

It made sense.

He squashed the surge of frustration that greeted that thought. Divorce made sense. He had married her, yes—because he had fancied her; because he had come round to thinking that a wife would be a handy accessory; and, of course, he had taken the company, and to take Robert

Bishop's daughter as well had seemed fitting retribution for the wrong that had been done to his father.

But life could hardly be called satisfying for either of them. He had not ended up marrying the woman he wanted to bed. He had ended up marrying a woman who had had her eye to the main chance.

He would be well rid of her.

Once he had cleared her from his system, which was what this little sojourn in the tropics would be about.

The same, he assumed, applied to her.

Having travelled the world, he was blasé about a lot. But now, as they were transported to his villa through small streets lined with the waving fronds of coconut trees, with glimpses of turquoise ocean glittering through the spaces, he had to admit that he had chosen a peach of an island on which to buy his villa.

It was tiny. They could cover it end to end in a handful of hours.

And Lucy...

She was as eye-catching as the scenery, as was her enthusiasm. He had never seen her as excited as this at any of the grand houses which had been at her disposal. She peppered him with questions, face flushed, eyes wide, like a kid in a toy shop.

How the hell had the Caribbean managed to pass her by? Wasn't that one of the bonuses of leading a pampered life? The long haul, over-the-top holidays?

How had *family holidays* passed her by? Unless Daddy had been too busy drinking and dipping his hands in the coffers to spare the time?

After the gluey, uncomfortable heat of summer in a city it was balmy here, with a breeze blowing lazily through the swaying fronds of the coconut trees, only just disturbing the exotic colours of the flora.

In the twenty minutes it took for them to reach his villa, they passed three cars and many more people on foot. The economy was exclusively tourism-based, and every so often glimpses of millionaires' holiday mansions flashed past, along with several boutique hotels. They drove through the town centre, which was colourful and without a single department store in sight.

As soon as he had decided where they would be heading, he had got his long-suffering secretary to sort out a wardrobe. It would be waiting for them in the bedroom when they arrived.

New experience, new clothes. Simple as that.

'Wow, Dio. This is…spectacular.' Lucy had never seen anything like it. The villa sprawled in gardens that led down to a private cove. Surrounding the entire house was a broad, wooden-planked verandah with pale, sun-bleached railings and, from the overhanging eaves, baskets of brightly coloured flowers spilled out in a welter of extraordinarily diverse colours. Coconut trees fringed the gardens at the back. She could just about make them out. In front, it was picture-perfect, from the blazing blue of the sky, to the ocean stretching out ahead of them seeming so impossibly close to the lush, tropical gardens leading down to the cove.

She gaped.

'I wish I'd been to this house,' she said a little wistfully. 'It would have made a change from the city apartments and houses.'

'You grew up in London. I took you for an urban girl.'

'My mother's family came from Yorkshire,' Lucy said abruptly. 'She was an only child but she remained close to her cousin after her parents died.'

Standing next to her, staring out at the open ocean, Dio frowned at the sudden edgy tension in her voice.

Was she having second thoughts? he wondered. She had certainly gone back to her formal dress, the suitable attire of a rich man's wife. Slim, silk, loose-fitting trousers, a silk top, discreet items of gold jewellery, make-up.

It irked him.

He didn't want to have a hot ten-day fling with the wife he had known for the past few months. He wanted to spend it with the girl he had confronted in that shabby building in East London.

Was he being greedy?

'So your family holidays were in Yorkshire...'

'Mum and I used to go there often.'

'And stay in the family home?'

'That was no longer available to us. We stayed with Aunt Sarah.'

'I see...' He wondered where her slimy father had been when these trips had been taking place. 'I don't recall you disappearing off to Yorkshire after we married.'

'Well,' Lucy said lightly. 'It's not as though we were around one another twenty-four-seven. A lot of the time you were abroad and, when we *were* sharing the same space, well...'

'Which makes it all the more special that we will be sharing the same space here...but in quite a different way...'

Lucy didn't imagine that long conversations were going to play much of a part in this 'special way' they would be sharing space. Considering she had always placed such high value on the quality of the relationship that defined marriage, considering she had sold herself short and made a horrendous mistake, she still couldn't shake the simmering excitement at what lay ahead for the next ten days.

Since when had she ever been interested in sex for the sake of sex?

It baffled her but she was helpless to do anything about it.

'Shall we go in?' She changed the conversation, wondering whether she should play the sexy kitten he expected. 'I'm dying to see what the villa looks like and I feel rather hot and tired.'

'I'll lead the way.'

Inside was as exquisite as the outside. Wooden floors, soft muslin blowing gently in the breeze through open windows, with pale shutters keeping out the blast of the hot sun, bamboo furniture and a short staircase leading to spacious bedrooms and bathrooms on the landing above the ground floor.

He had had someone come in and make sure the place was ready for immediate occupation, although he had done away with having staff on the grounds while they were here. There was a little Jeep, if they wanted to go into the town or to explore other beaches, and enough food and wine to see them through.

It was paradise for the extremely wealthy and she should have taken it in her stride, for she was well accustomed to the palatial splendour of his other properties, but she was still knocked for six as they did a quick tour of the villa.

There was nothing she didn't adore about it, from the furnishings and the feeling of space and light to the magnificent views and the distant sound of the sea.

They bypassed four huge bedrooms and finally she was standing in the room they would be sharing.

The smiling man who had brought them from the airport had deposited her and Dio's scant luggage on the king-sized four-poster bed and it suddenly hit her...

This was their honeymoon. The honeymoon that had never been. She was with her husband and, even though their union had been a cruel joke, she couldn't stop the piercing thrill that filled her when she turned to look at his darkly sexy face.

The windows in the bedroom were sprawled open and she strolled to stare out, breathing in the wonderful balmy air and enjoying the way the breeze lifted her hair from her face.

'Are you going to survive for ten whole days without staff waiting at your beck and call?' she asked, eyeing him, and then nearly subsiding into a frantic, nervous coughing fit as he began to unbutton his shirt, exposing a sliver of hard, brown chest.

'It's a sacrifice I'm prepared to make because I don't want to have anyone around while we're both here.' He slanted just the sort of wicked smile at her that sent her senses shooting off into la la land. 'Come.'

Lucy walked slowly towards him and fell into his arms. His scent filled her nostrils with the punch of a powerful aphrodisiac. She almost lost it and groaned.

It didn't matter how many times her head was telling her that this was a pretend honeymoon; right here and right now, it felt *real*.

She wanted this man as though there had been no muddy water under the bridge.

Dio tilted her chin and kissed her, a long, lingering kiss their tongues meshed and explored each other's mouths.

Lucy clung.

'You must be baking hot in this get-up,' he murmured.

Lucy thought that she was damned hot now and it had nothing to do with the temperature. In fact, the outfit was pretty cool, even though her body was on fire.

'I think we need to bath you...'

'We're going to shower...together?'

Dio laughed with open delight and led her to an amazing wet room in different shades of sand and tan marble. 'Now,' he said briskly. 'Clothes off.'

There was furniture in the bathroom. He proceeded to

sit on a clean, lined wicker sofa, legs indolently crossed, half-naked and all rippling muscle and sinew.

This felt very different from the safety of a darkened room.

'I can't.'

'Why not?'

'Stage fright.'

Dio threw his head back and laughed, a full-bodied laugh rich with genuine amusement.

'My virgin bride,' he murmured, his silver-grey eyes roaming appreciatively over her fully clad body. 'How about if I break the ice for you?' In one easy movement, he stood up and undressed, and Lucy watched, fascinated by his utter lack of self-consciousness.

'You make me feel so gauche,' she said nervously as he walked towards her, all powerful, all aroused and all one hundred percent alpha male.

'Touch me.'

Lucy took his heavy shaft between her slender fingers and a ripple of anticipation almost knocked her sideways. Her breathing quickened and her pupils dilated darkly as she played with him, enjoying the power she felt as he moved in her hand.

He controlled his surging response.

He was realising that he couldn't get within a metre of her without his body going crazy. Maybe it was just the natural after effect of all those months of keeping his distance. He should have handled this situation a hell of a lot sooner, but why go down that road? The fact was that they were here now and he intended to waste no time in exploring every single way he could discover his wife's sexy body.

The fact that she was so innocent was an unbelievable turn on.

'If you're self-conscious about doing a striptease for your husband...' he said unsteadily, holding her hand firm, because any more of what she was doing and he would respond in the only way he knew how '...then allow me to perform the task myself...'

Lucy succumbed. With every touch, she shed a little more of her inhibitions. This was what she had dreamed of when she had enthusiastically accepted his marriage proposal. Nothing had turned out quite the way she had expected, but she was determined to enjoy the physical pleasure he was offering her. Neither of them was looking for more than what was on the table.

They showered under jets of water that felt like warm rainfall. Halfway through, he switched off the jets and explored every inch of her with his hand and his mouth while she stood with the water drying on her, back pressed against the cool tiles, eyes closed, savouring every sweet lick. When he brought his mouth against the damp mound of her femininity, she parted her legs and let his tongue drive her to such dizzy heights that she could no longer contain the scorching orgasm that just seemed to go on and on and on as he kept his mouth firmly pressed against her, tasting her as she came.

The promised wardrobe was waiting for her when they finally made it out of the bathroom. Her body was singing.

'So, I had some clothes brought here for you.' Dio threw open the wardrobe doors and Lucy tentatively peered inside.

One by one she went through the things before turning to him where he lay sprawled on the bed in nothing more than a pair of unbuttoned jeans. His hair was still damp from the shower.

'But these aren't what I'm normally accustomed to wearing.'

Dio raised his eyebrows at her confused expression. 'I didn't think designer labels would be appropriate.'

Lucy tentatively stuck on a pair of small, faded denim shorts and the cropped top which could have come straight out of a department store.

These were the clothes she felt comfortable wearing and always had done. Even when she had been surrounded by money, growing up, designer labels had always made her feel like someone who had to be on show, the perfect doll which her father could parade in front of his chums to give an impression of the perfect family that had been far from the truth.

On the many trips she had made back with her mother to Yorkshire, she had ditched the silk and cashmere and enjoyed the freedom of wearing what she wanted. She had escaped the cloying confines of a life she didn't like and this was what it felt like now. A brief escape before she embarked on a whole different life. She was his wife and yet this felt like stolen time.

She told herself that her husband was a guy who knew what he wanted just as he knew what made women tick.

He wanted her and he was shrewd enough to work out that, yes, sophisticated London glamour would not set the scene for the sort of rapid-fire seduction he had in mind.

But there was still a treacherous part of her that was willing to overlook the cynicism behind his choices.

Not that he would have scoured department stores for the clothes himself. He would have told one of his minions what he wanted and that would have been the sum total of his contribution.

It was good that her head was still working, she thought.

'Nice,' he commented approvingly. 'I liked what I saw when I surprised you at that little club of yours and I like what I'm seeing now.'

'I'm not a puppet and you're not my puppet master.' And wasn't this just another form of him dressing her up for his own purposes?

'Is that what you've thought of me during our marriage? That I've tried to control you?' Dio's pale eyes flicked over her flushed face.

'Haven't you?'

'Most women would slice off their own right arm to be controlled by a man who gives them limitless spending money.'

'Dio, I don't want to argue with you about this. We're not here to…to argue…' They had never spoken as much during their marriage as they had done over the past couple of days and there had been times when Lucy had almost felt…*seduced* into telling him why she had pulled back from him the second the final guest had left on their wedding night. Whatever he thought of her and her father, she had wanted him to see her side of the story. She had had to remind herself that he had used her and that was the bottom line.

He had wanted her father's company, had been in a position to grab it for a knockdown price, and, even though he had certainly put right the wrongs her father had done financially, he had got *her* in exchange—the perfect hostess who could move seamlessly amongst his important clients, who actually *knew* some of them from times past.

She suspected that, had they consummated their marriage, he would have tired of her sexually within weeks and would have set his sights on other women.

Once, just once, she had done an Internet search on him to find out about the women in his past. There had been nothing aside from one photo taken from years and years ago of a curvy brunette clinging and laughing up at him as they emerged from a limo somewhere in New York. He had just signed a record-breaking deal.

That single photo had been enough to tell her the sort of women he was drawn to. It gave credence to her father's malicious taunt that Dio was little more than a jumped-up barrow boy who had made a few bucks and needed a suitable little woman to show off to the world that he'd come good.

She had overheard enough on her wedding night to know, for herself, that he was no saint when it came to manipulating an advantage. She had heard the low, cold intent in his voice when he had told her father that he had his company, and he could personally ruin him, but instead he would have his daughter, so he could count his blessings...

She hadn't needed to hear any more.

'No, we're not,' he told her softly. 'So why don't you come and sit here by me and show me why we're here...?'

'Do you ever think of anything but sex?' But she relaxed a little, pleased to close the door on that uneasy conversation between them.

'I'm finding it hard to in this particular situation,' Dio drawled, watching with satisfaction as she strolled towards the bed, looked for a moment as though she intended to take a flying leap on to the mattress but then gracefully settled next to him, though sitting up with her legs crossed.

'And, by the way, I don't like you referring to my project in East London as some *little club* of mine...' Lucy wondered where that had come from, considering she didn't want contentious subjects to get in the way of this arrangement of theirs.

'Following on from that, I've set things in motion to take care of all the finances there.'

'I know and I should have thanked you.' *But she'd had too much on her mind: him.* It made her cringe. 'Mark

phoned just before we left and told me. He was very excited and he's waiting until I return so that we can break
the news to the community together.'

'Cosy.' Dio frowned. Did she have a crush on the man,
whatever she chose to tell him? 'You didn't mention that
he called you.'

'I forgot,' Lucy told him honestly. 'Besides...' She lay
down at a distance next to him until he pulled her against
him and curved her so that they were facing one another,
bodies pressed together.

'Besides what...?'

'Besides, there's no law to prevent me from talking to
Mark, especially as we work together.'

'You can have however many cosy chats you want to
have with him, and with anyone else for that matter, once
you're no longer my wife.' Dio knew that he was overreacting. The man was a limp-wristed tree-hugger.

Except that was probably just the sort of guy Lucy
would be attracted to. In an ideal world.

The thought got on his nerves and he found that he
couldn't let it go.

'Who else comprises this little community of do-gooders?' he asked and Lucy tugged herself free of him and lay
back to stare at the ceiling.

'Why do you have to be so condescending?'

'I'm not being condescending. I'm expressing curiosity.'

'I would have thought that you, of all people, would
have sympathised with *do-gooders* who actually want to
do something to help those who aren't so lucky in life.'

'Let's not get into my background, Lucy.'

'Why not?' She looked at him, glaring. 'You always
feel free to get into mine.' Not that he knew the first thing
about what her background had really been about!

'You're avoiding my question. Who else works with you? How long have you known them? Did you approach these people or did they approach you, via some kind of mutual acquaintance?' Dio heard the rampant possessiveness in his voice with distaste.

Lucy was bewildered at the harshness of his voice. What, really and truly, did he care one way or another?

'I approached them,' she admitted. 'I wanted to do more with my life than just be a hostess looking after your properties and mixing with other women who were married to similarly wealthy men. I wanted to use my brain and I saw an ad online so I applied. And there are a few of us who volunteer on a part-time basis. Mark is the key guy but there are… Well, do you want me to name them all?'

'Like I said, I'm curious. Humour me.'

With a sigh—because she couldn't recall him ever being that curious about what she got up to when he wasn't around and she saw his sudden burst of curiosity as just another controlling aspect of his personality—she listed the five other members of their team: three women, all much older than her, and two guys.

'And, when the cat's away, you socialise with these people?'

'Off and on.'

'Whilst concealing who you really are: no wedding ring in sight…'

'I wanted to be taken seriously, Dio. If they knew… Well, if they knew that I was married to you, that I lived in the house I live in, chances are they would just write me off as some rich young girl playing at helping out. Why are we having this conversation?'

Dio wasn't entirely sure himself. He just knew that nothing she said was filling him with satisfaction. 'So none of those guys know that you're married.'

'Not unless they're physic.'

'And what are they like?' he asked with studied casualness.

Lucy thought about Simon and Terence. 'Really, really nice,' she admitted. 'They're both full-time teachers and yet they still manage to find the time to come in whenever they can. They do at least three after-school classes a week. Simon teaches maths alongside me. Terry covers English and history. I can't wait to break the news about what…what you're going to do about injecting some cash into the organisation. They'll be over the moon.'

'Indeed…' Dio ran his hand along her smooth thigh and felt her quiver in immediate response. 'And, when the delighted celebrations kick off, I think it's only fitting that I attend as the wealthy benefactor…wouldn't you agree?'

Lucy shrugged and tried to imagine her husband mixing with the teachers and parents. She had a mental image of a lion being dumped into a litter of kittens.

But of course he would want to see where his money was going. He wasn't a complete idiot. He might have used that as a way of getting her where he wanted her, but he was shrewd enough not to write off the cash as money that could be blown.

And yet, did she want him invading this very private part of her life? The part of her life that she had mentally linked to her bid for freedom?

A sudden thought occurred to her and it was unsettling. Would he actually want to do much more than just throw money at the project? Would he want to oversee things? Would he still be a presence in her life, a dark, powerful, disturbing presence, even after they were divorced?

'I don't think we should talk about this,' she murmured, reaching down to hold him, feeling a surge of power at being able to distract him simply by touching him. 'I think there are far better things to do than talk right now...'

Dio swept aside the uneasy feeling that, for once, he wasn't entirely sure that he could agree...

feeling which set her nerves fizzing and her blood roaring as he got closer and closer until, just like that, the
fine, settling comfortableness of feeling half asleep
would vanish and her body would take over.

CHAPTER EIGHT

OVER THE NEXT few days Lucy successfully managed to
suppress those niggling, uncomfortable thoughts that occasionally bobbed to the surface.

What was going to happen once they left this paradise
bubble they were in? Would he expect her to leave the
house by the time he returned to London after his Hong
Kong trip? Would he choose to keep working abroad until
the coast was clear? Naturally, they would have to talk
about the nitty-gritty business of the divorce. It wasn't
something that would happen at the click of his imperious
fingers but she had no intention of contesting whatever financial settlement he agreed to give her.

Strangely, the seductive lure of gaining her freedom
no longer shone like a beacon at the end of a dark tunnel.

She assumed that that was because she was having the
time of her life.

It amazed her, this ability to divorce her emotions from
a physical side of her she'd never known she possessed.

It was as though something so powerful had awakened
in her that it overrode all her common sense.

Sex. Everywhere and anywhere.

At night, they shared the same bed and, far from that
feeling weird and abnormal, it felt absolutely brilliant. She
enjoyed that period of being half-awake, half-asleep, curl-

ing into the warmth of his naked body and feeling it stir into instant response.

Everything else took a back seat. Misgivings. Unanswered questions. Simmering resentments. None of it mattered when they were making love. He'd been right. This so-called honeymoon, a time when they could both exorcise whatever it was they had to exorcise, was no hardship at all.

Today, a boat trip had been planned. Lucy looked up at the ceiling, missing the presence of Dio's body next to her because he had awakened at the crack of dawn and was in some other part of the villa working.

A little smile curved her mouth. Before he had left the bed, he had touched her, slipped his finger into her half-slumbering body and brought her to a climax while she had been in a glorious state of semi-sleep. It had been exquisite.

In a second, she would get up, have a shower, change into her bikini, with a wrap over her, and the flip flops which he had also managed to think about including in the wardrobe he had had imported from who knew where.

Right now, though, a nagging headache was sapping her of her energy and she remained in the bed with the overhead fan whirring efficiently over her and an early morning breeze wafting through the open windows.

Under the light sheet and blanket, her body felt hot and achy and she stirred, trying to find a more restful position.

She had no idea that she had fallen asleep until she heard his voice reaching her from a great height. At least, it felt like a great height, booming down into the room, making her feel a little faint.

'You're shouting,' she muttered, not opening her eyes and turning onto her side.

'I couldn't talk any lower if I tried.' Time had run away and it was after nine. Irritated by a pressing physical urge to take the steps two at a time, back up to the bedroom so that they could make love before setting off, Dio had controlled the impulse but now…

He frowned, standing at the side of the bed.

'It's nearly nine-thirty, Lucy…'

'Oh, no.' With a cry of dismay, she sat up and instantly fell back onto the pillow.

'What's wrong?'

'I…nothing; nothing's wrong. Just give me a couple of minutes. I'll get dressed and be down in, er, a little while.'

Everything was wrong, she thought faintly. Just three more days to go of living like this, far away from reality, and what did her body have to go and do? Fall ill!

She was in the grip of an oncoming cold at the very least. At worst, she was going to get the flu with all its nasty, debilitating side effects.

Right now, her head was banging, her limbs felt like lead, her mouth was dry and she knew that she was running a fever. She could feel it in the aching of her joints.

Disappointment speared her.

And if she was disappointed then she shuddered to think how furious Dio was going to be.

This was the honeymoon he had demanded and he had ended up with half of it and—worse—a wife who wasn't well. When she half-opened her eyes it was to find that he was still standing by the bed with a frown.

He reached down and pressed the back of his hand against her forehead.

'Nothing wrong? You're running a fever, Lucy!'

'I'm sorry.' Her reply was half-audible and addressed to his departing back.

She didn't blame him. He was so pissed off about the situation that he had headed back down to do something useful with himself. Like carry on working. Having had to cancel the boat and unravel the picnic hamper which had been delivered especially to the house the evening before.

Misery overwhelmed her. When she thought about leaving the island without having the opportunity to touch him again, she felt sick.

She didn't hear him re-enter the room until she felt his arm under her, propping her up into a sitting position.

He had a thermometer in one hand and a glass of water in the other.

'Why didn't you tell me that you weren't feeling well?'

'Because I was fine last night. I just…woke up this morning with a bit of a headache. I thought it would go away but I fell back asleep and…I'm sorry, Dio.'

Dio impatiently clicked his tongue and sat down on the bed next to her.

Sorry? Did she perceive him as that much of a monster that she would feel the need to apologise for not being well? He considered the way he had held the sword over her head, using the threat of sending her packing penniless as a means to an end. An end which he told himself he more than richly deserved.

He thought of the way he had announced, for all to hear, that renovation of the building that meant so much to them rested on her shoulders, doubly strengthening the case for her to get into bed with him.

He had seen taking her as a right which he had been denied. He had justified everything because she fancied him as much as he fancied her. Two consenting adults, all said and told, so what was the problem with that?

For him, he had had unfinished business and, typically, he had got exactly what he had wanted by using all the tools at his disposal—and gentle persuasion had not been one of them.

He was assailed by a rare attack of guilt and he flushed darkly as he stared down at her.

'I've phoned the island doctor.'

'Why?'

'Let me take your temperature.'

'There's no need! I have a cold, Dio. There's nothing anyone can do about that.'

'Open your mouth. Once I've taken your temperature, I've brought you some tablets.'

'What about the boat trip?' Lucy all but wailed. *What about the rest of our stolen honeymoon?* She was ashamed to find herself thinking about whether she could have some kind of IOU note, promising her three more days of snatched love-making once she was better. She found herself wishing his Hong Kong deal might not require his presence after all.

She found herself being *clingy...*

Appalled, she tried to recapture some of the hard-headed common sense that had been her constant companion for all the long months she had been married to him.

How had she suddenly become *clingy*? Was it because she was ill and far removed from her comfort zone? That line of reasoning at least made her feel a little less panicky.

'The boat trip is the least of your worries right now,' Dio told her drily. 'Now shut up and let me take your temperature.'

He did and then frowned. 'Okay, drink as much water as you can and take these tablets. You're running a high fever, Lucy. It's a bloody good job I called a doctor. He should be here any minute.'

'I told you, it's just a cold...'

'Mosquitoes can carry diseases in the tropics,' Dio said patiently. 'Not malaria, fortunately, but other diseases that can be almost as severe. Now, water—drink.'

Lucy did as she was told then she lay back, perspiring, eyes closed.

'You don't have to stay here, Dio. I know you probably have better things to do than tend to a sick wife.' She smiled but kept her eyes closed. Her words were composed and controlled but her thoughts were all over the place and she still couldn't seem to harness them. As fast as she got one under control, a swarm of others broke their leash.

'Name a few.'

'Work. It's the great love of your life.' She yawned and adjusted her position on the bed.

'It's had to be,' Dio murmured absently. 'When you have to drag yourself up by the boot straps, getting out of the quicksand becomes a full-time occupation.'

'And it's hard to let go,' Lucy said drowsily.

'And it's hard to let go,' Dio echoed, surprising himself by that sliver of confidential information he had passed on to her. 'Right. Don't move. The doctor's here.'

'Move? Where am I going to go? My legs feel like jelly.'

Dio grinned. His wife might have played the part she had been briefed to play perfectly over the past year or more, might have shown up at important events always wearing the right thing and always saying the right things and making the right noises. But he had learned what he had maybe suspected all along—that there was a feisty, stubborn streak to her lurking just below the surface, the same streak that had prompted her to break out of the box into which she had been sealed and look elsewhere for fulfilment.

He couldn't stand the thought of her having to look anywhere else beyond him, yet not only could he understand the urge that had prompted her but he reluctantly admired it.

Most women would never have thought to do anything but enjoy a life of stupendous luxury.

Most women would have slept with him.

He was finding it difficult not to think that there was far more to her than the opportunist working in cahoots with her father.

The doctor was a small, brisk man who bustled up to the bedroom, throwing little facts over his shoulder about germs, bugs and the innumerable things that could happen even on an island as small as theirs.

No snakes, he informed Dio crisply, shaking his head, but who said that mosquitoes couldn't wreak similar havoc?

There was a certain little mosquito...

Dio found himself bombarded with a litany of Latin names as he pushed open the bedroom door and followed the doctor into the room where Lucy was tossing restlessly on the bed, her cheeks bright red, her eyes glazed.

The doctor barely needed to examine her, although he was meticulous, taking his time and shaking his head before pronouncing his diagnosis.

Yet another long Latin term and Dio impatiently asked for clarification.

'Something similar to Dengue fever,' he pronounced, standing up and collecting his bag from the floor. 'Not as serious but nasty enough to wipe your wife out for as long as a week. No antibiotics needed. Just a lot of fluid and a lot of rest. The usual painkillers will do their best to fight the fever and the aching joints but, on the bright side, once it clears her system she'll be immune to catching this particular bug again.'

Lucy was appalled at the diagnosis. Drifting in and out of sleep, she woke as night was drawing in to find that Dio had brought his computer up to the bedroom and was working, keeping an eye on her. He hadn't signed up to any of this. She looked at him miserably. Even furious with her, which he would be, he still managed to draw her eye and hold it and, to his immense credit, he didn't show the annoyance on his face when he caught her staring at him.

'You're about to apologise again,' he drawled. 'Save it. You've caught something unpleasant from a mosquito bite and apologising isn't to make it go away. How are you feeling? You need to drink some more water and have something to eat.'

He stood up, stretched and strolled over to sit on the bed next to her. 'At least you're not so hot that I could cook a meal on you.'

'You're being very nice about this.'

'What would you have me do?'

'You don't have to be, you know. Nice. You don't have to be nice.'

'Are you giving me permission to be the sort of person you expect me to be?' There was an edge to his voice, although his expression was mild.

'This is supposed to be our overdue honeymoon.' Bitterness crept into her voice. 'A honeymoon is no place for getting sick.'

'And, on that note, I shall go and get you something to eat. My instructions are to keep you rested, fed and watered.'

He headed out to the kitchen where he banged his fist on the granite worktop.

How low was her opinion of him? Could it get any lower? This was supposed to have been an uncomplicated few days for him, during which he would get her out of his system the only way he knew how. And yet here he was now, frustrated by her unspoken insinuation that she might find him sexy, but that was as far as the complimentary thoughts went. On every other front, he was the sort of person she would have avoided at all costs.

She had apologised for being ill; had told him that getting ill had not been part of the honeymoon deal.

Was she afraid, deep down, that he would still see it as his right to have sex with her because he had effectively *paid* for it? He was repulsed by the idea.

Fifteen minutes later, he was on his way back up to the bedroom with a tray of food and her eyes opened wide when she took in the plate of bread and eggs and the long glass of fruit juice.

'You cooked this *yourself*?'

'You sound a lot better,' he drawled, setting the tray down on the bed next to her and dragging the chair closer to the bed. 'That sharp tongue of yours was missing in action while you were tossing and turning with a high fever. Headache gone? And yes, in answer to your question, I cooked it myself. I'd give myself a pat on the back if the meal was more complicated than bread and two scrambled eggs. Are you going to thank me profusely and tell me that producing some bread and eggs for you was not part of the honeymoon deal?'

Funnily enough, that had been on her mind, and she blushed and tucked into the food, losing her appetite after a couple of mouthfuls.

She had taken painkillers a couple of hours previously and she could feel all the aches and pains and soaring fever waiting to stage a comeback.

In the meantime…

'Maybe…maybe we should talk about the divorce,' she ventured hesitantly.

When he was touching her, she lost all power to reason or even to string a sentence together coherently. But he wasn't touching her now, *couldn't* touch her now, and she thought that it might be better to talk about the awkward elephant in the room rather than wait until they were back in London, when the barriers would be up again. Strangely, she didn't want to remember her final time with him as a cold war during which their communication was translated via lawyers and would revolve around money. At least if they sorted things out between themselves here in this setting, far removed from reality, they would part company with less bitterness between them.

Dio stiffened. He wondered whether she was making sure to pin him down to the details before the sex was over. Did she imagine that he would walk off into the sunset, having got what he wanted, without completing his half of the bargain? Maybe she thought that being ill had left her vulnerable to him having a rethink about the terms and conditions of their brief affair.

Despite the doubts he was beginning to have about all the assumptions he had made about her, Dio lost no time in allowing his imagination to jump to all the worst possible conclusions.

It was safe territory.

'Feel up to that, do you?'

'I'm not as groggy as I was earlier. I've got an hour or so before the painkillers really begin to wear off.'

'And why not use the time constructively?' He removed the plate of half-finished food, dumped it on the dressing table, returned to his chair by the bed and folded his arms. 'I get where you're coming from.'

Lucy breathed a sigh of relief. Should she try and explain that it would be better to get this awkward situation dealt with and put it behind them, like a boil that had to be lanced so that they could enjoy whatever brief time remained to them?

Or would that confession make her seem foolish? A bit of a loser? Over-sentimental?

And why should she feel sentimental anyway? Was it

some lingering after effect of having grown up to be the sort of girl who had believed in the sanctity of marriage? Had there been some part of her that still viewed divorce, whatever the circumstances, as a personal failure?

Even though this particular divorce couldn't happen fast enough...

It just showed how easily led the body was. It could veer off in a wildly different direction from the one the mind was telling it to stick to.

She wondered whether she could get over this stupid bug in double-quick time if she just stayed in bed for the next twenty-four hours. Then they could at least have the last bit of their stay here together...

It would be self-indulgent and probably a very bad idea but why not? And at least if they sorted the whole divorce thing out they wouldn't have that hanging over their heads like the Sword of Damocles...

She could pretend that it didn't exist, just like she had been pretending that this honeymoon wasn't what it really was.

'If you like, I can bring some paper and a pen and put my signature somewhere so that you don't think that I'm going to renege on the deal...'

'I...I just want to know when you'd want me out of the house.'

'This conversation is sordid.'

'Why?'

'You're sick and, even if you weren't, we haven't come here to talk about the details of our divorce. Call me mad but I've always thought that there's nothing more guaranteed to ruin a honeymoon atmosphere than talking about divorce.'

'I just thought...'

'The fact that you've been bitten by a mosquito and

ended up in bed ill won't affect your financial package.'
Dio knew that that was a brutal way of saying what he
wanted to say but he didn't take it back.

Nothing about what they were doing was real but, hell,
he was still enjoying it and the last thing he needed was
a reminder of just what had propelled her into his bed in
the first place.

'I wasn't thinking about the money side of things,' Lucy
said faintly.

Dio looked away, mouth drawn into a thin line. 'If
there's one thing life taught me,' he said with lazy cool-
ness, 'it's that when someone tells you that the last thing
on their mind is money it's invariably the one thing they're
thinking about.'

'If you don't want to discuss this then forget it. I just
thought that while we're both here it might be better to
talk face to face than for us to return to London and have
lawyers do it on our behalf. I mean, divorce is a really
personal thing.'

'And most divorces usually go down a slightly different route.' He raked his hands through is hair, outraged
that she would stubbornly persist with this even though it
must be obvious to her that it was an inappropriate topic
of conversation. More to the point, it was a conversation
he didn't want to be having.

'Most people usually end up facing one another across
a desk with lawyers at their sides after they've spent years
rowing and arguing. By the time most people hit the divorce courts, they'd tired and fed up of the arguments and
they're ready to bow down to the inevitable. That's a personal divorce, one where emotions have been exhausted.
This isn't one of those instances.'

'It doesn't make it any less personal.' She thought of her
parents and their lousy marriage. There hadn't been years

of shouting and arguing, just a quiet destructive under-current with insults and criticism delivered in a moderate tone of voice. Unless, of course, her father had been rolling drunk but even then he had never been a crashing around the house kind of drunk. Theirs had been a silent, failing marriage and was nothing like what she and Dio had.

'You're right. It's not.' She stared off into the distance quietly. 'But not all marriages that break down end up that way, after years of shouting and throwing plates. Some marriages just end up broken and useless with no shouting at all. In fact, shouting can be a good thing in a marriage. Anyway, I don't know why we're talking about this...' She shook her head and looked at him, resting back against the pillows. 'I shouldn't have brought this up in the first place.'

She did that.

Opened a conversation in which he had no desire to participate and then got him to a point where his curiosity had been stirred, only to back away, leaving him with a bit between his teeth.

Did she do that on purpose or was it just some fantastic ingrained talent she had managed to hone over the years?

He just knew that he now wanted to find out what she was thinking, why her expression had suddenly become so pensive. He wanted to know what the heck was going through her head.

'What are you going on about?' He placed one finger under her chin and directed her head so that she had no choice but to look at him. 'One minute you're telling me that you want to discuss our divorce so that you can make sure you get your financial settlement—'

'That's not what I said!'

'And the next minute you're generalising about broken marriages where there's no arguing. Are you talking about any marriage in particular?' It was a stab in the dark and he could see, immediately, that he had hit the jackpot. Her eyelids flickered and her mouth parted on some unspoken denial, her fingers compulsively twisting the thin sheet covering her.

'Some friend of yours, Lucy? Aunt? Cousin?' She didn't reply. 'Your parents?' he asked softly, for want of any other name to pull out of the hat, and she gave a terse nod.

Dio was astounded. He drew in a sharp breath and looked at her narrowly to see whether she was having him on but her eyes were wide and unblinking.

'I've never told anyone before.' Her head was beginning to throb. She closed her eyes, part of her knowing that she should just shut up because the fever and the aching limbs were a potent mix, making her want to say things she knew she shouldn't.

'And there's no need to now,' he murmured, instinctively knowing that once certain doors were opened they could never again be closed, and suspecting that this might just be one of those doors.

Did he want his assumptions overthrown?

Did he want to hear about her parents and their occasional well-bred tiffs? Frankly, when you thought about it, any wife in her right mind wouldn't have been able to stand Robert Bishop for longer than five minutes, because the man was a disaster area.

But the picture he had always had of the Bishop family had been one of the perfect nuclear unit blessed with beauty and wealth all round...

'You probably think that I had a great childhood,' she murmured drowsily. 'Actually, lots of people think that. Well, except for very close family friends and some relatives. Not many.' She slid her eyes over at him and smiled. 'In our circles,' she said with a trace of irony in her voice, 'it doesn't do to wash your dirty linen in public.'

'You should get some sleep, Lucy.'

'Maybe you're right. I guess I should.' She sighed and Dio grudgingly pinned his silver grey eyes to her flushed, rosy face.

'Tell me,' he commanded gruffly.

'Nothing much to tell,' she yawned. 'It's just that…we're going to be getting a divorce and I don't want you to go away thinking that I'm a prim and proper, pampered little princess who was born with a silver spoon in her mouth.'

'Which bit of that statement is not true?'

'You've always thought the worst of me, Dio.'

'God, Lucy. I didn't come over here so that we could end up having long, meaningful conversations about where we went wrong.'

'Because we should just have been out here pretending that we could spend time in one another's company and get through it with sex alone.'

'I thought we were managing just fine on that front.'

With every bone aching, Lucy still felt a crazy quiver at the wolfishness of his smile and the sudden flare of heat in his lean, handsome face.

A mosquito-borne virus made her feel less wobbly than his lazy, brooding eyes.

'I tried hard to forget that you only married me because you figured I would make a suitable wife.'

About to remove the tray of half eaten food on the bed, Dio paused and looked at her narrowly.

Fever made a person semi-delirious and he could tell that her fever was back. However, she sounded calm and controlled, even though her eyes were over-bright and there was a sheen on her face.

'A suitable wife…'

'Right background. You know.'

'Do I?' He sat back down. 'I'm not so sure that I do. Enlighten me.'

Lucy twisted the sheet between her fingers. 'On our wedding night,' she said so quietly that he had to lean forward to catch what she was saying, 'I overheard you talking to my father. Well, more of a heated conversation, to be honest. I heard you telling him that he had got what he deserved and that you were going to make sure that you took what was owed to you. The company...and everything that went with it...'

Dio cursed fluently under his breath as pieces of a jigsaw puzzle slotted into shape. She had heard snatches of conversation; she might have cast her own interpretation on what she had heard, but...

Was he going to provide a fuller explanation? No. He'd wanted revenge. It was something that had eaten away at him since he had been a young adult. He'd got it. But now he felt strangely disconcerted as he questioned that driving passion that had propelled him forward for years.

Stupid.

The man had deserved everything he had got, and not only because of what he had done to his father, but for what he had done to the people who had held shares in the company, the people he had been happy to throw to the wolves by embezzling their money.

So he'd been diverted by Lucy, had married her for not entirely honourable reasons, but her life had been pretty damn good.

Except...

'He told me that you married me because I was the sort of person who could give you social credence, you know. He said that...'

'That *what*...?'

'That you came from a deprived background and what

you wanted was someone who could promote your chances to go through doors you wouldn't normally be allowed to go through. That you might have made a lot of money but...but you didn't have...have...what it took to gain entry into certain circles.'

For a few seconds, Dio actually thought that he had misheard her, but as the meaning of her words sank in rage engulfed him.

If Robert Bishop hadn't been safely six foot under, he might have been tempted to send him there.

'And you believed him?'

'Why wouldn't I?' Lucy asked, confused. The dark anger on his face, which he was struggling to control, made her wish that she'd never broached the topic. 'Anyway, I'm beginning to feel really tired. Plus my headache's coming back and the fever...'

Fetching painkillers gave Dio a few minutes during which he suppressed a violent urge to punch something very hard.

Then, just like that, his thoughts veered off in a different direction and he was moderately calmer when he sat back down and watched her swallow the tablets and then lie back with her eyes closed.

'You're not going to fall asleep on me now, are you, Luce?'

Lucy didn't say anything. He hadn't called her that for a very long time, not since they had first started going out; not since they had been on one of those few early dates...

She was aching all over but still alert, fired up by the fact that she had confided in her husband for the first time in many long months. It felt liberating because what did she have to lose?

'When you said that your childhood wasn't what everyone assumed,' Dio said thoughtfully, 'what you really meant was that your father wasn't the man the world thought him to be.'

Her eyelids flickered and she sneaked a glance at him to see if she could figure out what was going through his head but Dio only ever revealed what he wanted other people to see. She knew that and right now he wasn't revealing anything at all about what he was thinking.

'Was his abuse...physical?' Just voicing those thoughts out loud was sickening but he had to know and he felt a wave of relief when she shook her head in denial.

'He was brutal to me and Mum but it was only ever verbal. My mother was such a gentle creature...'

'So you overheard our conversation and your father convinced you that the only reason I married you was because I wanted to use you to gain social entry to...God only knows where. It never occurred to you that I couldn't give a damn about gaining social entry to anywhere? No...' He pensively provided his own answer to that question before she could confirm his suspicions. 'It wouldn't because he appealed to all your insecurities...' And yet a lifetime of good schools where an ability to mask emotion and project the right image had stood her in good stead when it came to maintaining an air of cool.

'You mean you didn't...use me?'

'I mean...' Guilt seared through him as he trod carefully around his words. 'If you think I married you because you had the right background, or because I thought you could open doors for me, then you're very much mistaken.' He stood up, unwilling to go down any further roads, because those roads were riddled with landmines. 'And now, get some sleep, Lucy. Doctor's orders...'

CHAPTER NINE

LUCY WAS VAGUELY aware of time passing by over the next couple of days. The fever came and went in phases, as did the pain in her joints, making her feel as weak as a kitten.

However, when she did surface from the virus, her recovery was swift. She awoke to a room awash with pale light sifting through the closed shutters and the muslin drapes and the soft, overhead whirring of the fan.

A quick glance at the clock by the bed told her that it was a little after eight in the morning. Dio wasn't in the room.

She took time out to mull over certain flashbacks that floated to the surface.

He'd been around all the time. She could remember waking to find him sitting in the room with his laptop at a little table he had brought from some other part of the house. She could remember him bringing her food, which had been largely left uneaten, and making her drink lots of fluids. He had bathed her and helped her with whatever she had needed.

He hadn't signed up to look after her. She was pretty sure that he had never had to do anything like that in his life before and who knew? Maybe if they hadn't been stuck on an island where normal life had been temporarily suspended he would have called in people to pick up the slack so that he could remove himself from the thick of it, but they were on this island and he hadn't had a choice.

But he had risen to the occasion. Admirably.

She remembered something else, stuff they had talked about, and she was sure it wasn't her mind playing tricks on her. She had finally opened up about what her home life had really been like. Not given to personal confidences of that kind, it had been an enormous relief to let it all out. Growing up, not even her friends had known how much she had hated her father's mood swings, the sneering way he had of putting her down and putting her mother down, the atmosphere of tension that had been part and parcel of growing up. Her mother had maintained the front and a stiff upper lip and so, in the end, had she.

The last person she would ever have imagined talking to was Dio, yet she had, and she hadn't regretted opening up because he had proved to be a good listener.

And she'd been wrong. He hadn't used her. He'd said so. Her father had lied, had told her that Dio was a trumped up nobody who had married her for her social connections and her ability to fit in to the world he wanted to occupy—a world, her father had said, that was denied to him because he didn't come from the right background and didn't have the right accent.

She could have kicked herself for not really questioning that assumption. She should have known that Dio was so confident in himself, so much a born leader of the pack, that he wouldn't have cared less about any social pecking order.

But he'd hit the nail on the head when he had told her that her father had known how to manipulate her own insecurities.

She'd been wrong about Dio.

Whatever his reasons for buying her father's company,

and whatever bits and pieces of that awful conversation she had heard, she had misconstrued.

She'd had a lot of champagne and she had added up two and two and arrived at the wrong number and, because of that, they had had a sterile marriage in which all lines of communication had been lost. Indeed, she had ensured that those lines of communication had never been opened and he was far too proud a man to have initiated the sort of touchy-feely conversation he loathed.

He was proud, he was stubborn and…she was madly in love with him.

Her heart skipped a beat and she licked her lips, glad that she was alone in the room, because she would have felt horribly naked and vulnerable if he had been sitting in the chair, looking at her. Those amazing eyes of his saw everything.

She had fallen for him from the very first second she had laid eyes on him and she had papered over that reality with bitterness and resentment once they were married. She had told herself that he was just the sort of man she should have avoided at all costs; had told herself that the man for her was gentle, kind, thoughtful and considerate and that Dio was spectacularly none of those things.

How could he be when he had ruthlessly used her and married her for all the wrong reasons?

Now she felt as though the scales had been ripped from her eyes.

Not only had he proven just how considerate he could be, just how thoughtful and caring, but he was no longer locked up in that box that she had turned her back on.

The divorce, which she had insisted on, was a mocking reminder of how stubbornly she had held on to her misconceptions and panic swept over her in a rush.

She'd hankered after a bright, shiny new life, free from

someone who didn't give a damn about her, who had used her and who didn't care about whether she was happy or not.

But Dio...

She frowned.

Did he really care about her? She loved him. She knew that now. She had always loved him, which was why she had never been able to be in the same room as him without all her antennae being on red alert. She had fumed and raged but had still been so aware of him that her breathing became ragged whenever he was close to her.

But he had always been guarded around her and even here, making love, in the throes of passion, he had never—not once—let slip that he felt anything for her beyond lust.

She knew that she should take something from that, yet hope began to send out alarming little shoots.

Would he have been so solicitous if he didn't feel something for her?

Putting damp cloths on her forehead and cooking food, even if the food was usually the same fare of scrambled eggs and toast, counted for something...didn't it?

Alive to all sorts of possibilities, and feeling as right as rain, Lucy took herself off to have a shower. Then she slipped on the silk dressing gown hanging on the back of the door, making sure to leave her bra behind, and also making sure to wear some sexy lacy underwear, one of the few items of clothing she had brought with her.

She found him in the kitchen, some papers in one hand whilst with the other he stirred something in a frying pan. His back was to her and she took her time standing by the door, just looking at him.

She was seeing him in a whole new light. She had given herself permission to have feelings for this guy and now she appreciated the strength and beauty of his body, the muscular length of his legs, the powerful yet graceful arch of his back and the way his dark hair curled at the nape of his neck.

'I think you might be on the way to burning those eggs…'

Dio started and it took him a few seconds to register that Lucy was in the kitchen and looking so… So damned fresh-faced and sexy that it took his breath away.

She was in a dressing gown, loosely belted at the waist, flip flops on her feet, and she had draped her hair over to one side so that it fell in blonde, tumbled disarray over her shoulder.

No make-up. All one hundred per cent, natural woman.

His body clocked into a response that was fast, furious and immediate.

Just as it was, now, utterly inappropriate.

'What are you doing downstairs?' He salvaged the eggs. 'I was about to bring you your breakfast.'

Lucy strolled to the kitchen table and sat down. Here, as everywhere else in the villa, large windows allowed maximum light in and French doors led out to the lush back garden. It was already a warm, blue-skied day. The French doors had been flung open and a gentle, tropical breeze wafted in. She could smell the salty tang of the ocean air.

He was truly magnificent, she thought, in a pair of faded jeans and a white tee-shirt that did wondrous things for his physique.

'I woke up this morning feeling as right as rain.' She smiled and propped her chin in the palm of her hand. 'So I thought I'd come downstairs to have breakfast.'

'You should go back to bed,' Dio urged, abandoning the eggs to lean against the counter, arms folded.

'I know the doctor said that,' Lucy told him wryly, 'but I'm sure what he meant was that I could actually get out of it once I started feeling better…'

Dio gave her a long, considering look. She looked better. In fact, she looked in rude health, but was it an act? She had spent so much time apologising for her ill health getting in the way of why they were here that he wondered whether a sense of guilt hadn't propelled her into this act of sunshine and smiles.

'No need, Lucy.'

'No need for what?'

'Do you want breakfast? Of course you do. You need to eat.' Did he really want to get involved in a long, complex conversation? He'd already been knocked sideways by the last one.

And the last couple of days had thrown him off course even more. As marriages went, theirs had not been one that had involved any of the usual things he assumed were normally taken for granted. He had cooked meals—a first—and sat by her bedside, keenly aware that, whatever some doctor said, who knew whether this whirlwind virus would just miraculously disappear? He had mopped her brow and frankly put his own life on hold.

He'd barely managed to get any work done and his Hong Kong deal had been rearranged.

His life had always revolved around work so, like cooking meals, shoving it to the back burner had also been a first.

And she had told him things he had stupidly never suspected. How was it that it had never occurred to him that Robert Bishop, the man who had cold-bloodedly swindled his father, not to mention the people who had entrusted their pensions to him, might not have been the upstanding, loving family man he had assumed? If it walks like a duck, quacks like a duck and looks like a duck, then it was a duck. Robert Bishop had been a thoroughly unpleasant criminal, *ergo* he had been a thoroughly unpleasant man, full stop.

And Lucy...

So she might have got hold of the wrong end of the stick in one small detail, but if she only knew the half of it...

Yet his body was still on fire at the sight of her sitting there on the kitchen chair, looking as young and as fresh-faced as a teenager. The sun had brought out a scattering of freckles.

'Maybe we could have something aside from scrambled eggs...'

Dio forced a smile, while his mind continued to roam through all sorts of unexplored avenues. 'Are you telling me that you find fault with the chef?'

'Not at all. In fact, the patient couldn't be more grateful to the chef, although it has to be said that the chef's repertoire is very limited.'

'As you know only too well, I haven't made it my life's career to get to grips with a kitchen.'

'I'll help. Maybe we could cook something together. It'll do me good to be up and moving.'

Dio shrugged and Lucy stifled a sudden feeling of hurt but she stood up anyway and headed to the fridge, where she pulled out some ham, then she rifled through the cupboards and managed to locate enough ingredients for French toast.

'You sit, Dio. You've spent the past few days cooking for me; the least I could do is repay the favour.'

'Like you said, scrambled eggs don't exactly qualify as cooking.'

'I'll bet it's more than you've ever done.' She glanced over her shoulder and felt her heart constrict.

Had she disturbed whatever reading he had been doing? He couldn't have got much done while she had been ill and she knew that his Hong Kong trip had been postponed. He'd had to play the good Samaritan and she could hardly blame him if his mood wasn't all that great.

'You can prepare breakfast if you really want to, Lucy, but that's it. I'll get Enid in to take over the cooking arrangements for the remainder of the time that we're here. The last thing I need is for you to have a relapse.' This was what he had to do. Dio hadn't banked on long confessionals, and he hadn't banked on discovering what had really happened on their wedding night, what had led to her physical withdrawal from him. He got the uneasy feeling that something in her had changed towards him.

She had looked at him…differently after that little chat.

Maybe it was simply the fact that she'd been ill, running a high fever. Maybe that look in her eyes had been virus induced. Had she revised her rock bottom opinion of him because he had truthfully told her that he hadn't married her for her connections?

Did he want her to have revised opinions?

He recalled the way she had looked at him when they had been going out on their handful of dates. He had been charmed at the unexpected find of Robert Bishop's daughter.

Who'd have guessed…?

She had looked at him as though she were a starving waif and he were her specially prepared banquet.

He'd liked that too. What man wouldn't? He hadn't known just when it had occurred to him that she might play a part in the revenge plan that had been his companion for more years than he could remember. He didn't know whether that had been a conscious decision or not.

He just knew that emotions had never played a part in it for him. Emotions had never played a part for him in anything. He had absorbed one very simple reality growing up and that was that emotions were a train wreck waiting to happen.

Emotions had propelled his volatile, brilliant father into trusting a guy he considered a friend. It hadn't occurred to him to get signatures on a dotted line, to get lawyers involved when it came to his invention. He'd paid dearly for that oversight and they had all paid as well. Not just his father, but his mother, who had had to live with a bitter and disappointed husband and a son who had not been spared the details of a wrecked life.

No, Dio had learned from early on that emotions were not to be trusted. Logic, common sense, the intellect—those were the things to be trusted. They never let you down.

And money… With money came power and with power came freedom.

The only emotion Dio had allowed into his life was a healthy thirst for revenge and he had made enough money to ensure that, whatever form that revenge took, he would be able to cover it. His money had bought him the freedom to do just as he pleased when it came to ensuring that Robert Bishop paid for past sins.

He'd married Lucy because he'd fancied the hell out of her, because at thirty-two he'd been ready for marriage and the undeniable advantages it brought and because she'd been Robert Bishop's daughter—and how better to twist the knife than to parade her in front of her father as his wife?

But it would appear that nothing had been quite as it seemed.

He hadn't married a daddy's girl; he'd married someone who had been desperate to escape. For her the escape hadn't gone quite according to plan but, because she had been wrong about one small detail, did she now imagine that he was, in fact, the knight in shining armour she had originally placed all her trust in?

Because Dio didn't want that. Not at all…

She'd lost her virginity to him.

In the cold light of day, he was all too aware of the significance of that and it scared the hell out of him.

'I'm not going to relapse.' Lucy laughed uncertainly as she began focusing on food preparation.

'I've already had to postpone my Hong Kong deal…as you no doubt know.'

'Yes.' Tears stung the back of her eyes because he wasn't being cruel, he was just being honest. 'And I believe I apologised to you about being the cause of that. Several times over. But I'm happy to tell you again that I'm sorry I screwed up all your precious plans.' Lucy said all of this in a rush without looking at him.

Dio raked his fingers through his hair and glared. He could tell from the slump of her shoulders that she was close to crying.

'I'm not asking for your apologies. I'm making sure that you don't overdo it and end back up in bed.'

'I know.' She clattered and began dipping the bread in the egg and frying. She could detect the grim impatience in his voice and it dawned on her that the honeymoon was well and truly over. 'Don't worry. I'll take extra care to make sure I'm bouncy and in top form and, if I do feel a little tired, I'll make sure I don't bore you by saying anything. These are done, although suddenly I'm not very hungry.' She was mortified at the foolish hope that had propelled her down the stairs in a dressing gown and not much else. Still not looking in his direction, she spun round with the frying pan in her hand to find that he had somehow, stealthily, managed to creep up on her.

He should have been at the kitchen table. Instead, he was an inch away from her and now he was gently removing the frying pan from her vice-like grip.

'I've never been a fan of crying women,' he murmured.

'And I've never been a fan of crying.' Lucy's voice wobbled. 'So you're in luck.'

Dio sifted his fingers through her hair and knew that he

really shouldn't. She wanted out of the marriage and she would be a lot better off out. He was no knight in shining armour. He was, in fact, a lot worse than she had taken him to be.

What she needed—and he could see that, now that she had revealed her true colours—was a guy who could give her all those things she was looking for. Friendship, security of an emotional kind, a shoulder on which she could lean…

She needed one of those do-gooder, social worker types she had hitched up with at her out-of-hours teaching establishment. Her turbulent background had conditioned her for a guy whose ideal night in would be cooking together before settling down in front of the telly with just the dog between them. He didn't fit the bill, didn't want to and never would.

In which case, the kindest thing he could do would be to distance himself from her, starting from right now…

But when her hot little body was pressing up against him the way it was now, it was difficult to keep a handle on noble thoughts.

And she wasn't making things easy, either. She had pressed her face into his shoulder and he felt her body quiver as he stroked her hair with an unsteady hand.

Dio made a half-hearted attempt to create a little space between them and he wondered whether he was imagining that she held on to him just a little bit tighter.

'So you think I was being cruel when I reminded you of my deal in Hong Kong and the fact that I've had to reschedule it? You think I'm somehow blaming you?'

'I don't.' Her voice was muffled as she spoke into his shoulder. 'The only thing you really care about is work, isn't it?'

'How well you know me…'

A fortnight ago, had he said that, she would have shrugged and told herself acidly that that just about summed up why she didn't like the guy and never would—forget about what he had done to her, forget about how he had used her.

Now that she knew that he hadn't used her, she was seeing him in a different light—seeing his humour, the depth of his intellect and the way he had looked after her when she had been ill.

There was a warmth there she'd never known existed. He might tell her that the only thing he cared about was work, but there was so much more to him than that, whether he accepted it or not.

She had sensed that all along, hadn't she? Which was why her heart had remained his even though her head had tried to persuade her otherwise.

If she let him, he would turn her away. She sensed that. Maybe she should fight for him. Would it be possible for her to seduce him into a place where he might find her presence indispensable to him?

They had slept together! Why shouldn't they carry on sleeping together? Why shouldn't this marriage become the real thing? She couldn't remember why she had been so passionate about getting a divorce.

They could stay as man and wife, but their lives would change in so many ways! She could carry on doing her maths classes at the centre…at the new and improved centre! Of course, she would have to come clean about who she was, but why should that be a problem?

She wriggled against him and the silky dressing gown dislodged just a tiny bit.

She made no attempt to belt it back into shape.

Dio groaned softly as her soft breasts squashed against his chest. When he looked down, he could see the shadow of her cleavage, the gentle swell of her naked breasts, nipples tantalisingly half-concealed by the dressing gown.

All he had to do was shift his hand, dip it under the silky fabric and he would be able to cup her breast, feel its weight in the palm of his hand…

'I want you to touch me,' she said huskily, shocking herself with her forwardness. She guided his hand under the dressing gown and felt his big body shudder. Heady satisfaction overwhelmed her. She was damp between her legs and she shifted, rubbing her thighs together and, more than anything else, wanting to feel his hand down there…

Even here, she'd shied away from making love in broad daylight, preferring to have the curtains drawn, which he had found very amusing.

Now, though…

She clasped his hand and stood back. 'This isn't the place.'

Dio knew that he could step in now and make clear his intention to put this honeymoon behind them…

Unfortunately, his body had other plans.

Maybe, if she'd said 'bedroom', he would have come to his senses. Maybe if she'd been predictable in her wants…

But she inclined her head to the kitchen window, tugged his hand and smiled shyly.

Dio followed the direction of her gaze and felt a charge of supersonic adrenaline flood through him.

'You like the curtains closed,' he said gruffly.

'Maybe I'm ready to branch out.'

'Luce…'

Lucy took a deep breath, untied the barely tied belt on the dressing gown and then shimmied out of it, leaving it to pool at her feet so that she was stark naked aside from her underwear.

She watched the flare of his nostrils, the way his eyes darkened, and noted the sharp intake of breath.

She'd never wanted him more desperately than she wanted him now. She'd spent months making sure to keep her heart under lock and key and, now that it had been released from captivity, she couldn't bear the thought of them walking away from one another.

She'd misjudged him and that put everything in a whole new light.

'I want to make love on the beach,' she said, brazening out her absolute terror of her body being exposed in the full, unforgiving glare of daylight. She was long and slim but her breasts had always been smaller than she'd wanted, her figure not voluptuous enough. She wondered whether he was making comparisons with all those other women he had slept with, now that he was actually seeing her like this, then she squashed that thought which did nothing for her self-esteem.

This is still honeymoon time… Dio thought, waving aside the introspection that had led him to resolve that he had to get out of a situation that had developed like a swift-moving hurricane. That the man he was definitely wasn't the one she thought she'd unearthed; that he had done what he had set out to do—he had acquired the company that should have rightly belonged to his father, had acquired Robert Bishop's daughter. Job done.

Now she was standing there, bare-breasted, her rosy-pink nipples pointing at him, her skin paler where it had been covered by her bikini top…her long slender legs going on for ever.

How was any red-blooded man to resist?

He walked slowly towards her and decided, in a sudden brainwave, that it would be downright callous to turn her away. She had a lot of issues. He'd never realised that before, but he knew now. She'd grown into adulthood with deep feelings of insecurity, unable to enjoy the looks she had been given.

If he rejected her now, all those insecurities would return tenfold.

Would he be happy being responsible for that? No. So...

In one easy movement, he pulled his tee-shirt over his head and smiled wolfishly as her eyes dipped compulsively to his washboard-hard stomach.

He never failed to get a kick at the way she looked at him, as if she was compelled to and yet, at the same time, was mortified to be caught doing it.

She was looking at him like that right now.

He linked his fingers through hers and gently brushed her hair away from her face.

'If you're sure...' Dio drawled.

'I am. Are you?'

At this moment in time, with an erection bulging against his trousers, Dio had never been more sure of anything in his life.

Outside the sun was already hot. The villa was set in its own very private grounds and the only sound they could hear was the sound of the sea lapping lazily on the shoreline.

A couple of days in bed had dimmed Lucy's recollection of just how stunning the tiny cove was: powder-white sand, sea so clear that you could see every polished stone you were treading on as you waded out, a distant horizon that was blue meeting blue.

The breeze felt wonderful on her naked breasts. She turned to him, laughing, holding her hand to her hair to keep it out of her face and, for just a few seconds, she was literally dazzled by his masculine beauty.

'Are you going to make me beg you to remove the rest

of your underwear?' Dio's hand rested on the button of his jeans and he slowly pulled down the zip.

Lucy was riveted at the sight of him removing his jeans. The sun glinted over his bronzed body, exposing the flex of his muscles as he tossed the jeans behind him onto a rock, followed by his boxers.

Then, eyes not wavering for a second from her flushed, excited face, he touched himself and grinned.

'Okay. Your turn.'

Lucy slid out of her underwear, attempted nonchalantly to toss it to join his boxers, and then watched in dismay as a sudden gust of wind blew it into the sea.

Dio laughed and shielded his eyes from the glare. 'So...' He pulled her into him and she yielded without hesitation. His hard erection pressed against her belly made her quiver. 'Why the sudden sense of daring, my darling wife?' He nibbled her ear and she sighed softly and squirmed against him. 'What's happened to the shy little creature who wouldn't contemplate sex unless the curtains were tightly pulled?'

'Maybe you've kick-started a sense of adventure in me,' Lucy murmured and an unpleasant thought flashed through Dio's head like a depth charge...

Another man would be the recipient of her new found, so-called sense of adventure. He almost longed for the hesitant timidity that had made him keep those curtains tightly drawn.

His unexpected possessiveness was disturbing but thankfully short lived as he cupped her naked breasts in his big hands, teasing and thumbing the ripe swell of her nipples.

'Sand can be a nuisance,' he murmured, flicking his tongue against her ear, knowing just where she liked to be teased. 'So keep standing...'

He worked his way down until he was kneeling in front of her.

Lucy knew what he was going to do and her whole body thrummed with heady anticipation.

She loved it when he licked her down there. It had felt outrageously intimate the first time he had done it, and he had had to gently but firmly prise her legs apart so that he could settle between them, but having him tease her clitoris with his tongue was a mind-blowing experience.

She curled her fingers into his dark hair, arched back and parted her legs.

The sand was warm between her toes. She wanted to look down at his dark head moving between her legs but, on a soft moan, she closed her eyes and tilted her face up to the sun, losing herself in the wondrous sensation of the slow, inexorable build to her climax.

She cried out as she came against his mouth. Before she had time to return to planet Earth, he had hoisted her up, lifting her as easily as if she weighed nothing, and she wrapped her legs around him, feeling the thrust as he came in her.

No protection. And he was normally so careful. The realisation vanished as he pulsed inside her, driving her higher and higher until she was clinging, shuddering and coming in waves of intense pleasure, knowing that he was doing the same, feeling his release with an explosion of pure ecstasy.

Afterwards, they swam. Lucy would love to have been able to bottle the moment and treasure it for ever.

Failing that, as they returned to the beach towels he had brought down with him and lay on the sand, she wondered how she could engineer the conversation towards this very real thing that existed now between them.

Surely he must realise that things had changed?

They hadn't spoken about the divorce for days. She wondered whether her being ill had been a blessing in disguise. It had certainly been an eye opener for her. Had it been the same for him? So, he wasn't the kind of guy who was into long conversations about emotions, but that didn't mean that the emotions weren't there, did it?

She reached out and linked her fingers through his.

They were both gazing up, squinting at the bright blue sky through the fronds of the palm trees.

'So…' She allowed that one syllable to drag out tantalisingly.

'I should apologise.' Dio was down from his high and acknowledging that he had failed to take protection. He had known exactly what would happen out here, on the beach, and yet he had still failed to carry protection with him.

'Sorry?'

Furious with himself for overlooking something so vital, he stood up abruptly and strode towards the discarded clothing, slipping on his sandy boxers and jeans, which he brushed down.

Lucy immediately followed suit.

'I risked an unwanted pregnancy,' he said bluntly. 'I didn't use protection.'

Hearing him say those words, hearing the tone of his voice, was like a slap in the face and she almost stumbled back.

'I'm sorry if I sound harsh.' He raked his fingers through his hair and cursed himself for not having had the will power to resist her when he'd known he should have. Instead, he had fabricated a bunch of non-excuses for enjoying himself one last time. Maybe if he hadn't discovered just how innocent she really was, maybe if she had been the hard-nosed opportunist he had always assumed her to be, he might have felt better about himself.

No, he *would* have felt better about himself. He would have taken what he had seen as his right and he would have walked away. As things stood, by exposing her own vulnerability, by revealing a softness he had never, ever expected, she had likewise exposed him for what he was: cold, ruthless, a man who had played the long game to get what he wanted.

They were poles apart. He was a shark to her minnow and he wondered whether he would have been quite so keen to secure her in his bid for revenge had he known. Probably not.

'I'm sure,' he began, heading back towards the villa, 'that, like me, the last thing you would want is to discover that you're pregnant. Especially…' he turned to face her fully '…when you consider that we're going to be getting a divorce.'

'It's okay,' she whispered. 'We were caught up in the passion of the moment. I'm sure it will be fine.'

Pain assaulted her on all fronts. She was giddy with it. How could he look at her like that, as though they hadn't just shared the most amazing experience ever? And it wasn't just about making love. It was so much more that they had shared. At least, that was how it was for her…

How could he be so…*callous*?

Desperation ploughed into her with the force of a sledgehammer and she hated it.

'How can you be like this, Dio?' The pleading whisper made her wince.

'Be like what?'

'We've just…made love…'

Dio could feel the unexplained horror of something breaking inside him and, far, far worse, the knowledge that it was inevitable that he was now walking down this road. 'It's what we came here to do. To make love. To have our honeymoon…'

'I know that!' Stripped of words, she stared at him, heart pounding so hard that it hurt.

'Then…what?' This was where revenge had finally taken him, to this impasse, to the only place he had ever reached before where he was powerless. He had thought his heart to have been wrapped in ice, immune to pain. He was discovering that it wasn't.

'What we had… Do you feel *nothing*?' Lucy longed to be cool, to just let it go, because she knew that she was trying to fight a battle that she was destined to lose, but the black void opening up at her feet seemed to galvanise her into a terrifying urge to cling.

Dio banked down the wave of unfamiliar emotion surging through him.

Her hands were balled into fists, her body rigid with accusation, and he recognised the searing hurt that lay behind that accusation; knew that from that angry hurt would eventually come the return of the cold dislike she had nurtured towards him.

And he knew that it was deserved. Hell, he knew that with as much certainty as he knew that night followed day.

'I feel we've had our honeymoon.' The words felt like shards of glass in his mouth but, deprived of any choice, he ploughed on, every muscle in his body braced for the job at hand—because that was what it was. 'And now we have to have our divorce…'

CHAPTER TEN

LUCY STOOD AND looked around the brand-new apartment which would now be her new home.

She knew that she should be feeling as pleased as punch. When she had finally garnered her courage all those weeks ago to bring up the matter of a divorce with Dio, this was exactly the sort of outcome she had had in mind.

No. This was a whole lot better than the outcome she had had in mind.

She had spent two weeks at the London house, during which time he had made sure to be abroad. He had fulfilled every single one of his promises, even though she knew, from what her lawyer had told her, that there had been no need because she had indeed signed up to a watertight pre-nup without even having realised it, idiot that she had been.

He had been generous beyond words. He had immediately arranged the purchase of the breath-taking apartment in which she now stood. It was in a prime location and there wasn't a stick of furniture she didn't like. Just as he had glimpsed the part of her that was the girl with the pony tail, the girl she really was, he had made sure that some member of staff chose items of furniture that were homely, comfortable and cosy.

She wasn't amazed that he had managed to acquire the perfect apartment so effortlessly.

Having spent a year and a half married to him, she knew that the one single thing money got when it came to purchase power was speed. What Dio wanted, Dio got. And what Dio had wanted had been this spectacular apartment.

What he had wanted was her out of his life, having got the honeymoon he had demanded when she had asked him for a divorce.

She sat on one of the boxes cluttering the living room and stared miserably out of the window. Her view, from here, was of the sky, a grey, leaden sky that seemed to reflect her mood.

She should be counting her blessings.

She was financially sorted for the rest of her life. The run-down building which had been her lifeline was in the process of a startling renovation which would make it the most desirable place in that part of London to which deprived children could go to further their education after school hours. She had no doubt that dozens would find their springboard to a better life. She had signed up to a teacher training course, something she had always wanted to do until marriage and Dio had swept her off her feet, and she would be able to do it without worrying about money. There were so many things for which she should be grateful.

And yet…

With a little sigh of pure misery, she strolled over to the window and stared down at the street below.

For a little window in time, out there in paradise, she had actually dared to hope. She had opened up to him, thankfully only stopping short of telling him how she felt about him—not that she was in any doubt that he didn't know—and she had dared to hope that destiny might veer off in a different direction.

She'd been such an idiot.

He might not have used her in the way she had been led to assume, but he hadn't cared about her either. Why had he married her? Probably because he had fancied her and had decided that she could be an asset to him. It had been a lazy decision and he hadn't banked on having a sexless marriage. Once sex had been put on the menu, he had been happy to grant her the divorce she wanted.

She knew that at least he had parted company caring enough about her to ensure her physical wellbeing, except what was the good of that when her emotional wellbeing was in pieces?

He had been ultra-courteous to her before they had parted company in London.

The sad truth was that she didn't want his bland concern. She wanted…

Frustrated with herself, she began unpacking. It was not yet ten in the morning and there was so much to do that she hardly knew where to begin. She had left most of her designer clothes behind but Dio had insisted she take the jewellery.

'It's worth a fortune, Dio,' she had protested half-heartedly and he had shrugged as they had boarded the plane.

'What do you suggest I do with it all?'

She had been tempted to tell him that he could always donate the lot to her replacement. *She* certainly had no intention of showing up to teach dripping in diamonds.

Now, she opened the first box of jewellery. It all belonged in a safe but instead she shut the lid and began placing the boxes at the back of the wardrobe, knowing that in due course she would have to do something more secure with them. Stick it all in a vault somewhere. Or maybe flog it all and donate the proceeds to charity. That seemed like a good idea.

She was so absorbed in her task, her thoughts so given

over to silly, pointless rehashing over how her life had changed for ever, that she was barely aware of her entry phone ringing, at which point she wondered who it could be.

Maybe she half-expected it to be Dio but she was still shocked when she saw his grainy image on the little screen. He was glancing impatiently around him and then he stared up and she felt a quiver of nervous excitement invade her body.

'Are you going to let me in?' he asked tersely.

Lucy gathered her scattered senses to reply in a composed voice. 'What are you doing here?'

'I've come to…' *To what?* 'Just let me in, Luce. I need to talk to you.'

'Is it about the divorce? Because I thought it was all pretty straightforward.'

'I'm not enjoying this conversation on your entry phone.'

Lucy didn't think that she would enjoy a conversation face to face but she buzzed him in, knowing that he had probably come to check and make sure everything was okay with the apartment. He would be polite and concerned and she would want to scream with frustration.

'When did you get back?' she asked, as soon as she had opened the door to him. Her voice hitched in her throat. Never had he seemed so gloriously good-looking, his dark hair swept back, his lean, sexy face reminding her all too painfully of the intimate moments they had shared before his passion had given way to cool indifference.

'An hour and a half ago.' And he had had a struggle not coming sooner; had had to endure the slow, dawning realisation that he had made a terrible mistake.

He'd let her go. He'd allowed her to walk away and had then had to live with his uneasy conscience which would not let *him* go.

'And you came straight here?'

'I don't like putting things off.'

'Putting what off?' She had to tear her eyes away from his handsome face and was dismayed to find that she was perspiring, that her hands were shaking so that she stuck them behind her back before launching into a grateful speech about the apartment—about how wonderful it was, nervously laughing at the boxes still to be unpacked, offering him something to drink.

Dio glanced around him but he was driven to look at her. She looked scruffy. Her hair was tied back and she was in a pair of faded jeans, a baggy tee-shirt and some old, stained trainers. She couldn't have looked less like the polished beauty who had entertained clients as though she had been born to it.

But then, hadn't he already realised that that polished beauty was not her at all?

She also looked nervous as hell which, he thought wryly, could only be a patch on how nervous *he* was feeling. It was a sensation that was utterly alien to him. He knew that there was only one person in the world who could inspire that in him and that person was looking at him anxiously, as though half-waiting for some hidden hangman's noose to fall.

'Have you…had a period?'

'I beg your pardon?'

Dio raked his fingers through his hair and glowered. 'We made love without protection. Remember?'

'You've stepped off a plane and rushed over here to make sure I wasn't pregnant?'

Dio shrugged and frowned at her. He was hovering in the middle of the cluttered living room but now he sought out one of the chairs and sat down.

'I told you that it would be fine and it is,' Lucy said

tersely, arms folded, as the reason for him descending on her became clear.

He hadn't come to make sure she had settled in all right. He had come to make sure there was to be no inconvenient situation to be dealt with. Woe betide her if he had dealt with one inconvenient situation only to find that another had come along! One that might be a little trickier to deal with!

'So you didn't have to dash over here in a flat-out panic thinking that there would be some other mess for you to try and clear up!'

'Why would I have panicked at the thought of you being pregnant?'

Lucy refused to give houseroom to anything stupid like hope. She'd been down that particular road already and look where it had got her. Nowhere.

His challenging remark was greeted with stony silence.

'Why don't you sit down?' Dio urged.

Likewise that was greeted with stony silence until Lucy replied with simmering resentment, 'What for? You've told me why you came here and I've answered you. What more is there to talk about?'

'A lot, as it happens.' He hunkered forward, arms resting loosely on his thighs.

Lucy watched, bemused, as he slumped into silence. He was hesitant. Had she *ever* seen Dio hesitant? Even when she had asked him for a divorce, he had immediately and confidently responded with his demand for his denied honeymoon. He was the most self-assured person she had ever encountered in her entire life, yet right now...

'A lot...like what?' she asked, bewildered.

'I didn't marry you because of your background, Lucy.'

'I...I know that. I didn't at the time, but I know now. And you know I know.'

'But because I didn't marry you because of your background, doesn't mean that my intentions were entirely... honourable.'

'Dio, I have no idea what you're talking about.'

'It's a long story.' He sighed heavily and glanced at her with that same uncertainty in his pale eyes that filled her with apprehension. 'Your father wasn't entirely unknown to me when I decided to take over his company. In fact, I've known about your father for a very long time.'

'But how?'

'It goes back decades, Lucy. Before you were born. Our fathers knew one another.'

'I don't understand.'

'Skeletons in cupboards,' Dio said wearily. 'All families have them.'

'They do,' Lucy accepted, thinking of her own skeletons, no longer a secret from this man sitting across from her.

'Sometimes those skeletons have bones that rattle so much, they create all sorts of problems down the line. A long time ago, my father invented something pretty big and at the time he was friends with your father. They were at university together. My father was a boffin, yours was... what can I say? The life and soul of the party. I have no doubt that my father was somewhat in awe of your father's rich, playboy lifestyle. He was studious, poor, everything your father wasn't. When your father decided that he was worth investing in, my dad believed him. Unfortunately, his trust was somewhat misplaced.'

Comprehension was beginning to drip in and Lucy's eyes widened. 'My father...'

'Took everything. He took his family business and built it into something huge on the back of my father's hard work. I grew up with that and it... Let's put it this way, for a very long time I've been hell-bent on revenge. I waited my time, Lucy. I went to university and I made sure that I was better than good at everything I did. Fortunately, I seemed to have a knack for making money. I traded but quit that pretty quickly, just as soon as I had enough capital, along with a bank loan, to begin the business of acquisition. I made more money than I knew what to do with but there was only one thing I wanted to do with my millions and that was to wait until the time was right. I knew it would come because I knew what kind of man Robert Bishop was.'

'He was drinking himself into a hole…stealing from pensions.'

'He was and I knew just when to strike. The conversation you semi-overheard that night was when I told him exactly who I was.'

'He must have known before—he would have recognised your name.'

'Of course he did but the man was so arrogant, so sure that he was top dog, that it never occurred to him that he had become involved in a game in which there could only be one winner and that winner would be me.'

'So you went out with me…'

'I hadn't planned to. In fact, whilst I knew to the very last detail the progress of your father's company, I never had the slightest interest in the progress of his personal life. I didn't know you existed until I met you on that very first visit when I came to enquire about buying the company.'

'And my father encouraged us to go out…'

'I needed no encouragement, trust me on that, Luce. He knew who I was but he still stupidly thought that he could somehow con me into paying full whack for his company whilst keeping him on, honour intact. Maybe he thought he could use you as a bargaining tool to get an even better deal out of me. He'd swindled my father and he thought that we were cut from the same cloth. I have to admit that I didn't immediately disillusion him. I got involved with you and I was having…a good time.'

'You were having a good time…' Lucy said slowly, driven to search for an answer she knew she wouldn't want to hear. 'But did you plan on actually asking me to marry you?'

Dio looked at her steadily. He'd brokered hundreds of edge-of-cliff deals but never had he felt more nervous about the outcome of any situation…or more desperate to secure the outcome he wanted.

'No.'

'You planned on having some fun with me and then getting down to the main business of ruining my father as payback.'

'That's about the sum of it.'

'Why did you change your mind? Why did you decide to ask me to marry you?' Her puzzled, questioning eyes tangled with his steady, cool ones and it dawned on her that a man hell bent on revenge might find that revenge in all sorts of ways contrary to what he might have planned originally. 'I get it,' she said in a small, appalled voice. 'You figured that not only would you get the company but you would take me with it, and that way you would have wiped my father out on all fronts…'

Dio said nothing. He found it impossible to understand the whole business of revenge that had motivated him for such a long time, but then something so much bigger had come along and knocked him to the ground.

'How could you?' She sprang to her feet and paced the room, dodging the packing crates, her mind in turmoil, her stomach churning with his revelations.

With a flick of his hand he caught her as she jerkily paced past him and pulled her so that she toppled onto him, only to push herself back immediately, shaking with mortification and anger.

'I thought I'd misjudged you,' she flung at him bitterly. She clenched her fist because she wanted to slap his beautiful face so much that it was a physical pain.

'I know you did,' Dio told her gently. 'Just like I knew that finding out the truth would…hurt you. Why do you think I decided that the best outcome would be for me to walk away? Spare you the details?'

'Oh, how generous of you,' Lucy jeered with biting sarcasm. She could feel the heat from his body against hers and the steady beat of his heart under her arm, which was pinned into position. He was only holding her lightly but she still couldn't move an inch. Tears stung the back of her eyes.

'Generous and, as it turns out, impossible,' Dio murmured. He could sense the effort she was making not to cry. He felt powerless to ease the pain and enraged that he was responsible for causing it, even though when all this began he had no idea that this was the route it would end up going down.

'Not impossible,' Lucy whispered. 'You could have just left me believing what I did.'

'You deserved to know the truth, Lucy, especially as…' He sighed, shook his head and released her abruptly.

Freed from his clasp, Lucy was dismayed to find that her body didn't immediately behave the way it should have. It took her a few seconds to leap away from him and sprint to one of the packing crates, where she sat, glaring at him.

'Especially as…*what*?' She wondered how many more revelations he had tucked up his sleeve.

'This isn't quite the end of what I have to say…'

'What more can there be, Dio? What more can you *possibly* have to say to me?'

'I thought I married you as a fitting way of making sure the wheel turned full circle. I took you for a daddy's girl and, yes, I thought that I could deprive him of more than just his company in one fell swoop. It never occurred to me that what I felt for you went far beyond anything to do with getting even with your father.'

'Oh, please…'

'I knew I fancied the hell out of you; I just didn't realise that I felt much more than that, which was why I was just so damned furious with myself when you decided that sleeping with me wasn't going to be on the table. I figured you'd strung me along to get me to sign on the dotted line, thinking, like your father, that I would be a sucker for your pretty face.'

Lucy flushed because, although that had been a horrible misunderstanding, she didn't emerge as flawless. They had both had issues with one another.

'I made sure I got what was mine, though… But I spared your father the humiliation of a prison sentence because of you.'

'Surely that would have been the ultimate revenge?'

'I found I couldn't do it.'

'Even when I refused to sleep with you?'

'Even then. Maybe…' he smiled wryly '… I wasn't quite as hard-nosed as I thought I was, or maybe I just fell in love with you and couldn't bring myself to take that ultimate step.'

'Fell in love with me?'

'It's why I lost interest in all other women the minute you came on the scene. The only woman I went to bed dreaming of was you. I thought that it was because I had never had the chance to take you to my bed. I thought it was a simple case of wanting what had been denied me…'

'Which was why you wanted the honeymoon, so that

you could get me out of your system.' *He'd fallen in love with her?*

'I came here to tell you everything, Luce. I…I let you go, and I never should have done that, but I didn't know how to stop you, not when I knew that there was so much muddy water under the bridge.' He looked at her, wondered what was going on behind that beautiful, expressive face. If he lost her…

The thought filled his head like a blackness.

'When you say you *fell in love with me*…?'

'By that I mean I want you next to me for the rest of my life. I don't want a divorce, Lucy, although if you insist on one then I'll walk away. Unless,' he mused, 'I choose the other option of pursuing you relentlessly until you can't stand it any more and you just give in. I should warn you that I can go to great lengths to get what I want.'

Lucy threw him a wobbly smile. 'I can hardly believe what I'm hearing, Dio,' she confessed unsteadily. She sighed heavily. 'I fell in love with you the second you stepped into my life.' Her eyes flickered and got the response they wanted, the steady, tender gaze that warmed her to her very depths. 'It was like I was waking up for the first time in my life. I never thought…it never occurred to me that what was happening between us might not be real. I was so…inexperienced; when I overheard that conversation and then had it all confirmed by my father… You have no idea. It was like something inside me shrivelled up. I'd been bought, like something from a shop.'

'I was blind, Lucy. I hadn't been looking for love and I was arrogant enough to assume that it wouldn't find me unless I had been.'

'I was married to a guy I was crazy about but I was forced to tell myself otherwise. I knew that if I just confronted that truth I would break apart.'

'You played a part and I was responsible for that, my darling. You'd spent your life playing a part and then you were forced to continue…' And that hurt him. 'Little wonder that you were searching for an exit.'

'And I thought I'd found it. I could get back to what I had always dreamed of doing. I thought I'd be free, like a bird released from a cage, but then we went on our honeymoon and all the truths I'd shoved away out of sight began creeping out of their hiding places—and this time round I couldn't hide any of it from myself. I was still crazy about you. I'd never stopped…' Never had she felt more naked but that look on his face was still there, still warming her, taking her heart to heights she had never known existed.

'My darling…'

'I love you so much, Dio.'

'Revenge might not be an honourable emotion.' Dio stood up and walked across to her, dragging another packing crate so that their knees were touching. 'But I wouldn't have changed a second of those dishonourable emotions because they brought me to you, Lucy, and being with you is coming home. So…' He went down on one knee and looked at her with such tenderness that her heart melted. 'My darling almost-ex-wife, can I ask you not to divorce me?'

'I never thought I'd have a marriage proposal as weird as that!' Lucy's heart took flight and she reached forward and ran her fingers through his hair. 'So how can I say no? The past is behind us, all of it, and now…now we just have the future.' She laughed, leant to kiss him and lingered a bit more as their mouths met. 'My dearest husband for ever…'

* * * * *

A DEAL SIGNED
BY PASSION

LOUISE FULLER

For my children; Georgia, Eleanor, Hugo,
Archie, Agatha and Millicent.
Thank you for letting me stay in my cupboard.
I love you all x

CHAPTER ONE

IN THE DARKENED bedroom of his penthouse hotel suite Massimo Sforza gazed in silence at the illuminated numerals of his watch. It was almost time. He held his breath, waiting, and then there was a quiet but audible beep. He breathed out slowly. Midnight.

His lean, dark features tightening, he shifted his gaze and stared down dispassionately at the naked women sprawled over both him and one another in the emperor-sized bed. They were beautiful and wanton and idly he tried to remember their names. Not that it mattered. He would never see either of them again. Women had a tendency to confuse intimacy with commitment but he liked variety and anyway the 'c' word was simply not part of his vocabulary.

The brunette shifted in her sleep, her arms flopping onto his chest. Feeling a spasm of irritation, he reached down and lifted the tangle of limbs away from his torso and onto the rumpled sheets before rolling over and out of the bed.

His breathing quiet and measured, he stood up and began to pick his way between the shoes and stockings strewn across the soft pale grey carpet. In front of the huge panoramic window that covered the length of the apartment he noticed a half-empty bottle of champagne and, leaning over, he picked it up.

'Happy Birthday, Massimo,' he murmured and, lifting it to his lips, he tipped it up. He made a moue of disgust. Flat and sour—like his mood. Grimacing, he looked down at the street below. He hated birthdays. Particularly his own. All that faux sentiment and ersatz celebration.

A signature on a contract. Now, *that* was a reason to celebrate. He smiled grimly. Take the latest addition to his ever-expanding property portfolio: a six-storey nineteen-thirties building in the exclusive Parioli district of Rome. He'd had his pick of five properties, two in the most sought-after road in the area: the Via dei Monti. His eyes gleamed. He could have bought them all—he still might. But the one he'd finally chosen hadn't even been for sale.

Which was why he'd had to have it.

He gave a small tight smile. The owners had refused to sell. But their refusal had simply fuelled his determination to win. And he always won in the end. His smile widened. Which reminded him: those glitches in the Sardinian project should finally have been ironed out. He frowned. And about time too. Patience might be a virtue but he'd waited long enough.

Behind him, one of the women moaned softly, and he felt a frisson of lust shudder over his skin. Besides, right now, he was more interested in vice than virtue.

Savouring his body's growing arousal, he glanced at the sky. It was nearly dawn. The project meeting was scheduled for that morning. He hadn't been planning to attend—but what better birthday present could there be than hearing first-hand that the last remaining obstacle had been removed? And that work on his largest and most prestigious resort ever could finally begin.

His eyes narrowed as the blonde lifted her head, her lips curving into a suggestive pout. Coolly, he smiled back at her. Perhaps there was one thing…

He watched the brunette uncurl and stretch lazily and began to walk back to the bed.

Exactly fifty-one minutes later he strode into Sforza headquarters in Rome, wearing an immaculate navy suit and a deep blue shirt, his five o'clock shadow neatly trimmed.

'Mr Sforza!' Carmelina, the junior receptionist, gave a squeak of surprise.

'Carmelina!' he replied, smiling calmly.

'I—I wasn't expecting you in today, sir—' she stammered. 'I must have made a mistake. I thought it was—'

'My birthday?' Massimo laughed. 'It is. You didn't make a mistake, and I'm not planning on hanging around. I just thought I'd pop into the boardroom on my way to lunch at La Pergola. Don't worry! I'm a big boy now. I can wait until tomorrow for my present from the staff.'

He watched Carmelina blush. She was sweet, and clearly had the mother of all crushes on him, but he never mixed business with pleasure. Nor would he—unless there was a sudden global shortage in the number of beautiful, sexually imaginative women eager to share his bed.

He paused briefly in front of the door to the boardroom and then pushed it open. There was a sudden flurry of people pushing back chairs and standing up as he walked purposefully into the room.

'Mr Sforza!' Salvatore Abruzzi, the company's chief accountant, stepped forward, a nervous smile upon his face. 'We weren't—'

'I know.' Massimo waved him away with an impatient hand. 'You weren't expecting me.'

Abruzzi smiled weakly. 'We thought you might be otherwise engaged. But please join us—and happy birthday, Mr Sforza.'

Around the table, his colleagues murmured their congratulations too.

Massimo slid into his seat and gazed calmly around the boardroom. 'Thank you, but if you really want to give me something to celebrate then tell me when we're going to start work in Sardinia.'

There was a strained, simmering silence.

It was Giorgio Caselli, his head of legal affairs, and the closest thing Massimo had to a friend, who cleared his throat and met his boss's gaze. 'I'm sorry, Mr Sforza, but I'm afraid we can't give you that information at the moment.'

For a moment, the room seemed to shrink as though the air had been sucked out of it and then Massimo turned and stared unwaveringly at the lawyer. 'I see.' He paused. 'Or rather, I don't.' He gazed slowly around the room, his blue gaze colder than an Arctic ice floe. 'Perhaps somebody would care to explain?' Frowning, he leaned back in his seat and stretched out his long legs. 'You see, I was led to believe that all objecting parties had been—' His eyes narrowed. 'Removed.'

There was another strained silence and then Caselli raised his hand. 'That's what we believed too, Mr Sforza. Unfortunately the tenant of the Palazzo della Fazia is still refusing to accept all reasonable offers. And as you are well aware, she is legally entitled to stay on at the property under the terms of Bassani's will.'

Pausing, Caselli tapped loudly on the top of a document box on the table in front of him; several of the junior board members jumped.

'Miss Golding has made her feelings completely clear. She's refused to leave the *palazzo*—and, to be perfectly honest, sir, I can't see her changing her mind any time soon.' He sighed. 'I know you don't want to hear this, but

I think we might have to think about some sort of compromise.'

Seeing his boss's set expression, Caselli sighed again and tipped over the box. There was a muffled gasp from around the table as Massimo stared coldly at the sprawling pile of identical white envelopes. Each one was franked with the Sforza logo. All of them were unopened.

He lifted his head, his expression suddenly fierce, his eyes the darkest ink-blue. 'That's not going to happen.'

Now the accountant cleared his throat. 'I think on this occasion, sir, that Giorgio is right. Perhaps we might consider some form of conciliation—'

Massimo shook his head. 'No!' Leaning forward, he picked up one of the envelopes, his face blanked of emotion, the intensity of the gaze belying the quiet reasonableness of his tone. 'I don't compromise or conciliate. *Ever.*'

The eyes around the table stared at him with an unblinking mixture of fear and awe.

'But we've tried every option, Mr Sforza.' It was Silvana Lisi, his head of land acquisitions. 'She simply won't acknowledge our communications. Not even in person.' She exchanged a helpless glance with her colleagues. 'She's completely uncooperative and volatile too, apparently. I believe she threatened to *shoot* Vittorio the last time he visited the *palazzo.*'

Massimo surveyed her steadily. 'How volatile can some little old lady be?' He shook his head dismissively. 'Look! I don't care how old she is, or whether she looks like his *nonna*, Vittorio is paid to acquire land and properties. If he wants to care for the elderly, I suggest he looks for another job.'

His face pale with nerves, Abruzzi shook his head. 'I'm sorry, Mr Sforza. I think you must have been misinformed. Miss Golding isn't a little old lady.'

Lounging back in his chair, Massimo frowned. 'I thought she was some elderly Englishwoman?'

An awkward silence spread across the room and then Caselli said carefully, 'There *was* someone living at the *palazzo* when we first bought the estate—but she was a friend of Bassani, not a tenant, and she left the property over a year ago.'

'So she's irrelevant.' His boss's face darkened. 'Unlike the *volatile* Miss Golding, who appears to have single-handedly thwarted this project and run rings around my entire staff. Perhaps she should be working for me.'

Caselli gave a strained smile. 'I can only offer my apologies…' His voice trailed off as he saw the look of impatience on his boss's face. Sweeping the envelopes off the table, Massimo leaned forward.

'I own that *palazzo*, Giorgio. I own the estate and the land surrounding it. And we've had approval for the first stage of the project for nearly six months and yet nothing is happening. I expect more than an apology, Giorgio—I want an explanation.'

Hastily, the lawyer shuffled through the papers in front of him. 'Aside from Miss Golding, everything is on schedule. We have one or two more meetings with the environmental agencies. Just formalities, really. Then the regional council in two months. And then we're done.' He cleared his throat. 'I know we have permission to convert and extend, but we could just modify the plans and build a brand-new *palazzo* on some other part of the site. We'll have no problem getting it passed, and it would mean we can bypass Miss Golding entirely—'

Massimo stared at him, the cold blue of his eyes making the temperature in the boardroom plummet abruptly. 'You want me to change my plans now? To modify a project we've worked on for over two years because of one tricky tenant? No. I think not.' Shaking his head, he glanced angrily around the room. 'So who exactly *is* this mysterious Miss Golding? Can someone at least tell me that?'

Sighing, Caselli reached into a pile of folders on the table in front of him and pulled out a slim file. 'Her name is Flora Golding. She's English. Twenty-seven years old. She's moved around a lot, so there's not much detail, but she was living with Bassani until his death. Apparently she was his "muse".' The lawyer stared at his boss and smiled tightly. 'One of them, anyway. It's all there in the file.' Caselli licked his lips 'Oh, and there's photographs. These were taken at the opening of the Bassani Wing at the Galleria Doria Pamphili. It was his last public appearance.'

Massimo gave no indication that he had heard a word of this explanation. His eyes were fixed on the photographs in his hand. More particularly they were fixed on Flora Golding. She was clinging to the arm of a man he recognised as the artist Umberto Bassani, and looked far younger than twenty-seven.

She also appeared to be naked.

He felt suddenly dizzy. Wrenching his gaze away, he took a shallow breath and then felt his cheeks grow warm as he saw that she was wearing a dress of some sort of unbleached silk, perhaps a shade lighter than her skin. Noting the soft curves of her breasts and buttocks beneath the clinging dress and the triangle of pale gold skin at her throat, he drew a breath, feeling lust uncurling in the pit of his stomach.

She most definitely was *not* a little old lady!

He studied her face in silence. With that disdainful tortoiseshell cat's gaze and crooked crop of fine brown hair, she was an arresting, unorthodox beauty. But she *was* beautiful—there was no denying that.

A muscle flickered in his jaw as he studied the photograph intently. Beautiful and greedy. Why else would a woman like that surrender her body to a man more than twice her age? Suddenly he tasted bitterness in his mouth. She might look the part, clinging on to her lover's arm, her eyes lit with an oh-so-convincing adoration, but he knew from personal experience that appearances could be deceptive. More than deceptive! They could be damaging and destructive.

Staring down into those incredible tawny brown eyes, he felt a spark of anger. No doubt a steely will lay beneath the misty softness of their expression. That and a gaping hole where her heart should be. His anger shifted into pity. But what man was truly going to care what lay beneath that satiny skin and curving flesh? And, although he might have been one of the greatest artists of his generation, Umberto Bassani had still been just a man. A sick, elderly, lovestruck fool.

His face hardened. This girl must be quite something if she'd been willing to hook up with a dying man. A lot more than something if she'd lured him into letting her stay on in his home. He felt suddenly sick to his stomach. But was her behaviour so surprising, really? After all, who knew better than he how low a woman like that was prepared to sink in exchange for a share of the spoils?

Or a footnote in a will.

He snapped the folder shut. At least Bassani had had no children. Whatever Miss Golding's malign influence had been over the old man, it had now run its course. Slowly, he ran a finger over the clean lines of his neatly trimmed stubble. Soon her little protest at the *palazzo* would be over too, and then denuded of her former powers, she would be homeless and destitute.

Looking up, he studied the faces of the men and women seated around the table. Finally he said, almost mildly,

'Perhaps you're right. Maybe we do need a new approach with Miss Golding.'

Clearly surprised by this volte face, Lisi nodded nervously. 'We could use an intermediary.' She glanced at her colleagues for support. The lawyer nodded. 'I think distancing ourselves might be the solution. There are several companies here in Rome that specialise in these sort of negotiations. Or we can go farther afield—London, maybe—'

'That won't be necessary,' Massimo said softly. 'We already have someone working for the company who's more than capable of convincing Miss Golding that our way is the only way.'

Giorgio frowned. 'We do? Who?'

Massimo stared at him calmly. 'Me!'

There was a shocked silence and then Giorgio leaned forward, his forehead corrugated with confusion. 'As your lawyer, I would have to advise you against such a course of action. Let's do what Silvana suggested and find an intermediary. It won't take long but it would be better to wait…' His voice faded as his boss shook his head slowly.

'I've waited long enough. And you know how I hate waiting.'

'But, sir.' Giorgio's face was taut with shock. 'You really shouldn't get personally involved. This is business—'

'Yes. *My* business. And it involves me personally.'

'I understand what you're saying, sir, but I really don't think it's wise for you to meet Miss Golding—' The lawyer stopped, clearly horrified by the prospect of his uncompromising boss actually coming face to face with the shotgun-carrying, volatile Miss Golding. 'Anything could happen!'

Massimo felt his body stir. *Yes. It could!* His eyes flickered over the photographs of Flora, inexorably drawn to the beauty of her body and the challenge of her gaze. His chest tightened. She would be passionate at first, and then tender, those honeycomb-coloured eyes melting as she pulled him fiercely against her...

Closing his mind to the tantalizing image of a naked, feverish Flora, he smiled and the tension around the table evaporated like early morning mist.

'Don't worry, Giorgio. I'll be sure to wear my bullet-proof vest,' he said.

His lawyer grimaced and slumped back in chair. 'Fine. You can meet her. But only if I'm there to make sure you don't say or do anything you or more importantly *I* will regret!' He shook his head in frustration. 'I would have thought that you would have had something better to do, today of all days.'

Massimo pushed back his chair and stood up smoothly. 'I do indeed. I have a surprise birthday luncheon waiting for me at La Pergola.' His eyes gleamed beneath their dark brows. 'Reschedule it for this evening! That should give Miss Golding more than enough time to sign on the dotted line. And now you and I have a helicopter to catch.'

Two hours later, Massimo closed his laptop with a decisive click. The file on Flora Golding had made an entertaining read, but she hardly offered anything in the way of a challenge. In his experience pretty, greedy young women simply needed the correct handling to help them towards the sticky end they so richly deserved.

Leaning back against the plush upholstery, he stared at the Tyrrhenian Sea through the window of his private helicopter. Away from the coastline the water gleamed flat and bluer than a gemstone, while in the distance he could just make out where the waves lapped against the island's famous ragged granite outcrops.

He turned as the pilot leaned forward. 'Beautiful scenery isn't it, sir?' he shouted over the whirring buzz of the helicopter's rotors.

Massimo shrugged. 'I suppose so.' He glanced down at his watch and then shifted round to face the lawyer who sat, eyes squeezed tightly shut, his face damp with sweat.

'Open your eyes, Giorgio. You're missing the scenery,' he said mockingly. Frowning, he shook his head. 'I don't know why you insisted on coming. You know you hate flying. Just take deep breaths and we'll be back on terra firma before you know it.' He turned back to address the pilot. 'How long before we land?'

'Ten minutes, sir.'

Massimo frowned. 'That was quick!'

The pilot grinned. 'We made good time—but then this chopper's the best on the market.'

Massimo nodded. To him, the helicopter was simply a means of transport. He had no interest in the make or model. Nor did its stupidly high price tag excite him. In truth, all of his 'toys'—the cars, jets and luxury yachts— left him cold. What truly excited him was the pursuit of some unattainable deal. He loved going head to head with an opponent. And the more he—*or she*—tried to outma- noeuvre him, the more single-minded and ruthless was his desire to bring them down.

As Miss Flora Golding was about to find out.

The pilot pointed out of the window. 'That's the Palazzo della Fazia, sir. If you don't mind, I'll probably bring her down over there.' He gestured towards a large, flat patch of land at the end of the drive.

Massimo nodded, but his eyes were fixed on the honey- coloured building in front of him. The helicopter touched down lightly and as the rotors slowed, he stepped onto the parched grass, his gaze continuing to rest on the *palazzo*. He owned many large and impressive properties, but he found himself holding his breath as he stared at the golden stucco shimmering beneath the Majorelle blue sky. He was transfixed not by its grandeur but by its serenity and its sense of reassuring immutability—as though the building had grown up out of the land itself.

'Thank goodness that's over!'

Massimo turned sharply as Giorgio came and stood beside him, patting his pallid, sweating face with a handkerchief.

'How are you feeling?' he asked drily.

The lawyer smiled weakly. 'I feel okay.'

Massimo frowned. 'Really? You look terrible. Look… Why don't you wait here? I don't think you being sick in the flowerbeds is going to help close this deal, do you?'

Giorgio opened his mouth to object. Then took one look at his boss's face and closed it again.

Massimo smiled. 'Don't look so worried. This won't take long.'

The driveway definitely needed some attention, he thought critically, as he sidestepped a crater-like pothole. Up close, the *palazzo* too had clearly seen better days. Parts of the stucco were crumbling, and there were small plants poking through the plaster like loose threads on a jumper. And yet still there was something magical about its faded glamour.

He scowled, irritated by this sudden and wholly uncharacteristic descent into sentimentality. There was nothing magical about bricks and plaster. Especially when they were reduced to rubble. And as soon as Miss Flora Golding signed over her tenancy rights that was exactly what was going to happen.

Eyes narrowing, he climbed up the steps to the large front door and pulled purposefully on the bell rope. Tapping his fingers impatiently against the brickwork, he frowned and then pulled on the rope again. There was no answering jangle from inside and stifling a stab of irritation, he hammered hard against the peeling paint, resting his hand on the wood, the heat of it somehow feeding his anger.

Damn her! How dare she keep him waiting like this? Craning his neck, he looked up at the first-storey windows, half expecting to see a face, the eyes dancing with malice. But there was no face, and for the first time he realised that the windows—*all* the windows—were shuttered. Gritting his teeth, he straightened up. The message could hardly be clearer: Miss Golding was not at home to visitors. *Ever.*

His head felt full to spilling with rage. Turning on his heel, he walked down the steps and strode along an untidy path beside the *palazzo*, his shoes crunching explosively on the gravel. Each shuttered window seemed to jeer at him as he passed, and his anger swelled with every step. Reaching the end of the path, he found a gate, the latch broken and with what looked suspiciously like a woman's stocking tied around it to keep it shut. Irritably, he tore at it with his fingers.

Stalking past a pile of discarded masonry and rusting iron railings, he felt a quiver of excitement as he stepped through a crumbling stone archway into a walled garden. In contrast to the front of the building, all the shutters and the windows at the back of the building were open, and then, turning towards the *palazzo*, he noticed a half-empty glass of water and the remains of an apple on a marble-topped table. So she *was* here! But where, exactly?

Blinking in the sunlight, his spine stiffened as he got his answer. Somewhere in the gardens, a woman was singing.

He stared fiercely around the *terrazza*, but it was empty except for a handful of sunbathing salamanders. For a moment he was rooted to the spot, the pounding of his heart drowning out the song, and then, forcing himself to breathe more slowly, he lifted his head. But it was too late. She'd stopped singing.

Damn it! He turned slowly on the spot, his eyes narrow slits of frustration. Where the hell *was* she? And then he heard it—the same husky voice—and he felt another flicker of excitement. With light, determined steps, he ducked under an archway festooned with roses—and then stopped almost immediately. It was just another empty terrace. His disappointment aching like a blow to the stomach, he glanced through a fringing of leaves at a large sunken ornamental pond and a collection of marble nymphs.

What the hell was wrong with him? Chasing after a singing girl like some foolhardy sailor bewitched by a siren…

And then his breath stopped his throat and his heart seemed to miss a beat as across the garden he saw one of the nymphs reach out to touch a cluster of pale pink oleanders.

Dry-mouthed, he watched her bend and twist in silence, his breath still trapped somewhere between his throat and his stomach. With the sunlight gleaming on her wet body she looked like a goddess fresh from her morning bath. Her beauty was luminous, dazzling. Beside her the exquisite marble nymphs looked dull and blandly pretty.

Staring hungrily at the slender curl of her waist, the small upturned breasts, he felt the blood start to pulse in his neck. His eyes followed the soft curve of her backbone down to the firm, rounded bottom. The vertebrae looked both defenceless and dangerous and he watched, silently mesmerized as she lifted her arms, and stretching languidly, began to hum. And then his breath almost choked him as he saw that she wasn't completely naked but was wearing a tiny flesh-coloured thong.

The scrap of damp fabric tugged at his gaze.

His chest tightening, he stared at her hungrily, his blood pulsing thickly as she dipped her feet into the pond and then began to sing again in the same sweet, light voice.

Massimo smiled. He recognised the song, and with the breath spinning out of him like sugar turning to candy-floss he started to whistle the tune.

The girl froze, her head jerking upwards. Taking a step forwards, she frowned. 'Who's there?'

Moving out from under the archway, Massimo held his hands out in front of him. 'Sorry. I couldn't resist. I hope I didn't scare you.'

She stared at him fiercely, and he realised with surprise that she didn't seem scared. Nor had she made any attempt to cover her nakedness. But then given the beauty of that body, why should she? His own body hardened painfully as she looked up at him defiantly.

'Then perhaps you shouldn't creep about in the bushes. This is private property and you're trespassing. I suggest you leave now before I call the police.'

Her Italian was fluent, and bore no trace of an English accent, and he felt another stab of surprise and admiration too. But neither showed on his face as he smiled at her coolly.

'The police! That might be a little premature.' His English was perfect and, watching her eyes widen with surprise, he smiled grimly, gratified to see that he had got under that delectable skin. 'Don't you want to know who I am first?'

'I know who you are, Mr Sforza.' Her voice was clear and calm. She lifted her chin. 'And I know what you want. But you're not going to get it. This is *my* home, and I'm not about to let you turn it into some ghastly boutique hotel for loud, sweaty tourists, so you might as well leave.'

'Or what?' His eyes drifted casually over her naked breasts. 'If you're concealing a weapon, I'd really like to know where.' He stared at her mockingly. 'This is *my* property and *my* land and you are *my* tenant. As your landlord, I'm entitled to inspect what's mine. Although, to be fair, I think you've pretty much shown me everything there is to see.'

Flora glared at him, her eyes flashing with anger. So this was the famous Massimo Sforza—or was that infamous? The man whose arrogant swirling signature had dominated her days and dreams for so many weeks. He was everything she had imagined him to be: slickly clever, charming yet ruthless. But now, with that glittering blue gaze locked onto hers, it was clear she had underestimated the ratio of charm to ruthlessness. Meeting his eyes, she felt a shiver of fury run through her body. He clearly believed that his presence was dazzling enough to overpower her objections to his stupid hotel. If so, he was sadly mistaken. She'd had her fill of men simply assuming that she would fit in with their plans. Particularly one as smug as Massimo Sforza.

Her heartbeat began to quicken. He *was* completely, irredeemably loathsome. So why then was her pulse fluttering like a moth near a candle? Heat burned her cheeks and she shook her head in denial—but there could be no denying her body's treacherous, quivering response to his. Nor the fact that he was the most wickedly attractive man she'd ever met.

And the most dangerous.

She gritted her teeth, confused and angered by her body's response. It was so inappropriate and shallow and given who she knew him to be, frankly *wrong*. So what if he was handsome? Hadn't she seen his photo in enough newspapers and magazines to have grown sick of that sculpted head? Her body felt hot and taut beneath the intensely blue focus of his gaze, but she shivered. It was crazy: he hadn't even touched her. But nothing could truly have prepared her for the reality of his beauty or that air of power and self-assurance. With that sleek black hair, the flawless bone structure just visible beneath the stubble and that imperious gaze he might easily have been one of the bandits that used to roam the island's hills.

She scowled. Only now, instead of robbing rich travellers of their money and jewellery, he robbed ordinary people of their homes and livelihoods. He might be wearing the trappings of respectability and wealth—his suit and shoes were clearly handmade and expensive—but he had the morals of a common thief.

Her gaze skipped swiftly over the breadth of his chest. It might be broad—but not because he was big-hearted. This man didn't have a heart, and she would do well to remember that the next time she got dewy-eyed about his blatant masculine perfection.

'I didn't have you down as a prude, Mr Sforza,' she snapped back. 'Not given your well-documented fondness for scantily clad women. But then it doesn't surprise me in the least that you're a hypocrite. After all, you are the head of a multinational corporation—so it's sort of a prerequisite, isn't it?'

Massimo shrugged casually, but the intensity of his gaze made her breathing jerk. 'I'm not a prude. You caught me off guard. You see I don't generally discuss business with naked women. But then I don't tend to frequent strip joints.'

Her eyes glittered brighter than the Sardinian sun. 'I'm *not* a stripper,' she said frostily. 'And we are *not* doing business. This is my home and I can walk around in it any damn way I want.' She paused, her face twisting with scorn. 'Besides, unlike *some* people, I don't have anything to hide.'

Her pulse leaped as his face darkened with anger.

'Oh, you think nudity equates to honesty, do you? Interesting. In that case, I've got nothing to hide either.' Eyes glittering, he slid off his jacket and tossed it disdainfully onto a nearby rose bush, showering petals in every direction.

'Hey!' Flora took an angry step towards him. 'What the hell do you think you're doing?'

He glanced at her and instinctively she tensed as she saw the hostility in their cobalt depths. 'Me? I'm showing you the purity of my soul.' Holding her gaze, he slowly began undoing the buttons on his shirt.

She gritted her teeth. 'Really? You're *really* going to do this?'

Flora stared at him helplessly. This couldn't be happening. Surely he wasn't going to take all his clothes off in front of her just to prove a point? She watched in silence, a knot forming in her stomach, her heart beating frantically as he tugged his shirt off and threw it on top of his jacket. Meeting her gaze, he pushed his belt through the buckle and undid the top button of his trousers.

'No!' Turning round, she grabbed a faded sundress from the stone slabs and pulled it over her head in one swift moment.

'And I thought *I* was the prude!'

She heard the note of triumph in his voice and turned to face him with wide, scornful eyes. 'Not wanting to see you naked doesn't make me a prude. It's just a matter of taste. I know you must find it hard to believe, but I don't actually find you attractive enough to want to see you naked.'

'Oh, I can believe that. I'm clearly a little young for your taste. Perhaps I should come back in thirty years.'

Flora frowned. 'Thirty years?' she repeated stupidly. 'Why would that make any difference?'

Massimo shook his head. 'Don't play the innocent with me, *cara*. We both know I'm rich enough for you. But you like your men *old* and rich, don't you, Miss Golding? Or should that be Miss Gold-Digger?

Her eyes blazed with fury. 'How *dare* you?' She stepped towards him, her hands bunching at her sides. 'You know nothing about my relationship with Umberto.'

Her stomach muscles clenched, the knots inside pulling tighter. He was disgusting! A monster. Coarse, cold-blooded and corrupted. How could she have thought he was attractive? And he was such a hypocrite! Barging into her life and her home and judging her like that. Her breath felt sharp in her throat. Not just judging, but destroying something good and pure—sullying the memory of what had been innocent with his vile insinuations.

Scowling, she lifted her chin. Let him think what he wanted. She knew the truth. That she and Umberto had shared not passion but friendship, and a mutual desire to hide: she from her family's claustrophobic love and he from the knowledge that his artistic powers were fading.

'Just for the record, I don't have a problem with your age. Just your character! Umberto was twice the man you could ever hope to be, and you will never be capable of understanding what we shared. But it certainly wasn't his bank account.'

He smiled coldly. It was the smile of someone to whom such an outburst was a sign of weakness and imminent surrender. 'The lady doth protest too much. Although in your case…' he raised his eyebrow mockingly '… I think "lady" might be pushing it somewhat, don't you?'

Leaning over, he picked up his jacket and reached into the inside pocket. He pulled out an envelope and held it out to Flora.

'Save your self-justification for someone who cares.' His face hardened. '"Just for the record", I don't care who you sleep with or why. I just want you out of here— and, despite your damning little speech about my character, I think if you look inside that envelope you'll find that I understand pretty much everything about you, Miss Golding.'

His icy, knowing smile made her stomach flip over. She glared at him but he held her gaze.

'I like playing games as much as the next man, *cara*, but you don't have to play games with me anymore. And this *is* a game, isn't it? You holding out for more and me giving you what you really want?'

She stared at him in silence. His blue eyes were as deep and tempting as the Tyrrhenian Sea.

'Come on, *cara*,' he said softly. 'Umberto was a rich man, but accept my offer and you'll be a far richer woman.'

Flora stared at the envelope in silence. A rich woman! She could almost picture the cheque: could see that authoritative swirling signature.

He watched with grim satisfaction as she hesitated momentarily and then took it from him. 'Aren't you going to open it?'

She looked up at him, hating the note of triumph in his voice. 'No,' she said quietly, her eyes fixed on his face. And then with slow deliberation she tore the envelope in two and threw it at him. 'I don't need to. You see, there's nothing you can offer me that I will ever want. Except never to see your vile, arrogant face again!'

And before he even had a chance to reply she turned and darted through an archway and vanished as a light breeze blew the pieces of envelope and cheque across the flagstones.

CHAPTER TWO

MASSIMO STARED AFTER her in confusion. What the hell had just happened? Had she really just taken his cheque and ripped it up? Without even looking at it?

His stomach contracted. Everything he'd wanted had been almost in his grasp and now he felt stupid and out of place—almost as though she'd left him standing at the altar, with the pieces of envelope fluttering around his feet like discarded confetti. His breathing quickened. *Damn her!*

'Mr Sforza?' At the sound of Giorgio's voice he turned sharply. Looking pale and flustered, his lawyer hurried across the flagstones. 'I'm sorry I took so long. This place is like a maze. But I heard voices.' His eyes popped slightly as finally he seemed to register his shirtless boss, and then he looked quickly away. 'Er…is everything okay? I mean—'

Massimo's face darkened. He was well aware of how he must look, standing there half-naked and alone like some spurned suitor. His confusion was gone, replaced by a rage so pure, so absolute, that it seemed to fill his entire body.

'Everything is fine,' he snapped. 'I just thought I'd have a quick sunbathe.'

The lawyer gazed at him uncertainly. 'Really…?'

Massimo shook his head in exasperation, his body seething with a frustration that took him straight back to his childhood. 'No, Giorgio. Of course not. I was—' Grimacing, he shook his head again. 'It doesn't matter.' Breathing out slowly, he picked up his shirt and slid his arms into it. 'You can tell Lisi she was right, though. She *is* volatile.'

'That's the impression I was given, sir.' Giorgio nodded, a look of relief sliding over his face. 'That's why I think we should cut our losses and walk away before...' He glanced furtively across at his boss, who was buttoning up his shirt with swift precision. 'Before this gets any more out of hand.'

Massimo whirled towards him. 'Walk away?' Snatching up his jacket, he shrugged it on carelessly, his voice colder than marble. 'Oh, I've got no intention of walking away, Giorgio. Not before I've taught Miss Golding a long and clearly overdue lesson in manners. Come with me.'

He turned and began to walk swiftly in the direction that Flora had just taken. Ducking under the archway, both men came to an abrupt stop as they emerged onto a neatly trimmed grass lawn. Across the lawn a high yew hedge rose out of the ground, in the centre of which was another archway. There was no sign of Flora—

'This is getting ridiculous,' Massimo muttered. 'How many gardens does one *palazzo* need?'

They crossed the lawn and stopped in front of the archway. It wasn't a garden.

'It's a maze!' Giorgio gazed uncertainly at a small rusting sign. He looked up at his boss, his expression a mixture of astonishment and dismay. 'Do you think she's in there?'

Massimo scowled. Of course she was in there. No doubt laughing her pretty little head off at their expense.

He sighed. 'I should have ripped the damned house down with her in it. I know I said this before, but I'm going to sort this out once and for all and then I'll be back. And this time I really won't be long. After all, how difficult can it be to find her?'

The answer to that question was *really* difficult, he decided some twenty minutes later, after he'd turned yet another corner to find yet another dead end. With a groan of frustration, he ran his hands through his hair and cursed Flora loudly.

'I may not be a lady, but even *I* wouldn't use words like that!'

His body froze as her voice, fizzing with malice, cut sharply through his tirade.

'What's the matter, Mr Sforza? Don't you like hide and seek? I thought you liked playing games "as much as the next man".'

He spun round, his gaze boring into the thick, dark leaves. 'Oh, very funny. This is very amusing, I'm sure. But you can't hide from me for ever!'

'Probably not! But I've got a funny feeling that after an hour...' she paused, and sighed elaborately '...or *four* spent wandering around in here, you might just want to go home. If a bullying, greedy monster like you actually *has* a home.'

He gritted his teeth and then his pupils flared as from somewhere behind the high green hedge, he heard a twig snap. *Gotcha!* Slowly, with delicate steps, his heart hammering with excitement, he crept towards the end of the path and stepped swiftly around the corner. But there was no one there.

'You might as well give up and go home.'

Her voice floated through the foliage, the crisp, cool words acting like salt on his wounded pride. And yet despite his irritation part of him was enjoying this game they were playing.

His mouth curved into an almost-smile. 'If you knew me better, *cara*, you'd know that I never give up or give in.'

'Thankfully I will never know you at all. Anyway, carry on looking if you want, but I should warn you there's over a thousand metres of paths and only one of them will take you to the centre. Still…happy hunting!'

Massimo glanced up at the sky, and his breathing slowed. She was going to pay for this. And a lot sooner than she thought. Reaching into his trouser pocket, he pulled out his mobile phone and punched in a number.

Flora stared up at the thick, yew bushes and felt a surge of satisfaction. The maze had been designed by Umberto and had a particularly fiendish layout. Massimo Sforza would be stuck wandering around between its high, impenetrable hedges hopefully until the sun set. She smiled happily. Which should give him ample time to ponder the ethics of harassment and bribery.

Her smile faded. His casual, unfounded assumption that her reason for staying at the *palazzo* was to squeeze more money out of him and his stupid company made her skin tighten with anger.

If only there was some way to get rid of him for good. But like most rich, powerful men, he was used to getting his own way.

She felt suddenly tired. Was it so much to ask to keep her home? But it was always the same. Even reasonable, well-adjusted men seemed to assume that a woman could and should change her life to fit in with their plans.

Remembering James's angry disbelief when she'd refused to upend her life for his, she felt an ache spread inside of her. And it had been the same with Thomas too. He'd been bewildered and then furious with her for pursuing her own goals instead of supporting him.

Her lip trembled. Then of course there was her dad and

her brother, Freddie. They'd always been *protective* but since her mother's death, they'd treated her like she was a child; an adorable but foolish child who needed protecting from herself.

Still, at least they loved her and cared about her. Massimo Sforza, on the other hand, only cared about himself. But just because he was rich and used to getting his own way didn't mean she should give up her home so he could turn it into a stupid hotel.

She shivered. The stone bench on which she'd taken refuge was cold, and even though the sun was gleaming like a huge pearl in the flawless blue sky the seven-foot hedges meant that little of its heat was reaching her.

Damn Gianni! It was all his fault. If only Umberto hadn't left him the estate. And if only his feckless, greedy brother hadn't sold it on as soon as the deeds were in his hands, she wouldn't be here, hiding like a criminal on the run.

A twig cracked nearby, and she froze momentarily—then relaxed. It was probably just a lizard or a bird. Massimo Sforza might be rich and powerful but he'd need x-ray vision or wings to find her in here.

Her head jerked up abruptly. Above her, a Marsh harrier gave a shrill screech and, frowning, she slid off the bench, a shiver of apprehension scuttling down her spine. It might have been muted by the hedges, but it had definitely been a warning call. But before she could even ponder as to what might have caused the bird's alarm she heard a faint droning noise, and then a shadow fell across her upturned face and the droning become a loud rhythmic 'whumping'.

Open-mouthed, Flora stared up in astonishment at a large, sleek white helicopter. Where had it come from? And then she gave a sudden cry of rage. *Sforza!* It had to be. She'd assumed he'd driven to the *palazzo*, but who else would have such a showy boy's toy? She must have been swimming under the water in the pond when he'd flown over—

There was a crunch of footsteps on gravel behind her, and her heart leaping in her chest, she turned, knowing before she did so that it would be him.

'Thanks, Paolo. Yeah, I think I can find my way out. But I'll call you if I need your help.' Massimo clicked off his phone and examined her face, his eyes glittering with malice. 'So. We meet again.' He glanced at his watch and frowned. 'Not quite fifteen minutes!'

'Only because you cheated!' Hands curling into fists, Flora stepped backwards. Her calves collided painfully with the stone bench, but it was nothing compared to the injuries she would inflict on Massimo if she stood too close to him.

He shook his head. 'You're not going to have a tantrum about losing, are you, *cara*? I told you—I don't give up and I don't give in. And, besides, I hate waiting.'

She shivered as his face shifted, grew harder and colder than the marble bench pressing against her legs.

'And I never, *ever* lose.'

Flora stared at him stonily. 'What a wonderful mantra for life. Your parents must be so proud of you.'

His eyes flared, and nervously she realised that his broad body was blocking her only way of escape.

There was a short, tense silence and then he shrugged. 'And what about *your* parents, *cara*? Were they proud that their daughter was shacked up with a man old enough to be her grandfather?' He paused, his lip curling, his teeth bared so that for a moment he seemed to resemble a large, dangerous animal more than a man.

She lifted her chin and met his gaze. 'We can stand here all day and trade insults, if you want,' she said stiffly. 'But it won't alter the fact that I have a legal right to stay here as a tenant for as long as I wish. Nothing you can do or say will change that fact.'

For a long moment he stared at her steadily and then, to her astonishment, he smiled without rancour. 'That's true.'

She waited tensely as he continued to study her, his abrupt change of mood almost as unsettling as the growing realisation that they were only inches apart, alone, separated from the rest of the world by seven-foot hedges. Goosebumps tiptoed over her skin, and she swallowed uneasily. Why was he looking at her like that? It reminded her of the way buyers used to look at Umberto's paintings: cool, assessing, critical.

She shivered again, and he frowned slightly. 'You're cold! Of course, you must be.'

Before she could reply, he had pulled off his jacket and draped it over her shoulders. His hand grazed her skin, and she shivered once more, this time from the heat of his touch.

Feeling somehow disloyal—although to what or to whom, she wasn't sure—she tried to shrug it off, but he shook his head.

'It's just a jacket, *cara*. Not a white flag.'

Blushing, wondering how or when her thoughts became so transparent, she nodded mutely. She felt hot. Impatient. Restless. But where had all her anger and outrage gone? Wrapping her arms tightly across her chest, she stared mutinously past his head. *He* was making her feel like this. His tantalising nearness seemed to have driven all rational thought from her mind. And now, wearing his jacket, with the warmth of his body still clinging to the fabric, she felt even more confused.

Still staring straight ahead and desperate to at least appear cool and calm, she cleared her throat. 'I'll walk you out.' His gaze was burning her skin and, turning, her heart shivered as her eyes collided with his.

He nodded slowly. 'Then I won't charge you for the loan of my jacket.' Her eyes widened and he grinned. 'I'm kidding. Look. I can find my own way out—'

She rolled her eyes. 'No you can't. Come on. It'll only take a few minutes.'

It took seven. Giorgio was waiting at the entrance. He glanced anxiously at their faces. 'Ah, there you are. There you *both* are—'

Massimo interrupted him smoothly. 'Giorgio. I don't believe you've met Miss Golding. Miss Golding, this is my chief legal advisor, Giorgio Caselli. Our business is done here, Giorgio. I'll see you back at the helicopter.'

Looking both astonished and respectful, the lawyer nodded. 'It is? Excellent. Wonderful. It was a pleasure to meet you, Miss Golding.'

Flora stared after him, a sense of foreboding creeping over her skin. Was that it, then? After all these months of harassment, was he just going to give up and walk away?

She turned to face him. 'I don't understand. Are you saying I can stay? Or is this some game? Because I don't know how to play.'

His mouth curved at the edges. 'This isn't a game.'

'But it doesn't make any sense,' she replied fiercely. 'One minute you're jack-booting around like some crazed dictator on a rampage, and now you're being—' She stopped.

'What? What am I being?'

His blue eyes were fixed on her animated features and she frowned. 'I don't know—reasonable, nice!'

He winced. 'Reasonable! *Nice?* I don't think anyone has ever accused me of being that before!' His tone was teasing.

'I don't suppose they have,' she said cautiously.

He grinned, his handsome face softening. 'It's a low blow! *Arrogant, ruthless, crazed*...I can handle. Niceness, though... That's dangerous! Whoever heard of a *nice* CEO?'

She bit her lip.

He frowned. 'I'm serious. You have to promise me: what happens in the maze, stays in the maze. I can't have my reputation as a "bullying, greedy monster" ruined.'

Recognising her words, Flora blushed. 'You were a bit bullying,' she said carefully. 'But I suppose that doesn't matter now.'

He was watching her thoughtfully. 'I'd like to think it doesn't.' Pausing, he glanced across the lawn. 'Are there more gardens over there?'

Surprised by the change of subject, she nodded.

'I'd like to see them. Will you show me?' he asked simply.

Breathing in the drifting scents of blossom and warm earth, Massimo was surprised—impressed, even—by the scale and diversity of the gardens. He was no horticulturist, but even he could see that in stark contrast to the *palazzo* it looked as though someone was taking care of them.

Between narrow gravel-filled paths edged with meticulously trimmed bay hedges, the neat, square beds were filled with lavender, thyme, rosemary and sage, while espaliered fruit trees mingled with climbing roses, jasmine, honeysuckle and wisteria on the walls and arches.

Massimo ran his hand lightly over a topiary spiral. No doubt Bassani had taken up gardening when his career as an artist had begun to fade. Squinting into the sunlight, his face tightened. It was pretty, but gardening—like all hobbies—seemed a complete waste of time to him. He worked out with a personal trainer five mornings a week, but work fulfilled all his needs except rest and relaxation, which was why, in his leisure time, he liked to sleep and have sex.

His lip curled—although not necessarily in that order.

'It's beautiful,' he said finally. 'I didn't know Bassani was such a keen horticulturist.'

Flora looked up at him, her mouth curving into a pout, and he felt his groin tighten almost imperceptibly. How to describe those lips? Not red, not pink— He smiled grimly as the words came to him from school art lessons: *rose madder*. He stared at her critically. A tiny scar just above her eyebrow and a sprinkling of freckles over her nose and cheeks contrasted with the classical symmetry of her face and saved her from being just another pretty girl. But that mouth was a work of art: a mixture of challenge and seduction, determination and—surrender.

An image of Flora, soft-eyed, her body melting against his, those lips parting, exploded inside his head.

Struggling to keep himself from touching the plump cushion of her lower lip, he gestured offhandedly towards a cluster of dark red peonies. 'Did he choose everything?'

Flora shook her head slowly. 'Umberto didn't have anything to do with the gardens—' She checked herself. 'He liked sitting in them, of course, but he knew absolutely nothing about plants.' She wrinkled her nose. 'He couldn't tell a weed from a wallflower!'

Watching her eyes mist over as she talked about her lover, Massimo felt something twist inside him. The thought of Flora and Umberto together, her bewitching young body pressed against the older man's, made him want to snap the heads off the flowers—

Her voice broke into his thoughts. 'He sometimes helped me with the planting, though. Not the actual digging, but he always knew what plant should go where. I think that's because he was an artist; he had a wonderful eye for colour and composition.'

Massimo nodded. 'I know even less about colour and composition than I do plants. But I have a couple of properties on the mainland,' he said idly. 'I could do with a capable gardener.' His blue eyes gleamed. 'Maybe I could poach yours.'

She burst out laughing. He was impossible. Incorrigible. Infuriating. And for one bizarre moment, it actually felt like they liked each other. Biting her lip, she met his gaze. 'So now that you can't have my home, you want my gardener?'

Amusement lit up his eyes. 'I hadn't thought of it like that but—yes. It seems only fair.'

The gentle, mocking tone of his voice made her heart beat faster. He was still her enemy, she told herself frantically. He was a devil in disguise and she shouldn't let her guard down just because his eyes were like woodland pools and his voice was as sweet and silken as wild honey.

'That's not going to happen,' she said carefully, hoping that her face revealed nothing of her thoughts. 'Looking after these gardens—' she frowned 'Well, it's not just a job. It's more complicated than that.'

His eyes were dark and teasing. 'Compared to that maze nothing is complicated! Don't look so worried, *cara*, I'm not going to kidnap your gardener. I can see you don't want to lose his services.'

Their eyes met, and she felt her skin grow warm and tingling beneath his lingering gaze. His eyes were a beautiful, deep, dark blue of a forget-me-not, and she felt a sudden sharp heat inside as she stared at his lean jawline and the full, passionate mouth. He would be impossible to forget even if his eyes *didn't* demand that he be remembered: his lean, muscular body, the compelling purposefulness of his gaze and the intensity of his masculinity set him apart from every other man she'd ever met. And his smile— She felt a rush of longing. What woman *wouldn't* want to be the cause of that smile?

And then, as though the sun had gone behind a cloud, his smile faded. 'I'm sorry,' he said slowly. 'It must be the heat or something. I'm usually a little quicker on the uptake.' He frowned. 'You don't have to explain. I get it.'

'Get what?' The hair on the nape of her neck rose at the sudden tension between them.

'Obviously, he's a "friend" of yours.'

She stared at him, confused. 'Who?'

'Your gardener.'

The expression on his face was hard to define, but she could almost see him retreating, and she felt a rush of panic. 'He's not a friend of mine. I mean, he can't be. He doesn't exist,' she said breathlessly. '*I* do the gardening. *Me*. On my own.'

There was a moment's silence as he studied her face and then he smiled slowly, and once again she felt her nerves flutter into life and her skin grow warm. 'Is that so? You really are full of surprises, Miss Golding. No wonder Bassani was so smitten with you!'

There was nothing new in his words. She had heard them said in so many ways, so many times before. Normally she let them wash over her, but for some reason she didn't want this man to think that they were true.

'No—it wasn't like—' she began but her words stopped in her throat as he reached out and gently took her hand in his. Turning it over, he ran his fingers lightly over the hard calluses on her palm, and she felt her breath snag in her throat; felt heat flare low in her pelvis. Her heart was racing. She knew she should tell him to stop, should pull her hand away, but she couldn't speak or move.

Finally, he let go of her hand and said softly, 'So. This is why you want to stay.'

It wasn't a question, but she nodded anyway. 'Yes. Partly.'

She looked up at him hesitantly. She never talked to anyone about her real work. Most people on the island simply assumed that she was Umberto's muse, and it was true—she *had* often posed for Umberto. But she'd only modelled for him as a favour. Her real passion, ever since she was a little girl, was flowers, although not many people took her seriously when she told them—probably because they were too busy pointing out the fact that her name was Flora and she liked flowers: a joke which had stopped being funny years ago.

She took a deep breath. 'I'm actually writing a thesis on orchids. The island's home to some very rare species. That's why I came here in the first place.' Feeling suddenly a little shy, she gave him a small tight smile. 'I didn't even know about the *palazzo* or Umberto before I arrived. I just bumped into him in a café in Cagliari.'

Massimo studied her assessingly. She made it sound so innocent, so unplanned. As though her relationship with Bassani had been a matter of chance. His face hardened. Yet here she was with her name on the tenancy agreement. He gritted his teeth. However she spun the story, he knew she had been looking for some sort of sugar daddy, and in Sardinia there was only one man who fitted the bill.

A muscle flickered in his jaw. Women like Flora Golding did their homework. Nothing was left to chance. Because if their efforts succeeded then, like his stepmother Alida, they need never work again—although spending his father's money had pretty much been a full-time job for *her*. His body stilled as he allowed himself a brief memory of his stepmother's icy disdain, and then he gazed coolly at Flora.

No doubt she'd found out where Bassani had liked to drink and set the whole thing up. He could well imagine the older man's greedy excitement on discovering this beautiful young girl sipping cappuccino in some shabby little bar. And then all she'd had to do was pose for him. Naked. At the thought of Flora slipping out of her faded sundress, her eyes dark and shiny with triumph, he felt almost giddy with envy and lust.

For a moment he lost all sense of time and place, and then he breathed out slowly. 'How fortuitous,' he said smoothly. 'To find your own blank canvas here at this *palazzo*—the very place you have chosen to make your home.'

He stared broodingly across the garden, blind to its beauty. He should have been satisfied by this final proof that she was as disingenuous and manipulative as he'd suspected, but beneath the satisfaction was an odd sense of disappointment, of betrayal. And of anger with himself for responding to her obvious physical charms.

His jaw tightened. But wasn't it always so with women? Especially women like Flora Golding, who had duplicitous charms ingrained in them from an early age. *Flora*. It was a name that seemed to suggest a honeyed sweetness and an unsullied purity. And yet it tasted bitter on his tongue.

His gaze sharpened as she looked up at him, her light brown eyebrows arching in puzzlement at the shift in his voice. 'I do love the gardens, but it's more of a hobby than anything else. My real work is my dissertation and if I'm going to finish my thesis I need peace and quiet. And that's what I get living here.'

Massimo smiled. Her tone was conversational, her words unremarkable, but she had unwittingly given him the means to her end.

They had reached the front of the *palazzo*. Abruptly he

turned to face her. 'It's been an enlightening visit, Miss Golding. Don't worry—we won't be contacting you anymore. And there certainly won't be any more financial incentives. You've made it perfectly clear that you're not motivated by money, and I respect that.'

Flora blinked in the sunlight. Even though the day was now suffocatingly hot, she felt a chill run down her spine. His voice sounded different again—almost like a sneer or a taunt. But nothing had changed. Maybe it was just the heat playing with her senses…

'Good,' she said quickly, trying to ignore the uneasiness in her stomach. 'I'm just sorry you had to make a personal trip to understand how I feel.'

He stepped forward, and she felt a spurt of shock and fear for this time there could be no confusion. His face was cold and set.

'Don't be. I always like to meet my enemies face to face. It makes closing a deal on my terms so much easier.'

It took a moment for the implication of his words to sink in. 'Wh-what deal?' she stammered. The word echoed ominously inside her head. 'There *is* no deal,' she said hoarsely. 'You said so. You said you wouldn't be contacting me or offering me money again.'

He smiled coolly, a contemplative gleam in his blue eyes. 'I won't. You won't be getting a penny of my money. Not now. Not ever.'

She stared at him, chilled by the undisguised hostility of his gaze. 'I don't understand…' she began, but her words died in her throat as he shook his head.

'No. I don't suppose you do. So let me make it clear for you. Like I said earlier, *cara*, I *always* get what I want.' His face seemed to be no longer made of flesh and blood, but cold stone. 'And I want you out of here. Normally I'd pay, but as money's not an option I'm going to have to use some other method to get what I want. But believe me I will get it. And by the time I've finished with you, you'll be begging to sign any contract I put in front of you for free.'

She stared at him, her heart pounding against her ribs. 'What do you mean?' But already he had begun walking down the drive. 'Y-you're wrong! Y-you can't do anything!' she called after him. 'This is my home!'

She was panting, stuttering, her anger vying with her fear. He was bluffing. He had to be. There was nothing he could do.

But as she watched the helicopter rise up into the sky and slowly disappear from view she knew that it was she who was mistaken. She had thought he had come to the *palazzo* simply to broker a deal. And maybe it had started out that way. But that had been before she threw his deal back in his face. She felt a rush of nausea. Now there would be no more deals, for his parting words had been a declaration of war. And she knew with absolute certainty that when Massimo Sforza came back next time he would be bringing an army.

CHAPTER THREE

ROLLING OVER IN her large wrought-iron bed, Flora stared miserably out of the window at the cloudless sky. She'd slept badly again. Her night had been filled by images of Massimo Sforza, his eyes darker than his bespoke navy blue suit, beckoning her towards him only for the floor to open up beneath her feet.

Her cheeks grew warm, and she shifted uncomfortably beneath the bedclothes. The nightmares had been horrible, but the dreams were far more unsettling. Dreams of a naked Massimo, his lean, muscular body pressed against hers, those long, supple fingers drifting lazily over her skin and—

And what? Irritably, she sat up. He'd probably take the bed, with her still in it, and push it out to sea—and frankly she'd deserve it.

Gritting her teeth, she pulled on a faded black T-shirt and a pair of sawn-off jeans and stomped downstairs. Holding her breath, she forced herself to look at the letter cage hanging on the back of the door, but there was no heart-stopping white envelope to greet her, and she breathed out slowly.

It had been three weeks since Massimo had turned up at the *palazzo*, but still she sensed his presence everywhere. The thought that someday she would turn round to find him standing there, watching her, his face rapt and triumphant, made her feel dizzy.

But only until the anger kicked in.

In the kitchen, she took out a plate and a cup and glanced up at the deadbolts she'd fitted to the French windows. As a tenant, she was forbidden from changing the main locks, but there was nothing in her contract about adding additional security so she had bought new solid steel padlocks for all the gates too. Glancing up at the old iron range, she felt the tension inside her ease a little. There was only one key to the huge, solid oak front door and it was hanging there, between the skillet and the espresso coffee pot. Whatever happened, Massimo Sforza was not going to be able to barge his way unannounced into her home again.

She woke the next morning to the insistent ringing of her mobile phone. 'Okay, okay,' she mumbled, fumbling on the bedside table, her eyes still screwed shut. 'Hello? Hello!'

Opening one eye, she squinted into the sunlight filtering through the gap in the curtains. Who the hell was ringing at this time? And, more importantly, why weren't they saying anything? She gazed irritably at her phone and then her breath seemed to freeze in her lungs as the ringing began again—from somewhere downstairs.

For a moment she lay gripped with confusion, panic swelling inside her, cold and slippery as a toad. Wishing her heart would stop making so much noise, she strained her ears. Surely she'd imagined it—but there it was again. And then from nowhere came a high-pitched screeching that made her press her hands over her ears.

Still wincing, she rolled out of bed. She wasn't scared now. Burglars didn't use drills. She sniffed suspiciously. Or make coffee!

The noise downstairs was even louder than in her bedroom. Edging into the kitchen, she took a deep breath as her mouth fell open in horror. Everywhere she looked, there were people in overalls and boxes piled on top of one another.

Her lips tightening, she tapped the nearest man on the shoulder. 'Excuse me! What are you doing in my kitchen?'

But before he could answer a woman with a sleek shoulder-length blond bob, wearing a clinging grey jacket and skirt, slid past her, miming apologetically.

Gritting her teeth, Flora gazed furiously in front of her. She might not go shopping much anymore, but she knew a designer suit when she saw one and that little outfit probably cost more than her food bill for a year.

It also answered her question more eloquently than any workman could have done.

Her face twisting with anger, she stormed out onto the *terrazza*. 'I *knew* it,' she spat. 'I knew you'd be behind this! You are such a—' She swore furiously in English at the man lounging at the table, drinking coffee.

He frowned, his handsome face creasing with mock horror. 'Somebody got out of bed the wrong side.' His eyes gleamed maliciously. 'Good morning, Miss Golding! I hardly recognise you with your clothes on!'

'Ha-ha! Very amusing. Now, will you please tell me what the hell you're playing at?'

'I'm not *playing* at anything, *cara*. This is work.' His eyes pinned her to the spot. 'I'm sorry we got you up so early, but not all of us have the luxury of a lie-in.'

He was speaking in English too, and she stared at him mutely, trying to work out why. And then abruptly he stood up and languidly stretched his shoulders and all rational thought went out of her head as her body went on high alert.

'Don't mind us,' he said, stifling a yawn. 'We can just carry on down here and you can go back up to bed.'

Flora gaped at him. Why was he acting like this? He

was being friendly, pleasant. He was making it seem as though this was something she'd agreed to. Glancing round, she felt her skin grow warm as she saw two of the men on his team share a conspiratorial glance.

Did they think she and Massimo were—? She opened her mouth to protest—and then stopped as Massimo smiled malevolently at her outraged expression.

Their eyes met and his smile widened. 'Actually, I had a very early start. Perhaps I'll just come up with you—'

She glowered at him. 'No. You will not—' And then she jumped violently as a loud thumping started from somewhere further inside the house. 'What the *hell* is that noise?' Turning, she stalked back into the kitchen like an angry cat.

Following her, Massimo shrugged, his face bland and unreadable. 'I'm not exactly sure.' He gestured vaguely towards a box of cables. 'Something to do with improving the internet.'

His eyes picked over the two spots of colour on her cheeks and the pulse throbbing in her neck and something in their considering gleam made her want to take some of the cable and strangle him with it. But instead she gritted her teeth. Knowing him, he was probably hoping she'd do just that so he could exercise some medieval right to remove unstable female tenants.

She took a deep breath. 'You can't do this, Mr Sforza—'

'Call me Massimo,' he said smoothly. 'I know I'm your landlord, but there's really no need to stand on ceremony.'

She bit her lip—he was baiting her. Worse, he was enjoying watching her struggle with her temper. 'Yes. You are my landlord. Which means that you can't just walk in here whenever you feel like it.'

'You know, I thought you'd say that,' he murmured, reaching into his jacket pocket. 'So I had one of my staff print off a copy of your tenancy agreement. Here. You can keep it.' He glanced at the slanting pile of letters stacked against the wall. 'File it with all your other important documents.'

Staring at him mutinously, she snatched it from him. 'I don't need a copy. I know what it says, and it says that you can't just turn up without warning. You have to give me notice.'

He frowned. 'Did I not do that? How remiss of me. I can't imagine how that happened. And there was me, trying to be a good landlord—'

'You were not,' she retorted, her resolve to keep her temper hanging by a fibre optic thread. 'If you were, your men wouldn't be bashing holes in my walls—they'd be fixing the roof and the plumbing. You're just doing this to try and make my life difficult. So why don't you just take your stupid internet cable and all this other rubbish and leave before I call the police?'

He held her angry gaze, and she saw that flecks of silver were dappling his eyes like sea foam. Her heart began to thump painfully.

'Why bother?' he said easily, glancing at his watch. 'I'm meeting the Chief of Police in an hour for lunch. We're old friends. I can mention your concerns to him, if you like.'

The expression on his face was hard to define, but whatever it was it didn't improve her temper. 'Which presumably he'll then ignore?' she snapped. *Damn him!* Pretending he was concerned about her when they both knew the exact opposite was true.

'There's no need to get hysterical, *cara*.' There was a glint of satisfaction in his eyes. 'I'm only trying to help you.'

It was the last straw. Her voice rose shrilly. 'You're not trying to help anyone but yourself.'

He took a step towards her and held out his hands apologetically, placatingly. 'I am. Truly. And I'm sorry about all this noise and mess.' Turning, he barked out a few words in rapid Italian, and as if a switch had been flicked the hammering and drilling stopped and within seconds the kitchen was empty and silent.

She stared at him, confused.

'Here. Drink this.' He held out a glass of water and then as she took it, he shook his head and said softly, 'You see. You're already starting to wish you'd taken the money, aren't you?'

For a moment she floundered, shocked by his malice and sheer bloody-mindedness, and then anger, hot and damp like wet earth, rose in her throat. Breathing out slowly, she put the glass on the table. She wanted to kill him.

'Is that why you're doing all of this?'

He shook his head. 'No. I'm doing all this for my new tenant. Your new neighbour.'

She gaped at him. '*What* new neighbour?'

'The new tenant who's moving in today. It was in the email.' He paused. 'The one that wasn't sent.' He smiled blandly. 'Don't look so worried. I hand-picked him myself.'

It took all her will-power not to throw the glass of water at his head. Finally, she said flatly, 'Let me guess. He's a drummer in a band. Or maybe he breeds huskies or budgerigars.'

He laughed. 'Are you saying I'd *deliberately* pick an antisocial tenant to make your life hard?' He shook his head. 'Sorry to disappoint you but there's no dogs or birds. Just a nice, quiet businessman.'

Something wasn't right.

His words nudged each other inside her head and then she knew what it was. She went hot, then cold, and then hot again with horror.

'No!' She shook her head, her pupils flaring. 'No! You are *not* moving in here. You can't—'

'But I can.'

He paused, and her pulse soared as he smiled at her slowly—a dark, taunting smile that sent a shiver through her body.

'You're not scared, are you, *cara*? After all, it's a big house.'

She felt a jolt, low down, felt suddenly horribly out of her depth. It was a big house but she knew that he would dominate every inch of it. A lump rose in her throat. It wasn't fair. This house was her home—her refuge from the world. But how was she supposed to feel safe living with a man who looked at her with such absolute focus? Such predatory purpose?

Fear mingling with desire, she stared at him in silence, terrified that he might somehow be able to read her mind as the blue gaze lingered on her hot, flushed face.

Finally, he shrugged. 'I've taken the bedroom next to yours—the blue room.' Pausing, he smiled coldly. 'Of course if you don't like it you can always move rooms. Or move out.'

Her stomach clenched, and she could barely swallow her anger. 'Over my dead body.'

Massimo smiled coldly. Normally his business decisions were based on logic and reason. But his decision to move into the *palazzo* had been driven by pure, elemental rage. Flora had defied him and he'd wanted to punish her defiance—to rub his power in her face.

Giorgio had been appalled. His team astonished. It had been reckless and completely out of character. And yet he'd still gone ahead and done it.

His body twitched and he stared at her greedily, a memory of her near naked body stealing into his mind like a cat burglar. For weeks it had been the same story. He'd found it impossible to concentrate, his mind drifting off, distracted by images of a fierce-eyed Flora melting into his arms—

His breathing slowed. And why not, he thought idly. He'd tried money and threats and reasoning with her and none of those had worked. So why not seduction?

He smiled at her, feeling the tug of sexual tension between them. 'I'd rather be on top of your living one.'

Flora swallowed the lump in her throat. Fear spiked inside her. Until that moment it hadn't been real—this feeling, this longing. It had just been inside her head: private, shameful. Now it was out in plain sight. His gaze rested intently on her face, and she felt something hot and dry eddy over her skin like the air pushed out of a tunnel by an approaching train.

'You're disgusting,' she whispered.

He studied her face fully, his eyes narrowed, knowing, cruel. 'Just honest,' he murmured. His lip curled. 'You should try it some time.'

Her pulse beat loudly in her head; her mouth was dry. What was the matter with her? Was she really so shallow that her body could simply override what her brain knew to be true? Massimo Sforza might be heart-stoppingly handsome, but he was also a despicable human being.

She walked slowly across the kitchen and stopped in front of him. They were so close that she was dizzily aware of the warmth of his body and the scent of lavender and bergamot that clung to his skin. Her heart was hammering in her chest, her eyes huge as she looked up at him.

'You forcing your way into my home is a pretty scummy thing to do—and I'd honestly thought you couldn't sink any lower. How wrong I was! Sorry to disappoint you, but I don't do housework, listen to opera or sleep with men I hate.'

She felt a sting of satisfaction as his smile vanished. After so many months of feeling harried, it felt good to turn on her hunter.

His fine features twisted mockingly. 'Hate? Oh, you don't hate me, *cara*. You're afraid of me. Afraid of how I make you feel.'

They were inches apart, and she found herself staring helplessly at his full and sensuously curved lips. How could a man with so little integrity have such a beautiful mouth? It was cruel and unfair.

'You're right,' she said hoarsely. 'I *am* afraid. Afraid I might get sent to prison for beating you to death. As if I'd sleep with you after how you've treated me! You are literally the most arrogant, insensitive person I've ever met.'

His eyes were cold. He let the silence grow and swell between them until it felt as if it was bruising her.

Finally, he shrugged. 'I don't know why you're making such a big deal of it. I'm not asking you to do anything you haven't done before.'

Her whole body was trembling, as though the fury and outrage inside was trying to burst through her skin. 'Which is *what*, exactly?' she snapped.

He gave her a speculative look. 'Sleep with a rich man to make your life easier.'

With satisfaction he watched something flutter across her eyes even as her hands curled into fists. How far could he push her? And how hard would it be to make her forget her anger and give in to the tension that had been building between them ever since that first day in the garden?

He gritted his teeth. For his sake, he hoped it wouldn't be too long. His self-control was already being severely tested.

Flora felt fury sweep over her skin. 'You're not only

rude, you're wrong. *Your* girlfriends might act like that, but I'm not that kind of woman.'

'Oh, I think you're *exactly* that kind of a woman,' he said softly. 'But don't get me wrong. I'm just making sure we understand one another. It doesn't actually matter to me what kind of woman you are. After all, men and women don't need to like or respect one another to have sex. You of all people must know that.'

She felt her breathing change, anger layering on top of the pain. 'No. They don't. But they have to like and respect themselves—and I wouldn't be able to do either if I slept with *you*.'

There was a glint in his eye but his voice was surprisingly calm when he spoke. 'As you wish. And now I really *do* have work to do, so enjoy your breakfast.'

He turned and walked out of the kitchen before she had a chance even to register that he was leaving. For a moment, still seething with resentment, she stared after him in stunned silence. And then she shivered. Maybe she should have just taken the money and gone…

Her mouth tightened. But why should she have to give up her home? Whatever he might like to imply, he couldn't force her to her leave. She had the law on her side. And she had the measure of him now.

Stepping out into the garden, she blinked. Only that was proving less of a help than a hindrance—now she knew just what she was up against. Knew that he would use every weapon at his disposal to get his way. Unfortunately what she hadn't realised until now was that his most effective weapon was himself.

Hunched over a tray of seedlings in the greenhouse, Flora blew a strand of hair out of her eyes and, looking up, stared resentfully at the beautiful honey-coloured *pala-*

zzo. It had only been five days since Massimo Sforza had moved into the building but already she knew that he had changed her life. And she was not sure it would ever be the same again.

Her once peaceful home was now filled with a succession of painters and plumbers—and, of course, his glossy-haired, expensively clad entourage. And that was just the men, she thought sourly.

Standing up, she arched her back and let out a long, slow, calming breath. Why did all the women employed by Sforza have to look like extras from a Victoria's Secret show? Surely it couldn't be a prerequisite of working there: that would be vile, not to say illegal. She pursed her lips. Although what would a bit of male chauvinism really matter to a man like Massimo?

Wiping her hands on her shorts, she picked up the tray and slid it into the rack, her face darkening. She'd been determined to ignore his existence, or at the very least treat it with the indifference it deserved. But it was proving hard when everywhere she looked there was some reminder of his presence: a pair of carelessly discarded cufflinks on the kitchen table, a sleek black sports car parked in the drive...

Flora sighed softly. Her life and her home were no longer her own. And there wasn't anything she could do about it.

At least not if her brother was to be believed.

Freddie ran his own law firm in London and, having sat and stewed in a mixture of misery and frustration, she'd finally rung him and given him an edited version of what was happening.

Thankfully, he had a big case on and was more distracted than usual. Unfortunately he'd simply confirmed her suspicions that she had two choices: stay or leave.

But somehow hearing it from him had seemed to snap it into focus.

'The law's on his side,' Freddie had said, the grim note in his voice underlining her plight. 'Technically, he should have notified you...'

He'd paused, and she'd gripped the phone tightly, willing him to present her with some watertight legal argument that would wipe that smug smile off Massimo's handsome face.

'And...?' she prompted, and heard him sigh.

'Not and—but! But it just won't be worth pursuing it. For a start it'll take so long to come to court, and secondly—on paper, at least—he's a good landlord. I mean, you said he's doing all the repairs you wanted.'

Flora stared tiredly down at her bare feet. He was. And some she hadn't even asked him for—like installing a gleaming stainless steel cooker with a baffling array of dials and programmes.

'I'm sorry, Flossie!'

Her brother's use of her childhood nickname made a lump form in her throat.

'It's okay,' she said quietly, kicking a pebble into the sunken pond. 'It was just a thought. And thanks for looking into it. I know it's not your thing.'

She could almost picture the amused expression on his face. 'It's a little domestic for my tastes. But then again, Sforza's a big name. He's high-profile. I could easily stir the pot up a little.'

She sighed. 'No, thank you. I can handle him. It's just nice to know I can run things past you.'

Freddie cleared his throat. 'You know you can always ring me. It makes a nice change from all the usual horror.'

Freddie specialised in 'causes', not cases, but she knew he loved his work.

'Look…'

She heard the shift in his voice.

'I know you don't want to hear it, but you're wasting your time out there. There's plenty of flowers in England too, you know. Why don't you come home? Dad would love to see you. We both would. You can have your own room—'

Gritting her teeth, Flora interrupted her brother quickly. 'Thanks, Freddie. But I'm not leaving the *palazzo*. It's my home—'

But he'd already moved on. 'Okay. But just promise me you're not going to go looking for a fight. Just keep your head down and stay out of his way—'

Glancing at the seedlings in front of her, Flora sighed. Of course she had promised, and she had meant what she said.

She had no intention of giving Massimo Sforza the satisfaction of getting what he wanted, and launching an all-out battle against him would have done just that. He was clever and cool-headed enough to keep on goading her until she snapped—thus giving him the perfect justification to end her tenancy. So, much as she would have liked to take him on at every opportunity, she'd kept her promise and kept out of his way.

She bit her lip. And it was fine. Except that Massimo's arrival in her life had been so sudden, so traumatic, that living with him felt as if she was dealing with the aftermath of some natural disaster. Everything familiar and safe had gone. Now even something simple, like eating breakfast, was so highly charged with possible outcomes that just thinking about it left her exhausted.

At some point she would be happy to resume open warfare, but in the meantime she was like a shipwreck survivor alone on a raft at sea. Picking up another tray of seedlings, she sighed. What she really needed was time to come to terms with her new circumstances. Time to get her bearings. And time to plan her next step...

Thankfully, the following two weeks went by without incident. The house was finally free of dust sheets and ladders, and the smell of wet paint was starting to fade. Much as she had done before Massimo's arrival, Flora spent most of her days in the greenhouses, writing up notes for her thesis. And after a couple of days spent looking warily over her shoulder she'd finally begun to relax, for it was clear that whatever occupied her landlord's days it didn't involve venturing into what she thought of as *her* space.

The gardens, though, represented a somewhat trickier prospect. A sort of no man's land. It was galling to admit it, but she skirted round them to reach the greenhouses. However, she couldn't avoid going there for ever unless she was happy to see them all go to seed. Picking up her favourite trowel and a pair of secateurs, she shut the greenhouse door firmly. She would start today with the rose garden. It always needed the most attention.

Her cheeks grew warm. The fact that it was the garden farthest away from the *palazzo* obviously had nothing to do with her decision.

After days stuck in the greenhouses, it felt glorious to feel the sun on her skin and hear the birds chattering excitedly in the hedges. The air was thick and heavy: there would be a storm later, but probably not until the evening. She worked steadily, only stopping to eat a makeshift lunch of a *sebadas* and some grapes.

Finally straightening up, she noticed a beautiful apricot floribunda: Absent Friends. She had planted it after Umberto died. He had loved all roses, but that delicate coral colour had been his favourite.

'You poor old thing,' she said softly. Brushing the petals lightly with her hands, she inhaled the smooth, voluptuous scent with pleasure. 'I'm sorry I've haven't been
looking after you.' Gently, she trimmed back a couple of
straggling stems. 'There. That's better!'

Smiling, she turned to throw the discarded blooms into
her bucket—and it was then that she saw Massimo's tall
figure, leaning casually against the stone sun dial that
formed a centrepiece to the rose garden.

'I've heard of people talking to their pets. Or even to
trees. But I've never heard anyone talk to a flower before.'

Slowly, he began to walk towards her, his eyes fixed
on her face. Hypnotised, she watched him come closer,
her body stilled by the sudden tension in the air. Even the
birds had fallen quiet, their sharp cries replace by a taut,
expectant silence.

He stopped in front of her, and she felt suddenly almost
giddy. After so many days of harbouring a grudge against
him it was a shock to see him again. And a greater shock
to be reminded of how beautiful he was. Her eyes skipped
nervously over the curved, hard muscles of his arms and
chest. Dressed casually in blue jeans and a faded grey
T-shirt, he looked more indie rock star than autocratic billionaire businessman.

His gaze travelled lazily over her and despite the
warmth of the day she felt a shiver trickle over her skin.

'So. Do they talk back?'

He spoke gently, without any hint of mockery, but she
still felt her cheeks grow warm.

She gripped the roses tightly. 'Sometimes.'

The sun seemed to light up the bones beneath his skin,
emphasising the finely etched features, the firm jaw and
smooth, slightly angular cheeks. There was strength there,
and a compelling authority, but also restraint—as though

he were holding something back…some dark energy. Quickly, she looked away.

'What are they saying now?'

His voice was so cool and clear that it made her feel thirsty. Somewhere inside her head a warning bell was ringing faintly in time to the beating of her heart. He was too close, and suddenly her breath caught in her throat, hot and panicky, as around her the birds broke into sweet, high song and a trembling breeze shook the leaves on the bushes.

He alone was silent, watching her with eyes so deep and blue she thought she might drown in them.

Trying to ignore her heart thumping against her ribs, she cleared her throat. 'They're saying, *Why is this really annoying man trampling all over us*?'

Their eyes met, and her skin twitched, and heat flared in her stomach as his lips curved into an irresistible smile.

'Really? I thought they were saying, *Why did this really annoying woman cut off our heads*?'

'So you think it's *my* fault you trod on them? That somehow *I'm* responsible for your actions?'

He laughed softly. 'Definitely. That's what nymphs do, isn't it?'

She felt her cheeks flood with colour. 'I am not a nymph. And no, it is not what they do. They simply personify nature.'

'That's what all nymphs say. Right before they bewitch some helpless man with their beauty.'

He was teasing her, and those ridiculous eyelashes were flickering like sea anemones in a rock pool. Breathing in slowly, she tried to frown; tried her hardest not to respond to the dizzying pull of his smile but she couldn't resist.

'And that's you, is it? You're the helpless man?' She lifted her chin. 'Why didn't you say that in the first place?'

Massimo felt lust gnawing at his body. He thought himself a man of the world—if not debauched then occasionally decadent—but he didn't think he'd ever seen anything as erotic as Flora, wearing a loose T-shirt cinched at the waist with an old brown leather hunting belt, her bare feet pressing into the earth.

Her cheeks were flushed, and he studied her face, watching her dimples deepen. She was teasing him, testing him. And for a moment he forgot all about punishing her. He even forgot that he wanted her to move out. In fact, her leaving was the last thing on his mind. Like a child running to reach the sea, every inch of him was focused on one goal: getting her to surrender that delectable body to him.

Her eyes were exactly the colour of cinnamon, hinting at warmth and sweetness. And a whisper of fire. He felt his groin tighten. She would be like that in bed. Sweet and warm…that incredible lush pink mouth melting beneath his…those even white teeth nipping and biting in ecstasy—

'I didn't want you to take advantage of me.'

Flora swallowed. The garden was warm; the droning sound of insects soporific. But even though his eyes seemed drowsy, she knew he was watching her intently, and the heat on her back felt suddenly like a warning. A reminder that Massimo was not and never would be helpless and that it was he who was distracting and bewitching *her*.

Slowly, she turned to drop the dead roses in the bucket and then, trying to keep her voice steady, she said, 'I'm pretty much finished here. I should probably go and clean up…'

Her heart gave a lurch, her words petering out as slowly he stepped towards her. 'Wait!'

It was a command, not a request, and she wondered if

he ever relinquished his power to anyone. His eyes were the same blue-black as the storm clouds gathering on the horizon and she stared at them as though mesmerised, a pulse fluttering in her throat. Being near him was so confusing. She felt surrounded—overwhelmed, almost and yet she wasn't scared or suffocated by his power.

Like a bee seeking pollen, his gaze settled on her lips and suddenly the humming of her blood threatened to blot out the warning voices in her head.

'We should go inside. It's going to rain,' she said hoarsely. 'Can't you feel it?'

He smiled—a dazzling smile that made her heart split— and she felt a quiver of panic. How could something be so irresistible and yet so dangerous?

'Are you sure that's what it is?' he said softly.

Mutely, she stared at him, and then she felt heat flare up inside her as gently he reached out and stroked her hair. 'Wh-what are you doing?' she stammered.

'I'm checking to see if you're real.'

'Why wouldn't I be real?'

She felt his fingers move. 'Because you've got petals in your hair,' he murmured, holding out his hand to show her. 'And you're dressed like some woodland nymph.'

His gaze on her face was blunt and she felt her cheeks grow warm.

'I'm just a gardener.' Her voice was husky, her eyes both fierce and afraid. 'You, on the other hand, have been out in the sun too long if you think I'm some nature goddess. You should get inside.'

Shaking his head, he stepped closer—so close she could see the flecks of brilliant cobalt in his eyes.

'You'll have to do better than that. If you want me to leave then tell me and I'll go.'

She swallowed. 'I want you to leave,' she lied.

There was a moment of silence and then he nodded. 'There. That wasn't too hard, was it?'

The air seemed to tremble between them, and relief and regret and merged inside her.

'You see. We're both liars.'

And slowly he lowered his head and tilted her face up towards his. Her heart seemed to drop inside her and she felt suddenly glutted with longing, and the rightness of that longing, and the heat of that longing. The breeze and the birds fell silent and still and her breath stopped. And then like a diver on a springboard she curled her toes into the grass and, standing on tiptoe, kissed him gently.

Fire flooded her skin and the tension inside her that had been growing and growing burst as his mouth moved softly over hers. She felt his tongue drift teasingly over the curving flesh of her lips and, moaning softly, maddened by its firm, probing tip, she kissed him more fiercely, nipping his mouth with her teeth.

His fingers slid slowly over the nape of her neck and then her lips parted in surprise as he jerked her against him, his arms tightening around her slender body as he deepened the kiss. Helplessly, she arched herself against him, the heat of his body drawing out the heat inside her—a relentless, tugging, pulsating thread of longing and need.

She was losing herself; she felt breathless, euphoric. Her hands slid over the broad muscles of his back, caressing the hard body beneath his shirt. Her blood was singing, her nerves dancing in time to the frenzied beating of her heart. And then she heard him groan, and her stomach clenched in a sharp, almost painful spasm.

Hazily, she became aware that her skin, her dress, his hair was wet. Abruptly, she pulled away. Eyes wide, she stared at him dazedly, and then tugged her dress back onto her shoulder.

Massimo's expression was a mixture of frustration and amusement as raindrops splashed lightly onto his face and shoulders. 'It's only rain, *cara*!'

She smiled weakly. 'This is a bad idea. We should go inside.'

Her voice was breathy and uneven. For a moment he said nothing, just watched her in silence, making no attempt to hide either his desire or his triumph.

Finally, he nodded. 'I agree. Your bedroom or mine?'

CHAPTER FOUR

THERE WAS A SHORT, strained pause. For one brief, dizzying moment, Flora imagined his fingers curled round hers, imagined them running through a merry-go-round blur of hedges and walls, their feet moving up the stairs…

And then her skin grew cool. A shiver rose up her spine and her eyes widened in angry disbelief. 'What are you talking about?' she said slowly.

Your bedroom or mine? Had he really just asked her that question? His arrogant assumption that, having kissed, she would simply go to bed with him jarred inside her like an out-of-tune piano.

'Do you actually think we would—?' She stared at him incredulously. 'You are *unbelievable.*'

Like war paint, the leaves of the rose bush cast stripes of shadow across his face. His eyes were narrow, angry and thwarted.

'For wanting to have sex with you? I'm a man and you're a woman and we just kissed like the world was about to end. Of *course* I'm going to think about sex.' His eyes glittered. 'And you kissed me first, so I don't really know what you were expecting—'

'I didn't expect anything! Why should I? Nothing happened!'

'Nothing happened?' he ground out, his voice cold with fury. 'You call that *nothing*?'

She glanced up at the sky. Above them, a rainbow was shimmering, its gentle pastel arcs somehow at odds with the sharpness of his anger.

'No. I call it a mistake. One I don't intend to repeat.'

A faint blush suffused her cheeks and throat. She couldn't deny the heat humming in her veins. Or the fact that she had responded to him with a force and intensity that had never happened with any other man. But he wasn't just 'any other man'. He was the cold-hearted, manipulative man who wanted to make her homeless and she would have to be a certifiable lunatic to forget that for the sake of one kiss.

She glared at him. 'I don't have to explain myself to you. And as I only sleep with men I like and respect, I'm not going to have sex with you either. But I guess that's where you and I differ. Your standards are probably a little lower than mine.'

His face felt taut; the blood was pounding in his ears like a battle drum. He couldn't believe she'd turned him down. Had she any idea how many women would jump at the chance to sleep with him? His anger was slick and hotter than blood.

'A lot lower. They pretty much hit rock bottom a moment ago.'

Flora's heart thumped dully in her chest. The contempt of his tone as much as his actual words left her breathless, chilled. 'You're a pig,' she said shakily.

He studied her face, his mouth forming something between a smile and a sneer. 'I prefer pragmatist. As far as I'm concerned I don't need to like or respect a woman to want to have sex with her. And I want to have sex with you. Just as much as you want to have sex with me. Except you're too much of a hypocrite to admit it.'

Heat burned her cheeks. 'You're not only disgustingly arrogant, you must be deaf too! I already told you that I don't want to have sex with you.'

Something flickered across his face—subtle but deliberate and designed to goad.

'My hearing's perfect, *cara*. You told me you wouldn't sleep with me because you didn't like or respect me. You never said you didn't *want* to. As for the arrogance—I guess I *was* a little presumptuous. But only because I have cause to be. Women *like* me.'

She shook her head incredulously. 'No. They like your money!'

'Are you speaking from experience?'

His taunting smile made her want to drop the sun dial on his head. 'Fine. Have it your way. Every woman you've ever met wants to have sex with you.' She paused, her eyes flashing with anger. 'Until now! But don't take it personally. It's not as if I have to like or respect a man *not* to want to have sex with him.'

His eyes hardened. 'You're a very good liar, Miss Golding. Plenty of practice, I suppose? But that's the trouble with telling lies. You stop being able to recognise the truth. And the truth is that you want me like I want you. And pretending otherwise isn't going to change anything.'

His words were still ringing in his ears. Was that the truth? With shock, he realised it was. That using sex to gain her trust no longer seemed as important as ridding himself of this debilitating haze of sexual frustration.

She stared at him. His words had blunted her power of speech, their sharp, undeniable truth slicing through her skin down to the bone.

He studied her coolly, long enough for her to know that he knew exactly what she was thinking, and then lifting his gaze, he squinted up at the sky. 'Anyway, I'll leave you to your flowers—' his eyes gleamed '—and your righteous indignation. But let me know *when* you change your mind.'

There was a pulsing silence, and then he turned and walked calmly away without waiting for a reply.

A bubble of hysteria rose up inside her. 'You're wrong, Massimo Sforza!' she shouted. 'I don't want you and I never will.'

As she watched him disappear beneath an archway she shivered, feeling both the chill of his absence and the rapidly sinking sun. Pressing her hands against the cool stone of the sun dial, she breathed out slowly. Those few febrile moments in Massimo's arms had convinced her that having sex with him would not just be a mistake. It would be a disaster. And not because of who he was. But because of how he had made her feel for those few vivid moments.

She bit her lip. It was embarrassing to admit it, even to herself, but she wanted him. With a longing that was as hot and as real as the sun. But it wasn't lust or even shame that was making her feel like a startled deer. Something had happened even before his fingers had slid over her skin. Something new and unsettling and yet also familiar. Something that had made her heart ache and then start to race like a sprinter. That teasing banter, that soft encircling warmth of his smile had been a reminder of what two people could share.

Her face tightened. *And lose.*

Looking up, she stared at the arch of colours shifting and fading into the thunderous sky. Massimo Sforza was more than just a temptation. He was dangerous: a flashing red sign, a shrill, warning cry. And to ignore that fact would be like running towards the edge of a cliff in pursuit of a rainbow. Her independence, the sanctuary of calm isolation that was her life in Sardinia, these were solid and real and reliable. And she needed to remember that next time she felt like getting up close and personal with her landlord.

Massimo strode through the gardens, his gaze fixed on the path ahead of him, currents of confusion and anger tugging him sharply over the stone slabs and the gravel of the drive. Heat was pulsing out a telegraph of dots and dashes over his skin. The same message over and over again.

What the hell had just happened?

Sliding into the driver's seat of the black Lamborghini slung carelessly across the driveway, he forced his breathing to slow and tried to pull his thoughts into focus. And shift the painful throb of his erection.

She'd kissed him. And he'd kissed her back. And a kiss was just a kiss. So why the hell did it feel as though a hole had just opened beneath his feet?

It made no sense. Flora Golding was a nobody. Up until a few days ago she had been nothing more than a name—a glitch in his plans to make Sforza Industries the biggest hotel and resort company in the world. But now—

A memory of Flora, lips parted, eyes drowsy with desire, slid into his head and a teasing twist of lust spiralled lazily inside him. His heart throbbed in his throat. Glancing down at his hands, he saw that they were shaking, and he felt a spasm of fury at this sudden and uncharacteristic loss of control.

What was the matter with him? It was bad enough behaving like some adolescent schoolboy. But he couldn't shake the feeling that something had happened in that garden. Something more than mere sexual attraction. Something too blurred and just out of reach.

Gritting his teeth, he shook his head.

What was it about this skinny English girl with messy

hair and eyes like an angry cat? Even before he'd met her in the flesh she'd been messing with his head. Playing games. Pulling strings.

And he'd let her.

Even though he'd vowed never to let it happen again. Never to let his emotions rise up and drag him under to that place of dark misery that had been his childhood.

His stomach tightened as it always did at the thought of his stepmother and, grimacing, he pressed the ignition, letting the snarl of the engine override the jerky beat of his heart. He'd let that manipulative little witch get under his skin. But it wouldn't happen again. Whatever it was he thought he'd felt when he held her in his arms was just that: a thought. Fleeting, illusory—like a rainbow.

Shifting gear, he imagined the day ahead. He had a meeting with the architect. Then lunch with his land agent. Maybe afterwards he would take the yacht out. Invite a couple of 'guests' to join him. Find a deserted beach and lose some inhibitions.

Feeling calmer, he pressed his foot down lightly on the accelerator pedal. The hard stone of fear and doubt inside him was disintegrating, mingling with the dust whipped up from the road, and as he pushed the car up a gear, his head emptied of everything but the sound of the engine and the intoxicating rush of air.

'And six of the tomatoes, please.'

Flora gazed dully at the colourful fruit and vegetables spilling onto the dusty ground. She wasn't a keen cook, preferring meals of almost rustic simplicity, but this was one of her guilty pleasures: poring over the crates of lemons and artichokes in Cagliari market.

She had woken early and, hounded by the memory of what had happened the day before, had slipped out of the *palazzo* with no plan in mind other than avoiding Massimo. Now, wandering aimlessly around the town, she felt both listless and strangely on edge.

Crossing the road towards the café quarter, she felt a sudden sharp pang of envy as a pair of teenage boys shot by her on a scooter, shouting with laughter. Yesterday she had felt like that too: carefree and unfettered. But now everything had changed.

And it was all because of him: *Massimo*.

She bit her lip. It was so unfair! And irrational!

It wasn't as if she'd never been kissed before. She'd had boyfriends. Actual, real-life boyfriends whom she'd liked and respected. Her cheeks grew warm. Only their kisses had never felt like that.

Even now she could still feel the touch of his lips on hers, vivid and blazing like a brand. And, more worryingly, she couldn't stop thinking about what he'd said to her after she'd kissed him. It had been arrogant and crass and it should have repelled her. But it hadn't. Instead, she had felt something stir inside her—a tingling, flickering tug of desire that had tasted warm and sweet and smooth on her tongue—

She took a hard, fast breath and, stopping abruptly in front of a café, sat down and ordered a coffee. A folded newspaper had been left on the table and she threw it onto the unoccupied chair beside her, dropping her bag on top of it.

Glancing round at the smiling, happy faces, she felt a pinprick of fear. Surely there had to be rules about this sort of thing. It didn't make sense that he, of all people, should have such an intense physical effect on her. She bit her lip, goosebumps tingling over her skin. But was it really that incomprehensible? Massimo Sforza was the most beautiful man she'd ever met. Sexy and smart, and of course arrogant beyond belief. But nothing could detract from his dazzling, wild, mesmerising beauty.

Her phone buzzed inside her bag and, relieved to have an excuse to push away her unsettling thoughts, she pulled it out. Her relief faded and her breath jerked in her throat. It was Freddie.

Typically, he started speaking as soon as she picked up. 'I think you're right. You should stay put.'

Flora frowned. Her mind seemed to have stalled. Had Freddie just told her she was *right*? 'Okay...' she said hesitantly. 'Wow! That's great. It feels like the right thing to do. I mean, I can't just up and leave every time something gets tricky. Sometimes you have to stay and fight—like Spartacus.'

'So you're saying you're like a slave in Ancient Rome?'

Freddie's voice was pleasant enough, but the undertone beneath his words still stung. 'No,' she said hastily. 'In fact, it's actually got better,' she lied.

There was a silence, and then Freddie said softly, 'That's great!' He paused. 'If it was true. But I know when you're lying, and you just lied to me. Which means it's a whole lot worse than you're letting on. Which leads me back to why I rang you in the first place—'

'To tell me I'm right to stay here,' Flora interrupted, resenting Freddie's hectoring tone and feeling a familiar wave of panic rise up.

'No! To tell you that I'm coming over to help—'

'Oh, no, you're not, Freddie. You are *not* coming!' Curling over the phone, she pushed her coffee cup across the table with a shaking hand. 'I do not need you to fight my battles.'

'So you admit you're fighting with him?'

Flora breathed out slowly. 'Please, Freddie. Don't cross-examine me. I'm fine. I don't need your help.'

'Spartacus had help. And he still lost.'

She winced. Her nails were cutting into her hand. 'He had to fight the entire Roman Army,' she said breathlessly. 'I just need to stay put. Keep my head down. Like you said. Besides, I think we've reached a sort of understanding.'

'Meaning what?'

Colour touched her brow and cheeks. Meaning that she'd kissed a man she should despise. Not a peck on the cheek but a passionate, feverish kiss that even now sent scalding heat across her skin.

There was silence, and then in the background she heard a phone begin to ring.

'Damn it! Look, I have to take this call—but do me a favour, Flossie. Think about what you're doing and then maybe you can try and explain to me why you're putting yourself through all this—because I really don't understand what you think you're achieving.'

With relief, Flora hung up. She was never a match for her brother in full 'gown and wig' mode, but trying to explain her actions to him would be impossible—mainly because she had no idea how to explain them to herself.

Heart racing, she lifted her bag to find her purse—and then her blood suddenly seemed to stop moving as she caught a glimpse of a familiar face, gazing out at her from between the headlines. Slowly, with a hand that shook slightly, she picked up the newspaper and gazed at Massimo Sforza's unmistakable profile.

Except it wasn't *his* face that caused her to raise her hand in front of her eyes. It was the face of the woman he was kissing. His *fiancée*.

Her eyes barely moved as she read the story, but her thoughts were writhing. He was *engaged*! She felt a rush of blood to her head. He was despicable. Revolting. And faithless. She shivered.

'Your bedroom or mine?'

He'd actually asked her that! Worse, for one infinitesimal moment she'd actually given it some consideration.

She glanced circumspectly around the café, half expecting to see people pointing and staring at her, but everyone was chatting and eating quite normally. Folding the newspaper, she called the waiter over and ordered another coffee.

She felt dreadful. She had kissed a man who was about to get married. That poor woman! This was exactly why she liked being single. So what if she didn't have a date on Valentine's Day? At least there were no nasty surprises. No disappointments. No pain.

Laying down the paper, she nodded automatically as the waiter placed the coffee in front of her. And then she glared at the photograph of Massimo and quickly covered his cheating, unscrupulous features with the cup. A shadow fell across the table

'Sugar?'

It was the waiter again. Pinning a weak smile onto her face, she looked up and shook her head. 'No, thank you. I don't—'

Her words died on her lips and her smile dropped from her face. Wearing a pale pink shirt that seemed only to accentuate his flagrant masculinity, Massimo Sforza was gazing down at her, his impossibly handsome face perhaps the cruellest reminder she'd ever had that beauty truly was skin-deep.

'You don't what?' He slid into the empty seat beside her as waiters from either side of the café converged on their table like a pack of eager dogs waiting for a bone. Barely turning round, he rattled off his order and settled back in his chair, his blue eyes never leaving her face. 'What is it that you don't do?'

Ignoring his question, she sat up stiffly. 'I don't know what you're doing here or how you found me,' she croaked, 'but I don't remember inviting you to join me so perhaps you'd like to leave.'

He frowned. 'Really? That's not very friendly. You were a lot friendlier yesterday.'

His eyes gleamed maliciously, and she gripped her cup tightly. Her hand was aching with the effort of not throwing her coffee all over his infuriating face, but losing her temper in front of so many witnesses would not be a smart move. Especially as they were probably all plain clothes police officers on Massimo's payroll.

'Was I?' she said, forcing herself to lift her chin and meet his glinting gaze. 'It happens sometimes...'

He shook his head slowly, a cold smile tugging at his lips. 'So that's how you want to play it, is it? *Grazie!*'

Flora blinked as he nodded curtly to the waiter who had appeared at his side to deposit an espresso and a glass of iced water onto the table.

'I suppose I should be grateful you aren't pretending to have amnesia.'

She glowered at him. 'Is that what you do, then?' she said stiffly. 'When you're with your *fiancée*?'

He picked up his cup of coffee and drank it swiftly. 'Absolutely,' he said coolly. 'As I have no memory of actually having a fiancée.'

Their eyes met—hers furious, his a clear, challenging blue.

'Really? Does she know that?' Gritting her teeth, Flora breathed out slowly. 'I'm surprised you even feel the need to pretend. That would imply guilt, and you don't feel guilt, do you? Feelings are just for little people. The sort of people you trample over to get what you want. Because that's all that matters, isn't it? Getting what you want.'

He stared straight at her, his gaze so focused that she felt as though her skin was melting, and then, leaning forward, he gently tugged the newspaper out from under her cup and unfolded it.

'*Now* I understand,' he murmured softly.

He looked up at her, his expression relaxed and composed, and yet she knew he was watching her closely.

She scowled at him. 'I doubt that. You and I are at opposite ends of the spectrum.'

Her heart thudded against her chest as his eyes met hers. 'And opposites attract!'

CHAPTER FIVE

THERE WAS A pulsing silence. Flora stared at him, imprisoned by the dark, lambent heat in his gaze, and then he smiled—a lazy, knowing smile that made her whole body shiver.

'You really shouldn't believe everything you read in the papers, you know,' he said softly. 'Although naturally I'm flattered that you find me so interesting.'

Her face flared with anger and embarrassment. 'I do *not* find you interesting!' Reaching out, she tried to snatch the paper away from him, but he fended her off easily.

'No, no, *no*! I don't normally read this drivel, but since you were so kind as to buy a copy…'

'I did *not* buy it,' she said shrilly. 'Someone left it on the table!'

'Of course they did,' he murmured, his pacifying tone clearly designed to provoke more than placate. 'Now, let's see what I've been up to!'

Flora sat back in her chair, gritting her teeth as his eyes skimmed over the newsprint.

Finally, he looked up at her and shrugged.

'Is that it?' she snapped. 'That's all you've got to say?'

He frowned. 'I'm a public figure. Being in the gossip pages goes with the territory.'

She gave him an icy glare. 'I'm not talking about the

ethics of journalism. I'm talking about the fact that you're engaged to be married!'

Amusement flickered across his face. 'You want facts? Okay. I'm not engaged, so naturally there will be no summer wedding.' He rolled his eyes. 'Nor did I date her sister or her stepmother.' The corners of his mouth twitched. 'And I'm absolutely *not* going to expand into shipping. Which is fortunate as it sounds quite painful, don't you think?'

Flora swallowed. It would be so easy to smile back at him. He was so ridiculously handsome, with his tanned skin, jay's wing eyes and sleek dark hair—all gold and blue and black, like a portrait of some medieval prince.

But that curving smile was as dangerous and deceptive as any hairpin bend, and curling her fingers into her palms to stop herself from grinning back at him, she scowled. 'Okay. So she's not your fiancée,' she said stubbornly. 'But she's still your girlfriend.'

Massimo took a mouthful of coffee and frowned. 'Alessa? No. She's just—easy!' He met her eyes and shook his head impatiently. 'Not *that* kind of easy. I mean she's uncomplicated. She's single and fun. She doesn't have an agenda and she's photogenic. A dream date! At least according to my public relations team.'

Flora stared at him incredulously. 'Her name is *Allegra*.'

His face didn't change, but she saw something glitter in his eyes. 'Whatever. She comes to any name.'

She felt her face drain of colour. 'You're disgusting.'

His face hardened. 'I thought you wanted facts?'

She shook her head. 'I don't want anything from you.'

Massimo watched her closely. She was lying. Her body was betraying her. She wanted him. Just as he wanted her. Or she had done until he'd made that stupid crude remark.

Watching the tension on her face, he shifted in his chair. 'I'm sorry. That was a cheap thing to say.'

She turned towards him, her face flushed. 'Yes, it was.'

Her eyes met his, and he saw the green flecks dancing angrily in their tawny depths.

'Why would you talk about somebody like that? If you think that little of her, why are you even seeing her?'

A sharp, nameless pang shot through him. Why, indeed?

He pushed the thought away and stared past her at the crowd of mid-morning shoppers. 'That's precisely why I am seeing her, *cara*,' he said lightly.

'That doesn't make any sense!'

He saw the confusion in her eyes, could hear it in her voice. But how could he explain how he felt? That caring—truly caring for someone—was never going to be part of his life. Not now. Not in the future. His past had made sure of that. Even now, just thinking about it made him feel sick to his stomach. Just like when he was a child—

An all-too-clear memory of pleading down the phone at boarding school, begging his father to let him come home for the holidays made it suddenly hard for him to breathe.

For a moment, he stared fixedly at the empty coffee cup, waiting for his body to forget what his mind couldn't. Finally, he forced himself to meet her gaze. 'It makes perfect sense. Think of a relationship as a bank account. If you have one with a lower rate of interest, you're not going invest much money in it, are you?'

Shaking her head, her eyes flashed angrily. 'And that's what this woman is to you? A low-interest account? Wouldn't it be more satisfying to actually be with someone you *do* want to "invest" in?'

She was chewing her lower lip and he felt his body grow hard, remembering how that soft pink mouth had surrendered to his hungry kisses. 'It's sweet of you to worry about me,' he said slowly, 'but I promise you I get regular dividends.'

There was a slow, pulsing silence as he watched the colour rise over her throat and cheeks, and then she lifted her chin, her eyes challenging him. 'Oh, I'm not worried about you—I'm sure your relationships suit your *unique* personality perfectly.'

He burst out laughing. She was such an odd mix: stubborn and scrappy as one of those cats that roamed the Coliseum; yet teasing and tempting him with her soft eyes and sweet smile.

A tension he hadn't acknowledged before eased inside him. It was strange: normally he found it difficult—more like impossible—to talk about something as personal as relationships. Talking meant thinking, and thinking meant feeling, and feelings were like a summer sea: tranquil on the surface but underneath swarming with riptides and jagged rocks.

Only it didn't feel like that talking here, now, with Flora. Instead, he felt as though she'd walked into his life, throwing open all the windows and ripping the dust sheets off the furniture. And instead of exposed, he felt exhilarated—excited, even.

'You know, you're wasted stuck out in the gardens talking to flowers. You should go into politics. Or maybe you could come and work for me in my public relations department.'

Her fingers twitched. 'What? So you can boss me about at work as well as in my own home? I think not!'

'You think I bully my staff?'

'I think you bully anyone and everyone!' she said bitterly. 'Whatever it takes to get your own way. You were probably in nappies the last time you actually had to do something you didn't want to do!'

Around him, the noise of the café seemed to retreat like a drawn breath, and despite the heat of the midday sun, he shivered as her words pressed against the black bruise of the past.

'Actually, it was more recent than that.' His voice sounded wrong—flat and tired—and he felt the air shift around them.

Her head snapped up. 'What does that mean?'

A thread of anger fluttered inside him, and he grabbed it gratefully. 'It means that you're going off-topic,' he said coldly. 'I'm not here to discuss my character or even yours. Unless it's somehow relevant to what happened yesterday.'

Leaning backwards, he gestured lazily for another glass of water.

There was another long silence. He watched her face grow still and furtive and felt a sharp jolt of satisfaction. *Let her sweat!* She'd been so determined to chastise him about his supposed engagement that she'd forgotten all about their own little assignation in the garden. Unfortunately for her, he hadn't. And after that grilling she'd just given him he wasn't about to let her wriggle off the hook.

His gaze rested on her face until finally, scowling, she met his eyes. 'Fine! Look… It was wrong. *I* was wrong. I don't know why it happened, but it won't happen again—'

Reaching out, he picked up a piece of ice from the glass of water and sucked it between his lips. 'How do you know?' he said lazily.

She stared at him blankly. 'I— What?'

'How do you know it won't happen again if you don't know why it happened?' He studied her face, enjoying her discomfort.

Flora gritted her teeth. She could no longer deny that she wanted him. How could she when she could feel the beat of desire throbbing in her veins? But sleeping with

Massimo…even the idea of it set off alarm bells inside her head.

Her mouth was dry. More than anything, she wanted to flee—not just from the undercurrents of tension swirling between them but the intensity of her response to him. Only despite knowing she should run like hell from his compelling, disturbing presences, something vague, some wavering thread kept tugging them closer.

Only being closer scared her more than the thought of having sex with him. Her heart gave a leap as though it too wanted to escape. If only she could crawl under the table and hide. But she could tell simply by looking at the set of his jaw that running away would only prolong her agony.

'I don't,' she said flatly.

He frowned. 'So it could happen again? That's a little worrying, don't you think?' The corners of his mouth twitched. 'I mean, what if you lose control and try and take advantage of me?'

She lifted her face to his and he saw the fear and the longing in her eyes, and in the shake of her head, and the fluttering pulse at the base of her throat. She wanted him. But she was going to fight him every inch of the way. The thought both exasperated and excited him unbearably.

Licking her lips, she stared at him confusedly. The sudden shift of his mood from tormenting to teasing made her insides lurch. And then slowly he smiled, his blue eyes flickering over her skin like a naked flame, cutting off her breath in her throat.

Around her the pastel-coloured stuccoed buildings began to waver in the sunlight. Desperately, she clutched the table like a lifebelt, and then her heart gave a quivering lurch as he reached over and took her hand.

'Why don't we stop this, *cara*? We're both adults. And we both want the same thing. So let's stop playing games—'

His hand was warm and light on hers. His thumb moving gently, caressing her skin like a warm tide.

Her head was spinning. It would be so easy to surrender to the golden glow of his touch. Taking a small, shallow breath, she glanced helplessly around the cafe. An elderly man and his wife were smiling at her, their lined faces soft with approval. No doubt they thought she and Massimo were some young couple—a pair of newlyweds, maybe. She breathed out sharply. Whatever they thought they were seeing, they were wrong. And she must have absolutely no sense of self-preservation if she was going to let that beautiful, lethal smile blind her to the perils of getting involved with him any more than she already had.

For where would that involvement end? Probably he would grow bored with her the minute she surrendered her body to his. And that would be humiliating. But humiliation was the *most* positive outcome here. What would happen if she fell in love? Her stomach twisted. A memory of her father slid into her head: hunched, shrunken on a sofa, clutching her mother's cardigan, his face wet with tears. Her face tightened. Then her pain would be infinitesimal and immutable.

She shivered.

Love! She'd read the poems and listened to the songs on the radio. But love wasn't just about devotion or even passion. It was about sacrifice too. And if you had that sort of love—a love that exploded inside you and sent shock waves to the tips of your fingers—then at some point you would end up paying. And it would take everything you had. Your strength, your health, your happiness, your sanity.

She bit her lip and abruptly withdrew her hand from his. 'You're right. We do want the same thing. But the difference between us is that I know that's not enough of a reason to have sex.' She spoke quickly, her desire to be gone giving force to her words.

Beckoning for the waiter, she pushed back her chair and threw a handful of coins onto the table.

His face hardened. 'Why are you fighting this?'

'Because it's *wrong*,' she shot back. 'Wrong. And stupid.'

'You didn't think that yesterday!'

His voice was filled with frustration, but it was the chill in his eyes that whipped the breath from her throat.

'That was then—' she said hotly.

'Oh, please!' His scorn, sharp-edged, sliced through her denial. 'If I kissed you now you'd kiss me right back.'

The truth felt like a blast of cold air. She took a deep breath. Why *was* she fighting it? Would it really matter if she took his arm and led him to some anonymous hotel in the town? For a moment, she could almost feel the weight of the door key in her hand. Could feel the shimmering heat between their naked bodies—

She straightened her shoulders. Sex made everything *seem* so simple. All it required was some bodies and the right mix of hormones. But no matter how much she ached to feel the weight of his body on hers she wasn't going to give in. No amount of ecstasy was worth risking the pain and loss her father felt.

She breathed out slowly as, behind her, a bus pulled noisily into the square. 'Yes. I kissed you,' she said defiantly. 'And I'm not going to pretend I didn't enjoy it or that I don't find you attractive. Only it's not enough. Not enough for me to sleep with you. It might have been if we felt the same way. But we both know your motives have nothing to do with passion and everything to do with paying me back for getting in your way.'

Massimo stared at her, caught between anger and admiration. She was right to question his motives although she was also wrong: he *didn't* want to pay her back. Maybe at first he'd simply intended to exploit their powerful sexual attraction and thereby make her more malleable. But now his motives seemed to be growing more complex and confused. Just as the ache in his groin grew ever more intense and painful.

Watching his face harden, she felt her heart beat high in her throat—and then the tension seemed to drop inside her. Suddenly, for the first time in days, she felt calm. Wanting sex for its own sake wasn't wrong. But she knew deep down that Massimo's desire for her was motivated more by power than lust. Her refusal to move out had simply fuelled his desire to have his own way: if he couldn't have the *palazzo* he would have her instead. And that was wrong.

Her heart was thumping painfully hard and, feeling almost light-headed, she came to a sudden decision.

'Like I said, it's not a reason to stay but it *is* a reason for me to move out.' Snatching her handbag from the table, she stood up abruptly. 'I'll send someone to pick up my stuff. Congratulations. You've got what you wanted!'

She heard Massimo swear softly, saw his hand reach out to stop her, and then she turned and darted across the pavement towards the bus, slipping between the doors as it started to rumble away from the square.

Switching off the shower, Flora wrapped herself up in the towel provided by the *pensione* and stared glumly at herself in the small chipped mirror above the sink. Last night she'd been on a high, but now things felt slightly different. Her elation had dissipated, leaving behind the miserable realisation that, while she might have succeeded in having the last word, she had made herself homeless in the process.

She sat down on the bed and watched the cafés in the street below set up their tables.

So what was she going to do now? She couldn't stay holed up in the *pensione* for ever. Sooner or later she would have to go back to the *palazzo* to pack. And then it hit her. She hadn't just made herself homeless: her seedlings and plants, including her precious night-flowering orchids, would soon be on the streets too.

She bit her lip. Unless Massimo would agree to let them stay in the greenhouses. But it seemed unlikely. He would probably just laugh in her face. Tears pricked her eyes and she angrily swatted them away and took a deep breath. Tonight. She would go tonight and collect her orchids and leave the rest of her life behind. Start again. Live light. It would be an adventure. Besides, much as she loved the *palazzo*, the thought of being responsible for it had always made her feel edgy and uptight.

Feeling a little happier, she began to dry her hair.

Incredibly, she'd managed to hitch a ride most of the way to the *palazzo*, but it was still nearly nine before she finally slipped through the side door. The house was dark and strangely silent in a way that it hadn't been for weeks and she sighed with relief.

He was out! Probably celebrating her departure. But at least it meant she wouldn't have to see his stupid, smug face.

Feeling her way around the furniture, she made her way carefully through the house until finally she saw a glimmer of light. Her first thought was that at least she wouldn't break her neck on the stairs, but then, as she stepped into the hallway, something like fear scraped over her skin.

The front door was wide open and moonlight was shining straight through the doorway into the hallway. On legs that felt as though they were made of glass she walked softly across the floor. Looking nervously out into the darkness, her heart stopped as her thoughts tumbled into one another.

Massimo's car was still parked on the gravel beside the limousine. So he *was* home. Unless he'd taken a taxi. But then if he wasn't home why had he left the front door open?

She turned round and stared into the darkened house. And then the air seemed to shrink in on her as, with a sudden, paralysing lurch of fear, she heard something or someone move tentatively in the stillness. She froze, her stomach slowly turning to ice. But it was no good pretending she hadn't heard it. Somebody was inside the *palazzo*. Somebody who didn't want to be seen.

For a moment her body was rooted to the floor, her breath coming in panicky little gasps, and then there was a crashing sound, a muttered curse, and it was as though a pin had been pulled inside her. Anger, bright and blinding white, rose up and blossomed like a flare.

How dare they?

Gritting her teeth, she thought longingly of Umberto's ancient shotgun. It was broken and unloaded, but it still looked pretty damn scary. Only it was locked up in one of the outhouses. And then suddenly she saw the broom... leaning against the banisters, gleaming in the moonlight like some magical mythological weapon. Breathing out slowly, she picked it up and walked swiftly across the hallway and kicked open the kitchen door.

She had barely stepped into the room when she felt hands grab her. Strong male hands, gripping her round the waist and neck, twisting and crushing her. She lashed out with her feet and arms but her attacker was stronger, much stronger than she had ever imagined, and in sheer animal terror she sank her teeth into his arm.

'Let me go!'

He swore and, feeling his grip loosen, she yanked herself free. There was a cracking sound, and she staggered backwards with a cry.

'F-Flora?'

Her heart was crashing against her ribs so loudly that for a moment she wasn't sure if she was hearing things, and then she heard him curse softly in the darkness. Breathing out, she reached behind her and flicked on the lights, squinting as brightness filled the room.

'M-Massimo! What on—?'

He was suddenly beside her, his hands gripping her arms, his eyes the exact colour of a stormy night sky. 'You damned little fool! What the hell do you think you're doing, creeping around in the dark in the middle of the night? I could have broken your neck!'

Through the beating of her heart Flora could hear the shock in his voice. But she didn't care. A fury wilder than any storm reared up inside, splitting her open.

Tearing free of his grip, she thumped him hard in the chest. 'What do you mean? *You're* the one creeping around in the darkness. And how dare you tell me what I can and cannot do?'

Tension was shimmering off him like a heat haze. 'What *is* it with you? Don't you ever get tired of fighting me? It's like you're on some kind of mission!'

She glared at him, her eyes wide with disbelief. 'You *attacked* me!'

He stared at her incredulously. 'Then how come I'm the one bleeding?'

'You were hurting me!'

They were inches apart. She could feel the heat of his

body. He smelt of salt and leather, and despite her anger she felt heat spike up inside her.

He held up his hand. 'You bit me!'

'Good!' she snapped. 'It's the least you deserve after how you've treated me.'

'How I—' He stepped towards her, and she heard his sharply drawn breath. 'If you were a man—'

Her eyes narrowed. 'I'd wipe the floor with you.'

Her hands formed fists, but he was too quick for her. Grabbing her wrists, he pulled her against him. 'That's enough! Stop acting like a wildcat or—'

She tried yanking herself free, but he clamped her body closer.

They stared at each other, the tension pressing down on their skin, the air tightening around them.

'Or what?' she said hoarsely. 'You can't—'

'Oh, but I can,' he snarled and, lowering his head, he covered her mouth with his, stifling her protest with a kiss that tasted of fire and danger.

He pulled her closer, hard and fast, his body pressing against hers so that she could feel the thickness of his arousal. His mouth was hot, his tongue probing fiercely between her lips, teeth nipping, tugging, her body tingling, growing tighter and tighter—

Her breath shuddered, jerking out of her with a gasp as his fingers slid over her collarbone and over the thin fabric of her bra. She wanted him. More than she had ever wanted any man. His touch was like fire on her skin, melting her from the outside in. She shivered. Pleasure, like sunlight falling on leaves, swept over her. Her body burned with need. Her heart was racing...wild, frantic—

And then, like a drum beating out a warning rhythm, she heard the kitchen clock chime the hour and it saved her.

'No—' She broke away from him, stepping back clumsily.

'What—?'

He didn't move, but she saw something flicker in his eyes, only her brain seemed to be spinning on its own axis and she could barely speak, let alone make sense of his body language. 'No. We're not doing this. I told you.'

He was angry: his breathing unsteady, his gaze hostile and frustrated. 'Then why the hell did you come back?'

She blinked. Why *had* she come back? The question seemed to slip away from her, like a coin in a penny fall machine. Slowly, her thoughts began to level out and she met his eyes squarely. 'To get my orchids.'

He stared at her, his jaw tightening.

Catching the disbelief in his expression, she lifted her chin. 'They're *bulbophyllum nocturnum*,' she said defensively. 'Night-blooming orchids. They're very rare. It took me almost a year to convince Professor de Korver to send me some seeds.'

He frowned. 'Are they dangerous?'

She gaped at him. 'No! Why would they be dangerous?'

There was a short, tense silence and then he shrugged. 'I thought maybe you might be raising an army of ninja orchids. All armed with brooms, primed to attack me.'

Flora swallowed. He was teasing her, trying to lighten the mood. She wasn't ready for that but despite his earlier accusation, she was tired of fighting him. She shook her head.

'They're actually pretty ordinary, really, except they only flower at night. Usually I check in on them about eleven o'clock.'

'Do you tuck them up as well?' he said coolly.

Their eyes met and she bit her lip. 'I just want to collect them and then I'll leave,' she said stiffly.

A muscle flickered in his cheek. 'Then I'll *just* get my jacket.'

She stared at him in horror. 'I don't need an escort. I know my way—'

'And I need to know where you are. So. Either I go with you or you leave without your precious orchids.'

They walked in silence through the gardens, Flora stalking ahead like an angry cat.

Despite the almost tropical heat of the greenhouse she shivered in the darkness. It had been bad enough being alone with Massimo in the brightly lit kitchen. Now, in the sultry, sticky warmth of the greenhouses, with the leaves brushing against her face, it felt as if he was some big predator, stalking her through the jungle.

Holding a torch in one hand, she made her way carefully through the foliage. Behind her there was a muttered cursing as he banged into a watering can.

Turning, she frowned and said tersely, 'Be careful! You'll break something.'

'Yes. Like my neck,' he said irritably. 'Is that why you brought me out here? To finish me off?'

'Don't blame me! It was your idea to co—'

Abruptly, she stopped. 'Oh! I don't believe it! It's flowering. It's actually *flowering*!'

Massimo leaned round her and stared, bemused, at a small yellowish-green plant. 'It is?'

She nodded happily. 'I know it doesn't look like much but it's such an incredible plant. It's so stubborn, so determined to survive. And it's unique. There's no other orchid even remotely like it.' She let out a sigh of contentment. 'I can't believe it. I'm just so happy.'

Massimo stared at her in silence. The air around them tasted warm and perfumed, and something in her unguarded enthusiasm touched him. His heart was speeding and he took a step closer, his arm brushing against hers. 'So… Is that it, then?' he said hoarsely. He paused, his words jamming in his throat. 'Do you want to take them and go, or—?'

She looked up at him. His eyes looked almost black in the torchlight, the shadows making his face look younger, more vulnerable. She felt her stomach swoop down, as though she'd stepped off a diving board. Her breath was twisting in her throat. She should run. Or bite him again. Or maybe hit herself with the torch. Anything to stop this soft, gauzy heat creeping over her skin. She needed to focus, to concentrate on the facts. He was the enemy. Worse, he was an enemy who had managed to tear through all her carefully built up layers of logic and reason as though they were tissue paper.

But then what were they really but memories of her father's grief? Maybe now was the time to lay those ghosts to rest. After all, Massimo wasn't the love of her life: and this was only ever going to be sex.

Looking up, she saw the night sky, blue-black like a bruise, and suddenly she wanted to dive into it and lose herself beneath the inky surface. 'Or what…?' Her voice was husky, slipping and sliding with fear and longing.

'Or this…' he murmured softly, and slowly he lowered his head and kissed her.

It was a different kind of kiss. Softer. Slower. Sweeter. His pulse jumped as her lips parted, and he felt his groin tighten painfully. Groaning, he pulled her closer, his hands curling around her waist so that she was pressed against the full length of his arousal. Tearing his lips from her mouth, he kissed her neck, licking and nipping the petal-soft skin. He could feel her fingers tangling urgently through his hair, feel her breath coming in shuddering gasps as she dragged him closer.

'Massimo—'

His body stiffened even as his brain seemed to melt. Hearing her say his name was like a spike of adrenaline in his heart. He felt light-headed.

And then, moaning softly, she jerked away from him. 'Not here—'

They ran, stumbling, through the empty gardens and into the kitchen.

'Where do you want to—?' he began, but she stepped towards him, eyes blazing, and he reached out for her and jerked her into his arms, crushed her mouth against his.

She kissed him back, her lips parting as, breathing unsteadily, he nudged his knee between her legs, pushing her back against the table. His hands framing her face, he kissed her again and again with an urgency he'd never felt before. She tasted clean and cool—of springtime and green woods. His lips moved lower, kissing her neck, her throat, licking the salt from her skin. Hunger jack-knifed in his stomach as he heard her breath catch, felt her pulse flutter.

Flora felt her body tense as his hand slid under her T-shirt, her muscles spasming, a tingling heat swamping her. Her breath shuddered in her throat and desire…warm, sweet, liquid…rose up inside her as he moved between her thighs, flattening her body against his.

She shifted against him, frantic to soothe the sting of heat in her pelvis, and then she gasped as he tugged her dress down over her shoulders, down to her waist, and a sudden rush of cool air hit her overheated skin. Gripping the hard muscles of his arms, she shuddered as his fingers slid over her breasts, stroking and caressing her nipples, and then she moaned softly as she felt his lip curl around the rigid tip, grazing the soft dimpled flesh with his teeth.

She could feel the beat of his blood, pulsing over her skin, beating in time to her snatched breaths; her skin was prickling…pinpricks of fire threading out in every direction. Suddenly she wanted more and, body arching, she squirmed against him, frantically yanking at his belt—

Grunting, he reached down and tugged his trousers over his hips, then tore her panties down. His hand slid between her legs and she pressed against it. Heat was building inside her, dissolving and sparking into silver and white and a thousand kinds of gold.

'Touch me…'

She slid her fingers over the soft skin of his belly and then lower, over the cluster of dark curls, then lower still, until he groaned softly and grasped her head in his hands as a knife-sharp spasm of pleasure shuddered through his body.

As she locked her arms around his neck he shifted her weight and fumbled in his pocket. Reaching down, she took the condom and with hands that shook slightly, stroked it over the hard length of him. Hands reaching under to cup her buttocks, he lifted her in one strong movement, up and onto the table, and then he thrust into her so that she grabbed his shoulders, her nails digging into the smooth flesh.

With each thrust of his hips he drove into her deeper and harder, and she moved against him, rocking her hips faster and faster, until her body shuddered and, closing her eyes, she gripped him tightly as he groaned again and tensed inside her.

For a moment they stayed there, spent and sated, arms around one another, their bodies juddering with the aftershocks of their passion. She felt his lips brush against her hair. His arms tightened around her and as he gently withdrew she buried her face against his shirt.

She didn't want to look at him—didn't want to see her mistake in the curl of his lip. Not for a little while anyway. Not while his hands were still caressing her and while she could still feel the warmth of his body and the soft beating of his heart.

He would move soon enough.

But he didn't. And finally she forced herself to look up at him again. He was watching her, his face calm and serious. For a moment he said nothing, and she tensed, fearing his hesitation. And then, tilting her face upwards, he lowered his mouth and kissed her.

'Let's go to bed,' he said slowly. 'Together.'

And, reaching down, he scooped her into his arms and strode out of the kitchen and up the stairs.

Later, still shaken by the intensity of what they'd shared, she lay in his arms, watching him sleep. She felt stunned and sated and happy. Not that anything had changed really, she told herself carefully. They had simply had sex. And no matter how warm and safe, how tender she might feel right now, he was still as ruthless and single-minded as ever—just as a tiger in a zoo was as dangerous as a tiger in the jungle.

His arm was resting across her stomach and carefully, so as not to wake him, she rolled towards him to watch the play of dappled light across his lean chest. It didn't feel real, him being there. It was like a dream.

But what would happen when he woke up?

She tensed, fear scraping over her skin. And then, beside her, Massimo shifted in his sleep, his hand tightening possessively over her hip, and her fear dropped away.

Feeling calmer, she curled her arm over his chest. And as her eyes drifted shut she wondered drowsily what exactly he'd been doing in the dark in the kitchen. But it was too late to answer that question, for the next moment, lulled by the heat of his body and the comforting sounds of morning birdsong, she had fallen swiftly and deeply asleep.

CHAPTER SIX

MASSIMO BREATHED OUT SLOWLY.

Finally, she was asleep.

Staring up at the ceiling, he gritted his teeth and tried to work out exactly what was happening. It certainly wasn't what usually happened. Usually at this point he would have forgotten the woman's name—if he'd even known it at all—and, satiated by a night of passion, he would have been waiting for the earliest possible opportunity to leave.

And it should have been the same with Flora—in theory at least. Last night he'd taken her into his arms with the sole aim of working her out of his system—the same way he'd done time and time before with every other women he'd desired.

But from the start nothing had been straightforward with Flora. And now, at some point between last night and this morning, everything had changed again.

With her arm curled loosely around his body, it felt different between them. For a start he doubted he would ever forget her name…not after what had happened last night—he smiled tightly—and twice this morning.

His heartbeat shivered. His sex life was hardly vanilla. But Flora was the most erotic woman he'd ever known. Her feverish response to his touch had taken his breath away. She had been like fire and light in his hands, her body molten with heat. It had been incredible.

At the memory of just how incredible she'd been, he felt his body grow painfully hard and, shifting beneath the sheets, he frowned. What the hell was the matter with him?

So she was sexy... So what?

It wasn't as if there was a shortage of beautiful, eager women clamouring to share his bed. Flora was nothing special.

He gritted his teeth.

So why was he fighting an impulse to lean over and pull her closer? To press his lips softly against hers and wake her with a kiss? He'd never felt like that before. No matter how good the sex had been, he'd never once wanted to indulge in any sort of post-coital affection. He'd always wanted to break free, some deep-rooted need driving him on to the next one-night stand.

His heart banged painfully against his ribs. It didn't make any sense except— She wasn't just sexy, he admitted a moment later. She was beautiful.

And smart and determined.

And, unlike every other woman of his acquaintance, he lived with her.

Which was *clearly* the real reason he was still holding her in his arms. He felt a sudden swift stab of relief. Of *course*. It was obvious. Why would he drag himself out of one bed to get into another in the room next door?

Feeling calmer now that he'd rationalised his uncharacteristic behaviour, he turned his attention to more predictable matters: work! Swiftly, he clicked through his day's schedule. He had a conference call planned for just after ten, and then a lunch with an overseas investment bank.

He needed to prepare for both. But he was finding it impossible to concentrate on anything but Flora's warm body curving against his, her skin so smooth and soft and just begging to be touched.

He felt a rush of raw desire and, glancing down at her, his breath snagged in his throat. What was happening to him? It didn't make any sense.

Working…his job…the business he had built up from scratch had never taken second place to a woman before. Somewhere inside, something shifted and stirred, a shadow rising. He grimaced.

He knew what had happened. And when. It had been yesterday, in that café. For one tiny moment, he'd let Flora get under his skin. He never talked about personal matters but for some inexplicable reason, he'd let his guard down. *Hell!* He'd even hinted at his miserable childhood, he thought angrily. He let out a long, slow breath. Thankfully, though, he'd come to his senses before losing control completely and telling her the whole sordid story of his life.

His stomach tightened. He'd been close to blowing it all; dredging up feelings he'd buried in the furthest corners of his soul. He'd let lust and frustration impair his judgement.

But it wouldn't happen again. Flora might be sexy and beautiful, but she was dangerous too. Whenever he was with her—like yesterday—he didn't recognise himself. But whatever might have happened in that café, it didn't mean that he trusted her. His mouth twisted. Since his father's betrayal he hadn't been able to trust anyone, and he couldn't see that changing any time soon. Probably never. And he was glad. That way the pain of the past would stay in the past.

Beside him, Flora shifted in her sleep, moaning softly. Glancing down at her, he smiled grimly, his confusion forgotten. He'd been careless, that was all. Soon, she would join the long list of women with whom he'd shared a one-night stand. But before that happened, he wasn't about to turn down what she was offering. After all, he was a normal red-blooded male with natural urges. So why argue with nature?

And, gently lifting her arm, he shifted down the bed and woke her with a kiss.

Much later, Flora woke again to the sound of running water. The bed was empty and, stretching slowly, she wriggled free of the sheet and sat up. She could just see Massimo in the shower. His gorgeous male body was blurry through the glass, but she felt a shiver of pleasure as she remembered his golden skin and the hard muscles of his chest and back.

For a moment she lay and watched him, her body twitching at the memory of his dark touch, his strong, firm hands drawing out her desire, smoothing her skin, roaming over her body, so intimate, so possessive.

It had felt so *right*—the weight of his body on hers and the way she'd moved and cried out and begged—

A blush swept over her skin and, closing her eyes, she pressed her face against the cool cotton of the pillowcase.

Not that she was ashamed. It was just that she hadn't known sex could feel like that. So wild and intense and beautiful. It certainly hadn't ever been like that for her before. Her cheeks grew warmer. The truth was, she had barely recognised herself.

She'd been like a wild creature, driven by a fierce hunger such as she had never known—a hunger that had swamped her and pulled her under so that she had lost herself in the darkness.

Rolling onto her back, she breathed out deeply. But she had survived. Better than survived. She was fine. She felt calm and happy. For the thing she had dreaded hadn't happened.

She had feared that at some point her feelings would get tangled up in their feverish coupling. And that no matter what she did she would find herself ensnared: feeling, caring, loving.

She shivered.

But it hadn't happened. She might have surrendered to his touch, but she knew now that she would give nothing more. And why should she? Who needed feelings when they could have that fire of passion?

Her eyes were still closed when she realised that the shower had stopped—and then, almost before she had a chance to process the implications of that thought, she knew that Massimo was in the room. Her skin began to tingle and her stomach flipped over. Nerves humming, she opened her eyes.

He was watching her, leaning against the doorjamb with an easy animal grace that made her heart quiver. He was wearing nothing but a towel knotted round his waist, his bare chest still damp, the smooth lines of his muscles knife-sharp, like sculpted marble.

But it wasn't just his muscles that looked like stone. His face was lean and hard and unsmiling, and she suddenly realised two things: one, she was holding her breath, and two, in her haste to examine her own response to what had happened she had pretty much forgotten all about Massimo.

Her sense of calm started to drain away. It was easy telling herself that passion was enough. That she could choose when and what she should feel. But now, with his gaze pressing down on her skin, she realised that not only was that untrue, it was dangerously premature and presumptuous.

She waited, her nerves humming, but he seemed in no hurry to speak; he just studied her face with eyes that were the same cool blue as an Alpine sky.

Finally, when she was on the verge of screaming out loud, he said calmly, 'Did you sleep okay?'

His voice was cool too. It felt like shards of ice skittering over her skin. It was the voice of a stranger or an adversary. She stared at him, confused; after what they'd shared last night she'd been expecting some small degree of warmth. But then, given that up until last night they'd spent most of their time sparring with one another, perhaps this moment was never going to be anything but awkward.

She nodded warily. 'Yes. How about you?'

He nodded and there was a tiny, sharp silence, and then abruptly he held out his hand, and she felt a curl of happiness rise up like smoke inside her. He was offering her an olive branch. That meant everything was okay between them. That maybe last night had given him as much pleasure as it had given her.

Lifting her hand, she smiled up at him—and then her stomach seemed to go into freefall as, frowning, he pointed past her to the bedside table. 'Could you pass me my watch? I need to know what time it is.'

Her cheeks felt as if they were on fire. She felt stupid and small. But what had she really imagined would happen today? Last night might have left her breathless and dazzled. But to a man like Massimo—a man whose sexual escapades were splashed over the newspapers—it was clearly commonplace, and there was no point in getting upset about that quite obvious fact.

She lifted her chin, feeling her temper rise. Getting upset was at the bottom of her agenda. Her pride demanded that she stayed cool and unemotional—or that she appeared to do so at least. In fact, if she was going to survive this fling with any shred of her dignity intact she needed to remember this moment. Remember how it had made her feel.

She picked up the watch, glancing at it swiftly before

she handed it to him. 'Is that the time? I should get up,' she said briskly.

Rolling over, she slid out of the bed and pulled on her dress.

He watched her with that clear blue gaze that left scorch marks on her skin, and despite her anger and disappointment she felt a fluttering sensation low in her pelvis. She gritted her teeth. It was not fair that he should still have this effect on her. Far worse though was the thought that he should know it and instantly she met his gaze, determined to match him look for look.

He smiled then—a cool, curling smile of such arrogance and ownership that her hands curled into fists—and her breath felt suddenly hot and tight in her throat. Why was he looking at her like that when moments earlier he'd been acting as though he couldn't wait for her to be gone? No doubt it was some technique he'd picked up in business— some trick to intimidate a rival. Shape-shifting so that it was impossible to know what he would say or do next.

Looking up, she read the challenge in his gaze and felt her skin start to prickle.

Was it any wonder the sex had been so hot and fierce and wild? she thought shakily. It was just an extension of how they interacted outside of the bedroom: pushing boundaries, playing games; taunting one another. Every word, every touch, was just another move in their desperate power struggle.

She clenched her teeth. It was bad enough that this man had such a strong effect on her. Indecent, almost. But if she didn't make a stand then she would more or less be giving him carte blanche to walk all over her.

She took a deep breath. 'Actually, I should probably be going. I've got a load of notes to write up.'

She saw his eyes harden and felt a rush of satisfaction.

Now he knew how it felt when somebody blew hot and cold. The fact that she really did have loads of notes to write up was actually beside the point; she would happily have told him she needed to fly to Jupiter to collect rare orchid seeds if it meant she could leave his disturbing presence with her pride intact. Or at least with his a little dented.

His eyes narrowed. 'Really!' he said softly. She took a small step backwards, suddenly desperate to get some distance between them.

He was dangerous. And desirable. Or maybe they were the same thing. She didn't know any more. Didn't know anything except that she needed to go somewhere she wouldn't be tempted to reach out and touch him.

'Yes. And I'm sure you've got meetings and stuff,' she insisted, pressing her knees together in an effort to stop the teasing ache between her thighs.

He moved away from the door with a languid grace that made her insides melt and she inched backwards.

'Stuff?' he repeated. 'What kind of stuff?'

She looked at him blankly. Every atom of her body was straining with the effort of not turning and running away and her head seemed empty of thought. 'You know... Shouting and jack-booting around.' Her voice was tightening up, and nervously she watched his eyes flicker over her face.

'Shouting and jack-booting isn't until tomorrow,' he said quietly, taking a step towards her. 'Today I thought I'd work from home. Maybe brush up on disciplinary procedures.'

Her cheeks flooded with colour, her lips parting. She stared at him wordlessly, trying to think of something smart and flip to say, but she could hardly breathe much less think straight. Then suddenly she didn't care about being smart or cool. All she wanted was to get out of the room before he demolished all her self-control and reason.

She took a deep breath. 'Look, I know there's probably some slick way of asking this, but I don't know how to do it. So I'm just going to ask you straight. What are we doing here? I mean, was this it? Or do you want to sleep with me again?'

Massimo studied her face in silence. Her words seemed to hover and hum in the air between them, and he almost reached up to brush them away. He hadn't expected her to act like this. Although, truthfully, he'd hardly given any thought at all to how she would react to what had happened between them.

Probably he would have imagined her just as she had been a moment ago, lips parted, cheeks flushed. No fear: just fire. But this was different. *She* was different. Her eyes were wide and clear. Not challenging, just grave and real.

He knew those eyes. Knew what they were asking. Knew too how hard it was to ask. It had had taken a lot of guts.

The silence stretched out between them, dissolving and blurring into the silences of his childhood. How many times had he waited, his heart in his throat, for answers to questions he'd had no choice but to ask? For a moment he was lost, alone in the past, and then her face slid into focus and breathed out slowly.

'I want you and I know you want me too,' he said bluntly. Her lashes flickered up and she met his gaze, her face wary but with a flicker of curiosity in her eyes. 'Besides, that was the best sex I've ever had.'

He smiled at her slowly and Flora felt a shimmering pleasure unfurl inside her even as her heart contracted at his stark choice of words. She nodded slowly. 'Okay, so let me get this clear. This is just sex.'

'That's right. Unless you fancy doing my laundry...?' he drawled.

He was teasing, and part of her wanted to be teased. But she needed to know. 'And it's just the two of us?'

It was supposed to be a statement, only it came out like a question and her nails bit into the palms of her hands as something flickered across his eyes. Slowly, he glanced down at her fists and then back to her face.

'I'm all yours,' he said softly. 'And you, *cara*, are all mine.'

His hand on her skin was warm and firm, and she gave a start of surprise as leaning forward, he slowly began to undo the buttons on her dress. His arm slid round her waist and he pulled her closer. 'And I'm not sharing you with anyone.'

Her head was spinning. Desperately, she tried to hang on to her self-control. She'd told him she had to leave and she should go. Another minute and she would be lost, all caution gone, her mind sliding away, claimed by the fierce pull of his gaze and the light, teasing touch of his fingers.

'I really should be going...' Her voice was husky and she couldn't keep the shake out of it.

He lifted his hand from her dress and stroked her face, his fingers light and tender, tracing the line of her cheekbone, brushing over her lips. And then, as she opened her mouth to repeat herself, he lowered his head and kissed her.

He tasted of mint and salt, and she felt her stomach tense as he parted her lips with his tongue and kissed her hungrily. She pressed against him as his hands travelled over her skin, pulling her against him so close that their bodies felt as one. His breathing was raw, almost savage against her throat, his pulse jerking with hers as he licked and kissed the skin of her neck.

She bit into his shoulder as his fingers curved under the

swell of her buttocks, firm and sure, their touch so precise and so in control. Every touch, every breath was changing her. The room was growing lighter and lighter in time with the tantalising beat pulsing through her body.

And then from somewhere outside the window she heard the faint humming of a bee, and with an almighty effort she pulled away from him. 'No. Not now—'

His eyes narrowed. 'What are you talking about?' He glanced down at the thickness of his erection through the towel. 'Do you think I can put this on hold?'

She glared at him. 'I don't know. Anyway, why are you yelling at me? It was you who started it. You didn't have to kiss me.'

'I'm not yelling. And what was I supposed to do? You were waiting to be kissed—'

'I was not!' Her eyes flashed angrily. 'We were just talking. Getting things straight. I'd already told you I have work to do.'

'Work!' He blew out a long breath. 'I think it can probably wait, don't you?'

She glowered at him. 'You mean it's okay to put that on hold?'

He shook his head slowly, his eyes glittering. 'Why are we even having this conversation?'

She stared at him furiously, her cheeks flushed with anger. 'Because you didn't listen to me.'

His face twisted irritably. 'I didn't realise you were being serious.'

'No. What you meant was that you don't think my work is serious. Well, it is and I am. I actually do have work to do.' Not that it was really about that. She just wasn't about to let him walk all over her. 'Look… Maybe this wasn't such a good idea after all.' She bit her lip and glanced away.

He stared at her in silence.

Work aside, this was probably the longest conversation he'd ever had with a woman. Probably the *only* conversation he'd ever had with a woman. And he still wasn't exactly sure why he was having it. She wanted to have sex and so did he. That was what they'd agreed. His face tightened. Only now she was saying she had to work! And that their sleeping together wasn't a good idea.

Was she seriously going to choose her thesis over him? As if that compared to running a global company. Although truthfully neither his business nor even the *palazzo* project seemed as important as convincing her that this affair could work.

He gritted his teeth. Who the hell did she think she was? And what possible reason would he have to hang around while she *wrote up her notes*? Didn't she know how many women would be more than willing to satisfy his needs? But for some inexplicable reason he didn't want just *any* woman. He wanted this stubborn, maddening woman standing in front of him.

Abruptly, he held out his hand, frowning as she eyed it warily. 'It's okay. I'm not going to jump your bones.' Reluctantly, she took his hand and, curling his fingers around hers, he pulled her closer. 'You're right. And I'm sorry. I can wait…'

He breathed out slowly and drew away.

'Go on. Go and do your work.' His gaze locked onto hers. 'But only if you promise to let me take you out to lunch.'

He stared at her intently, watching the indecision in her eyes. He hated having to negotiate with her. It reminded him of his childhood. Of the fear and uncertainty of life with his father and stepmother. But let her play her games—let her think that this act of defiance would somehow change the balance of power between them. He'd soon show her exactly who was in charge.

She nodded slowly, her face softening. 'Okay. But you have to let me pay half. That way it won't feel like a date.'

She met his gaze, and he nodded, but as he watched her walk out through the door his smile faded. She might think she was going out to lunch in Cagliari, but a crowded restaurant was not the place for what he had in mind. He needed somewhere private—somewhere he could strip her naked and play a few games of his own.

In the meantime, though, he needed to take another shower. And the colder, the better.

Pushing the gearstick hard to the left, Massimo dropped down a gear and effortlessly steered the Lamborghini down the curving hillside. It was a beautiful day, with a clear delphinium-blue sky and a warm breeze. Glancing at Flora, he grinned as he saw the golden flecks in her eyes. She was enjoying herself.

As though reading his mind, she turned to him and gave him a smile of such sweetness that he almost crashed the car.

'It's incredible!'

He laughed. 'I like it—even though it is a bit of cliché!'

She frowned. 'Does that make me a cliché too?'

He laughed again. 'You definitely aren't a cliché, *cara*!' His eyes slid approvingly over her short green dress and bare legs. 'I like that colour on you. It brings out the green in your eyes.'

She smiled at him mischievously. 'It's called absinthe— after the drink.'

'Is that right?' He shook his head. 'So instead of fighting me, you're trying to drive me mad!'

Glancing at him sideways, she giggled. 'No. I thought it was an aphrodisiac.'

'Then *you* must be mad! An aphrodisiac is the last thing I need when I'm with you.'

Before he'd even thought about what he was doing, he reached over and gently rumpled her hair. He felt her arch her head beneath his hand, and as heat rushed through him, he slid his fingers over her collarbone, his thumb circling the pulse beating at the base of her throat.

'Maybe we could just go back to the *palazzo.*'

She heard the heat in his voice and, turning her head, she smiled. 'You're incorrigible. And I'm hungry and you promised me lunch. So keep your mind on the road and both hands on the wheel—otherwise you'll end up driving us both into a ditch.'

Ten minutes later they'd reached the outskirts of Cagliari.

'So where are we going?'

'I thought—' Massimo stopped. His phone had started ringing.

'Do you want to answer that?' she said quickly. 'I don't mind.'

He shook his head. Picking it up, he switched it to silent. 'It's not important. What did you ask me? Oh, yes. Where we're eating. I don't think you know it.'

Flora nodded. 'Oh. Okay. What kind of food is it?'

He shrugged. 'Seafood. Unless you don't like seafood?'

The change in him was so subtle that at first she thought she might have imagined it. But as he turned to check the oncoming traffic she saw that there was a slight tension in his shoulders, and the easy warmth in his eyes had been replaced by a dull anger. Not the raw antagonism that seemed to characterise their confrontations but a hard, icy, controlled fury that made a knot form in her stomach.

She stared at him uncertainly. 'I do. So, is it in the town centre?'

He nodded, and Flora frowned. 'But why are we at the marina then?'

She glanced past Massimo to where at least fifty huge yachts sat on the shimmering turquoise water, their gleaming white hulls like huge gulls.

He switched off the engine and turned to face her. 'Slight change of plan. But I know you'll love it.'

Sliding out of the car, he had walked round and opened her door before she'd even had a chance to open her lips.

'What do you mean, change of plan—?'

But he stifled her words with his mouth. Then, lifting his head, he gave her an irresistible grin and taking her hand firmly in his, began to walk towards the jetties.

'Where are we going?'

She was having to run to keep up with his long strides and suddenly she felt a little nervous. Everywhere she looked there were gorgeous women standing on decks, long legs gleaming in the sunlight, perfectly manicured hands resting on chrome rails that glittered almost as much as the jewels around their necks.

With horror, she realised that he was steering them towards one of the boats—the biggest, in fact—and she began to drag her feet.

'What is it?' He turned to face her, his handsome face creasing.

She hesitated. 'It's really very kind of you, but I can't just turn up at some party with a load of super rich, super loud, super confident friends of yours. It's just not my thing.'

He frowned. 'They're not really that rich. Or confident.' He tugged her gently towards the gangway. 'But they are super quiet. Listen.'

She listened, but all she could hear was the gentle slap of the waves against the side of the boat and the odd shrill cry of a gull. 'I can't hear anything.'

Gently, he rubbed at the worry lines between her eyes. 'That's because they don't exist.' He sighed. 'Why would I do that? Arrange an intimate lunch with you on my boat and then go and invite hundreds of guests along for the ride?'

She gaped at him. '*Your* boat? You *own* this?'

Something in her voice seemed to cut through the hard lump of tension inside him. For a moment back there, when his phone had started ringing, he'd almost changed his mind. But now, watching her eyes widen with astonishment, he felt calmer. Grinning, he tightened his grip on her hand and tugged her after him.

They were halfway up the gangway now and, looking up, Flora could see several men wearing shorts and T-shirts starting to assemble on the deck. 'Who are *they*?' she squeaked.

He glanced up. 'They're the crew.'

Crew! Flora felt her stomach flip over. But it was no good digging in her heels any more. They were on the boat now, and Massimo was shaking hands with the members of his crew.

Staring dazedly across the deck, she felt his hand around her waist and, taking a deep breath, she turned to face him. 'Isn't it a little small?' she murmured.

His eyes gleamed. 'It's eighty metres!'

She met his gaze, a smile tugging at her lips. 'So it's not true then, what they say about men with big boats…?'

He laughed softly.

She smiled up at him, and he felt his body grow hard at the soft, teasing look in her eyes. 'So, do I get to wear a uniform while I'm on the boat?'

'I don't know if we've got anything in your size,' he said, running his fingers along the bare flesh of her arm.

Inside his pocket he felt his phone vibrate, but today was going to be all about him and Flora. Nothing was going to come between them.

Probably not a uniform.

And certainly not his past.

CHAPTER SEVEN

'I CAN'T BELIEVE how soft this is. It feels just like powder.'

Reaching down, Flora picked up a handful of sand and let it run through her fingers. Her eyes narrowed thoughtfully as she glanced over her shoulder at the dunes that edged the beach.

'I wonder what grows here. Euphorbia, maybe? Anyway, it'll probably be something quite hardy—something that doesn't need many nutrients.'

Crouching down beside her, Massimo sighed. 'Probably,' he agreed. 'But I *do* need nutrients, *cara*. So can we please go and eat? Much as I love sand, you can't eat it—and I'm absolutely starving.'

He pulled her to her feet, and slowly they began to walk up the beach.

'Are you sure this is okay?' She looked up at him, not anxious, just curious. 'I thought you were going to work from home today?'

His gaze held hers. 'I'm the boss, *cara*. I make the rules. I don't follow them. Besides, today *is* about work.'

Her heart gave a thud. Of course—he'd probably brought her here to hassle her about the *palazzo*. She felt a sharp twist of anger. If only she hadn't allowed her stupid body to start calling the shots she might actually have seen that one coming.

'What do you mean?' she said dully.

His face was expressionless. 'One thing business has taught me is that you need to plan for the worst.'

'And what's that?' she croaked.

'I lose my job. My business. So, as I see it, spending time with you is just like training for a new career. If I can stop you from picking a fight with me, I reckon I could easily get a job as a diplomat. Give me a couple of weeks and I might even sort out peace in the Middle East—no problem.'

For a moment she couldn't breathe. She was too shocked… angry…relieved. Then, looking up at him, she saw that he was laughing. And after a moment she started to laugh too.

Massimo hesitated briefly and then took her hand in his. Her grip was firm, but not too tight, and it felt strangely relaxing walking beside her. It wasn't something he'd ever done before. He smiled grimly. Usually with a woman his hands were otherwise occupied. But he liked the way her fingers curled loosely around his.

He glanced at her sideways. She was such an intriguing mix of contradictions. One moment teasing him about bringing his wallet, the next bombarding him with questions about the boat. But he liked that too.

His mouth twisted.

Not that it really mattered either way. She was here because he wanted her here. It was a demonstration of his power, not some affirmation of her charms.

And, of course, it was a chance to enjoy the pleasures offered by that delectable body with no interruptions. Pushing his free hand into his pocket, something shifted inside him, as he felt the space where his phone should be.

'It's like paradise!'

Flora gazed happily at the clear blue water and the long, curving crescent of white sand and then turning to him, she frowned. 'But I don't understand why nobody else is here.'

He looked at her with amusement. 'Probably because it's private property!'

Catching sight of the confusion in her eyes, he grinned. 'Don't look so worried. I'm an old hand at trespassing. Remember?'

She felt a tingling warmth tiptoe over her skin. It was a good thing their relationship would only ever be about sex, she thought weakly. It would be perilously simple to start craving that curling smile; to start dreaming of ways to become the focus of that steady clear blue gaze.

She punched him lightly on the arm. 'I can't believe you brought me here. That's makes me some kind of accomplice!'

He gave her a long, slow smile. 'I wanted to see where your boundaries are—'

Transfixed by the many possible and all equally unsettling implications of his words, Flora decided it was definitely time to move the conversation on.

'So why is it so empty, then?' Unsettled by his glittering gaze, she spoke too quickly. For a moment, he simply stared at her so that she was holding her breath, her heart hammering in panic that he might have read her thoughts.

But after a long pause, he said coolly, 'Like I said. It's privately owned. Fortunately I happen to know the owner and he said we could stop off for lunch.'

She stared at him suspiciously. 'You're not the owner, are you?'

'One day, perhaps.' His expression was gently mocking. 'I might make him an offer when I'm ready to buy.'

He spoke calmly—as though he were discussing the possibility of buying a neighbour's car.

Suppressing a sigh, Flora nodded politely. Living

with him day to day, she'd been aware that Massimo was wealthy. But there was wealthy and then there was the sort of mind-boggling wealth that was quite impossible to picture. No wonder he'd been so furious when she'd refused to move out of the *palazzo*. If he could afford to buy an island, it must have come as a bit of shock when his money had failed to change her mind.

She felt another flicker of panic. Earlier, she'd felt strong and sure of herself. Despite wanting nothing more than to tumble back into bed with him, she'd forced him to see her not just as a conquest or a commodity but as a person. But now, transported by his luxury yacht to an exclusive piece of paradise she felt vulnerable and out of her depth—alone on an island with a man who not only didn't live in her world but clearly didn't expect to play by its rules either.

'You're very quiet.'

Massimo's voice broke into her thoughts.

'I was thinking.'

'I've got a cure for that.'

She felt his gaze sweep over her and, looking up, she found him watching her curiously. 'Thinking isn't a bad thing.'

He looked past her out to the open sea. 'Depends what you're thinking,' he said cryptically.

It was on the tip of her tongue to ask him what *he* was thinking. But just in time she remembered. This was just sex.

She didn't need to know what he was thinking and she certainly had no intention of sharing her thoughts. In truth, she'd rather die first.

She smiled up at him. 'Actually, I was just thinking that I would never have got to see the Spiaggia Rosa if you hadn't brought me out on your boat today.' She hesitated.

'So thank you.' She shook her head slowly. 'I still can't believe it's actually pink.'

He laughed. 'The clue's in the name.'

She rolled her eyes. 'I know it's called that. But lots of things have names that sound like one thing and then they turn out to be completely different. Like Leeds Castle,' she said triumphantly. 'Leeds is in Yorkshire but the castle's in Kent.'

There was short, taut silence, and then he said quietly, 'It was built next to a village in Kent which is also called Leeds. That's why it's called Leeds Castle.'

'How do you know *that*?' She stared at him in astonishment but he simply shrugged. For a moment she hesitated. This definitely had nothing whatsoever to do with sex but— 'Are you interested in castles, then?' she said tentatively.

His pace had slowed, and she sensed that he was deciding whether or not to tell her something. Finally, after several strides, he shook his head.

'I went to school in Kent. One year my class had to do a project on Leeds Castle.' His voice was flat and he was staring straight ahead. 'That's how I know so much about it. I don't actually remember much about the castle itself, except that it has a maze and a moat.' He smiled stiffly and let go of her hand. 'But then I was only seven, and seven-year-old boys find history pretty dull.'

Flora looked at him blankly. 'I didn't know your family lived in Kent. I thought you grew up in Italy. What were they doing in England?'

There was a stilted pause and then Massimo frowned. 'My family didn't live in Kent. I went to boarding school there. They were in Rome.'

His heart was beating slowly, like a funeral march. He gritted his teeth. What the hell was he doing? She didn't need to hear this stuff any more than he wanted to remember it. Except that saying it out loud, sharing it with Flora, made it feel different somehow.

He'd always thought that talking about it would bring back the pain. And it had. Only not in the way he'd imagined. It still hurt—how could it not? But this was not the dull, throbbing pain of loneliness and rejection. It felt more like the prickling ache that came when a wound was healing.

He felt her turn towards him and then saw her look away.

'Oh!' She swallowed. His words had shocked her, but it was the tension in his voice that made her flinch. 'Wow. That must have been quite hard for you. I mean, I still get homesick now and I'm twenty-seven. I can't imagine what it would have been like, going away from home when I was that young.'

He shrugged, holding up his hand almost defensively, as though to deter her sympathy.

'I didn't know any different. And it was actually a very useful life lesson. It taught me that you can only ever rely on yourself. That you don't actually need anyone in your life.'

Flora nodded. It was a brief, too brief glimpse into his mind and she badly wanted to ask him more. But the cool inflexibility of his voice was like a shutter coming down, and she knew that the topic was no longer up for discussion.

She smiled at him weakly, stunned and saddened. It might have been the slimmest of revelations but it went a long way to explaining the man he was. No wonder he was so detached and clinical. His parents hadn't just sent him away to school. They'd sent him to a different country. But they must have had some reason, she thought shakily. Only she knew that her own parents would never have made that choice.

'Fantastic. Lunch is ready!'

Massimo's voice bumped into her thoughts and, looking up, she felt her feet stutter to a halt.

Across the sand a huge canvas canopy was rippling gently in the breeze. Beneath it large, brightly coloured velvet cushions were strewn across a huge Persian rug. And in the middle, laid out on a low wooden table, was lunch.

Her hand flew up to her mouth.

Turning, Massimo studied her face as though assessing her reaction. 'I know I said I'd take you out to lunch, and I hope you're not disappointed, but I thought it would be more fun to have a picnic.'

His mood seemed to have lightened, and she felt a warm rush of relief. She didn't exactly know why, but she wanted him to feel happy. Maybe because he had made her happy. Her gaze drifted over the suckling pig, roasting over a pit of ash, and then moved back to the bottles of champagne chilling in a huge copper ice bucket. Who wouldn't be happy with this?

'It's not a picnic. It's a banquet!' she murmured.

'Are you sure you don't mind about the restaurant?' His face softened. Reaching out, he ran his thumb gently down her arm. 'I wanted it to be just the two of us. I didn't want to share you.'

His gaze slid slowly over her throat, dropping down to the curve of her breast, and then his eyes locked on to hers and she felt her heart beat faster beneath their shimmering, teasing gaze.

She breathed out slowly. He was probably just talking about sex again, but still, they could have just stayed on the yacht. So it had to have been his choice to bring her to this beautiful, idyllic beach...

Her shoulders stiffened. But perhaps he brought all his conquests here. After all, what woman could resist paradise?

'No,' he said softly, lifting up his hand to touch her face. 'I've never brought anybody else here. That's what you were thinking, wasn't it?'

She stared at him. 'There are a lot of islands in the world,' she said grittily.

'And there are a lot of women. But I haven't taken any of them to any island.' His eyes gleaming, he drew her into his arms. 'But I love it that you care that I might have done.'

'I *don't* care,' she lied, pushing him away. 'It would just be awkward if you'd left any of them behind.'

He burst out laughing and reached out for her. 'There are no women hiding in the bushes. I promise. But there's going to be one unhinged man on this beach if I don't eat soon!'

The food was delicious. After the crew had cleared away the plates and glasses with swift, soundless efficiency, Flora lay back on one of the cushions, her head resting on Massimo's shoulder. She was trying not to stare at him but it was difficult. With his shirt unbuttoned and his hair mussed up by the breeze drifting gently over the sand he looked more desirable than ever.

Feeling her gaze on his face, he leaned over and kissed her softly on the mouth. His lips were cold and tasted of honey and berries.

'Penny for them?' he said, tracing a finger up the bare skin of her thigh so that she squirmed against him.

'You'd get change,' she said lightly.

He frowned. 'What does that mean?'

She tilted her head back. He was watching her intently

and the feel of his eyes on her was making it difficult for her to breathe. 'It was something my mum used to say...' she said finally.

He waited for her to continue.

She shrugged. 'I don't know. I've been thinking about her a lot today. Before she died we used to go sailing together. Not your kind of sailing.' She gave him a quick, tight smile. 'We had a little dinghy and it was just the two of us. My dad and Freddie—my brother—they both got seasick, so it was just the two of us. Me and Mum.'

Glancing up at him, she hesitated, expecting him to look bored, but instead he nodded. 'When did she die?'

'When I was twelve. But she was ill for a couple of years before that.' Her shoulders tensed and she looked down at her hands.

'I'm sorry.'

He meant it. She could hear it in his voice.

She nodded. 'Me too.'

'So, do you still sail?'

His voice was so gentle that she had to curl her fingers into the palm of her hand to stop tears from filling her eyes. 'No. At first I didn't want to. But later my dad...' She paused. 'It made him worry. He couldn't help it,' she added almost defensively. 'He'd just lost my mum, and sailing *is* dangerous.'

'Did he remarry?'

Looking up, she was shaken by the intense blueness of his gaze. 'No. No, he didn't. He never really got over her death. You see, they were like soul mates.'

Trying to ignore the scratchiness in her voice, she gave him another quick, tight smile.

'They met at school. He was the year above her but *she* asked him out.' She bit her lip. 'He was just so lost without her. Some people can't be apart,' she said slowly.

She fell silent. Beside her, Massimo was silent too, and for a moment there was no sound except the waves washing over the sand. Looking across the beach, she watched the foam rise and fall, feeling awkward. Not that she really blamed him for having nothing to say. In her experience death was a no-go area for most people, and certainly not the most fitting topic of conversation for a picnic on a deserted island.

'My mother didn't really like the water very much.' His voice jolted her from her thoughts, and slowly she lifted her head. He smiled tautly.

'When she took me swimming she used to pile all her hair up on top of her head and do this incredibly slow breaststroke so as not to splash herself.'

Flora nodded but her head was spinning so fast she hardly knew what she was doing. Up until today Massimo had been like a dot-to-dot puzzle: she'd just filled in the lines, creating a picture of a man who was unscrupulous and ruthless. Only now she saw a different man. A man who'd once been a boy, struggling as she had with grief and guilt and loneliness and loss.

Leaning forward, Massimo ran his finger lightly over the pattern on the carpet. 'She had this sapphire necklace my father gave her when I was born and she always refused to take it off in the water. It drove my father mad. But he'd always back down. I think he liked it that she loved it so much.'

Flora looked at him. 'She sounds like she knew her own mind!'

'She did. She was very strong-willed.' His eyes met hers and he smiled reluctantly. And then his smile faded. 'She was strong too. Right up until the end she'd get dressed and do her hair and put on her make-up…'

'And her necklace?' she said softly.

Massimo nodded. His finger stopped moving. He'd never talked to anyone about his mother's death. When she'd died he'd been too young. And then later he'd been too angry. He felt sadness settle around his heart. It had been so long since he'd even spoken her name. He hadn't meant to do it, but in his grief for what he'd lost he'd edited her out of his life.

Chewing her lip, Flora stared up at his profile. He looked remote, untouchable, hard-edged. But she knew now that was how he'd learnt to manage the pain. Knew too that he hadn't always been that way.

Anxious not to break this new mood of intimacy between them, she breathed out quietly. It was strangely calming, sitting beside him, watching the play of sunlight beneath the canopy. Usually thinking about her mum left her feeling resentful and wrung out. But here, with the warmth of his body drawing her closer, she felt okay. Maybe it was because he actually understood how she felt; his mother's death had obviously had a huge impact on him. And his father too.

'How about your dad?' she said quietly. 'How did he cope after your mum died?'

Flora had a beautiful voice. Soft and husky and soothing, like the sound of summer rain, but nothing could relieve the pain caused by her innocent question. And nothing would ever induce him to share that pain with anyone.

Massimo gave a humourless laugh. 'He managed.' His voice was cool with a definite edge to it.

It was time to change the subject. Glancing across the beach, she said lightly, 'I don't know about you, but I quite fancy a swim.' Gripping his hand, she stood up, pulling him to his feet. 'The only trouble is I don't have a bikini. You don't have one on the boat I could borrow, do you?'

'I don't think you'd fit mine,' he said sadly.

She nipped his hand with her fingers. 'I didn't mean *you*...' She hesitated 'I just thought maybe one of your guests might have left one behind.' Colour was spreading over her cheeks and collarbone but she met his gaze defiantly.

He gave her a long, considering smile. 'By "guests", I suppose you mean female guests? But, as I've never taken a woman on the boat before today, I'm afraid I can't help you. If it's any comfort, I don't have any trunks with me either.'

He paused, his eyes roaming lazily over her body, and the sand seemed to shift beneath her feet. She felt as if she'd been drinking. Adrenaline and anticipation were spiralling up inside her like the curl of lemon in a martini. And fear too. Fear that she was confusing sensation for emotion. If this was going to work she needed to stay in control of herself. She needed to make it just about sex. Just as they'd agreed.

'In that case,' she said softly, 'I suppose I'll just have to go naked.'

The air was thickening around them like a sea storm about to break. Even the waves seemed to have stopped beating against the shoreline.

Breathing unsteadily, she took a step backwards and in one swift move pulled her dress over her head. Proudly, like some island princess, she stood in front of him, the green satin of her bra and panties gleaming like damp leaves beneath the shade of the canopy.

A dark flush stained his cheeks; his narrowed eyes sent darts of bright blue light over her skin.

With shock, Flora realised that she *liked* him looking at her like that.

Her pulse slowed. More than liked... It made her feel alive: wild and strong and beautiful. And she wanted him to keep looking. Wanted him to want her.

But every time they had sex everything got a little messier inside her head. It scared her how badly she wanted him. But what scared her more was the fear that she might grow careless—might grow to want more. She didn't want to care. She didn't want to feel *any* emotion. Emotion was dangerous. Watching her dad suffer had shown her exactly how dangerous. What she needed was pleasure and passion. Pure and simple.

Reaching round with a hand that shook slightly, she unhooked her bra and let it slip through her fingers.

'Last one to the sea has to swim home.'

Their eyes met, then before he could reply, she turned and ran towards the surf.

He caught her moments later, his arm around her waist as the water foamed over her feet.

'You cheated,' she said breathlessly as he pulled her against him, the damp fabric of his trousers slipping against her skin. 'You've still got your clothes on.'

They were deeper now, the water splashing against their knees. His eyes were shimmering with passion. 'That's your fault,' he said hoarsely. 'You make me break the rules.'

And then he pulled her closer and kissed her feverishly.

Her lips parted as his hands slid over her body, every touch sending an exquisite flickering flare of heat over her skin. Cupping his hands beneath her bottom, he lowered her into the water and then, raising her up again, put his mouth to her breasts and delicately licked the salty droplets from each swollen tip.

She gasped, her body jerking forward. Reaching for him blindly, she pressed his head against her nipple. But it wasn't enough. Heat was swelling inside her, impossible to ignore. Desperately, she grabbed his hand and pulled it between her shaking thighs.

This was what she needed. To clear her mind of conflict and doubt and fear. Maddened, she clenched his hand, pressing down hard against the knuckles. Heat spiked inside her and, reaching down, she pushed his fingers beneath the wet satin, bit down on his shoulder and shuddered, muscles spasming, her pulse beating against the palm of his hand.

She heard him groan, and as he reached into his trousers for protection she clawed clumsily at his belt. Panting, he held her still against him, his hands circling her waist, and then as his mouth covered hers he surged inside her.

She clung to him, her hands gripping the muscles of his arms, gasping into the sea breeze, and then she felt his lips brush the side of her face.

'Oh!' She gave a start of surprise as some tiny orange and white fish flickered swiftly through the water beside them.

'Rainbow wrasse,' Massimo said quietly. 'The tide must be going out. We ought to get back to the yacht.'

She nodded and let go of his arm. Their eyes met and for a moment he hesitated, and then, frowning, he pulled her against him, kissing her fiercely. As they broke apart he began to laugh softly.

Looking up at him, she frowned. 'Why are you laughing?'

He shook his head. 'This suit is dry clean only.'

She started to laugh too. 'Serves you right for not taking it off.'

He dropped a kiss lightly onto her forehead. 'You want to know what's even funnier…?'

'I didn't know you could actually launder money.' Picking up the damp five-hundred-euro note, Flora gazed at it thoughtfully. 'It's bad enough having to wash everything else. How's your wallet?'

Massimo rolled his eyes. 'Clean!' he said drily. 'As are my clothes.'

Flora giggled. They had returned to the yacht, showered, and made love again before making their way up to the lounge area on the foredeck. 'At least you left your phone behind. Otherwise that would have been ruined too.'

He nodded, but with a shiver she saw that his face had taken on the same blank, shuttered look as earlier. Reminding him about his phone had been a stupid thing to do, she thought miserably. No doubt it had also reminded him of all the hours he'd wasted with her today.

'I don't want to talk about my phone,' he said firmly. 'It reminds me of work. Look… We've only got a few hours of daylight left, so I thought maybe we could go and take a look at Caprera.'

He lounged back in his chair, and she saw with relief that his face had softened and that he was smiling. 'It should be right up your street. Unspoilt, wild and rugged. A bit like me!'

Flora poked him gently with her foot. 'You might be wild and rugged, but you are definitely spoilt.'

She gave a yelp as he leaned forward swiftly and caught her ankle with his hand. Slowly and deliberately, he wrapped his fingers around the heel of her foot.

'What exactly do you mean?'

Her lashes fluttered. 'I mean that you own an eighty-metre yacht—'

'She's actually eighty-*three* metres. I just rounded it down to make things easier for you.'

She rolled her eyes. 'Fine. You own an eighty-three-metre yacht, a *palazzo*. Probably a house—' He held up his hand and she frowned. 'You have *five* houses?'

Laughing he shook his head. 'Apartments—not houses.

And I have nine. I just couldn't hold up enough fingers. I thought you might kick me if I let go of your foot!'

She giggled. 'I have two feet, actually. Or did you round them down as well?'

He grinned and slid his hand down over her foot, pressing his thumb into the soft pad of flesh at the base of her toes.

Shifting in her seat, she tipped back her head. 'That feels amazing...' she mumbled.

'This part of the foot is supposedly connected to your neck,' he said slowly.

'That's *so* weird. My neck is actually tingling.'

She moaned softly. His fingers were caressing the underside of her heel, curling round to the hollow beneath her anklebone, drawing small, light circles over her skin. Leaning back against the chair, she felt boneless, her body melting beneath the sure, firm touch of his fingers.

And then her spine tightened and she arched upwards, heart pounding. 'What's *that* connected to?' she asked shakily.

'Can't you tell?' he murmured.

Her breath caught in her throat and, lifting her head, she stared at him dizzily. His eyes met hers and she swallowed at the dark intensity of their focus.

'Massimo. You can't—' She breathed out unsteadily.

But he could.

Soon his fingers had found the spot that made her squirm. Her heart was beating slow and hard, her thighs trembling, her breath coming in gasps. She shifted in her seat, desperate to ease the aching tightness in her pelvis, but his hand tightened, securing her. She wriggled helplessly, her whole body straining against his grip, but he kept stroking her with same deliberate, light touch.

'Please!' she gasped.

His eyes locked onto hers, and he loosened his grip. But only momentarily.

'I'll scream,' she said hoarsely.

He smiled. 'I know.'

And then he lowered his head, and her fingers splayed out across the arms of the chair as she felt his tongue start to circle her anklebone with merciless, measured precision. Rolling back in her seat, she let go, crying out softly as her body split apart and a bright, wild sweetness spread over her skin.

For a moment every thought was blotted out. From somewhere far away, or maybe nearby, she felt him reach forward and pull her towards him. Her hands twitching against the hard muscles of his stomach, she lay against him until finally her breathing returned to normal.

She'd had no idea that was even possible. Or that she would respond like that. Her face grew warm and, feeling slightly embarrassed by her lack of sexual sophistication, she shifted position.

And gasped.

He was hard—not just hard. The thickness of his erection pressing against her felt shockingly large. Looking up at him, eyes wide, she opened her mouth to speak but he stopped her, pressing his finger gently against her lips.

'It's fine,' he said quietly, his eyes clear and steady. 'I can wait. If it's you, I can wait for ever.'

CHAPTER EIGHT

MASSIMO'S WORDS HAD been more poetic than truthful, Flora admitted later as she stared out to sea, watching the sun slowly sink below the horizon. Not that she was complaining. It had been just as much her idea as his to keep things simple between them.

No feelings. No future. Just sex.

Well, she had certainly got what she wanted.

Having made it to his suite of cabins, they had spent the rest of the afternoon in bed, where Massimo had touched and teased her to orgasm after orgasm until finally she had pleaded exhaustion.

She felt her face grow warm. It had been so fierce, so intense. And so good. A fluttering rush like the wings of a hummingbird ran over her skin and, stretching out on the bed, she stared down at herself appraisingly. Then, pressing her legs together, she smiled, relishing the ache between her thighs.

Being with Massimo was a revelation. She'd enjoyed sex before, but she'd never realised it was possible to feel so *aroused*. It was an education—the positions, his intuitive understanding of what she would like. But it was more than that. *She* felt different when she was with him.

Flora curled her knees up to her chest and hugged them tightly. Of *course* she felt different. Massimo lived in another world. Of limousines and chauffeurs. Of helicopters and homes on several different continents. He was friends with people who owned islands—actual islands. It wasn't that his wealth mattered to her: it didn't. But there was no point pretending that she was oblivious to it either.

She heard the door open and, turning, she sat up and started to laugh as Massimo came in wearing a pair of swim shorts covered in large luminous green dollar signs.

'Are those yours? I'm not surprised you left them on the boat.'

He grinned at her. 'Sadly, I didn't. I thought we might want to use the pool later, so I sent Tommaso to go and buy us some swimwear.' He frowned. 'It was dollar signs or giant bananas. Apparently the selection was a little limited.'

She giggled. 'Was it, though? Was it *really*?'

'I suppose you'd have chosen the bananas?'

Still laughing, she met his eyes. 'Only if they didn't have any covered in very tiny chillies.'

He was still grinning. 'It's a pity you weren't there to help him choose. A *real* pity...' he said slowly.

She stared at him and then gave a yelp. 'What did he get for me? Show me!'

Her mouth dropped open as Massimo reached into the pocket of his trunks and pulled out what appeared to be nothing more than three tiny triangles of bright orange fabric.

She stared at it in horror. 'What is *that*?'

'It's a micro-bikini,' he said helpfully. 'Tommaso's girl-friend has one just like it. Only hers is pink.' His eyes gleamed. 'Bet you wish you had some trunks like mine now!'

She stuck her tongue out at him and, laughing, he dropped lightly onto the bed beside her and pulled her willing body against him.

Her pulse flickered. Even in those ridiculous shorts he looked utterly gorgeous, and his lean, tanned torso pressed snugly against her skin felt just as good as it looked.

Looking up, her heart gave a jolt as she met his gaze. His eyes were so blue that looking into them made her feel as though she were slipping beneath the sea. Instantly, her skin began to tingle.

'We could share,' she said huskily; her fingers were itching to touch him so badly she could hardly speak. 'Maybe.' He rubbed his face against hers, the bristles from his beard grazing her cheeks. 'It depends. What will you give me in return?'

Staring down at her, he felt a happiness he'd forgotten existed—sweet and cold and sharp like a shot of *limoncello*. She was so incredibly sexy. He loved how responsive she was to his touch. Sex with her was like no sex he'd ever had. His heartbeat slowed. But it wasn't just the sex. He *liked* her. She intrigued him; she made him laugh, and she teased him constantly, and yet this afternoon she'd managed to draw some of the pain from his heart.

Her hand slid over his stomach, her fingers tracing the line of dark hair disappearing beneath his shorts, and he pushed his thoughts away.

'What do you want?' she whispered.

In reply, he gave her a slow, sweet smile and began to tug deftly at the buttons of her shirt.

Somewhere across the room, his phone rang. His fingers faltered, and he glanced over his shoulder, feeling his stomach muscles knot together. It was his own fault. He should never have switched his phone back on. But either way he wasn't going to answer it.

He shrugged. 'It's fine. They can wait. If it's important they'll ring back.'

Flora nodded. He was probably right. But something in his voice made the hairs on the back of her neck stand up.

The phone was still ringing and, unable to stop herself, she said quickly, 'Why don't you answer it? I don't mind—'

'But I do,' he said flatly.

He could feel it starting to rise up inside him. That same dark misery he'd felt as a child. Except he wasn't a child any more, and he didn't have to explain himself to anyone.

Frowning, he shook his head. 'I didn't mean to snap. It's just—' The phone stopped and he breathed out sharply. 'It won't be important.'

She wanted to ask him how he knew, but deliberately he reached out, curving his hand under her chin. Lowering his face, he kissed her hungrily. *This* was what he wanted, he thought urgently. This was all he needed to make the rest of the world vanish. Just him and Flora. Untouchable. Perfect. Like a scene in a snow globe.

Except—except that he would never *need* anyone. Need was just another word for hurt. He'd needed his father and his father had betrayed him. He would never forgive nor forget that pain. But he knew a way to blot it out—

Flora gave a soft moan as he kissed her again, parting her lips roughly. She gave herself up to the shivering heat creeping over her skin and then her breath jolted in her throat as he jerked her closer. Some part of her brain registered that there was tension, almost anger in his gesture, but she pushed the thought away for his lips were soft and sure on hers, his fingers surer still as they slid under her shirt, seeking the hard peaks of her nipples—

The phone rang again and she felt him flinch. At the same moment he broke away from her, cursing angrily under his breath.

She stared at him unsteadily. His skin was stretched taut

across his cheekbones, his anger radiating to every corner of the room. She knew his fury and frustration weren't directed at her, but somehow that didn't make her feel much better. Biting her lip, she took a deep breath and touched him lightly on the arm. 'What is it?'

He didn't look at her, just shook his head. 'Nothing!'

The phone kept ringing and, running his fingers distractedly through his hair, he shook off her hand and stood up abruptly. It was intolerable. It was harassment.

'I'm not doing this—'

Flora gaped at him. Doing what? Was he talking to her? Or about the phone call?

She watched in silence as he strode across the room and snatched up the phone. Yanking open the door, he disappeared into the corridor and a moment later she heard his voice.

Crouching on the bed, she felt her stomach turn over with misery.

She'd seen him angry. When he'd been upset with her he'd been wild and stormy. But this was far worse. This anger was coldly controlled. His clipped, staccato voice as lethal and hostile as machine gun fire. What could have happened to make him that furious?

But the answer to that was obvious, she thought, and her own anger was cold and hard, like a small, sharp stone. For even without being able to hear what was being said, it didn't take a genius to work out that he was talking to a woman. Probably that Allegra girl he'd been so disparaging about in the café yesterday.

Her heart felt slow and heavy inside her chest. Was it only yesterday she'd sat in that café and listened to his lies? She felt a flicker of irritation. How could she have been so stupid? So gullible? All that talk of not wanting to share her when all the time he was fully intending to keep on sharing himself! But just because she might have been stupid enough to believe his lies once, it didn't mean she had to let him treat her like a fool now.

She let out a shaky breath. She felt cold and shivery, and if she'd been the crying type it would have been a good time to cry, but instead she stood up and padded across the room. Picking up her clothes, she dragged them over her limbs, barely registering whether they were inside out or upside down. She had just slipped her feet into her shoes when the door opened and Massimo walked in.

He stared at her blankly, almost as though he didn't recognise her. 'What are you doing?'

'Leaving,' she said coldly.

His eyes narrowed. 'Because I took a phone call?' He stared at her incredulously. 'Isn't that a little extreme?'

She took a quick breath. He was so manipulative! Twisting the facts and implying that she was overreacting when he'd just got off the phone from his girlfriend!

She glowered at him, so hurt and angry that she could hardly speak. 'I'll tell you what's extreme. Your selfishness. Just because you're rich and powerful and I'm not, it doesn't mean you can just use me—'

Massimo interrupted her sharply. 'How have I used you? We have an agreement—'

'Had!' she snapped back at him. 'I told you I was happy to have sex with you if there was no one else involved.'

The confusion on his face was so genuine, so convincing, that she wanted badly to believe him and some of her anger faded. She frowned. 'I heard you. You were arguing with someone—' Her anger flared again. 'And don't try and tell me it was work. I'm not an idiot.'

There was a long, strained silence, and then Massimo said quietly, 'No, you're not. But it's not what you think it is.'

Biting her lip, she looked away, her eyes drawn to a beautiful flame-coloured sunset outside the window. He was telling the truth. But it wasn't enough. She wanted— no, needed some kind of explanation.

'So who was it, then?'

His expression shifted. He met her gaze but didn't say anything. Finally, he shrugged. 'It doesn't matter.'

Her heart began to pound. 'How can you say that? Of *course* it matters. You were upset—'

'It's not your problem.'

Feeling numb inside, Flora forced herself to focus on the sunset. It was so beautiful, so simple. Just as today had been. Until now.

At what point had she become so stupid? She'd thought she was being so smart, so 'modern'. But seriously, how could she ever have thought this would work? Of course it had been easy in theory, agreeing just to have sex. But the reality was far more complicated and growing ever more so because the truth was she no longer just wanted him, she cared about him too.

Glancing at Massimo's still, set face, she swallowed what felt like a hard little lump in her throat. She cared that he was hurting. Even now, when he'd made it perfectly clear that he didn't want or need her help, she still cared.

Because she liked him.

She liked him a lot, she thought miserably.

She might only have intended to share her body with him, but now she was in danger of sharing her heart. The lump in her throat swelled. Except that he didn't want her heart. And, judging by the closed expression on his face, he certainly didn't want to share his feelings.

Watching her swallow, Massimo gritted his teeth. He knew he was hurting her. But he didn't know what else to do. He couldn't tell her truth. Let her stay as she was:

soft and light, shimmering with promise like the dawn of a spring morning. There was no need to blight her life by revealing how cruel the world really was.

But even though he couldn't tell her the truth about the past, he could tell her how he was feeling now.

'I didn't mean to upset you, *cara*. Truly, it's the last thing I want to do…' He hesitated and stepped towards her. 'If I could tell you I would. But I can't. Please don't hate me for that.'

She looked up at him, her gaze searching his face, and he felt his heart contract with shock—for there was no hatred in her eyes, just something that unbelievably looked like concern.

'I don't hate you,' she said quietly. 'I just don't understand you. And that seems like a reason to leave to me.'

His heartbeat slowed. She was wavering. He could hear it in her voice. Impulsively, he leaned forward and pulled her closer. She pushed her hands against his chest, but it was a token gesture of resistance. Feeling a rush of triumph, he closed the gap between them.

'I don't understand me either,' he said softly. 'But I do know that I don't want to fight with you.' He shook his head. 'I want it to be like it was earlier.'

She bit her lip and then nodded slowly. 'I do too.'

He watched a flush of colour spread over her cheeks and, feeling a sudden overwhelming need to touch her, he reached out and gently stroked her face.

She looked so young and, remembering the sadness in her eyes when she'd told him about her mother's death, he felt a sudden urge to protect her. To turn the yacht out to sea and sail away into that glorious, cinematic sunset.

He sighed. 'I'm sorry. I know I said we could spend the night on the boat but we can't,' he said slowly. 'I forgot I've

got a dinner. Tonight. And I can't not be there. It's business. Well, politics and business. I'm having dinner with
the prime minister.'

Watching her eyes widen in shock, he shook his head.
He still couldn't quite believe that it had slipped his mind.
It had certainly never happened before. Eyeing him sideways, Flora felt a rush of disappointment but as he met her
gaze, she held out her hand.

'It's fine. Give me that bikini. I can swim home.'

She was back to teasing him. Relief swept over him and
then swiftly faded. He didn't want to leave her behind. Nor
did he want to be stuck in some soulless hotel room with
just the mini-bar and his thoughts for company.

But why should he be alone?

He slid his arm around her waist and pulled her firmly
against him. 'How would you like to go to Rome with me?'

'I think—perhaps—if we do this…' Frowning, Massimo
got to his feet and, standing in front of Flora, folded the
shimmering blue fabric below her collarbone. 'Would that
work?'

Elisabetta, the tiny and incredibly chic head assistant at
the Via dei Condotti fashion house, nodded approvingly.
'It would indeed, Signor Sforza.' With swift fingers, she
deftly pinned the silk in place and then, turning to Flora,
she smiled. 'Perhaps you would like to see yourself now,
signorina?'

Smiling weakly back at her, Flora nodded and stepped
tentatively in front of the mirror. She stared at herself in
silence, jolted by her reflection.

It fitted perfectly. As it should, she thought wryly, after
two hours of pinning and pinching. It was all so exciting.
She'd never had a dress made for her before, and she'd

loved every moment. More exciting though was the way Massimo had dominated the huge fitting room, not a single stitch escaping his glittering blue gaze.

Watching him, it had been easy for her to see why he was so successful in business: he had given her dress the same focus as he gave to driving his sports car or teasing her to orgasm with his tongue.

And lucky for her that he did, she thought, gazing raptly at her reflection in the trio of huge mirrors that lined one end of the room. The dress was utterly divine.

She caught sight of Massimo watching her in the mirror and blushed. 'Thank you,' she said softly. 'It's lovely, really, and incredibly generous of you.'

He took a step closer, his eyes never leaving her face. 'It's my pleasure. Truly. And the dress *is* lovely, but it would be nothing without you, *cara*. You take my breath away.'

She smiled mechanically. His voice was soft, his gaze softer still, but that didn't make his remark true any more than it made the evening a date.

Heart hammering, desperate not to let him see how much she wanted his words to be true, she reached up and pressed a trembling finger against his lips. 'Then don't say any more,' she said lightly. 'I don't want you collapsing on me.'

It had been like a rollercoaster ride.

They had flown to Rome in Massimo's helicopter and a chauffeur-driven limousine had met them at the airport and whisked them across the city to the salon just as it had been about to close. It was yet another reminder that Massimo was no ordinary man. And that in his world shops were always open, restaurants always serving food.

Now the limousine was slipping smoothly through the traffic-clogged streets. She blinked as a flash of blue light swept past them.

'I still can't believe we've got a police escort. I thought only world leaders had those.'

Massimo squeezed her hand. 'I don't normally have one. But we're guests of the prime minister; that's why security's a little over the top.'

Lounging beside her like a modern-day Roman emperor in a dinner jacket and dress shirt, he looked as though he could rule not just the country but the universe, she thought helplessly. He was just so perfect. As though sensing her focus, he turned, his gaze locking onto her and horrified that he might actually be able to read her thoughts, she took refuge in humour. 'It certainly is. Your ego is bulletproof. You certainly don't need any encouragement—'

She broke off, her breath snagging in her throat, as he jerked her towards him and she felt the hard length of his arousal through his trousers.

'Not with you, I don't.' He groaned softly. 'I can't bear being this close to you and not being able to do anything.'

She felt her skin began to burn as his eyes roamed slowly and appreciatively over the clinging silk, and then she shivered as he slid his hand through the slit in the back of her dress and pressed his cool palm against her hot bare flesh.

'And I am definitely not going to be able to keep my hands off you in that dress for much longer—'

There was a discreet cough over the intercom.

Gritting his teeth, Massimo looked up sharply towards the front of the car.

'We're nearly there, sir,' said the chauffeur. 'There are quite a lot of photographers, so do you want me to take you to the front or use the service entrance—?'

'The front entrance will be fine.'

'What *is* this place?' Flora said shakily. She had never seen so many paparazzi or security guards.

'The Palazzo del Quirinale. It's the official residence of the Italian President,' Massimo said smoothly.

'I thought we were meeting the Prime Minister?'

'We are. And the President too.'

She bit her lip. 'Is that all?'

He hesitated. 'No. Not exactly.'

She stared at him nervously. 'How many other people are going?'

'Not many. Probably about fifty or sixty,' he said casually. Her mouth fell open, but it was too late to say anything now. They had arrived. The car slid smoothly to a stop and he gave her hand a quick squeeze.

'I'll be with you the whole time,' he said firmly.

As the doors opened she smoothed her dress down over her legs and stepped out onto the road into a roar of sound. Around her camera flashes exploded in every direction, and then Massimo was by her side, his hand locked tightly in hers.

'Don't look so worried. Just keep looking at me like you're crazy about me!'

His eyes gleamed, and she pinched him on the arm. 'I'm a gardener. Not an actress!'

'You won't need to act.'

He grinned at her, that sweet, slow grin that made her skin slip from her bones, and then, lowering his head, he kissed her. Lights flashed. But whether or not they were just inside her head she couldn't tell. All she knew was that there was nothing and no one that mattered but him and the fierce pressure of his kiss.

He lifted his head. 'See! No acting required,' he murmured.

His eyes were the darkest blue, as though he'd swallowed the night sky. She stared at him in confusion, her body tingling, her head still swimming. Behind them the photographers were calling out Massimo's name, and with shock she realised that it wasn't just the two of them any more. This wasn't the kitchen at the *palazzo* or even his yacht. This was public. It was *real*.

She felt a sharp stab of longing. Did that mean it was more than sex for him too now?

'Wh-why did you do that?' she said shakily.

Taking her hand, he led her along the red carpet, past the lines of security guards.

'We're in the city of love, *cara*. What else could I do?'

She gazed up at him, transfixed by the light in his eyes. 'I thought Paris was the city of love?'

He frowned and shook his head slowly. 'A Frenchman told you that, right?' He sighed. 'I'd be charitable and say he made a mistake, but I know that guy and he is not to be trusted. Rome is *definitely* the city of love.'

It was only later that she realised he'd been trying to distract her, no doubt prompted by her poorly concealed panic. But despite her nerves she started to relax—in the main because at every opportunity Massimo materialised by her side and slid his hand into hers. Almost as though he wanted everyone to know she was with him. Although that was most likely wish fulfilment on her part rather than fact.

'Thank goodness,' he muttered in her ear as the doors to the dining room opened. 'Don't worry—I tipped one of the waiters to put us next to one another. That way I can make sure you don't run off with the Minister for Trade!'

The Minister for Trade turned out to be a large, florid man in his mid-sixties, whose wife was sitting next to Massimo.

'She seemed nice,' Flora said later as they sat in the *salon della feste* enjoying their coffees.

'Carla? Yes, she is. They both are. It's his second marriage. His first wife died. They had a daughter about your age who's in a bit of a mess. She's not really coping.'

Flora bit her lip. 'That's so sad.'

He nodded, his eyes resting on her face. 'I hope you don't mind, but I told her about you.'

'You did?'

'I thought maybe you could talk to her. You don't mind, do you?'

She shook her head. 'No. I don't mind. But I'm not sure how much use I'd be.'

He frowned. 'What do you mean?'

Stalling, she picked up her coffee. 'I'd feel like a fraud,' she said stiffly. 'It's not as if I'm *really* coping.'

There was a brief silence, and then Massimo leaned forward. 'Why do you think that?' he asked quietly.

She shrugged. The air was shifting around them— thickening, tightening. 'Because if I was I'd be at home in England.' She put down her coffee cup. 'I only came out here in the first place because I couldn't cope with being at home.' She sighed. 'My dad and my brother were always quite protective when I was growing up. But after my mum died they just completely stopped listening to me.'

Looking up, she gave him a small, stiff smile.

'They treat me like a five-year-old. So in the end I ran away. I told them it was so I could get my head together and finish my thesis. But really it was to get away from them.'

A faint flush of pink crept over her cheeks.

'That's why I got on so well with Umberto. I know what everyone thought. But we were never lovers. We just understood each other: he was on the run too. From his wives and his mistresses. And the fact that he couldn't paint like he used to. So you see I didn't cope. I ran away.'

She fell silent. Around them the noise of laughter and people talking swelled and faded like a tide.

'Could you talk to your dad, maybe? Or Freddie?'

His voice was gentle. *Too* gentle. She felt her chest grow tight. How could she explain her father's grief? If *she* was struggling then he was hanging on by a thread. And Freddie was a lawyer. If she spoke to him she'd just end up agreeing with him as she always did.

'It would hurt him,' she whispered. 'And he's so broken. So fragile.'

Just thinking about her father, his face still anxiously scanning crowds, hoping for a glimpse of her mother, made her want to cry.

'I don't ever want to be that reliant on anyone,' she said angrily. 'What's the point of loving someone and caring for them if it makes you feel like that?'

She looked up at him, but he'd glanced away to where the waiters were clearing tables, and she felt despair, sudden and sharp enough to cut her skin. Of course! Why would Massimo be interested in her pain?

'It's what makes life worth living.'

His voice was so quiet at first she thought she might be hearing things.

But then he turned and said softly, 'If you don't feel sad when someone isn't there... If you don't care if they're happy or not...then there's no point.'

His eyes fixed on hers and, leaning across, he took her hand and pressed it against his mouth.

'Mr Sforza—?'

Flora turned and looked up dazedly. It was one of the waiters.

Massimo stared at him coolly. 'What is it?'

'I have a telephone call for you, sir.'

It was as though a switch had been flicked. Flora froze as Massimo shifted in his seat, his jaw tightening.

'Can't you see we're busy?'

His tone was so harsh she was surprised it didn't strip the gilt off the salon's golden walls. Glancing at Flora's frozen expression, the waiter hesitated.

'I'm sorry, sir. But there's been an accident—'

Massimo's face went white. 'Is she hurt?'

The waiter shook his head. 'I don't know, sir—'

Massimo turned to Flora. 'Wait here. I'll be back as soon as possible.'

She'd barely had a chance to drain her cup of coffee when he reappeared looking, if possible, angrier than he had on the yacht.

She got to her feet. 'Is she okay?' She had no idea who this mysterious 'she' was but she could feel Massimo's pain and she wanted to help him.

He stared at her, his features distorted with pure, blank-eyed rage. 'Of *course* she's okay. She lied just to get me to come to the phone.

Flora felt her heart start to pound. What kind of person would lie about being in an accident?

'Why would she—?'

'I don't want to talk about it,' he said coldly, his voice as flat and dangerous as black ice. She stared at him numbly, seeing the anger in his eyes and for a moment she hesitated. They'd already had a huge row that day. And some problems were just too big to solve. Like her father's grief…

Her stomach tightened. She hadn't wanted to deal with her dad's misery or his over-protectiveness so instead of confronting him, she'd run away. Feeling something like shame or guilt prod her in the ribs, she lifted her chin. This time though, she wasn't going to run away.

'Tough!' she said slowly. 'You can't just expect me to ignore this, Massimo. What's the big secret? Why won't you tell me who keeps ringing you?'

'I'm not prepared to discuss it with you,' he said roughly.

'But you *are* prepared to have sex with me?' she snapped.

Around them the room fell quiet. There was a moment of tense, expectant silence and then everyone began speaking at once.

They stared at each other for a moment, and then his eyes slipped away across the salon.

'Fine,' he said, his breath catching savagely on the word. 'Have it your way! But not here.'

He grabbed her roughly by the hand and dragged her out of the salon. He was walking so fast she had to run to keep up with his strides. Glancing up at his set, cold face, she felt dread scuttle across her skin.

What had she done?

But it was too late for regrets. Pushing open a door, he pulled her through with him, and suddenly they were outside.

He stopped and dropped her hand as though it were burning him. Glancing round, she saw that they were on a huge, terraced balcony and beyond that there was nothing but darkness.

She could hear his breathing—sharp, unsteady—and, turning slowly, she stared at his profile.

'Who is she?'

There was a silence, and then finally he said curtly, 'She's my stepmother.' He turned and looked at her. 'Her name's Alida.'

The rawness in his voice made her wince, but she said as calmly as she could, 'Why won't you speak to her?'

He laughed—a harsh laugh without any humour in it whatsoever. 'Because she made my life a misery.'

She hesitated. 'When did she marry your dad?'

His lip curled back into a snarl. 'Just after my mother died. When I was five.'

Watching his body tense, she shivered. She knew he

was remembering the hurt and the loneliness in every nerve and muscle, and the misery on his face made her feel sick.

'Is that why you were sent to boarding school?'

His eyes, narrowed and hostile like a cornered animal's, met hers. 'She told my father she couldn't manage me. That I was too difficult to handle.'

Flora felt a knot in her stomach. 'But you were only five,' she said slowly, 'and your mum had just died. I don't understand. Why didn't your dad stand up to her…?'

Her voice trailed off as Massimo's mouth curved into a grim smile.

'My father always took the path of least resistance. I don't think he wanted to oppose her. He hated rows, confrontation—'

'But surely he didn't want you to go away?'

A muscle jumped in his cheek and he stared out into the darkness. 'I don't know what he wanted. After he married Alida I barely saw him.' His eyes glittered coldly. 'I spent most holidays at school. When I was allowed home they went away travelling. I used to get sent to live with my father's handyman and his wife.'

Her head was spinning. But she needed to stay focused. Her shock and horror were not important beside his pain.

'What happened next?'

His mouth twisted. 'He died when I was sixteen. The last time I saw him properly was about five months before his death. I was summoned so he could tell me he'd changed his will.' The anger had faded from his voice. There was nothing in it now—no life, no feelings and tears rose in her throat.

'You can probably guess in whose favour.'

He made a movement somewhere between a shrug and

a shiver and fell silent, leaning back against the wall as though exhausted.

Flora breathed out shakily. It was cruel. More than cruel, it was abusive. How could anyone treat a child like that? It was incomprehensible. Alida was obviously selfish and spiteful, but Massimo's father— She shivered. How did anyone survive a betrayal like that? But with shock, she realised she knew how: by offering love and support.

Except that there didn't seem to be much of that in Massimo's life.

He had money and power, the envy and respect of his rivals and the admiration of his staff. But nothing approximating to tenderness or care. Even his many affairs seemed to have offered him nothing more than sexual gratification.

He was like a plant that had been forced to survive in the darkest, driest corner of a garden. If only he *was* a plant, she thought helplessly. It would be so much easier. She would know exactly what to do.

Even before her brain had started to process that thought her body responded and, leaning forward, she slid her arms around him. For a moment he didn't move, and then slowly he pressed her against him.

And there, wrapped in his arms, she knew.

Knew without a shred of doubt or denial that she loved him. Her heart missed a beat. Surely it couldn't be true.

Love was dangerous. Love hurt. Even years after her mum's death, her father was still tormented by her loss. But she saw now that none of that mattered. All her fears and all those careful plans she'd made to stay single and safe had been for nothing. She didn't get to choose. Her heart did. And, no matter how disastrous the consequences might be for her, it had chosen Massimo.

Words of joy bubbled up inside her but she stemmed the

flow. There had been enough talking for one night. Right now Massimo needing some tender loving care, and what she had in mind didn't require words.

She felt his lips brush across her hair and, looking up, she smiled. 'Let's go home.'

CHAPTER NINE

IT WAS THE early hours of the morning when they walked back into the *palazzo*.

Tired though she was, Flora didn't think she'd ever been happier. Yes, they'd quarrelled, and it had been difficult and upsetting, but for the first time sex hadn't been their 'go-to' to blot out the pain of the past or resolve the tension between them. Instead, they had talked and faced Massimo's demons together.

No longer two people just having sex. But equals coming together, side by side, to take on the world.

Walking up the stairs to his bedroom, Massimo kissed her with a tenderness and soft warmth that seemed to Flora to complement perfectly the golden glow of the dawn and their new mood of openness.

His eyes steady on hers, he touched her face almost reverently, his thumb brushing lightly over the smooth skin of her cheeks. And then, coaxing her lips apart with his tongue, his breath quick and warm against her mouth, he kissed her. It was a kiss she would remember all her life. A kiss that tasted of hope and dappled sunlight and everything crisp and green and new.

The sex felt different too, the incredible, raw physical attraction they felt for one another deepening into something more intimate, something bred from trust and openness. Riding a wave of sensation and arousal, they made love slowly, letting the memories of the past slip away in each other's arms, leaving only pleasure and longing behind. It felt like the most glorious dream... Time ceased to matter...sharp edges blurred into spinning circles of colour and light...

She didn't remember falling asleep.

But waking beside him, his body curved around hers, she knew that it hadn't been a dream. It was real. He'd even suggested that she return to Rome with him for a couple of days so he could show her the sights properly.

Wriggling down into the warmth of the bed, she felt a rush of happiness. Beside her, he shifted in his sleep and, looking over at him, she felt her breath catch in her throat. Sleeping, he looked younger, more defenceless—and she shivered, remembering everything he'd told her last night.

Even now the facts of his childhood horrified her, for she knew now how much it had damaged the adult Massimo. She knew too how much it must have cost him to reveal the truth to her. To trust her with his pain. A tiny hope sparked inside her. But he had trusted her *and* needed her. Needed her for more than just sexual gratification.

That had to mean something, didn't it?

She breathed out softly. Last night he had let her in; he'd shown her the 'real' Massimo. Not the über-cool, autocratic billionaire businessman, polished and harder than a diamond, but the man beneath the image.

The man she loved.

Her heart contracted and suddenly she wanted to leap out of bed and cartwheel around the room.

Was this how love felt?

Was this really what she'd been hiding from all these years?

She stared up at the ceiling, feeling reckless and wild

and alive. If she'd been an artist, like Umberto, she would have tried to paint her emotions. Just to see what they looked like. But instead she lay on her side and watched the sunlight and shadows play slowly across Massimo's face.

She loved him.

Frowning, she closed her eyes, shaken by how obvious it was to her now that what she'd been feeling for him was love.

It hardly seemed possible.

For so long she had pushed away all thoughts of ever giving her heart to anyone. She'd had boyfriends, but nothing that serious or permanent. In fact, in the past few years, she'd probably been closest to Umberto, and she hadn't even been romantically involved with him. Not that she had minded. She'd been content to watch others fall in love; she'd never wanted more.

Until now.

Until Massimo.

She breathed out slowly. When her mum had died it had been as if a fuse had blown inside her head. Alone and confused in the dark, she'd started to fear what lay outside. But Massimo had changed everything. He had brought light and hope into the darkness.

And she knew now that she'd rather feel *everything* with him—happiness *and* despair—than nothing on her own. He was worth the risk.

But would he feel the same way?

Feeling suddenly impossibly restless, she slid out of bed quietly, so as not to wake him, tugged on a pair of denim shorts and a T-shirt and tiptoed towards the door. It was too difficult to lie beside him, hoping that he might wake up feeling what she was feeling. Particularly when she'd barely come to terms with those feelings herself.

In the kitchen, she paced nervously around the table,

trying to order her thoughts. They barely knew one another, and up until a few hours ago their relationship had been based almost entirely on sex. It would be foolish, not to say disastrous, for her to imagine that was a good foundation for a future together.

But what was happening inside her head and her heart had nothing to do with sex. It was love.

Why else would she no longer want to fight with him—but *for* him? And why else would she finally be ready to pull down the emotional barriers she'd built to protect herself from the pain of caring?

In the past, she had been so scared of getting hurt, it had been easy to corral her emotions, to keep her distance. But being with Massimo had made her want to get closer. He'd quelled her fears, unlocked her life and given her the chance to dream again.

A sweet, shimmering happiness spread over her skin and suddenly she wanted him to know. Wanted him to know that she loved him and share her happiness.

Heart pounding, she turned towards the door—just as her stomach gave a loud rumble. Except she couldn't do it on an empty stomach. She would need a strong cup of coffee first. Or better still, some eggs and bacon!

Stifling a yawn, Massimo rolled onto his side. From downstairs he heard the sound of water running, cupboard doors shutting and, leaning over, he picked up his watch. He frowned. It was nearly two o'clock in the afternoon! Still, it was hardly surprising they'd slept in so late. They hadn't got to bed until three. He gave a smile of pure masculine satisfaction. Or to sleep until five.

His smile faded. It wasn't just their fevered lovemaking that had wiped him out. Last night had been emotionally draining too. He'd pretty much told her everything about his past: every hellish detail. He hadn't planned to—he still didn't really understand how he'd ended up doing so—but…

He braced himself against the bed. Until he'd met Flora his childhood had always been a locked room inside his head. And for good reason. His memories had power: the power to make him feel like a desperate, unhappy little boy again. Thinking about it, let alone discussing it with anyone, had simply not been an option. And he'd worked hard to keep it that way.

But somehow, yesterday, Flora had not only picked the lock, she'd kicked the damn door off its hinges.

How had she managed to do that? To blow his mind, his life, wide open like that?

Probably because she'd known grief too, he thought quickly. It had nothing to do with who she was as a person. Remembering her anxious face watching his, he shifted uncomfortably in the bed. Except that it did! She had put her own grief to one side and let him rage. She had listened, and she had forced him to face his feelings, and somehow that had lessened their power to hurt him. She hadn't actually held his hand, but she had been there by his side. And instead of feeling claustrophobic, it had felt liberating. His breathing slowed.

What if she was always there? By his side?

His phone juddered on the bedside table, and still reeling from the idea that his relationship with Flora could be more than just a no-strings fling, he picked it up without thinking. Glancing at the screen, he froze.

There were eleven messages.

All from Alida.

Deep inside he felt a familiar shifting sensation—a sense that his footing was not stable—he frowned. But why? Last night, Flora had helped him face the past: now he would face the present. And this time it would be different. He would be different: calm, detached, unassailable.

Standing up, he took a deep breath and punched a number into his phone.

'Finally! I would have thought you could have at least rung to see how I was.'

Even though he'd known what to expect, her voice sliced through his nerves like a scalpel. It was as polished and deadly as her glossily painted fingernails, and instantly he felt his bravado fail and once again, he was small and young and stupid.

Breathing out jerkily, his fingers tightened around the phone. 'I thought we agreed last night it wasn't serious?'

He heard her laugh—a tight, bitter sound that made his heart bang against his ribs.

'You mean compared to dining with the Prime Minister?'

He swallowed. 'There wasn't anything I could do—'

'There never is. Not now. Now you're far too important to be bothering with me.' Her voice was spiralling higher and higher. 'Too busy making all that money and sleeping with all those women to have time to talk to *me*.'

'I spoke to you yesterday—'

'You lost your temper with me yesterday! I can't imagine what your father would have said if he was still alive.'

'Can't you? I think that's highly unlikely. He'd have said exactly what you told him to say.'

Even before he'd finished speaking he knew his tone had come out more accusatory and emotional than he'd intended.

'Oh, here we go.'

He flinched. She was spitting the words down the phone at him, bile and bitterness ricocheting over the line.

'You needed boundaries. I was simply supporting your father. And you were so difficult to love. Always crying or having a tantrum. *Poor little Massimo!* Only you're *not* poor, are you? You're rolling in money. But what do I see of it? You barely send me enough to keep a cat alive—'

He was shivering uncontrollably, his heart beating like a trapped bird.

'I'll arrange for some money to be transferred this morning,' he heard himself say. 'I have to go now—'

With a hand that shook slightly he switched off his phone and sat down on the bed.

Earlier, he had felt so calm—lighter, almost. But the conversation with Alida had changed everything. Now his heart was racing, his nerves screaming like a car alarm.

How could he have been so stupid? Telling Flora about his past had been foolhardy and self-indulgent—for surely that same past had taught him that letting someone into your life, your head and, worse, your heart was tantamount to giving them control over you. He felt sick to his stomach. Look at how his father had changed after marrying Alida. Look at how Alida still knew exactly which buttons to press to make him feel helpless and trapped—

He should have followed his instincts to keep his private life private. Confiding in Flora had undermined all the efforts he'd made to keep control of his life. It had been careless, reckless even—he winced. How could he have thought he might want something other than sex with Flora?

He gritted his teeth. She'd caught him off guard. But it wouldn't happen again.

He couldn't let himself feel differently. Any more than he could alter his past. What he and Flora had was purely physical. He knew that now. And he needed to remind her of that fact as soon and as firmly as possible.

Picking up his clothes, he began to get dressed.

* * *

Humming softly, Flora picked up the heavy cast-iron skillet and put it on the hotplate. Next she filled the kettle with water and put it beside the skillet. Frowning, she looked round for the coffee pot. It wasn't in its normal place at the back of the stove. Nor was it in the dishwasher.

Bending over, she opened the doors of the huge dresser that nearly reached the ceiling and peered along the shelves. It wasn't there either. Sighing, she straightened up—and found Massimo watching her intently.

'Hi!'

She stared at him uncertainly. Despite privately acknowledging her feelings for him, she didn't really know what to expect from Massimo. Some awkwardness, maybe. But definitely closeness, given what they'd shared last night. Only he didn't seem awkward. Nor did he seem particularly inclined to be intimate. Standing just inside the doorway, hands deep in the pockets of his jeans, he looked more wary than anything.

His manner set her teeth on edge. It was hard to believe that she had been about to cook this man breakfast. Let alone tell him that she loved him.

But last night had been pretty intense for both of them. Probably he just needed a little time to relax.

'I can't find the coffee pot. The blue one,' she said, turning back towards the dresser. 'Have you seen it?'

He shook his head. 'No. But it might be in my study.'

He walked slowly across the room, his impassive face jarring against her nervous, hopeful excitement and quite suddenly the kitchen felt small and oppressive. 'I'll go and get it,' she said hurriedly. 'You can get the bacon—I mean the pancetta—out of the fridge.'

Standing in the hallway, she breathed out slowly. It had all felt so clear and right earlier.

Loving him had felt right.

Only now she wasn't so sure.

He was acting so strangely. Aloof and on edge—almost as though he was waiting to say something…

Pushing open the door to the room Massimo had appropriated for an office, she saw the coffee pot immediately. It was on his desk.

Sighing, she picked it up and turned to leave—and then, glancing down at the papers scattered across his desk, she felt the handle start to slip from her fingers. She gripped it more tightly. Inside her chest her heart had started to pound painfully hard.

She must be mistaken…but she knew she wasn't.

Massimo had moved. He was standing next to the stove, staring across the kitchen, his eyes dark and unreadable.

As she walked through the door he looked up at her, and she felt a surge of fury at his cool expression.

Trying to hold on to her temper, she put the coffee pot down on the worktop with exaggerated care and then casually, almost as an afterthought, dropped the plans she'd found in his study onto the kitchen table.

'These were on your desk.'

She felt it in the air first: the shift between them, the quivering rise in tension. Suddenly the room seemed to shrink around them.

Looking up, she met his gaze. 'They're plans for a development. Here. At the *palazzo*. But then you knew that, didn't you?' Her throat seemed to have closed up. Lifting her hand, she pressed it against her neck. 'I'm just wondering why didn't you tell me?'

Even saying the words hurt so much she could hardly breathe. He had held her in his arms, pushed inside her body, and yet he'd kept this from her.

How could he have *done* that?

Furiously, she realised how naive she'd been. At first, she'd assumed Massimo wanted the house for himself. Later, his furious determination to get her out was finally explained when the plans to convert the *palazzo* into a hotel were made public. But it had never occurred to her that there might be an even bigger picture.

But there was. And it was much, much bigger than she could have ever have imagined.

She looked back at the plans and shock hit her again like a punch to the stomach. Anger was rising inside her. And outrage too. These weren't plans for a development.

They were plans for an occupation.

'This is my home. You can't just decide that you want to knock it down and build some massive resort in its place.' Her voice was rising. 'There must be nearly fifty villas on those plans. And a golf course. It's huge—'

Massimo's eyes narrowed, his gaze on her flushed, angry face. Part of him knew that her anger was justified. And that she deserved some kind of explanation at the very least. But something cold twisted in his stomach. Why should he have told her anything? Or explain himself then or now? This was *his* property and she was nothing more than a tenant.

Just because last night she'd coaxed him into sharing grisly details about his childhood it didn't mean that he owed her anything. He shrugged.

'I don't know what you want me to say.'

Leaning back against the stove, he stared at her coldly. This was the only kind of conversation he liked. One that required cool detachment and logic. And absolutely no mercy.

Flora flinched and then her eyes flared. 'How about, "Flora, I thought you might be interested to know that I'm going to demolish your home and build a massive resort and golf course instead"?'

'Why would I tell you anything about the resort? It's none of your business,' he said coldly.

'How do you work *that* out?' She stared at him, feeling slightly sick. 'In the first place, I live here...'

Her voice faded as he shook his head slowly.

'Even without consulting a lawyer, I can tell you that your tenancy agreement is meaningless. It's certainly not going to stand in the way of hundreds of jobs, or the money this resort will bring to the community here.'

There was something soft and dangerous growing in his voice, but her own anger felt more acute, more pressing and so she ignored it.

'Is that all you think about? Jobs and money?' Her skin was trembling with rage, and the sort of hurt she hadn't felt since her mum died.

He shrugged. 'What else is there?'

She almost laughed. Only the pain and anger tangling inside her wasn't funny.

'There's *me!*'

He didn't move, but something flared in his eyes— something dark and formless. 'And who are *you* to tell me how to run my business?'

'I don't want anything to do with your damn business. But I thought...' She hesitated, her hands curling into fists at her sides. Did she really have to spell it out?

His gaze met hers and her stomach plummeted.

Apparently she did.

She lifted her chin. 'I thought I was something to do with your life. I can see why you wouldn't tell me at the beginning, but I thought things were different now. Between us. So why didn't you tell me after everything changed?'

'I didn't tell you because nothing has changed. Not with my plans for this building. Or with us,' he said coldly. His face was expressionless, but there could be no mistaking the distance in his eyes. 'It couldn't. Because there is no "us".'

For a moment her voice wouldn't work. Anger was clawing inside her like an animal, trying to climb out of a pit. 'How can you say that?' she said, her voice high and shaking. 'We haven't just been sleeping together. We've shared meals; we went to Rome—'

He looked at her incredulously. 'When I said we were just going to have sex, I didn't mean that literally. I'm not a Neanderthal.' Flora blinked. His eyes were staring through her, as though he had already deleted her from his life. 'But that doesn't make this a relationship.'

Shock and anger and misery rose in her throat, and for a second she thought she was going to throw up. 'But what about yesterday and last night?'

'What about it?'

Watching her eyes widen with shock and hurt, his skin tightened. He'd been right: he'd let her get too close. That was why she was so angry at him now. And that was why he needed to make sure she never did it again. Letting her know that his plan for the resort was off-limits was as good a way as any of proving to her that she was in his life for one reason and one reason only.

She stared at him wordlessly. She knew how hard it had been for him to tell her about his father and stepmother's treatment of him. So why was he acting now as though none of it had mattered?

A white ball of anger was swelling inside her chest and she swallowed, battening down the pain. 'Didn't what happened between us mean anything to you?'

His eyes on hers were cold, incurious. 'It was just a conversation—'

'It was *not* just a conversation.' She interrupted him,

eyes blazing. 'I told you things about myself, and you told me about your dad and your stepmother. We *shared* something.'

'Yes. Too much alcohol and too little sleep.'

The chill in his voice made her feel faint.

'Why are you being like this?' She breathed out unsteadily. 'Something happened between us. I know it did. I felt it, and I know you felt it too.'

Her heart was pounding but she wasn't going to walk away from this without a fight. Massimo found it difficult to trust. She knew that was why he was in denial about what had happened between them. All she needed was to find some way to make him trust her.

'I know what you're doing,' she said carefully. 'I know you want to push me away. And I know *why* you want to push me away. It's because you're scared.'

She took a small step towards him, trying to find the words that would make him see that she would never hurt him.

'But you don't need to be. Not any more. Not with me. You can trust me.' She took a deep breath. 'That's what I was going to tell you—'

His face looked glittering and hard and impenetrable, like a diamond. 'What were you going to tell me?'

For a split second she felt as though she were standing on a window ledge. Fear, thicker and blacker than smoke, filled her lungs and then, shaking her head, she gave a small, strangled laugh.

'I was going to tell you that I love you.'

He stared at her, the expression on his face so still and blank that she thought he hadn't understood her.

And then he said slowly, 'Then it's probably a good thing that you found those plans now. Keep your love, *cara*, for someone who wants it.'

He watched her face, saw the flash of pain and knew that he wasn't being fair or kind. But that simply seemed to wind him up more tightly, and he couldn't stop the rush of anger rising inside him.

She might trust him, but he sure as hell didn't trust *her*—or anyone else for that matter. And he would certainly never trust anyone enough to love them.

It wasn't his fault.

It was just how it had to be.

And he'd been fair. He hadn't promised what he couldn't give. Nor had he lied about what he wanted. And he didn't want her love. Hell, he'd never even asked for it. Yet now she was trying to make him feel guilty about that!

'I didn't intend for any of this to happen,' he said roughly. 'You and I. Us.'

Her head jerked up. 'I thought there *was* no "us",' she said, unable to hide her bitterness. 'There's not even really a me, is there? You're the only one that matters—aren't you, Massimo?'

She watched him, saw his face close and harden.

'So when were you going to make yourself homeless?'

His eyes met hers. 'I don't know. I didn't think that far ahead.'

In part it was true. Since he'd arrived at the *palazzo* his life had been turned upside down. Normally his days were micromanaged to the last minute. Now, though, he seemed to have lost the ability to think beyond the immediate present.

He frowned. It was also true that he'd deliberately avoided even thinking about the development—let alone broaching it with Flora. But so what if he had? It was nothing to do with her. And if she didn't like that fact, that was her problem. She shouldn't have tried to make things personal.

Flora felt something shudder through her bones. He was

lying. For weeks now she'd seen him at work. He was on top of everything. No detail escaped his eye. With a stab of misery she remembered her dress fitting. No, he *knew*: he knew exactly when he'd been going to tell her.

And suddenly so did she. It would have been when he took her back to Rome in a couple of weeks.

Blood was roaring inside her head and shakily she reached out to grip the back of a chair.

'You *used* me!' She was so angry that she was glad there was a table between them. 'Of all the low things you've done, this is the absolute—'

'What are you talking about?'

Her eyes met his. How could she have been so gullible? A man like Massimo could have sex every hour on the hour with a different woman if he wanted. Yet not once had she ever questioned his attraction to her. She clenched her teeth. But then she didn't have his low morals; she couldn't just use anything or anyone to get what she wanted.

'I thought you wanted this house. And then I thought you wanted sex. But this was never about the *palazzo*. And it wasn't about the sex either. It was always just about the *deal*. Building that resort.' She gestured towards the plans in disgust.

For a moment she thought of how it could have been. Of what it might have been like to love Massimo and be loved by him. And suddenly she was fighting tears. Gritting her teeth, she breathed in sharply. It was *not* the end. It was the beginning. For now she knew that love was no longer something to be feared or shunned. And one day she would give her heart to someone who would treat it like the priceless gift it was.

She lifted her face and stared at him. What was she doing? Why was she having this pointless, excruciating conversation? There was nothing more to be said. And nothing more to do here.

With shock, she realised that she didn't need to keep hiding in Sardinia. Massimo Sforza had just trampled on her heart. If she could survive that then she could face her father and her brother. It was time to go home. To England. To her family.

She held his gaze for a moment and then, turning, walked swiftly out of the room.

Massimo stared after her. Not a muscle had moved on his face but inside he felt something like panic stir inside him. Never had a conversation spiralled so badly out of his control. Every word he'd spoken had simply seemed to make things worse.

But it wasn't his fault, he thought angrily. Last night had unsettled him—for obvious reasons. And she knew that.

So why couldn't she just have backed off? Instead of grilling him about matters that didn't even concern her? And telling him she loved him?

What the hell did she expect him to do with *that* piece of information?

It was her choice to feel like that. She could have kept it to herself. But instead she'd had to go and tell him. But why? Did she think he was going to fall down on bended knee and propose to her? Well, he wasn't. He wasn't the right man for her. And she shouldn't have put him in the position of having to say so. Nor should she have got upset at hearing the truth. It was far better *for both of them* that he made it clear right now that their relationship was always going to be purely sexual.

He gritted his teeth. Why should he have to remind her of that, anyway? Just because he'd told her about his past it didn't mean he owed her anything.

His stomach tightened painfully.

Except that he did.

Remembering the warmth and worry on her face as she'd listened to him talking about his father and Alida, he felt his anger slide away. She had helped him face up to his childhood. Even though he'd lashed out at her she'd stood her ground, pushing back when he pushed her away. Until finally she'd broken through the layers of protection he'd put up between himself and the world and freed him from the burden of his past.

He breathed out unsteadily.

Was he really not going to go after her?

Heart racing, he walked quickly out of the kitchen and ran up the stairs two at a time. Her bedroom was empty. His too. Mouth drying, he stepped back into her room. At first glance it looked unchanged. Her clothes were still in the wardrobe. A book she was struggling to finish lay spine-up on her bedside table.

Turning sharply, he felt a rush of pain. Her rucksack was no longer hanging on the back of the door. Nor was the folder containing her thesis on the dressing table. Blood was pounding in his ears. Feeling light-headed, he stumbled into the bathroom intending to splash his face with cold water—and then he saw it. Her dress. The blue silk lay draped over a chair, like the discarded skin of some mythical creature. And resting on top of it, scribbled on the bottom of her tenancy agreement, was a note.

Congratulations. You win. You got what you wanted.
You closed the deal.

CHAPTER TEN

SLUMPING BACK IN his seat, Massimo stared at the men and women sitting around the boardroom table and frowned. All of them were white-faced and trembling. Some of the women seemed close to tears.

He'd lost his temper. It had been spectacular, brutal and unfair. But he didn't feel fair.

He felt angry.

And spread out on the table in front of him was the reason why.

The plans for the Sardinia resort. Nine weeks ago they'd been a glittering prize, waiting to be held aloft at the end of a challenging, arduous race. Now, though, the mere sight of them made him want to kick the table across the room.

Abruptly, he stood up and walked towards the floor-to-ceiling glass windows that ran the length of one wall, his eyes tracking the small clouds drifting slowly above the humming centre of Rome.

Where were they going? At some point would she look up and see them too?

At the thought of Flora, he felt his stomach clench painfully. And suddenly he wanted to be alone—alone with his anger and frustration.

'There's a lot to think about,' he said tersely, not bothering to turn round. 'Let's take the weekend and reschedule for Monday.'

The meeting was over.

Behind him, the sound of shuffling feet and papers told him that his staff were leaving. After a few moments he heard the door to the boardroom close with a soft click.

Sighing heavily, he added remorse to the list of feelings churning around inside his chest. His behaviour hadn't just been unreasonable; it had been completely incomprehensible as far as his staff were concerned. The Sardinian development was ready and waiting for the contractors to move in. Work on-site could have started today or yesterday or even a week ago.

So why the delay?

Remembering his fury when someone had asked him that very question, he gritted his teeth.

He knew the answer, of course. That was why he'd lost his temper. But what else could he have done? He certainly couldn't tell them the truth.

But now, alone, with no one to answer to except himself, his anger seeped away, leaving an aching hole in the pit of his stomach. The truth was there was no good reason to wait. There wasn't even a bad one. There was nothing except a feeling—a sense that once the *palazzo* was demolished what had happened between him and Flora would finally and irretrievably be over.

He felt a sudden, painful sting of frustration and, turning, he began to pace the room.

What was he thinking?

It couldn't be over because it had never actually started. Aside from the cohabiting, their affair had been exactly the same as every other he'd had. Probably the only reason he was even still thinking about her at all was because she'd stormed out on him.

His mouth twisted as he remembered how he'd sat and waited for her in the kitchen—hoping, believing that she would change her mind and come back. How finally, after several hours of increasing anger and frustration and despair, he'd got in his car and driven round the island looking for her. He hadn't found her. And instead of having the chance to throw her accusations back in her face he'd been left alone to brood in an empty house, where every single room was filled with reminders of her absence.

Was it any wonder he couldn't just forget her?

He was still mulling over that thought when there was a soft tap on the boardroom door.

'What is it?' he said irritably.

The door opened slowly and a hand slid through, waving a red paisley handkerchief.

Massimo frowned. 'Is this some kind of mime show or are you stripping? Because, as stripteases go, I have to say it's not doing that much for me.'

He watched as Giorgio stuck his head round the door. 'It should really be white.'

Massimo smiled reluctantly. 'So why are you surrendering?'

Stepping into the room, the lawyer glanced at him nervously. 'I've got a family so I need to stay alive!' He shot his boss a furtive look. 'Apparently it was a bit of bloodbath at the board meeting.'

Massimo sighed. 'Is that what they're saying?'

Giorgio shook his head. 'They're not saying anything! But given that it looks a bit *28 Days Later* out there, I just took an educated guess.'

There was a long, strained silence, and then abruptly Massimo yanked the nearest chair away from the table and sat down heavily. 'I was a little short,' he admitted finally. 'But I just need a bit more time…'

His words trailed off and, leaning back in the chair, he rubbed his hand slowly over the top of his neck. A headache was forming, and more than anything he just wanted to lie down in a dark room and go to sleep. Except that wouldn't actually happen. Since arriving back in Rome he'd barely managed more than an hour or two a night on the sofa. He'd lost his appetite too—which probably wasn't helping the headaches that punctuated his days and nights with monotonous regularity.

As though reading his mind, Giorgio cleared his throat and, pulling up a chair beside him, he said quietly, 'You look exhausted. Why not have an early night? Use the weekend to recharge. Get some focus.'

Massimo stared up at the ceiling. That was the other problem. He couldn't focus on *anything*. Certainly not work. He'd tried upping his exercise regime, to no effect. And his standard go-to for clearing his brain—a night or three with a beautiful, eager woman—held no appeal for him whatsoever. Not since Sardinia. Not since Flora.

The lawyer frowned. 'I mean it. Go home!'

Glancing at Giorgio, Massimo gave him a small, tight smile. 'That's a good idea—'

And it was—in theory.

Only the truth was he didn't have a home.

He owned properties: he'd added another three to his portfolio only last week. But none of them was a home, and the thought of spending a long weekend sitting alone in one of his hotel suites made a spasm of disproportionate misery squeeze his stomach tightly.

'But I really should get up to speed with everything,' he said slowly.

Nodding, Giorgio pulled out his phone and swiped rapidly across the screen. 'In that case there's a dinner tonight with the Minister of Finance. A lot of foreign investors are going to be there—including that Chinese consortium we worked with last year.' The lawyer hesitated, his face carefully expressionless. 'And we have a meeting in about an hour to discuss first-stage publicity for the Sardinia development.'

There was a sudden stillness in the room.

Massimo felt his skin tighten. The muscles in his back were rigid and it hurt to breathe. Did every damn conversation he had have to come back to Sardinia? He didn't even want to think about the development, let alone spend an afternoon discussing it in detail.

Frowning, he pressed his fingers against his forehead, where a new ache was starting to form. 'I thought we'd agreed to push everything back on that?' he muttered.

Giorgio shrugged. 'We did. But there's no harm in talking.'

Massimo shivered. 'Maybe I will take the afternoon off after all. I don't feel great. Is there such a thing as Sardinian flu?' he joked weakly.

There was a sudden shifting silence, and the lawyer cleared his throat. 'There could be.' He frowned, as though considering the possibility. 'What are your symptoms?'

Massimo hesitated for a moment and then shrugged. 'Nothing specific. I can't sleep. My appetite's shot. I've got no concentration.'

Irritably, he glanced around the empty boardroom. What kind of illness made you snap at your staff until they cried? Or made you so distracted they had to repeat everything they said to you?

Something was nagging at him—something obvious, yet nameless, and just out of reach.

Feeling Giorgio's gaze, he shifted in his seat. 'Ever since I got back to Rome I haven't felt myself. Joking aside, do you think I *might* have picked something up in Sardinia?'

'Maybe,' Giorgio said quietly. 'Although perhaps it's not what you picked up but what you left behind.'

'I didn't leave anything behind…' he began confusedly. 'The *palazzo* was empty—'

The air seemed to swell, as though it were holding back a secret, and Massimo felt his heart start to pound.

'The house was empty…' he said again.

'But *she's* still there somewhere, isn't she? Miss Golding, I mean?' Giorgio prompted gently. 'She won't have left the island. It's her home.'

And suddenly Massimo knew what was wrong with him.

He knew why he couldn't sleep or eat.

Or concentrate on anything for more than a few minutes.

And he knew why he didn't want to knock down the *palazzo*.

He was in love with Flora.

And the *palazzo* wasn't just some random building. It had been their home, somewhere he'd felt excited, happy, relaxed and safe. Safe enough to face his past. Only he couldn't have done it without Flora—with her, he had become whole.

Looking down at his lap, he saw to his surprise that his hands were shaking. Lifting his head, he found Giorgio watching him, his broad face creased with kindness.

'How did you know I was in love?' His face twisted. 'I mean, when…?'

The lawyer smiled. 'I saw the two of you together—' he cleared his throat '—in the garden, remember?'

Their eyes met, and Massimo breathed out. 'Oh, yes,' he said slowly. 'I forgot you were there.'

Giorgio laughed. 'That's when I knew. You only had eyes for each other.'

Massimo stared at him dazedly. Had Giorgio really been there that day? He had no memory of him at all. Or of the rest of the day, for that matter. All he could picture was Flora, singing softly to herself, her near naked body still damp from the pond.

'I don't understand,' he said shakily. 'I *can't* be in love. I don't know *how* to love.'

Patting him on the shoulder, Giorgio smiled ruefully. 'That's what everyone says. I certainly did when I fell in love with Anna. I actually broke up with her because it scared me so much.' He started to laugh. 'Then I saw her one evening, all dressed up to go out, and I walked into a door. That's what it took to knock it into my thick head.' He grinned. 'Then all I had to do was find Anna and tell her how I felt—'

Lowering his head into hands, Massimo groaned.

'I don't know where she is,' he said slowly. He looked up at Giorgio, his expression strained. 'We had a row and she stormed out.'

'We can find her,' the lawyer said firmly. 'It won't be that hard. She doesn't exactly blend in, does she?'

Massimo shook his head. 'It won't make any difference. After the way I treated her she's not going to want anything to do with me.'

Giorgio stood up. 'Then you *make* her want to,' he said, slapping Massimo around the shoulders.

'If you can't then you don't deserve her. And you're not the man who persuaded me to join his start-up business for less than half the salary I was getting from my previous job.'

Massimo's eyes gleamed. 'I was worth it, though, wasn't I?'

'Don't tell *me* that. Tell *her*!'

Gritting his teeth, he felt a rush of determination—hot

and strong-flowing, like blood. He'd been a fool. Never in all his business dealings had he been so blind, so utterly clueless. All the signs that he loved Flora were there. He'd looked forward to spending time with her. Not just having sex but talking and teasing, being teased. Listening to her talk about her mother's death, he had *cared* that she was hurting. More than cared: he'd wanted to take away her pain.

But it had never occurred to him that he was falling in love with her.

He hadn't even realised it was love he was feeling.

All he'd sensed was that for the first time since his childhood he'd felt vulnerable. Caring, loving, needing were all reminders of a past that had left deep and painful scars. So when he'd started to care about Flora, he'd got scared. Scared that a woman might once again have power over him—power over how he should feel, power to hurt him. And he'd panicked. So terrified by what he was feeling that he'd pushed her away, his fear blinding him to her kindness and her courage. Even to her love.

He breathed out slowly. That fear felt like nothing now. Not beside the realisation that he'd made the biggest mistake of his life: that having rejected her, he needed Flora and her love in order to live.

Pushing back the chair, he straightened his shoulders and stood up. Grabbing Giorgio's hand, he shook it firmly. 'You're a good man, Giorgio. A good friend too. I'm going to take your advice, so I won't be joining you for dinner.'

The lawyer frowned, then nodded. He was watching his boss intently. 'Do you want me to reschedule a meeting with the Chinese next week?'

Massimo glanced around the boardroom. It represented his life's work. His legacy. But it wasn't enough. His eyes

flared, but his face was calm and certain. 'That depends…
On when we get back.'

Giorgio raised an eyebrow.

Massimo grinned. 'I'm going to Sardinia to find her,
Giorgio. And when I do I'm going to prove to her that I
love her. However long that takes.'

Flora flopped back against the faded sofa cushions and
stared miserably out of the window at the rain-sodden garden. After Sardinia, England felt incredibly cold and grey
and wet. And, as if the weather outside wasn't bad enough,
inside the house it was distinctly stormy too.

She frowned. It was her own fault. Turning up on her
dad's doorstep, having clearly been howling her head off,
and then trying to pretend nothing was wrong had been
asking for trouble.

Sighing, she got up from the sofa, dragged on a pair
of boots and a coat and stomped out the front door. The
trouble was that her father had never really come to terms
with her being an adult. Obviously he knew how old she
was, but he just couldn't accept that she was capable of
making her own decisions.

And now she'd done the worst thing possible. She'd
proved him right.

Her dad had been horrified to see her so upset and then,
having recovered his equilibrium, he'd immediately started
to take charge of her life. Within twenty minutes he'd got
hold of a friend who ran a horticultural business and arranged an interview for Flora. Next he'd cajoled her into
choosing new wallpaper and curtains for her bedroom.

Still reeling from the shock and pain of Massimo's rejection, she hadn't had the strength to argue. It had been
easier just to acquiesce to his wishes. But then Freddie had

come home yesterday, and she'd remembered exactly why she'd fled to Sardinia in the first place.

It was hard enough trying to stand up to her father, but against her dad and Freddie united it was impossible.

It had stopped raining now, and the sun was trying to push its way through the drifting clouds. In the park, two small children were playing under the watchful eye of their father. Staring at them, Flora felt a shiver of despair. Being protective was perfectly natural, but Freddie and her dad were so overprotective it was stifling.

At least she'd managed to stop Freddie from flying out to Sardinia. Remembering her brother's fury when finally she'd given him a severely edited version of the truth, Flora winced. He'd actually been far angrier with himself than with Flora, but that had actually made her feel worse. Him thinking that she couldn't cope… As if she was useless or helpless or both.

The park was empty now and, glancing at her watch, she saw that it was nearly lunchtime. Reluctantly, she began walking home. After leaving Sardinia, it had taken her a few days to realise when she needed to eat. At first she'd confused the near permanent ache inside in her chest with hunger, until finally it had occurred to her that it had nothing to do with food. And everything to do with Massimo.

Unbidden, hot, swift tears rose in her throat. She missed him so much. And instead of diminishing day by day the pain in her heart seemed to be growing stronger—driven in part by the knowledge that perhaps, had she channelled that last devastating conversation differently, she might not even be back in England. But it had been so hard and he'd been so unapproachable, so brutal.

She felt a sudden flash of anger. It wouldn't have mattered what she'd said or how she'd said it. The outcome would have been the same. Massimo didn't love her. She wasn't even sure he knew how to love.

Glancing up, she saw that she was back at her dad's house and, with a sigh, she pushed open the back door.

'Where have you been?'

It was Freddie. His face was creased with exasperation. 'I went for a walk.'

His eyes narrowed. 'And you didn't think to tell Dad?' Punching buttons on his phone, he shook his head. 'I need to tell him you're back. He went out looking for you in the car!' He stopped. 'Yes…No…She's here…No. She's fine. I'll see you in a minute.'

Feeling like a child who'd been caught with her hand in the biscuit tin, Flora hung up her coat shakily. 'I was only gone a few minutes, Freddie.'

Her brother stared at her, his face flushed, his grey eyes dark like storm clouds. 'You were gone for nearly an *hour*, Flora.'

Her face grew still. He was right. She'd looked at her watch and seen the time for herself. Only it hadn't registered. Nothing really registered at the moment.

Freddie shook his head. 'You are *so* selfish sometimes. Do you have *any* idea how worried Dad's been about you?'

'I didn't—' she began.

But Freddie interrupted her. 'I'm not talking about now. I'm talking about all the time you were away. All that time—day and night—he was waiting for a phone call to say you'd been hurt or worse. It was bad enough that you ran away like that—'

Flora swallowed. It wasn't fair of Freddie to try and make her feel guilty about what she'd done. She *had* run away—but only because if she'd told them she wanted to go they would have talked her out it.

Her brother stared at her irritably. 'And then when something *does* happen you don't even tell us.'

'There was no point,' Flora said quickly. 'I was coming home. And nothing really happened.'

'He *hurt* you. How can you say that's nothing?'

'I'm not.' She glowered at him. Her temper felt thin and worn about the edges. 'He *did* hurt me, but being hurt is part of life, Freddie. I can't stay in my bedroom all my life, playing make-believe!'

Her brother scowled at her. 'I should never have let you go over there. And I certainly shouldn't have let you stay on living there when that snake Sforza moved in.'

Flora felt a flash of anger. 'It wasn't up to you, Freddie. I'm a grown-up—'

The door opened behind her and, seeing the anxiety and worry on her dad's face, she felt her anger give way to guilt.

'Flora, darling! I was so worried about you—'

Her father pulled her into his arms and she felt a rush of love mingled with irritation as she felt his racing heartbeat. She pulled away. 'I'm fine, Dad. I just needed to get out of the house. I took a coat and everything.' She smiled weakly.

'Everything except your phone,' Freddie snapped.

'Why would I need my phone? I was walking round the village.' She glared at him. 'The village we grew up in. Look, I know you both worry about me, but I'm not a child. I went to university. I've had jobs. And I've lived in a foreign country. On my own.'

Freddie snorted. 'And look how *that* turned out!'

Something inside her seemed to tear apart.

Turning, she faced her brother, her teeth pressing hard against each another. 'It turned out fine. I don't know what you think happened out there, but I left on *my* terms. And I'm going back on my terms too.'

There was a short, frayed silence, and then her father said slowly, 'Flora! I don't understand. You can't seriously be thinking about going back?'

'She's not,' said Freddie, staring at his sister with naked frustration. 'She's going to stay here, where we can keep an eye on her.'

Their eyes met. Normally this was the moment when she'd back down. Even before he'd become a lawyer she hadn't been able to fight the way her brother did. But since he'd become a barrister he was just in a different league when it came to questioning and confrontation.

'It's for your own good, Flora. It's not like there aren't orchids in England. You can easily finish your dissertation here.'

She nodded dumbly and, sensing her capitulation, he smiled. 'It's the right thing to do, Flossie.' He was calming down, his voice losing that implacable force. 'Dad and I— We're not trying to be mean. We just don't want to see you get hurt again. And I promise you it's not about stopping you from doing what you want to do. If you could think of one good reason to go back to that *palazzo* then we wouldn't stand in your way. But you can't, can you?'

One good reason.

Flora stared at him in silence. She *could* think of one very good reason to go back to Sardinia. In fact, it wasn't just a good reason, it was the best reason in the world: *love*.

Lifting her chin, she nodded slowly. 'Yes. I can. And that's why I'm going back, Freddie.' She turned to her father. 'I know you miss Mum. I do too. And what happened to her was awful. But it happened *here*, because bad things happen everywhere.'

Reaching out, she took her father's hand and then, after a moment's hesitation, she took Freddie's too.

'I know you love me, and I love you both—only you can't keep me safe and sound.' She bit her lip. 'But you *can* trust me to look after myself. I know it's hard, and I know I haven't always given you reason to believe me, but—' she squeezed both their hands tightly '—I *need* to do this,' she said firmly. 'So, will you please let me go back?'

Slowly her father nodded, and then finally Freddie nodded too.

'But you have to promise that you'll call if you need us.'

She smiled weakly. 'I'll always need both of you. But right now someone else needs me more.'

The sun was reaching its peak in the sky, high above the *palazzo*. Massimo stared moodily across the *terrazza*. It was too hot to be inland and he'd half considered taking the yacht out. But he couldn't bring himself to leave the house—not even for an afternoon.

He wanted to be there, just in case Flora came back. Picking up his glass of wine, he drank slowly and deliberately.

Not that there was any reason to think that she *was* coming back. In all honesty there was no reason to think that he would ever see her again.

It had been nearly eight days since he'd told Giorgio that he was going to find Flora. Eight days of false leads and dashed hopes. It had sounded so promising at first. He'd tracked her to Cagliari, and then over to England. But since then there had been no trace of her. She'd simply disappeared.

Lifting his gaze, he watched a jewel-bright dragonfly hover lazily above the fountain. He had been so sure he would find her. So sure he'd be able to win her back.

But now he saw that his certainty had been based solely on optimism. Not on statistical probability. After all, on a planet of six billion people, what were the odds of him finding her?

Truthfully, she could be anywhere.

And after the way he'd treated her the chances of her ever stepping through those kitchen doors again were minimal. Less than zero, in fact.

He poured another glass of wine. This was definitely the one place on earth she'd never want to set eyes on again. *Hell!* He shouldn't even *be* here. Only he couldn't seem to leave.

He glanced round the garden, his skin tightening. Or rather he didn't *want* to leave. Here, he could let his imagination drift. He could almost see her disappearing under an archway at the end of the garden, hear her laughter from inside the kitchen.

Sitting up straighter, he shook his head. If he was chasing shadows…phantoms, it must be time to move. Standing up unsteadily, he picked the bottle off the table and began to walk slowly across the lawn. Beneath his bare feet the grass felt hot and parched, and he could feel the wine working its way through his blood.

Softly he began to hum under his breath. He couldn't quite place the tune, but he knew he remembered it from somewhere.

And then he heard it.

Someone was singing—singing the words to the song he was humming.

His heart started to pound. It was a woman's voice. Soft, husky, familiar.

Squinting up into the sun, he let the alcohol and the heat mingle with his memories. It wasn't her. He knew that, of course. It was just his imagination. But he didn't care.

Slowly, as though mesmerised, he followed the voice across the lawn. But as he stepped through the arch that led into the water garden the singing stopped. Hesitating, he stared through the foliage, his heart pounding painfully in his chest, hope twitching in every muscle.

But of course she wasn't there.

For a moment he stood, swaying slightly, and then carefully he walked towards the large rectangular ornamental pond that gave the garden its name. The surface was dotted with water lilies, their waxy white petals splaying up towards the sun, and he stared at them in fascination. And then suddenly he jerked backwards, grabbing the arm of a beautiful marble statue to keep his balance, as a naked woman broke the surface of the water, rising up slowly.

She had her back to him.

But he would know the curve of that spine anywhere—even in the darkness. It was Flora.

His head was spinning; his breath was hot and dry in his throat.

It couldn't be her.

He must be imagining it. Or it was some kind of optical illusion. Any moment now the sun would go behind a cloud and she would disappear for ever.

Holding his breath, he watched as with effortless grace she pulled herself onto one of the marble slabs edging the pond, smoothing her hair back over the contours of her head.

He took a deep breath. It didn't matter that she wasn't real. He was happy just to stand there and watch her. He frowned. Maybe he could even get a little closer.

Letting go of the statue's arm, he put the bottle down on the ground and stepped forward just as she turned around.

She stopped, one foot slightly raised like a deer at the edge of a meadow. And then slowly she frowned and folded her arms. 'I know you're the landlord, but tenants have rights too. Including privacy while bathing. It's in my contract.'

Massimo gazed at her dazedly. 'Flora?'

She stared at him impatiently. 'Is that the best you can do? Pretend you don't know who I am?'

'I— No— I *do* know who you are. Of *course*. I thought you were…' He hesitated. 'It doesn't matter.'

He watched, transfixed, as she picked her way across the stones and came towards him, his eyes following the droplets of water trickling down over her naked breasts and stomach.

She was real. What was more, she was *there*, standing in front of him.

'What are you doing here?' he murmured.

She glowered at him. 'I live here, remember? This is my home.'

His eyes met hers and she almost flinched. She'd forgotten how it felt to be the object of that gaze. How tight and hot and restless it made her feel.

But she hadn't come back for that gaze.

This time it wasn't enough.

This time she wanted more.

But he had to want it too.

'Never mind about me,' she said hoarsely. 'What about you?' She glanced slowly round the garden. 'I thought you'd be long gone and all this razed to the ground.'

They stared at one another in silence.

Finally, he shrugged. 'Things have changed.'

He watched her lip curl, his heart beating in his throat. How had he ever imagined she was a figment of his imagination? She was so clear and vital. Beside her everything else seemed smudged and dull and imprecise.

'What things?' she snapped.

He smiled then, that same sweet smile that made her feel hot and dizzy and restless, and suddenly she felt more naked than when she'd climbed out of the pond.

Abruptly, she turned and picked up a faded blue shirt. Tugging it over her head, she breathed out slowly, grateful for a chance to break free of that dark, disturbing gaze. Being so close to Massimo was playing havoc with her body temperature. But she wasn't going to give in to the heat rising inside of her.

He shrugged, his gaze never leaving her face.

'It's complicated but in all probability the resort won't happen, *cara*.'

She stared at him suspiciously. 'Have you got that in writing?'

He laughed out loud. 'You know, you sound exactly like your brother. Thankfully, you don't *look* like him.'

Her face twisted. 'How do you know what my brother looks like?'

The air around them twitched. Her heart gave a jolt as he stepped towards her, his face tightening.

'I met him. Your father too.'

Suddenly she could hardly breathe. 'When?' she said woodenly. 'Where?'

'A couple of days ago. In England. You have the same colour eyes.' Gently, he reached out and touched her cheek, and her heart began to pound so loudly she thought her chest would burst.

'Why were you there?' she said hoarsely.

His eyes were soft and blue and loving. 'Why do you think?'

She shook her head. 'No. You *say* it, Massimo. But only if you mean it.'

He stepped closer...so close that she could feel the heat of his skin through his shirt.

'I went to find you so I could tell you that I love you. And that I need you. Now. And tomorrow. And for ever.'

Her eyes filled with tears. He pulled her closer but she pushed hard against his chest. 'Why should I trust you? You *hurt* me.'

'I know. And I'm sorry. Sorrier than you'll ever know.'

Her heart quivered. Massimo was apologising. In some strange way she knew that was as big a step as his declaration of love.

But still she needed more. 'I told you I loved you and you told me to keep my love for someone who wanted it.'

'I *do* want it. I love you, *cara*.' His face was pale and taut, but his gaze was clear and unwavering. 'More than I ever believed I could love anyone. And it was you that made me believe. It was you who made me whole and strong. Strong enough to let the past go and fight for my future. Fight for what I want.'

'What about this place? You wanted that?'

He nodded. 'I did. But not any more. In fact, as of yesterday, I don't even own it.'

Seeing the confusion and fear in her eyes, he shook his head. 'Don't worry. The new owner wants it left just as it is.'

'How do you know?' she said shakily. He smiled.

'Because she told me she wouldn't let me turn it into some "ghastly boutique hotel for loud, sweaty, tourists"!' Flora gasped.

'What have you done?' she whispered.

'I've signed this place over to you—'

'But— Is that why you're here?' Her hands gripped the

front of his shirt. He shook his head, his eyes suddenly too bright.

'No. I came back to wait for you. And to do what I should have done when you told me you loved me.'

Reaching into his pocket, he pulled out a small square box and, opening it, he held it out to her. It was a beautiful diamond ring, edged with sapphires.

'I want you to be my wife, Flora. And I want this to be our home. Some of the time, anyway.'

Searching his face, Flora felt her heart contract. There was no anger or bitterness or doubt. He looked happy and utterly assured.

'Will you marry me?' he said softly, taking her hand in his.

She stared at the ring fiercely. For so long marriage had represented everything she feared most.

But now, looking into his unguarded face, she was no longer afraid to hope or to believe in love.

Smiling up at him, she nodded, and he slid the ring smoothly onto her finger. And then his mouth came down on hers and he kissed her with a passion that was hotter and fiercer than the Sardinian sun.

Finally, they broke apart. Looking up, she knew that the expression on his face exactly matched the way she was feeling and then, loosening his grip, he glanced down at her and frowned.

'Is that my shirt?'

She shrugged 'I might have found it in your wardrobe.'

She watched his eyes glitter with amusement, and something dark and warm that sent shivers of longing dancing down her spine.

'I think the word you're looking for, *cara*, is *stole*!'

Her insides quivered as with slow deliberation he slid his hand beneath the shirt.

'I found it. So now it's mine. Possession is nine-tenths of the law!'

Suddenly the intensity in his eyes matched the probing pressure of his touch.

'I wouldn't argue with that!'

She stared at him, her skin prickling. 'You wouldn't?'

He shook his head, his hand curling possessively around her hipbone. 'No. You see, I found you in my garden. Which is now your garden. That means I'm yours. And you're mine. *All* mine.'

'What about the other tenth?' she whispered.

He smiled that slow, sweet smile again and her pulse began to race as she felt the soft, probing progress of his fingers over her bare skin.

'I rounded it up to make things easier.'

And, lowering his mouth, he kissed her slowly and hungrily.

* * * * *

CARRYING THE KING'S PRIDE

JENNIFER FAYE

For my mother who is quite simply the best person I know. Your spirit and love of philosophy inspired this book. Your belief in me has always been such a big part of how I get to 'the end'.

And for Stella for your help and for being one of those people you meet once and know it can't be for the last time.

CHAPTER ONE

SOFÍA RAMÍREZ PUT a Manolo Blahnik–clad toe out of the classic yellow Manhattan taxi, her shoe meeting pavement still radiating heat from a sultry, steamy New York summer day.

She followed up the iconic shoe with a slim leg that caused a tuxedo-clad male on the sidewalk to turn and watch, a champagne-colored, beaded cocktail dress that accentuated her voluptuous figure without flaunting it and a Kate Spade clutch a shade deeper than her dress.

Suitably assembled on the sidewalk, she paid the driver, ran a palm over her sleek French twist to make sure it was intact and made her way toward the entrance of the glimmering, stately Metropolitan Museum of Art.

As the co-owner of one of Manhattan's trendiest fashion boutiques, she knew the importance of dressing for the occasion. Overdress in this city and you looked as if you were trying too hard. Underdress and you would be talked about all night by the highbrow crowd.

She thought she'd gotten it just right as she swished through the front doors of the museum, where one of her most important clients was hosting a benefit for the arts. But could any outfit ever really prepare a woman for her other, perhaps more important, task of the evening—

saying thanks, but no thanks, to her relationship with one of Manhattan's most powerful men?

Not just a man. A prince. The sexy, charismatic second in line to the throne of his tiny Mediterranean kingdom, Akathinia, Prince Nikandros Constantinides, in attendance tonight. *The untamable one*, as the women who had dated him were wont to say in quick sound bites to the press, the slight hint of bitterness to their tone the only outward sign they were in any way chastened at being yet another of his castoffs.

For didn't they all know their time with the prince was limited to the length of his attention span? That once his interest wandered, the clock was on?

She had known it. And what had she done? Waited for him to call when he'd come back from Mexico, his much-lauded free trade deal in hand, obsessively checking her phone for a message from him every fifteen minutes only to find nothing until tonight when he'd known they would be at the same party.

Her stomach curled with a fresh burst of nerves as she handed her invitation to the greeters at the door of the Egyptian-themed Temple of Dendur exhibit. Getting herself into a state over a man, even one as gorgeous as Nik, was something she'd sworn she'd never do. Couldn't allow herself to do. So she was going to do what any smart, sensible woman would in her situation.

End it. Cut it off before he broke her heart. Before he made her want things she couldn't have. Things she'd long ago determined weren't attainable for her.

Her attendance verified, she wound her way through the glitzy, bejeweled crowd to look for her hostess, Natalia Graham, a well-respected philanthropist who came from one of Manhattan's historic, moneyed families. Business first, heart-pounding personal matter later.

The Temple of Dendur, a gift to the United States from Egypt in the late 1960s, then bequeathed to the Met, was lit up this evening as the centerpiece of the event. Harkening back to the age of the pharaohs and the gods they worshipped, it was breathtaking.

Several acquaintances stopped her to talk, all of them clients. She spent a few moments with each, summoning the polite small talk she had studiously taught herself over the years, because when you came from the opposite side of town these people did, where this world had once only been a dream in your daily existence, you weren't equipped with those skills.

"Sofia." Natalia found her moments later, drawing her into a warm embrace. "I'm so glad you made it."

"I'm sorry I'm late. It was a crazy day."

"And you probably want off your feet." Natalia drew her toward the bar. "No Katharine tonight?"

She shook her head at the mention of her partner. "Her father is in town."

"And no gorgeous man to escort you?" Natalia gave her a wry look. "I would have thought the men would be lining up to date you. Unless," her friend said slyly, "the rumors of you and the prince are true?"

"I don't have time to date," she said smoothly, sliding onto a bar stool. "You know I'm always working."

"Mmm." Natalia gave her a speculative look. "Martini?"

"Please." A healthy shot of potent alcohol might go a long way toward the liquid courage she needed at the moment.

She and Natalia caught up, working their way around to the joint endeavor they had been planning, a fashion show in support of one of Natalia's charities. They were discussing the details when the philanthropist's gaze sharpened on the crowd behind them.

"Speaking of the prince," she drawled, "he just sat down behind you."

Her pulse picked up, thrumming a steady beat in her throat. A prickly sensation slid up her back. She didn't need to turn around to know Nik had spotted her. She could feel the heat of his gaze, eating her up as it always did.

"Well, I guess that answers my question," Natalia murmured.

Sofía took a sip of her martini. She and Nik had managed to keep their relationship out of the tabloids after they'd met at a hospital fund-raiser, but rumors had been circulating of late. Since their relationship would be dead after tonight, she saw no reason to confirm it to Natalia.

"It's nothing." She shrugged. "You know what he's like."

Natalia lifted a brow. "If that's his *it's nothing* look, I'd like to see the *something* one."

She dug her teeth into her lip. Unable to resist, she swiveled on the stool, directing her gaze toward the group of men populating the lounge area behind them. It didn't take her long to locate Nik. Tall, dark and swarthy-skinned in a nod to his Mediterranean heritage, he looked…breathtaking.

The jacket of his silver-gray suit lay discarded on the back of his seat as per the jackets of the other men at the table, his white shirt open at the throat, his every physical cue as he lounged, long legs spread out in front of him, that of supreme confidence.

Her stomach twisted, her agitation intensifying. He looked like sex poured into an exquisitely made suit. Lethally powerful. *Dangerous.*

She lifted her gaze to his light, magnetic one that contrasted so vividly with his olive skin. Blue, an icy blue, it was focused on her in a not-so-discreet perusal, full of a sensual promise that took her breath away.

A wave of heat consumed her. He was just that *virile*.

Turning around, she reached for her glass and took a long sip with a hand that trembled ever so slightly. *Remember how discarded, how vulnerable you felt waiting for him to call this week.* That had to be her armor tonight.

You are going to do this, Sofía. You are not going to back out again. Muster your willpower.

"Bar bill says she will."

"You're on."

Nik pulled his attention away from Sofía and frowned at his two closest friends. "What's the wager for?"

"You." Harry, his best friend since college, flicked him an amused smile. "I bet the bar bill the eye candy over there breaks your self-imposed slump. Jake says she doesn't."

Nik could have told him she already had. That he and Sofía had been seeing each other for a couple of months. But he liked things the way they were. Private. *Uncomplicated.* Sizzling hot.

He took a sip of his whiskey, savoring the smoky flavor of the spirit before pointing his glass at Harry. "I've spent the past six months negotiating a free trade deal. A *landmark* free trade deal, I might add. It's not a slump. It's a lack of bandwidth."

Harry gave him a speculative look. "Still, you've been off. Your head isn't here. What gives?"

He wished he knew. Hadn't been sure what had been eating at him for a long time. All he *was* conscious of was that he *wasn't* himself, had been consumed by a restless craving for something he couldn't put his finger on.

What should have been the peak of his career, negotiating a free trade deal between his country and Mexico, a deal the critics had said couldn't be done, hadn't brought with it its usual adrenaline rush. Instead it had left him flat. Empty. Uninspired. A bit dead inside if he were to be honest.

But to try to explain that to his high-flying friends, still deeply immersed in the highs of their ultrasuccessful legal and banking careers, seemed pointless. That he, manager of a multibillion-dollar portfolio for his nation, a prince with unquestionable influence who could flick his fingers and have his heart's desire at a moment's notice, was having an identity crisis.

For what else could it be? Surely he was too young to be experiencing a *midlife* crisis?

He downed the last of his whiskey as their hostess slid off the stool beside Sofía, resisting the urge to delve too deeply into his head, because it never ended well, these ruminations of his. Thinking too much could make a man crazy.

"Maybe I need some inspiration," he murmured, getting to his feet.

"Yesss!" Harry held up a hand in victory. "I *knew* it."

Nik headed for Sofía, ignoring the group of women who had been sending unsubtle signals to their table for the past half hour. The closer he got, the more spectacular his lover became. Eschewing the rake-thin trend that always seemed de rigueur in Manhattan, Sofía had an hourglass figure that harkened back to the Hollywood starlets of the '50s and '60s. Curves that actually gave a man something to hold on to when he made love to her.

Her dark hair was up tonight, a fact that would have to change. It was the only accessory, he knew, she would need in his bed.

She was twirling a lock of her hair that had escaped her updo around a finger as he dropped down on the stool beside her, an uncharacteristically fidgety move for his ultracomposed lover. Her face was as spectacular as the rest of her as she turned to look at him: lush lips, a delicate nose and those startlingly beautiful long-lashed dark eyes.

"Your Highness," she greeted him huskily.

His mouth twisted at the game they played. "You know," he said, leaning toward her and lowering his voice, "you get punished when you call me that."

Anticipation would usually have sparked in her beautiful eyes at the exchange. Instead they darkened with an emotion he couldn't identify.

He frowned. "What's wrong? Bad sales day?"

She shook her head. "It was great. I—" She pushed her martini glass away. "Can we get out of here?"

He'd been on his way to suggesting the same thing, but there was something about her demeanor he didn't like. Those walls he'd broken down were back up.

He took out his wallet, threw some bills on the bar to cover the tab and stood up. "Meet me at the Eightieth Street entrance. Carlos will be waiting."

Sofía made a discreet exit while Nik bade good-night to his friends. A chill, at odds with the sultry heat, slid through her as she exited the building and walked toward the Bentley Carlos was pulling to a halt at the curb. He got out, greeted her by name and held the door open.

She slid into the car, its sleek leather interior filling her head with the scent of privilege and luxury. Her head swirled in a million directions as she waited for Nik. Should she tell him it was over here in the car? Short and sweet, no big scenes, which Nik would hate, then he could take her home? Or should she wait until they were at his place?

Nik joined her in the car minutes later. Instructing Carlos to take them to his penthouse on Central Park West, he lowered the privacy screen between them and the driver and sat back in his seat, his gaze scouring her face.

"What's wrong, Sofía?"

She swallowed hard. Decided the car was not where she wanted this discussion to take place. "Can it wait until we're at the penthouse?"

He inclined his head. *"Kala."* Fine.

She breathed an inward sigh of relief and sat back against the seat. Nik sank his hands into her waist, dragged her onto his lap and captured her jaw in his fingers. "You haven't properly said hello."

A wave of heat blanketed her. "We're in the car…"

"It's never bothered you before. " He lowered his head, his firm beautiful mouth brushing against hers. "And it's only a kiss."

And yet a kiss from Nik could be disastrous. Her lashes lowered as he captured her mouth in the most persuasive of caresses. Gentle, insistent, he claimed her again and again until her traitorous body responded, lighting up for him as it always did. Her lips clung to his, seeking closer contact.

Gathering her to him, Nik deepened the kiss, his fingers at her jaw holding her captive as he explored the softness of her lips, the recesses of her mouth. *All of her.*

A soft sound left her throat, her fingers curling in the thick hair at the base of his neck. Nik lifted his mouth from hers, a satisfied glitter in his eyes. "Now you don't look like a cardboard cutout. You look insanely beautiful tonight, Sofía."

"Efharisto." Thank you. A word he had taught her in his language. "And you," she murmured, "had your usual throng of fans."

His eyes glittered. "Jealous? Is that what has you off center for once? If so, I like it."

The taunt knocked some common sense into her head. She pushed a hand against his chest and forced him to let her go. Sliding off his lap, she took her seat back and straightened her hair. Searched desperately for a source of innocuous conversation to fill the space.

"Congratulations on your big deal. The analysts half expected it to fall through."

He inclined his head. "I thought it might at one point. But making the impossible happen is my forte."

She smiled. *No ego there.* But why wouldn't there be? First in his class at Harvard, a genius with numbers and forging high-stakes deals, the Wizard of Wall Street as he was known, he had turned his tiny Mediterranean island of Akathinia, a glittering former colonial jewel that hosted much of the world's glitterati, into a thriving, modern economy over the past decade, his reckless, some would say suicidal, deal making paying off with deep dividends for his country. It was the envy of the Mediterranean.

She shook her head. "Your need to win is insatiable, Nik."

"Yes," he said deliberately, his gaze trained on her. "It is."

A flush heated her cheeks. He had set out to win her after her initial resistance to his invitation to dinner and succeeded. Not a fair game, really, when she'd discovered the reckless, rebel prince had far more layers than anyone thought. Brilliant and deep with a philosophical side few knew about, he was undeniably fascinating.

She leaned her head back against the seat and eyed him. "What happens when winning isn't enough anymore?"

His lashes lowered in that sleepy, half-awake big cat look he did so well, when he was anything but. "I think I'm in the process of finding that out."

She blinked. It was the first deeply personal insight he'd given her. To have it come tonight of all nights was confusing. Tangled her up in a knot.

Carlos dropped them off. They rode the elevator, reserved exclusively for the penthouses, to the fifty-seventh floor and Nik's palatial abode.

Sofía kicked off her shoes while Nik opened a bottle of Prosecco and walked through to the salon with its magnificent views of the park, the floor-to-ceiling windows encasing the luxurious space offering a bird's-eye view of the Empire State Building and the sweep of the city with its breathtaking 360-degree perspective.

A light throb pulsed at her temples as she stood in front of the windows and took in the view. Lights blazed across the smoky, steamy New York skyline, as if a million falling stars had been embraced by the sweeping skyscrapers.

Nik's spicy aftershave filled her senses just before he materialized by her side with two glasses of sparkling wine. Tipping her glass toward him in the European-style version of the toast he preferred, her eyes on his, she drank.

Finding Nik's seeking gaze far too perceptive, she looked back at the view, following a jet as it made its way across the sky, silhouetted against the skyscrapers. It reminded her of what tomorrow was. Had her wondering if that was why she had chosen tonight to end this. Because it had reminded her of her priorities.

"You're thinking about your father."

"Yes. Tomorrow is the twentieth anniversary of his death."

"Has it gotten any easier?"

Did it ever get any easier when your father's plane dropped from the air into the Atlantic Ocean because of faulty mechanics that, properly addressed, could have saved his life? When it had cost *her* the guiding force of *her* life?

"You learn to let it go," she said huskily. "Accept that things don't always make sense in life. Sometimes they just happen. If I had allowed my anger, my sadness, my bitterness at the unfairness of it all to rule me, it's I who would have lost."

"An inherently philosophical way to look at it. But you were only eight when it happened, Sofía. It must have affected you deeply."

That seemed too slight a description for what had unraveled after that phone call in the middle of the night—her mother in her grief—her childhood ripped away in the space of a few hours with one parent gone and the other so emotionally vacant she might as well have been, too.

"I have an understanding of what it's like to lose something precious." She moved her gaze back to his. "It makes you aware of how easily it can all fall apart."

"And yet sometimes it doesn't. Sometimes you go on to make something of yourself. Create and run a successful business…"

Her mouth twisted. "Which could also fall apart if the market changes."

"*Any* business could fall apart if the market changes. It's the reality of being in the game. You don't anticipate failure, you believe in your vision."

She absorbed the verbal hand slap.

"How did you fund the business?" he asked. "You never did tell me."

"The airline was at fault for my father's accident. Faulty mechanics. The settlement was held in trust for me until I turned twenty-one. I put myself through design school on a scholarship in the meantime."

"What was the ultimate intention? The business or the designing?"

"Both. My first love is designing, but I put that on hold when we started the business. We needed to get the store in the black, pay off some investments. Now I finally feel like we're getting to the point where we can hire some staff and I can work on a line for the store."

"How many years have you been open now?"

"Six."

"Six years is a long time to wait on a dream, Sofía."

Heat singed her cheeks. "These things don't happen overnight. Interviewing is time-consuming, not to mention finding someone I can trust my baby with."

"Perhaps it's *you* you don't trust." Nik's softly worded challenge brought her chin up. "When you want something badly enough, you make it happen. There are no *can'ts* in life, only barriers we create for ourselves."

"I'm getting there." She hated the defensive note in her voice. "We don't all cut a swath through our lives like you do, Nik, impervious to anything or anyone but the end goal."

His gaze sharpened on her face. "Is that how you see me?"

"Isn't it true?"

He studied her silently for a moment. She looked away, his criticisms broaching an uncomfortable truth, one she'd been avoiding examining too closely. Putting off the designing had been practicality in the beginning when establishing Carlotta and finding a steady clientele had been a matter of survival. The problem was the longer she put it off, the harder it was to pick up her sketch pad again. Doubt had crept in as to whether she had what it took.

"You know what I think?" Nik said finally. "I think you're scared. I think you talk a good game, Sofía, but you aren't nearly as tough as you make yourself out to be. I think you're scared of investing yourself in something you care so much about because there's a chance you might fail. And it's personal, isn't it, designing for you? You're putting yourself out there. What if you do and New York rejects you? What if it *all falls apart*?"

She blinked at how scarily accurate that was. "I think that's a bit of a stretch."

"I don't." He stepped closer and reached up to trace a finger down her cheek, an electric charge zigzagging its way through her. "*I know how easily it can all fall apart.* Your words, not mine."

"Philosophical musings," she denied.

His fingers dropped to her mouth, tracing the line of her bottom lip. "I think my first impression of you at that benefit that night was right. You don't fully engage with life, you hold a part of yourself back so you won't get hurt. So there's no chance it *will* fall apart. But that's a delusion you feed yourself. Nothing can prevent a tragedy or a failure or someone walking away because it isn't right. To reap the reward you have to take the risk."

She had no answer for that because she was afraid it was true. All of it. But if it was true about her, it was equally, if not more so, true about him.

"And what about you?" she countered. "You hide yourself under this smooth veneer, Nik. No one ever really gets to know the real you. What you dream of. What you hope for. Tonight, what you said about winning, about not knowing what happens when it isn't enough anymore, it was the first time you've admitted anything truly intimate about yourself to me. And soon, my time will be up, won't it? You'll decide I'm getting too close, your attention span will wane and I'll receive a very nice piece of jewelry to kiss off and fade into the sunset."

His gaze darkened. "I never promised you more, Sofía. It's the way I am. You knew that."

"Yes," she agreed. "I did. We are two birds of a feather. Unwilling or unable to be intimate with someone else. Which is why I think we should end it now while it's still good. While we still like each other. So it doesn't get drawn out and bitter. We did promise ourselves that, after all, didn't we?"

His eyes widened, then narrowed. "You arranged to meet me tonight to *end* things between us?"

She forced herself to nod. "Be honest. You were going to do it soon, weren't you? Your silence this week was your way of demonstrating to me I can't depend on you."

His mouth tightened. "I was swamped this week, Sofía. But yes, I did think we should end it soon. I was waiting for the chemistry to burn its natural course."

Which it hadn't. She had a feeling it would be a long, long time before that happened. But it was about more than that for her now, more about who Nik was and how they connected on a deeper level. She'd thought it might be more for him, too, sometimes she could swear that it was, but apparently she'd been wrong.

She lifted her chin, her chest tight. She'd wanted to be different from the rest. Realized that's what tonight had been about. Wanting him to say they *were* different. And now she knew her delusion had been complete.

Nik closed the distance between them. There was a

dark glitter of emotion in his eyes she couldn't even come close to identifying. "It was good, Sofía."

"Yes," she agreed, shocked at how steady and resolute her voice was. "We were."

His gaze held hers—probing, searching. "Is *this* how you want to end us?"

"No." She stepped closer and lifted up on tiptoe, her eyes on his as she cupped the hard line of his jaw. "I wanted to end it like this."

CHAPTER TWO

HEAT FLARED IN Nik's gaze, wiping out the cool blue perusal that was his default expression and replacing it with a banked fire she knew preceded extreme pleasure.

He kissed her then, his lips parting hers with none of his earlier gentle coaxing. This time he demanded her acquiescence, *insisted* she give in to the electricity between them, and despite her better sense, she wanted this. She had known it would end like this, known it would *have* to end like this between them because their chemistry had always been beyond compare.

She sank into the kiss, gave herself permission to taste the lush depths of his mouth. The familiar, intoxicating flavor of him, enhanced by the wine, was deadly to her senses. She slid her arms around his waist to rest against the smooth fabric of his shirt. His hand came up to cup the back of her head, every bone in her body going liquid at the sensation of being back in his arms.

He released her lips to explore the curve of her jaw with butterfly kisses. She arched her neck to give him better access, sighing as he found the ultrasensitive spot between neck and shoulder. His fingers found the zipper of her dress and pulled it down, his palms sliding beneath the fabric, the heat of his fingers on her skin a brand she craved.

She pressed closer as his hands shifted lower to shape her hips against him. The heavy, potent force of his arousal imprinted itself on her; stirred a sweet, deep ache low in her abdomen.

"Nik..."

He pulled away from her and reached up to tug his tie loose. "Take off the dress."

She eyed him. "Was that an order?"

"What do you think?"

She couldn't deny the command was a turn-on. Power and his outrageous sex appeal were a lethal combination.

Electing to acquiesce, she slipped the straps of her dress off her shoulders, letting it fall to the floor. Nik stripped the tie off and reached for the buttons of his shirt. His eyes never left hers as he worked his way methodically down the row.

She stepped out of the dress. He crooked a finger at her. "Come here."

"I like these orders." She closed the distance between them. "You do the prince thing so well."

His mouth tipped up at one corner. He closed his fingers around hers and brought them to his unbuttoned shirt. "Take the rest off."

She slid the shirt off his broad shoulders, the anticipation of exploring all that masculine power making her feel all tied up inside. Her breath jammed in her throat as she dropped the shirt to the floor. He was so beautiful: powerful biceps and forearms honed at a Manhattan gym with a world-class boxer as a sparring partner every morning, his chest a work of art with its deep ridges defining rock-hard muscle. The sexy V that forged his lower abdomen drew her eyes to the potent masculinity straining against his trousers.

The low-grade intensity of his stare as she flicked the

button of his pants open and lowered his zipper made her stomach clench. Swallowing past her fervent anticipation, she tunneled her fingers underneath the waistband of his pants, bent and pushed them off his hips to the floor. Her position kneeling before him was undeniably provocative. As if she had been summoned to satisfy the prince's desire.

She found the thick, rigid evidence of his lust for her and freed it from his close-fitting black boxers. He was silky and mind-numbingly virile as she took him in her hands and ran her fingers from the base of him to the tip.

His hands curled in her hair. "In your mouth, Sofía. Take me in your mouth."

The rasp in his voice heated her blood. He had always loved it when she did this for him. It made him crazy. Desperate. But she didn't give him what he wanted, not right away. She teased him with her tongue first, tracing the throbbing veins that etched his shaft, exploring each one until his muffled curse filled the air. Only then did she take him deep into the heat of her mouth, again and again until his fists bunched tight in her hair and his patience failed.

"Enough."

He wrapped his fingers around her wrist and pulled her to her feet. A heady satisfaction filled her as he slid an arm beneath her knees and picked her up in a thrilling display of strength and carried her through to his bedroom. Dark and masculine it was dominated by an enormous four-poster bed. She landed on the whisper-soft silk bedspread. Nik stripped off his boxers and came down beside her.

Bracing himself on an elbow, he ran a finger across her bottom lip. "I have been craving this wicked mouth for weeks. On me, under me…"

Her heart slammed into her chest. She reached for him, curving her hands around his muscular torso. He caught her mouth in a kiss that was a blatant seduction, his tongue stroking the length of hers in a long, slow caress that made her shiver. The slide of his thumbs over her nipples deepened her shudder. They were already hard from wanting him, but his expert touch brought them to a rigid tautness that made her stomach curl, her insides ache. It had been too long since she'd had him and her body was crying out for release.

He broke the kiss, reached underneath her and unhooked her bra. The heat of his gaze on her turgid flesh made her tremble. He pushed himself upright to come down over her, his palms cupping her breasts. "I have missed these, too, *glykeia mou.*"

She closed her eyes as he took a rigid peak in his mouth. His tongue and teeth worked her nipple, the hard suction he applied intensifying the sweet ache inside of her. She moaned his name as he transferred his attention to her other nipple, his thumb teasing the damp, throbbing peak he'd left behind.

It was too much. Too much.

"Nik..."

His mouth still at her breast, he nudged her legs apart and slid his palm up her thigh. She trembled at the pleasure she knew he could give her, spreading wide for him. A guttural sound of approval left him. Her flesh was moist, ready for him as he pushed her panties aside and traced the line of her most intimate part.

God. She pressed her head back against the bed as he brought his thumb to the hard nub at the center of her at the same time he slid one of his long, masculine fingers inside of her. Her body tightened around him, missing him, aching for his touch. Nik knew how to work a woman until she begged; always made sure she was never anything less than fully aroused before he took her. Made her *wild* for him.

His eyes were hot on her face now, watching her reactions, absorbing every sound of pleasure she made. Slowly, deliberately, he brought her higher, until her hips were writhing against his hand. Then he added another finger and filled her so exquisitely, her vision glazed over. Her hands clenched the silk coverlet as the pleasure built and built until she was drowning in it.

Eyes glittering, he brought his mouth down to hers, their breath mingling. "Come for me, Sofía. *Now.*"

His sexy command pushed her over the edge. The insistent caress of his thumb against her nerve endings strung tight with tension sent her spiraling into a white-hot release that curled her toes. A release only Nik could give her.

His mouth closed over hers as he kissed her through every mind-numbing second of it, murmuring his husky approval of her response against her lips. She shuddered and grasped his powerful biceps to ground herself as the aftershocks tore through her.

He lifted himself off her, ready to retrieve a condom. The magnificence of his virility in full arousal was heart-stopping. *Indescribable.* "No," she said, curling her fingers around his arm, wanting, *needing* the intimacy of them together, just them, this last night. "I'm protected. You know that. Can't it just be us?"

He hesitated, his hand midway to the bedside table drawer, then he came back to her, settling his hard body between her thighs. *"Nai,"* he murmured, bringing his mouth down to hers. "I want that, too."

In bed, out of it, in the elevator to his penthouse, their lovemaking had not lacked in creativity. But tonight, he palmed her thigh and brought it around his waist in the most traditional of positions.

"So I can watch your face," he murmured, reading her expression. "I want to see you as I take you apart, Sofía."

The dark emotion in his eyes marked him angry. Angry that she was ending it, not he. He would ensure she thought of nothing but this in the future and she was sure, in turn, he would be right.

He notched himself into her slick opening and slid into her welcoming body. She gasped as he buried himself to the hilt, pressing an openmouthed kiss against her throat as he stayed motionless deep inside her. She felt him everywhere, stimulating every nerve ending, making her entire body feel alive.

He withdrew and took her again and again, the silky sensation of his body sliding against hers incredible, imprinting itself on her mind in a possession that claimed every last piece of her. She blinked, holding back the emotion storming through her. Nik brought his mouth to her ear telling her how sexy she was, how good she felt, refusing to take his own release until she came again with him.

When she cried out against his mouth and he stiffened and allowed himself to join her in a powerful orgasm that shook them both, she had never experienced anything so exquisitely intimate as the sensation of Nik joining his body with hers without reservation.

She collapsed on his chest, catching her breath as Nik smoothed a hand over her hair. Long moments passed, moments that felt suspended in time. She should go, she told herself when their breath evened out in the shadows of the silent room. Tonight was not the night to linger. Not when it felt as if Nik had taken all the control she'd walked in here with and decimated it.

She slid out of bed, found the beautiful champagne-colored dress, slipped it and her underwear on, then found her shoes in the salon. Nik followed her, watching her silently as he leaned against the wall in the entranceway, clad only in boxers. She slipped her shoes on, pulled the last of the pins from her hair, long since having lost its updo, and smoothed a hand over it.

"Regrets?" Nik asked as she came to stand in front of him.

"No." She stood on tiptoe to brush a kiss against his cheek. "No regrets."

She left before the conversation could drag on into something painful and awkward. Carlos was waiting for her downstairs, that same pleasant smile fixed on his face as had been there earlier. She slid into the back of the car, unable to summon a smile in return, and rested her head against the back of the seat as Carlos climbed in and set the car into motion.

A raw, achy feeling invaded her. She wrapped her arms around her chest to ward it off. She'd lied to Nik upstairs, perhaps to save face. Because if this was what taking risks felt like, she didn't need them in her life. She'd rather feel empty than feel any more pain.

Fully awake and unable to sleep after Sofía left, Nik pulled on shorts and a faded Harvard T-shirt and took a glass of Prosecco into the salon.

Ending things with Sofía had been the right thing to do. She had been starting to get attached. He could see the signs; they were unmistakable for a man who'd spent his life avoiding commitment. And perhaps he'd already let it go on for too long, because hadn't he always known Sofía was different from the rest of the sycophants he'd dated? Tough with a vulnerable underside… Content to keep their affair between the two of them because she didn't care about the rest.

Content to keep it uncomplicated. And yet tonight it had gotten complicated. He had hurt her.

His insides twisted. His rule never to allow a woman too close, to trust *anyone* in his position, was based on experience. He was a target for fame seekers, for those who sought to use him to further their own agendas. Charlotte, his ex-girlfriend, who'd sold her story to the tabloids and almost destroyed his family's reputation was a prime example.

Not that he put Sofía in that category. She was different. He had trusted her. He thought, perhaps, he was more angry than anything. Angry she'd broken things off first. Angry because he'd thought their relationship still had legs—the sexual part of it that is. It was the first time a woman had initiated an end to a mutually beneficial relationship. He couldn't deny it stung.

A wry smile curved his lips. Perhaps he'd had that one coming for a long time.

He pulled out his laptop, deciding to work through a few emails he'd left earlier to attend the event. His personal aide, Abram, who must have seen the light, knocked and entered from the adjoining staff quarters.

Equal parts friend, butler and highly trained fixer, Abram was sometimes dour, frequently circumspect, but *never* flustered. And yet, right now, in the heart of the Manhattan night, he looked distinctly agitated.

"What is it now?" Nik asked. "Don't tell me—King Idas has somehow managed to put my brother's nose out of joint with yet another expulsion of hot air."

Abram fixed his faded green gaze on him. The tumultuous light he saw there made his heart skip a beat.

"Crown Prince Athamos has been in an accident, Your Highness. He is dead."

The room dissolved around him. He rested a palm against the sofa, his head spinning. "An accident," he repeated. "It's not possible. I just spoke with Athamos last night."

Abram dipped his head. "I'm so sorry, sir. It happened last evening in Carnelia. It's taken time to verify the reports."

His blood turned to ice. His mind raced as he attempted to process what his aide had just told him. His brother had been raging about Akathinia's overly amorous suitor last night, its sister island Carnelia and its king, Idas, who wanted to annex Akathinia back into the Catharian Islands to which it had once belonged over a century ago. Insanity in this age of democracy, but there were enough examples around the world to put everyone on edge.

Nik had talked his brother off the ledge. *What the hell had happened after that?*

"What was he doing in Carnelia?"

"The facts are thin at the moment. There was an argument of some sort over a woman. Prince Athamos and Crown Prince Kostas of Carnelia decided to settle it with a car race through the mountains, the same route the ancient horse race used to take." His aide paused. "An onlooker said Prince Athamos took a curve too steeply. His car plunged off the cliff and into the ocean."

An argument? Over a woman? His brother was as levelheaded as Nik was passionate and reckless. And yet he had gotten into his car and raced his arch nemesis through the suicidal cliffs of Carnelia? *His enemy's domain?* A man known to have as much fire in his veins as his hotheaded, tyrannical father…

He worked to free his throat from the paralysis th̲
claimed it. "Are they sure…?"

"That he is dead?" Abram nodded. "I'm sorry, sir.
Witnesses say there is no possibility a man could have
emerged alive from that drop. They are working to recover his body now."

"And Kostas," Nik grated. "He survived?"

Abram nodded. "He was a car length behind. He saw
the whole thing happen."

A red rage blurred his vision, mixing with the agony
that gripped his insides to form a deadly, potent storm.
He got up and walked blindly to the windows, the spectacular skyline of Manhattan unfolding in front of him.

All he could see was red.

The clink of crystal sounded behind him. Abram came
to stand beside him and pressed a glass of whiskey into
his hand. Nik raised it to his mouth and took a long swig.
When he had emptied half the glass, his aide cleared his
throat. "There is more."

More? How could there be more?

"Your father took the news of the accident badly. He
has suffered a severe heart attack. The doctors are holding out hope he will survive, but it's touch and go."

A complete sense of unreality enveloped him. His fingers gripped the glass tighter. "What is his condition?"

"He is in surgery now. We'll know more in a few
hours."

He lifted the tumbler to his lips with a jerky movement
and downed another long swallow. The fire the potent li-
quor lit in his insides wasn't enough to make the reality
of losing both his father and his brother in one day in any
way conceivable. His father was too strong, too vigor-
ous to let such a thing fell him. It could not happen. Not

when their estrangement ate at his insides like a slow-moving disease.

He flicked a look at his aide. "The jet is ready?"

Abram nodded. "Carlos is waiting downstairs to drive you to the airfield. I thought you might want to gather some things. I will stay behind and take care of the outstanding details, cancel your commitments, then join you in Akathinia."

Nik nodded. Abram melted into the shadows.

Alone at the window, Nik looked out at Manhattan sprawled in front of him, his brother's voice, crystal clear on the phone the night before, filling his head. Athamos had sounded vital, belligerent. *Alive.* Despite the different philosophical viewpoints he and his brother had held, despite the wedges that had been driven between them in the past few years as Athamos had prepared to take over from his father as king, they had loved each other deeply.

It was inconceivable he was dead.

The sense of unreality blanketing him thickened into a dark fog with only one thought breaking through. *He* was now heir to the throne. *He* would be king.

It was a role he had never expected to have, never wanted. He had been happy to allow Athamos to take the spotlight while he did his part in New York to make Akathinia the thriving, successful nation that it was. Happy to keep his distance from the wounds of the past.

But fate had other plans for him and his brother...

Sorrow and rage gripped his heart, engulfing him like the inescapable gale force winds of the *meltemia* that ravaged the Akathinian shores without warning or mercy. His hand tightened around the glass as the storm swept over him, immersing him in its turbulent fury until all he could see was red.

Abram's horrified gasp split the air. He followed his

aide's gaze down to his bleeding hand, the shattered remains of the glass strewn across the carpet. The dark splatter that seeped into the plush cream carpet seemed like the stain on his heart that would never be removed.

Nik reached his father's bedside at noon the following day. Exhausted from an overnight trip during which he hadn't slept, worry for his father consuming him, he pulled a chair up to the king's bedside in the sterilized white hospital room and closed the fingers of his unbandaged hand around his father's gnarled, wrinkled one.

The king's shock of white hair contrasted vividly with his olive skin, but his complexion was far too pale for Nik's liking.

"Pateras."

Light blue eyes, identical to his own, opened to focus on him.

"Nikandros."

He squeezed his father's hand as the king opened his mouth and then closed it. A tear escaped his father's eyes and slid down his weathered cheek. The weight of a thousand disagreements, a thousand regrets crowded Nik's heart.

He bent and pressed his lips to his father's leathery cheek. "I know."

King Gregorios shut his eyes. When he opened them again, a fierce determination burned in their depths. "Idas will never get what he wants."

An answering fury stirred to life inside of him. "He will never take Akathinia. But if he is behind Athamos's death, he will pay for it."

"It was no *accident*," his father bit out. "Idas and his son want to provoke us into a conflict so they can use it as an excuse to swallow us up to cover their own inadequacies."

He was well aware of the reason Carnelia wanted Akathinia back in the fold, but he sought to keep a rational head. "The grudge between Athamos and Kostas has been going on for years. We need the facts."

The king's mouth curled. "Kostas is his father's errand boy."

Nik raked a hand through his hair. "The Carnelian military is twice the size of ours. Akathinia is prospering, but we cannot match what they have built up, even to defend ourselves."

His father nodded. "We have made an economic alliance with the Agiero family to acquire the resources we need. Athamos was to marry the Countess of Agiero to tie the two families together. The announcement was imminent."

His head reeled. A marriage had been in the works while Athamos had been carrying on an affair with another woman? Why had his brother not mentioned it to him?

His father fixed his steely blue gaze on him. "I will never rule again. You will marry the countess once you are coronated king. Cement the alliance."

He swallowed hard, all of it too much to process. His father's gaze sharpened on his face. "You must be a leader now, Nikandros. As strong as your brother was. The time has come to step up to your responsibilities."

His responsibilities? Hadn't he been bankrolling this nation with his work in New York? Hadn't he made Akathinia the talk of the Mediterranean—the place to visit—where almost every one of his people had a job? Antagonism heated his skin. What had it taken, five, six sentences for his father to start drawing comparisons between him and his brother? *Unfavorable* comparisons.

His father and Athamos had always been in lockstep,

their philosophies on life and ruling at polar opposites of his own. He was progressive, rooted in his experiences abroad; they remained stuck in the past, preferring to cling to outdated tradition.

He had always been the afterthought. The prince embedded in New York, quietly building the fortunes of his country while his father and brother took the credit.

His desire to make peace with his father faded on a surge of antagonism. Always it was like this.

The machine at the side of the bed started beeping. Nik lifted a wary eye to it. "You must rest," he told his father. "You are weak. You need to recuperate."

His father sank back against the pillows and closed his eyes. Nik released his hand and stood up. To battle the enemy was one thing. Locking horns with his father another campaign entirely. The latter could prove to be a far more stubborn, drawn-out war of wills.

CHAPTER THREE

SOFÍA WAS CONSCIOUS of the fact that chocolate was emotional gratification of the highest level, emotional gratification that would dissipate as rapidly as it left her bloodstream. But since nothing else was working, she was giving it her best shot.

In the weeks following her final assignation with Nik she'd promised herself she would move on. She'd been fairly successful at it, throwing herself into her work at the boutique and interviewing for a new staff member—what she considered the silver lining of her and Nik's split—the knowledge that she did, indeed, need to pursue her dream, *now* not later. But somehow, after all their weeks of keeping their relationship out of the public eye, a photographer had documented her and Nik's departure from Natalia's benefit. Had immortalized their final adieu.

Putting the whole thing behind her had become an exercise in futility. Which would all have been bad enough, if the rumors of Nik's pending engagement to the Countess of Agiero hadn't added fuel to the fire. The press were having a field day comparing her to the stately countess. If she heard herself described as the fiery temptress of Latin descent versus the icy, cool aristocrat Nik was about to marry one more time, she was going to start living up to her nickname.

Tearing the paper off the bar of dark European chocolate she'd purchased at the corner store, she shoved a piece in her mouth and began the walk back to the boutique.

She was also hurt, she acknowledged. That Nik was to be engaged to a woman weeks after their own affair had ended stung. That she was just *that* forgettable. Her rational brain told her there were political factors behind it given the countess's powerful family, but Vittoria Agiero's stunning beauty was a kick in the ribs. As was the fact she was a blue-blooded aristocrat whom Sofía would be more likely to dress than ever rub elbows with.

She tore off another piece of chocolate and popped it in her mouth. Emotional gratification had never tasted so good. Not when her mixed cauldron of emotions also included her sorrow for Nik. Her heart went out to him for what he was going through. She wanted to be there to comfort him in the storm he was facing. And how crazy was that, because he'd made it clear he didn't want her.

Still, it made her heart ache to look at the photos from his brother's funeral, from his coronation day, which had taken place a month after Athamos's death. He had looked stone-faced through all of it, devoid of emotion. But she knew it was all a cover for a man who carried his feelings bottled up inside of him.

Katharine gave the chocolate bar in her hand a wry look as Sofía made her way through the chime-enabled doors of the boutique.

"That's one a day this week. You going to let him ruin your figure along with everything else?"

Sofía scowled at the woman who'd been her best friend since design school. "This has nothing to do with him. I was too hungry to wait for lunch."

Katharine hung the dress she was holding on a hanger.

"I think you have depression hunger. The *to hell with it* kind."

"I'm also starving." Sofía set the chocolate bar down on the counter and reached for the bottle of water she'd stashed behind the register. "Like nauseous hungry if I don't eat lately. It must be the exercise."

She'd been sweating it out in a fitness class every night to take the place of her dates with Nik. It was definitely helping her figure, despite the chocolate.

Katharine gave her a funny look. "You know what that sounds like, right?"

Sofía blinked. Blanched. "*Oh, no.* It couldn't be. We were always careful. *Obsessively* careful."

Katharine shrugged. "I've just never seen you eat junk food."

A customer popped out of the fitting room at the back of the store. Her partner went to assist her. Sofía put the bottle down on the counter, a jittery feeling running through her. *There was no way she was pregnant.* She was on birth control.

She pulled her phone from her purse and checked the calendar. The blood drained from her face. *Dear God.* She was late. She hadn't even noticed given the insanity of her life of late.

"Back in a minute," she blurted to Katharine, grabbing her purse and hightailing it out the door. There was only one way to dispel the impossibility of what was running through her head.

At the drugstore, she snatched two pregnancy tests from the shelf, paid for them and flew back to the boutique, where she locked herself in the bathroom and administered them. Two solid blue plus signs later she stood looking at a disaster in the making.

"Sofía…" Katharine banged on the door. "Are you okay?"

"Fine."

Katharine's tone was grim. "Open up."

She opened the door. Held up the stick.

Katharine's face dropped. "Did you do more than one?"

Her head bobbed up and down.

"Okay," her friend said slowly, "This is what we're going to do. You're going to remain calm until you see your doctor. Then you can panic."

Except seeing her doctor the following morning only triple confirmed what she already knew. She was pregnant. And no amount of denial or panic was going to change it.

Nik lifted his gaze from the seemingly endless document recapping plans for the immediate expansion of the armed forces, his eyes having glazed over ten minutes ago. Undoubtedly it was a complex, tightly timed schedule on how the government should move forward, but he failed to see how it required fifty pages to bring him up to speed. He'd gotten the gist by page five.

Exhaling deeply, his gaze slid to the pile of newspapers on his desk. Admittedly, part of his distraction might have to do with the picture of Sofía on the front page of the society section of one of the New York papers, her face turned down as she left her apartment. Beautiful Sofía Trumped by a Countess Licks Her Wounds blared the headline.

Aside from being patently untrue—spirited Sofía could never be found lacking versus his chilly soon-to-be fiancée—the racy headlines weren't helping his merger with the Agiero family. Although when it came to Vittoria, it was hard to tell if it was just her stiff demeanor or that her nose was, in fact, out of joint. He had dined with her three times now and was actually wondering how he was going to psyche himself up to bed her. Beautiful she might be; engaging and personable she was not.

Unfortunately, he and the countess were announcing their engagement next week and his choice of who to bed would be forever taken away from him. As it had been with everything else.

His chest tightened at the thought of what he'd had and what he'd lost. Things that would never be given back to him. His brother. His life. The world as he'd known it. It was like opening a can of worms, thinking about it. He'd tried not to.

His life had been a living hell since he'd come back to Akathinia, his father's recovery slow, his country's recovery from its crown prince's death equally lengthy and sorrow-ridden, particularly given Carnelia's failure to deliver anything other than a formally worded apology via messenger. *As if that would ever do.*

His coronation had been a blur. He was fairly sure he had processed little of it, his only focus his increasingly verbose neighbor who continued to insist Akathinia was better off back within the Catharian island fold—a desire that Nik knew was motivated by economic reasons. Carnelia's economy was struggling, had been for years, and Akathinia was prospering. It wasn't hard to put two and two together.

And, if he were to be honest, he wanted, *needed* to prove to his father and the people that he had the ability to lead this country as well or better than Athamos would have. It was something that kept him up at night.

Exhaling a long breath, he took a sip of his coffee, set

the cup down and returned his attention to the report in front of him, skipping to the conclusion. His attention was pulled away once again when Abram knocked on the door and entered.

"Sorry to interrupt, sir."

He lifted a brow.

"You asked me to keep an eye on Ms. Ramirez, given the news coverage."

His fingers dropped away from the papers. "Is she all right?"

"She's fine." Abram clasped his hands together in front of him. "There has been a development."

"Which is?"

"Ms. Ramirez is pregnant."

"Pregnant?" He repeated the word as if he couldn't possibly have heard it right.

"We had a detail on her as you requested, with so many photographers still trailing her. She purchased a pregnancy test earlier this week, then saw her doctor."

Thee mou. His brain attempted to absorb what his aide was telling him. It was *inconceivable.* They had been so careful.

A buzzing sound filled his head. "And the doctor? We know for sure it was confirmed?"

"Yes."

He got to his feet, his head spinning violently. It was impossible. *Impossible.*

He excused Abram. Paced the room and attempted to wrap his head around what he'd just been told. He was going to be a father. Sofía was carrying the heir to Akathinia. It was a disaster of incalculable proportions.

It occurred to him Sofía hadn't told him because the baby wasn't his. But as soon as the idea filled his head, he discarded it. Sofía hadn't had a lover before him for a long while. *They* had been exclusive. That he knew.

So why not tell him? What was she waiting for? An image of that last time they'd been together filled his head. Woke up old demons. Sofía running a finger down his cheek. *I wanted to end it like this.* The emotion he'd read in her eyes that said she'd gotten too attached. How she'd stopped him when he'd reached for a condom... *Can it be just us tonight?*

Blood pounded his temples. Had she bedded him that night with the intention of getting pregnant? It seemed so at odds with Sofía's independent personality. With her acceptance of the no commitment rules of their relationship. Yet didn't he know from personal experience just how far a woman was willing to go to keep a prince? To preserve a relationship she knew was ending?

His head was in only a slightly better state when he found his father taking a mandated walk in the formal gardens. He curtly broke the news, without preamble. The king's leathery old face turned thunderous.

"*Pregnant? Thee mou*, Nikandros. We have all turned a blind eye to your philandering, but to have her conceive your heir? Have you lost your mind?"

His jaw hardened. "It was not planned, obviously."

"By *you*. What about by her?" He shook his head. "Has history taught you nothing?"

A red mist descended over his vision. "Sofía is not Charlotte."

"You wouldn't hear ill of your first American plaything either. Then she sold her story to the tabloids and seriously damaged the reputation of this family."

And his father would never let him forget it. Never mind the fact that Gregorios had indulged in countless affairs during his marriage, had torn this family apart and was far from a saint.

His father waved a hand at him. "No use dwelling on your irresponsibility. We are on top of this. It gives us a chance to deal with it. Consider our options."

His heart skipped a beat. "What *options* are you referring to?"

"We need this alliance with the Agieros."

What his father *didn't* say rendered him speechless. When he did recover his voice, his tone was as sharp as a blade. "This is the heir to the Akathinian throne we're talking about. What exactly are you suggesting?"

"We can make this go away. There will be other heirs."

Stars exploded in his head. He clenched his hands by his sides. "Do not utter that thought ever again."

"Don't be naive about her, Nikandros. Women are your downfall. They always have been."

Nik gave him a dismissive look. "I'm flying to New York on Friday."

His father gaped at him. "You can't leave the country right now."

"Idas is not going to start a war overnight. I'll be there and back in twenty-four hours."

"And if it gets out you've left Akathinia at this crucial time?"

"It won't."

"Send Abram."

Nik pinned his gaze on his father. "As you've just said, the country is on tenterhooks right now. I am trusting no one to deal with this extremely sensitive issue but me. I know Sofía. I know how to reason with her. We'll be back within twenty-four hours."

His father clenched his jaw. "This is insanity."

Nik shook his head. "Insanity was when Athamos

decided to take Kostas on in a suicidal race neither of them should have survived. *This* is practicality. Sofía is carrying my heir. Marriage is the only answer."

Sofía turned the sign on the boutique door to "closed," kicked off her shoes and carried them to the register, where she started doing the nightly deposit. Working was preferable to facing up to the question of when she was going to tell Nik she was carrying the royal heir.

When she unleashed a ticking time bomb with the potential to rock a nation and its leader at a time when it needed it the least...

From the timing the doctor had given her, she had conceived her and Nik's baby the night they'd ended it. When she'd questioned the effectiveness of her birth control pills, the doctor had informed her the migraine medication she was on could have interfered with the pill's effectiveness, a fact she hadn't been aware of. A fact she'd desperately wished she'd been in possession of.

That she'd gotten pregnant that night seemed to be the only thing she *was* certain of. That and the fact that she was keeping this baby. *Treasuring* it.

Her initial shock had faded into sheer, debilitating panic as her life shifted beneath her feet once again. How could this be happening *now*, when this was her time to shine? Her time to begin her design career with her business thriving. She'd even hired someone last week to make it happen.

She knew how difficult it was to bring up a child on your own. She'd watched her mother attempt to do it after her father's death and fail under the unrelenting pressure of the responsibility. *She* had been the one to parent her mother when her mother had lapsed into a deep depression. And yet what choice did she have? Nik was marrying someone else, he hadn't wanted her and it was up to her to figure this out, regardless that the life of an entrepreneur was completely unsuitable for what she was about to take on.

Overriding it all, however, had been the elemental, protective instinct that had risen up inside of her. That had always been in her DNA. The need to treasure what she'd been given. The need to protect the fragility of life. Although the sheer, debilitating panic still came in waves, something she had to keep a handle on, using the coping techniques the doctor had given her after her father's death, lest it get out of hand. Not a place she wanted to be.

She counted the twenty-dollar bills for the third time, her concentration in tatters from all the possible scenarios running through her head. The door chimed. Katharine went to intercept the customer who'd ignored the closed sign. Sofía kept counting. Her gaze rose as a funny sound escaped her partner's mouth.

The tall, dark male standing inside the door swept both of them with an enigmatic look. "You should lock the door if you're closed. This is New York, ladies."

The deposit bag slipped from her fingers. Eyes trained on Nik, she knelt and picked it up. He walked toward her, bent and scooped up two loose twenty-dollar bills, then straightened to tower over her. Their eyes locked. Her heart jumped into her mouth. Nik in full-on intensity mode was ridiculously intimidating.

She swallowed hard. "Nik— I— What are you doing here?"

"We need to talk, Sofía."

Her mouth went dry. *He couldn't know.* She had *just* seen her doctor. Then what was he doing here when tensions were running high in his country over its aggressive neighbor? Why did he have that furious glint in his eyes?

Katharine cleared her throat. "I have plans with my sister for a drink. I'll see you tomorrow."

She wanted to beg her not to go. Would have preferred a buffer between her and Nik until she figured out how to handle his unexpected appearance. How to tell him about the baby. Instead she nodded, a sinking feeling in her stomach. She had to get it over with now. She'd already waited too long.

She forced a smile. "See you in the morning."

The store was vastly, terrifyingly quiet after Katharine left. Sofía set the deposit bag on the counter and looked up at Nik. "I'm so sorry about your brother. About everything that's happened."

He inclined his head, his abrupt nod toward the deposit bag dismissing the subject. "Finish the deposit. We'll talk afterward."

The heated expression on his face made the hairs on the back of her neck stand up. She counted the rest of the money with trembling hands and shoved it in the deposit bag. Tried to convince herself Nik was in New York on urgent business and had simply dropped in to see her.

It seemed very unlikely.

She set the deposit bag on the counter and closed the register. Nik nodded toward the bag. "We'll drop it off, then talk."

She crossed her arms over her chest. "We can talk here."

"No." He picked up her purse and handed it to her. "We'll do it at home."

She was too tired, too frazzled to argue with him. They dropped the deposit into the slot at the bank, then Nik tucked her into the back of the Bentley and slid in beside her.

She tried to ignore how much she wanted to throw up.

What he would say when she told him her news. *How* she was going to tell him.

Lost in her thoughts, vainly trying to devise a strategy, she frowned as the driver took an unfamiliar exit. "I thought we were going home."

"We are. To Akathinia."

She jackknifed into an upright position. *"What?"*

"I can't be here. The fact I left the country with Idas breathing down my neck caused my advisers considerable anxiety. We'll talk in Akathinia."

She gaped at him. "We are *not* talking in Akathinia. I have a business to run. Take me home and we'll talk there."

His gaze turned incendiary. "You lost your chance to set the rules of the game when you elected to keep your pregnancy from me, Sofía."

Dear God. He knew. She swallowed hard and forced herself to stay calm. "I was going to tell you. This week."

"This week?" He yelled the words at her, his iron control snapping. "Do you have any idea what this means?"

Her insides flip-flopped. "Of course I do. Which is why I haven't said anything yet. Because I knew you would appear just like you have now and start making decisions. And I need to understand how I feel about this first. What I want to do."

His gaze narrowed on her. "What you want *to do*?"

Heat rushed to her cheeks. "I didn't mean that. Of course I'm having this baby. It's the logistics I'm not sure of."

"Logistics we should have discussed days ago."

She stared at him. So she'd been wrong in not telling him. Did he think this was any more convenient for her with her lifestyle? Any less than a disaster than it was for him?

Her chin dipped. "We can talk about this over the phone."

He caught her jaw in his fingers, the rage burning in his eyes making her heart pound. "We aren't talking about it on the phone. Akathinian law says this child we have conceived will succeed me to the throne. It doesn't matter if he or she is born in or out of wedlock. Which means I cannot marry the countess. My alliance is dead, an alliance I needed to fund a potential war." His fingers tightened around her jaw to ensure he had her attention. "It's a huge problem, Sofía. One we need to work out *now*."

Her insides twisted. She hadn't known Akathinian law well enough to draw that conclusion. Hadn't *wanted* to know.

She took a deep breath, inhaling past the tightness in her chest. For the first time she noticed how deep the lines bracketing Nik's eyes and mouth were. How stressed he looked. This pregnancy was a disaster in the current circumstances and she had made it worse by keeping it from him.

Guilt slammed into her, swift and hard.

"Come with me," he said flatly. "Before my actions set off a national security crisis. We'll talk and figure this out."

She pursed her lips. "I would need to see if Katharine can handle the shop by herself."

"Call her."

She fished out her mobile and dialed her partner. Katharine assured her she'd be fine for a couple of days.

"All right," she said to Nik. "I'll go. We talk. And then you fly me back."

He nodded. *"Efharisto."* Thank you.

It occurred to her as they boarded the plane at a small

private airfield outside of the city that she was putting herself on Nik's turf, where he yielded complete power. The power of a king. Perhaps not the wisest of decisions, she acknowledged as the tiny jet took off and left the lights of Manhattan behind. But she couldn't add any more stress to his life. Not now.

She waited until she'd endured what was always a white-knuckle affair for her in the takeoff before curling up in one of the chairs in the seating area of the luxurious jet. Then she attacked the elephant in the room. Or aircraft, as it would be...

"I know this has huge ramifications for you, Nik, but it does for me, as well. How do we deal with the distances? How am I going to juggle a baby and the shop?"

He leveled his gaze on her. "You aren't. You're the future Queen of Akathinia, Sofía. Queens don't work."

She stared at him. *Queen?* That would entail her being married to him... "You can't be serious."

His mouth flattened, the determination on his face making her heart pound. "Unless this baby turns out to be someone else's, which I highly doubt, then yes, I am entirely serious."

She didn't like the edge to his voice or the look on his face. "Of course it's yours. How can you even ask that?"

He looked at her as if she was naive to be asking the question. "How far along are you?"

"Eight weeks."

"A blood test will confirm it, then." He lifted a brow. "Funny how we were obsessively careful not to allow a pregnancy to happen and yet, magically, it happened on that last night when you asked me not to wear a condom."

She stared at him. "*Tell me* you are not suggesting I manufactured this pregnancy."

He shrugged, his face as hard as she'd ever seen it. "It wouldn't be the first time in history it's happened."

The blood drained from her face. She yanked off her seat belt and launched herself at him, her palm arcing through the air toward his cheek. He caught her hand before it got anywhere near his face and yanked it down to her side, pulling her onto his lap.

"Bastard," she hissed at him. "I can't believe you have the nerve to say that. To *me*, Nik. *Me* of all people. I was perfectly fine with the rules. *I* ended it."

"After you *told me* how you wanted to end it." His eyes scoured her face. "Were you using a little reverse psychology on me, Sofía? Being the one to end it first so I'd realize my mistake? Then along comes a baby?"

"You are insane," she gritted out, unable to free her hands to claw his eyes out. "Have you lost your mind over the past few weeks, Nik, because clearly you know me well enough to know I would never do that."

His mouth flattened. "I *thought* I knew you. But I also know how you were acting that night. I know the signs. You were getting too attached. Women can do uncharacteristic things when they want to hang on to a relationship."

Her head felt as if it was going to explode. "I *ended* it."

"You knew I was going to."

He *was* crazy. She tugged hard on her arm but he held her tight. "I am not marrying you."

He gave her a weary look. "We will. It's the only solution."

"No, it isn't. I don't want to get married. I live in New York. I have a business there. I'm not leaving it."

"What we both *want* doesn't figure into this. The only thing that matters is that you are carrying the royal heir. End of story."

Her blood ran cold. "There are other ways to make this work."

"I'm afraid there aren't." His beautiful mouth tipped up on one side. "Think of it this way. There is now no limit to how many times we can have each other. In fact, the more the better. A spare to the throne is clearly ideal. We can work out the rest of that explosive chemistry of ours."

His hard thighs burned into her bottom. The memory of what they'd done in exactly this position in the back of the Bentley sent a heated flush to every inch of her skin. She pushed a hand against his chest. "You *have* lost your mind."

A wry smile curved his mouth. "Surprisingly, I think I've kept it over the past few weeks. And believe me, Sofía, it was no mean feat."

She stopped fighting. Her breath jammed in her lungs as her brain caught up with what was happening. "You set this up. You told me we were going to talk at home so I'd get in the car and you could get me on this plane and my will would be taken away from me."

"So smart," he mocked, lifting a hand in an indolent gesture. "And so right."

She called him the filthiest name she could think of.

His smile grew. "I'm a king, Sofía. I do what I have to do."

CHAPTER FOUR

SOFÍA PACED THE palace library, oblivious to the stunning, chandelier-accented glory of the gold-and-mahogany-hued room. She wished she knew where among the exquisite first editions and precious bound volumes she could find a thesaurus. It might help her to put a label on her current set of emotions toward Nik, because *fury* seemed too little a word.

Anger, rage, wrath—they couldn't come close to encompassing the tempestuous feelings enveloping her in waves. How *dare* Nik trick her into coming here. How *dare* he assume she would give up her life in New York and marry him, just because she was having his child. Yes, she was carrying the heir to the Akathinian throne, but *she* wasn't Akathinian. She had a business in Manhattan to run. A business that meant everything to her.

Her insides roiled, sending the heat in her cheeks even higher. And then there was the utterly inconceivable accusation he'd thrown at her. *That she'd planned the pregnancy.* That she'd wanted to *trick* him into marriage. She knew Nik was cynical in the extreme, hardened from his life in the spotlight and those who would have used him had he allowed it, but to accuse her of all people of that? It was ludicrous.

Her fury and anxiety at being so helpless, so far from

home, so *out of control* of this situation had her breath coming fast and furious. Throwing herself into one of the leather chairs near the windows, she forced herself to take deep breaths, to calm down as she watched the million-dollar yachts bobbing in the harbor.

She might not be able to change the fact that she was here, but she could tell Nik how unreasonable he was being when he returned from his meeting with the Agieros, where he was attempting to avoid a diplomatic crisis as he broke off his engagement, given the results of the blood test had proved conclusively the child she carried was his. That giving up her business, uprooting her life and moving here to a little island in the middle of the Mediterranean to become his *queen* was a crazy, untenable idea.

They would talk, she could get out of here before his mother and sister returned from a charitable engagement in Athens and all would be good.

No need to meet his family when the idea of marrying Nik was preposterous.

Nik's meeting with the Agieros did not go well. In fact, it went far worse than he'd anticipated. Clearly the family could be expected to be disappointed at the loss of the opportunity to marry into the royal family and the power and prestige that came with it, but he had not been prepared for the overt antagonism Maurizio Agiero, the head of the family, had displayed upon hearing the news Nik would wed an American and not the Countess of Agiero.

He suspected it was Maurizio's deep political ambitions that lay behind the animosity. Yes, the media was abuzz with speculation surrounding an announcement of an engagement, but Vittoria had seemed to take it in her stride, cool as usual, when he'd taken her aside to personally apologize, only raising an eyebrow when he'd referred to what was an "unexpected" turn of events.

Pulling his car to a halt in front of the white Maltese stone Akathinian royal palace that stood set back from the harbor on a rolling hill that overlooked the Ionian Sea, he handed the keys to a palace staffer, then took the steps of the wide, sweeping stairwell two by two. The Agiero alliance eliminated, there was only one other partnership that would give his family the power it needed to fund a war, and it involved his arch nemesis, Akathinian billionaire Aristos Nicolades.

His father would immediately reject the idea of an alliance with Aristos because of what the real estate developer would undoubtedly demand—a casino license for the island—but there was no alternative now. Akathinia had to protect itself.

He expected to have a fight on his hands. Fortunately for both his father's heart and Nik's exhausted body, the former king had retired early. Which meant he could attack his other pressing issue: Sofía.

He headed toward his private wing. Sofía was waiting for him in his salon, staring out the window that overlooked the gardens, the tense set of her body warning him he had a battle on his hands. She whirled around, antagonism written across her beautiful face. "You fly me here to talk and then you leave me alone all day while you go to a meeting? How is that solving our problem?"

He shrugged out of his jacket and threw it on a chair. "I apologize. My meeting took longer than I thought."

She glared at him. "I am not marrying you, Nik. You are off having all these conversations, *deciding things*, when you have no idea what I'm going to say."

He worked his fingers into the knot of his tie and

pulled it loose. "I know exactly what you're going to say. What you just did."

She blinked. "So you understand we need to negotiate how this is going to work?"

"*Negotiate* isn't the right term." He pulled the tie off and tossed it on top of his jacket. "Come to terms with our situation is more accurate."

"*I* don't have a situation. *You* do."

He started undoing the buttons of his shirt. "You are carrying the heir to the throne. You are on Akathinian soil. You most certainly do have a problem to resolve."

She stuck her hands on her hips. "You *tricked* me into coming here. This is a democratic nation. You can't hold me here against my will."

"A democratic nation in which *I* retain ultimate authority." He stripped off his shirt and dropped it to the floor. "And I seem to remember you getting on that plane of your own free will."

"Because you played on my sympathies." Her eyes narrowed as he undid the button of his pants. "What are you doing?"

"Taking a shower so we can eat." He stripped the pants off, dragging his boxers over his hips along with them. Her gaze dropped to that part of him she loved so much. "Unless you'd like to join me in the shower first?"

She shifted her attention back to his face. "No, *thank* you."

"Later then." He turned his back on her and headed for the shower. "Pour me a drink, will you? I'm tired and I'm in a filthy mood."

Later? Sofía fumed. *How about never again?* She threw a mental dagger at Nik's beautiful backside as he walked into the bathroom. He could not force her into a marriage she didn't want. She was going to say her piece and leave.

His wet hair slicked back from his face, Nik joined her on the terrace a few minutes later. In jeans and a white shirt rolled up at the sleeves he didn't do much for her equilibrium. He'd always been spectacular in a suit, but in casual clothes, he was all muscular, earthy male. Devastating.

She lifted her chin. "Why are we not having dinner with your family?"

He took a sip of the drink he'd poured himself and rested his elbows on the railing.

"I don't think you're ready for it."

Her stomach tightened. "I'm sure they must be overjoyed to have me here. Your pregnant American lover who destroyed your alliance."

His mouth thinned. "I think we should focus on the point at hand."

"I'm not marrying you, Nik. There has to be some other way to make this work. Why can't the baby stay with me in New York? We'll do regular visits back and forth, and when he or she is older, they can choose whether they want to live in New York or Akathinia."

He gave her a scathing look. "The heir to the Akathinian throne is not being raised in Manhattan. This child is a symbol of the future of the monarchy, one the people desperately need right now. Our child will grow up here. Learn the customs and intricacies of the country they will one day rule."

"But *I* don't want to live here," she argued. "I have equal say in this decision, and *I* live in New York."

"Don't be naive." His razor-sharp tone sliced over her skin like a whip. "We aren't a stockbroker and an office assistant negotiating a custody settlement. I am the King of Akathinia. And if you think I'm letting you leave this country while you're carrying my heir, you're clearly deluded. Have the baby, then leave. It's your choice. But the child remains here."

The blood drained from her face, a buzzing sound filling her head. "You aren't suggesting what I think you are."

His expression was like the Hudson on a glacially cold day. "I've told you my preference. A child needs its mother. We are good together, Sofía. We *were* good together. We can make this work."

Her heart started to race, a frozen feeling descending over her. He would take her child away from her if she didn't agree to marry him. She knew that look. Knew he was dead serious.

She pulled in a breath, but the sultry, steamy air felt too thick, too heavy to deliver the oxygen she needed. Her head whirled, the strain of the past few weeks, of wondering what she was going to do, the press invading her every quiet moment, *Nik's threats*, descending over her like a dark cloud. Inescapable. Unnavigable.

She set a palm to the railing and pulled in another breath, but it was as if the air was being sucked out of her. A layer of perspiration blanketed her brow as the dusky night spun around her. She distantly registered she was going to pass out a second before Nik's arms closed around her, catching her before she could.

He sat her down in a chair and put her head between her knees. Knelt beside her, his hand on her back, commanding her to breathe. Minutes passed before the dizziness decided which way it was going to go. Finally, her gasping pulls of air slowed to rougher, longer breaths and her head began to clear.

Nik sat her up in the chair, retrieved some water from

the dinner table and pressed the glass into her hand. "A sip," he instructed. She obeyed, hand trembling as she brought the glass to her mouth. When she'd taken a couple of swallows, she handed him back the glass. Nik set it on the table, sat down opposite her and pinned his gaze on her face.

"What was that?"

"Too much," she muttered shakily. "It's all too much." She took another deep breath. "I hardly had any lunch. I get nauseated if I go too long without eating."

He shook his head. "Unless you're an A-list Hollywood actress, that was a full-blown panic attack, Sofía."

Her mouth twisted. "Isn't that what you've already established I am?"

A glitter filled his eyes. "You know I have the patience of Jove. I will wait you out all night if I have to."

"It's everything," she said quietly. "Forcing me to come here, the plane ride, threatening to take my child away. It's too much."

He shook his head. "I'm not forcing you to stay. I'm telling you my child will remain here. The rest is up to you."

"You know that's no choice."

"Then stay. Marry me."

She gave him a frustrated look. "You don't understand what you're asking."

He studied her for a long moment. "Then tell me. Make me understand."

Her gaze dropped away from his. She had never told anyone about her panic attacks. Never told anyone what her father's death had cost her. Only Katharine and even she didn't know the depth of it. But if she was going to make Nik see reason, she had to tell him.

She fixed her gaze on him. "My father was going

on his first big business trip to London the night he died. He had worked his way up through the ranks of an investment banking firm after my parents emigrated from Chile to New York when I was two. His credentials weren't recognized the same way there as they had been back home. He had to work his way up the ladder. He'd just gotten his first promotion before the trip. He was so excited. *We* were so excited.

"I remember him telling me the night he left, before I went to bed, with this big smile on his face, 'This is just the beginning for us, *chiquita*. It's only up from here. We'll be taking trips to all sorts of exotic places.'"

A lump formed in her throat, tears scalding the backs of her eyes. She blinked them back, intent on getting through the story. "The phone call came at 3:00 a.m. from the airline. They told my mother my father's plane had gone missing somewhere over the Atlantic. That they weren't sure where it was or what had happened. My mother sat up all night waiting to hear. When she woke me up for school, I knew something was wrong. She looked like a…ghost."

She swallowed hard, but she couldn't hold the tears back. They slipped down her face like silent bandits. Nik took her hand and curled his fingers around hers. "They found the first piece of the fuselage at two o'clock in the afternoon," she continued. "My father's body was recovered the next day."

"So long," he said quietly. "That must have been torture."

Not the torture he must be feeling knowing he might never get his brother's body back… Never get that closure.

"I'm not telling you this story for your sympathy. It explains *me*, Nik. What I'm feeling. When you said that night in New York my father's death must have affected me deeply, it's hard to even describe what it did to me. I was so young. I was only eight. I didn't really understand the concept of death. I was dependent on my mother to help me understand, but she wasn't there."

He frowned. "Where *was* she?"

"Emotionally, I mean. Mentally she was…gone. My father and she, they were a team when they came to America. They'd fought so hard to make a life there. But when he died, I don't think she knew what to do. She had me…so much fear about the future. She fell into a deep depression that lasted for years. It was only because of my aunt that I wasn't taken from her."

Nik's gaze darkened. "That must have been very scary for a little girl."

She nodded. "I was lucky to have my aunt. She helped until my mother could function again. Hold down a job. But my mother was never the same. It's only recently that she's started to recover some of who she once was. She is going to marry a surgeon in the fall—a doctor who works across the street from the café where she's worked for years."

"A good ending, then."

It was so, so much more complex than that simple statement. But it was easier to nod and agree than get into it. "What I am trying to tell you is that the ground shifted beneath my feet that morning, Nik. Life as I knew it ceased to exist. Everything I thought was predictable became unpredictable. Everything that was stable was suddenly unstable. I developed severe panic attacks I had to learn how to manage. I *coped* by having to have control at all times, by being self-sufficient in every aspect of my life."

He shook his head. "That's impossible, Sofía. No one has control over their lives. We all have to work with the cards that are dealt to us." He waved a hand. "*This*, this I did not expect to happen. But it's what *is*. We all have to make sacrifices in this situation."

She thought about what he had just been through. Was still going through. "I know this is a difficult situation for you. I understand what you're saying. But my business, my life in New York is what keeps me grounded, what gives me the stability I need. I've spent the past seven years building Carlotta up. You can't ask me to throw that away."

"I'm not asking you to give it up. I will fund the business. You can hire the staff you need to help Katharine. And you can spend your free time here designing the line you've always wanted to."

"*Thousands of miles* away from my friends and family."

"They can visit. You can make regular visits to New York to check on the business."

She slid her hand out of his. She knew what it was like to grow up with only one parent, with an ever-present ache in your chest for what had been taken away from you. She would never do that to her child. But stay here with Nik, a man who didn't trust her? Who thought she'd trapped him into marriage? Was that even possible?

Nik's gaze held hers. "You of all people will be able to understand the chaos our child will undergo as heir to Akathinia. The pressure. The need for a support system. They will *need* you."

Her stomach tightened at his unfair bargaining techniques. "Always the hard-nosed negotiator, Nik. Going for the jugular."

His jaw hardened. "Our child cannot be raised anywhere but here, Sofía. You know it and I know it. The only question is what you do. What I can promise *you* is that *I* will be here for you. I will protect you. Things will not *fall apart*. We will give our child the security and stability you were left without. We will do this *together*."

A cloud of confusion descended over her. She couldn't deny this baby was bigger than the both of them. The part of her that had always trusted Nik knew he was telling her the truth, that he would protect her. But would it be enough for them to make this work?

A knock at the door signaled the arrival of their dinner. She wasn't in the least bit hungry, but Nik made her sit down and eat anyway, a few bites of each thing so she wouldn't pass out on him likely.

She'd expected him to go off and work in his office after dinner. Instead he made a few phone calls and sent a couple of emails from his laptop in the salon while she got ready for bed. Maybe he was afraid she was going to bolt and run? But where? His security would catch her before she got thirty feet from the palace.

She took a long, cool shower, thinking that might help. Standing in front of the mirror afterward, about to brush her teeth, she realized she didn't have her toothbrush. Anything to sleep in... This was *insane*.

She stalked out to the salon, a towel wrapped around her. "I have nothing to sleep in."

Nik gave her an even look. "Abram had one of the palace staff pick you up a few things. They're in the wardrobe. There are toiletries in the bathroom, as well."

She went back to the bedroom. Opened the doors of the beautifully carved antique wardrobe. Lined up beside Nik's suits were a half-dozen dresses, a couple of bathing suits and a short, sheer ivory negligee.

He had been *that* sure of her. Also seemingly assured she would grace his bed in the sexy lingerie.

She slammed the wardrobe shut. Walked out into the salon. "Give me one of your T-shirts."

He blinked. "There's something to sleep in in there, too."

"I am not here for your amusement. Give me a T-shirt, Nik."

He got to his feet, walked into the bedroom and returned with a white T-shirt.

She yanked it out of his hands, went into the bathroom and got ready for bed. She was still attempting to get to sleep when Nik joined her. She stayed on her side, curled up, wondering how one night, one decision, could so hugely impact her life. Wondering how, even now, when she hated him, she could still feel the physical pull that drew her to the man on the other side of the bed.

They had never shared a bed and not made love. It was a strange and alienating feeling that added to the fury she felt, making it impossible to quiet her head. But apparently, a self-righteous, convinced-that-he-was-right Nik wasn't having any issues sleeping. His breathing had evened out and he wasn't making a peep.

She punched down her pillow. Tucked in again. Finally admitted what she knew to be true. Her and Nik's child would be born into a firestorm. He or she *would* be a symbol of hope for a nation. As terrified as she was of what was to come, she had to forgo her own selfishness and be there for her child. So they knew they were loved. So they would carry the burden they would assume without it destroying them. It was the promise she would make to them.

Even if it meant giving up everything she knew. Even if it meant spending her days protecting her heart from Nik. Which might prove to be the biggest challenge of all.

CHAPTER FIVE

NIK WAS UP at the crack of dawn for his journey to the neighboring island of Cabeirius to meet with King Idas on neutral ground in an attempt to put an end to the tensions between the two countries. Democracy and a desire for its independence had spoken in Akathinia over a hundred years ago and it would continue to be its guiding principle.

Idas elected to be his usual provocative self in the meeting, many of his statements based on falsehoods and misleading information. Nik might have been able to counter them more effectively had his advisers been better prepared on the points in question and been able to provide him with comebacks on the fly. He had been away from Akathinian politics too long to have every fact at his disposal.

Things went from bad to worse. By the end of the meeting, he had been left flat-footed one too many times, his fury catching fire. "Your commentary is inflammatory and untrue," he bit out, slamming his coffee cup down on the table. "You are making the markets and people uneasy, Idas. Push me much further and you'll give me no choice but to shut you up."

The white-haired, craggy-faced king eyed him, his lips twisting. "So passionate, Nikandros. So unlike your brother, who listened to reason. You are living up to your reckless reputation. I wonder what will be left of Akathinia when you're done with it."

Blood pounded his head, blinding him to the room around him. He stood up, fixing his gaze on Idas. "Let me know when you are willing to act like a reasonable man."

He was still shaking with anger as the Akathinian military helicopter lifted off from Cabeirius. It wasn't until they were halfway home to Akathinia that his brain right-sided itself. He had let Idas goad him into saying things he hadn't intended to say. Into issuing threats he hadn't intended to issue. Perhaps he would have called the Carnelian king's bluff eventually, but not until he had Aristos Nicolades in his back pocket and an enhanced armed forces behind him.

It did not make his dark mood, inspired by Sofía's recalcitrance, any better, he conceded, staring out at an endless vista of blue. She had acted like a woman wronged when he'd brought her here, determined to hang on to her story that she hadn't planned her pregnancy. And although he'd been moved by the account of her father's death, by where the vulnerabilities he'd always seen in her came from, she needed to agree to this marriage. He needed this particular item off his to-do list. He had only so much head space.

Was she second-guessing her gamble of getting pregnant when it had become clear this was only a marriage of convenience for him? That he would never offer her the part of him he'd suspected she'd been beginning to want? His heart, something he wasn't sure he even had anymore.

Or maybe she'd realized just how far-reaching the consequences of her actions were and was balking at the prospect of becoming a queen?

Whatever it was, he thought grimly, it didn't matter why Sofía was acting the way she was. Dissecting her guilt wasn't his problem. What mattered was that she accept the reality of their situation before the explosive news of a royal heir got out, causing yet more uncertainty among the people. There could be no more blows to this monarchy.

Sofía stood with her hand poised on Nik's office door, a sleepless night of decision-making behind her. She knew what she had to do. *Doing it* just seemed so much harder.

She pulled in a breath, knocked as Abram had told her to, then entered on Nik's command to do so. He looked up from where he sat behind his desk, a distracted, somewhat black look on his face. When he saw it was her, he put his pen down and sat back in his chair.

"Everything all right?" she asked cautiously.

"*Kala.* Fine. Have you reached a decision?"

"Yes." She shoved her hands in the pockets of the capri pants she'd found in the closet and came to stand in front of his desk. "You were right to appeal to my past in your arguments, Nik, because you know I will never abandon my child, nor will I expose them to an overdose of the pressure you were speaking of. To that end, I want to have the final say on any choices relating to our child. I want to be a hands-on mother. I don't want nannies taking over my relationship with my child. I'll be the one to set the schedule."

"We will discuss that as required."

"No." She lifted her chin. "That is my condition for agreeing to this, Nik. As well as that I want to be able to travel frequently back to New York to check on the business as you promised. I need to be part of it."

He nodded.

"I would also like to pursue my designing, so I would appreciate it if you would find me a space in the palace to do so. A quiet space with lots of room and good light."

"Done."

"As for *us*, I will play the role of your wife as required in public, but until we learn to understand each other, there will be no intimacy between us."

"Define *understand*."

"You need to believe me when I say I didn't engineer this pregnancy. We need to have trust between us if we are going to be able to do this."

He cocked his head to one side. "How am I supposed to believe a pregnancy wasn't in your head when you suggest we forgo a condom, then all of a sudden we're pregnant?"

Heat stained her cheeks. "I don't know what possessed me to say that. I don't know, I wanted that intimacy between us. But it wasn't *planned*. The doctor is fairly sure it was my migraine medication that reduced the efficacy of the pills. I had no idea it would do such a thing."

"Right." He gave her a look as if to say he hadn't been born yesterday. Her blood boiled. "Does it really matter at this point?" he suggested harshly. "It's a foregone conclusion we're having this baby."

"Yes, it does. You want to lump me in with all the other women who have abused your trust. I won't do it, Nik."

He stared at her for a long moment. "My remaining celibate for the duration of our marriage is not an option."

"Well, then I guess we have a disagreement we have to overcome, don't we?"

"Quite." He hit the button on the intercom to call Abram in. "We can get the ball rolling on an engagement announcement, then. The sooner the better."

"What about the baby? It's too early to confirm that."

"We won't." His mouth curved in a sardonic twist. This is the time we'll use to convince the people of Akathinia their king has made a last-minute, impulsive decision to pursue his happily-ever-after. A love match. We won't confirm the baby for another few weeks, unless we have to. Abram has taken steps to ensure the confidentiality of your doctor in New York."

Her stomach dropped. He had everything figured out. He was totally in control. And where was she? Completely at his mercy. Completely at the mercy of a palace machine that would strip her life of everything she'd built as soon as this announcement went out.

From this point forward, her life was never going to be the same.

Sofía's stomach was still a mass of knots as she dressed for dinner with the royal family. An announcement of her and Nik's coming nuptials was being prepared for release the next day, along with an invitation for the toast of Akathinian society to join them to celebrate the royal engagement at a party in two weeks' time.

She had balked at the tight timeline, but calming her as he would an overexcited filly, Abram had assured it was all easily done by the palace event machine. All she had to do was be a stunning *queen-to-be*.

A thousand butterflies traced a swooping path through her insides as she smoothed the beautiful violet dress around her hips that she'd chosen from the selection in the wardrobe. The palace was flying in her favorite designer next week with a dozen dresses to choose from for the engagement party, which might seem like overkill, but when you were going to be photographed by the world, your dress pulled apart piece by piece by the fashion media, you made sure you got it right.

Her mother had sounded ecstatic when she'd called, too happy with her own engagement to pick up on the reticence in her daughter's voice. *Dreamy*, she'd called Nik. "And a prince at that, Sofía."

The fact that her mother and she were still so far apart emotionally had brought back a familiar ache. The resentment at never really having had a mother who had been there for all the big events of her life, so lost in herself as her mother had been.

How some things never changed.

Pursing her lips, she scooped her hair off her neck and twisted it atop her head rather than ruminate about things she couldn't change. Up, her hair looked elegant; down, it looked a little wild with the curls the salty Akathinian air was inspiring.

Nik appeared in the mirror behind her, sleek in a dark suit that made him look like a particularly lethal jungle cat. Her pulse sped up into an agitated, jagged rhythm as his blue gaze slid over her in a slow, thorough perusal. "Wear it down."

She pulled her gaze from him. "It channels a bit of Grace Kelly if I wear it up."

His mouth curved. "There is no Grace Kelly in you, Sofía. You are all fire with some ice thrown in to keep things interesting. Be yourself."

She reached for a clip and secured the curls into a loose chignon. Nik's eyes glittered as she turned to face him. "If I told you you look incredible in that dress," he drawled, "would you put something else on?"

"Quite possibly," she retorted. "So please refrain. We're out of time."

She went to move past him to find her shoes. Nik

caught her hand in his. A current ran through her, as if she'd curled her fingers around a dangling electrical wire, jamming her breath in her throat. *Dammit.* She had to get over this. *Him.* She *hated* him for thinking the worst of her.

He lifted his other hand, a jaw-droppingly beautiful square-cut pink sapphire held between his fingers. "This could make a nice accessory."

Her breath caught in her throat. Surrounded by a double row of tiny white diamonds, the brilliance of the light pink stone was further enhanced by pave-set diamonds that covered the entire band.

It was unbelievably beautiful. Utterly perfect.

"Do you like it?" Nik prodded.

She sank her teeth into her lip. Once, when she and Nik had been walking down Madison Avenue after dinner out, they'd passed a swish jewelry store, the appointment-only kind. She'd jokingly commented to Nik that the pink sapphire in the window could persuade her to get married someday.

He had remembered.

She stifled the desperate urge to tell him she couldn't put *that* ring on her finger and perhaps he should take it back and get another.

"You could fund the entire Akathinian army with that ring," she said huskily.

"I bought it personally. And no, I don't think it would quite do it."

He lifted her hand to slide the ring on, moving it past her knuckle to sit on her finger like a blinding pink fire.

"It's beautiful," she said woodenly. Minus the heart-felt sentiment behind it.

She pulled away from him and crossed the room to

retrieve her shoes. Nik's piercing blue gaze followed her, probing, assessing. "Are you all right?"

"Perfect." She bent to slip a shoe on.

"Greet my father first," he said. "Don't bow, he hates it, wait for him to take the lead. My mother won't wish formalities, either."

"And Stella?"

His mouth tipped up at one corner. "Stella eschews formality whenever she can get away with it."

He took her arm and escorted her down the massive circular staircase to the gold-accented foyer and through to the drawing room, where Nik's family was gathered for drinks before dinner.

Her first impression of King Gregorios as he sat in a high-back chair near the windows was of flashing blue eyes the exact light aquamarine color of Nik's, a thinning head of pure white hair and a lined face that seemed to tell the colorful story of his almost four decades of rule.

Nik placed a palm to her back and directed her to his father's chair. King Gregorios stood as his son made the introductions, his vivid blue eyes inspecting her from head to foot.

"Ms. Ramirez," the king said, inclining his head. "We had anticipated welcoming a countess to the family, but life takes unexpected turns, doesn't it?"

Stella gasped. Nik's fingers tightened against her back. "*Behave*, Father."

The heat that she was sure heightened color in her cheeks was the only indication Sofía allowed that the king's barb had landed. Queen Amara stepped forward and took Sofía's hands. She was just as elegantly beautiful as her photographs, her silver hair caught up in a knot at the back of her head, her dark brown eyes discerning beneath sharply arched brows. "Sofía," she murmured, brushing a kiss to each of her cheeks, "it is so good to meet you."

The queen pulled back, a wry twist to her mouth. "Don't mind my husband. The men in this family have a tendency to speak their minds as I'm sure you've learned from Nik."

She forced a smile to her lips. "Somewhat. It's an honor to meet you, Your Highness."

"Amara, please. You are going to be my daughter-in-law after all."

She blinked at the unreality of that. Then there was another Constantinides to meet as Stella stepped forward. More arresting than beautiful, the cool, blue-eyed blonde with those signature Constantinides eyes took her in with unabashed curiosity.

"So lovely to meet you," Stella murmured, brushing a kiss to both her cheeks. "Don't mind my father," she said under her breath as she guided Sofía toward the ornately carved bar on the other side of the room. "He is who he is."

Sofía kept her gaze firmly averted from King Gregorios. "It's so nice to meet you, too. Nik has told me how close you are."

"That I am the renegade princess, I expect?" Stella lifted a brow, eyes dancing. "And you are the scandalous American lover who destroyed an alliance. It's a match made in heaven."

She gave Nik's sister a wary look as she poured her a glass of lemonade. "If it makes you feel any better," Stella murmured, handing her the glass, "I can't stand the countess. She is a cold fish. Nik would have been miserable."

Sofía's eyes widened. She wrapped her fingers around the glass. "What is *that*?" Stella demanded, manacling her fingers around Sofía's wrist to twist it so she could see the sapphire. "I can't believe Nik broke with tradition."

"Tradition?"

"All Akathinian royal engagements are celebrated with a rare type of Tanzanian sapphire named for the Ionian Sea upon which we sit. *You* will be the first not to wear an Akathinian sapphire. Well, except for Queen Flora's daughter."

"What did she have?"

"Her eldest daughter, Terese, refused to have an Akathinian sapphire. She hadn't been married two years when she and her husband had a huge argument. Terese took the car out and got in an accident. At the time, the queen was convinced it was because of the ring. Because she'd broken tradition. She was very superstitious."

Right. Yet another strike against her and Nik.

"So the legend goes." Stella waved a hand at her. "It's foolishness. I'm so glad Nik's not the superstitious type. I'm not wearing one if I ever marry. I'm a canary diamond kind of girl."

Queen Amara strolled over to see the ring. "Nik has always been of his own mind. His coronation ceremony was very simple, bucking tradition. I hope he won't deprive us of too many traditions around your wedding. We have such lovely ones."

Nik joined them. "On that note, we're planning an engagement party rather than a garden press conference."

The queen brightened. "That's a lovely idea. When will you have it?"

"In two weeks' time."

His mother looked horrified. "Two weeks?"

"It will be good for the people. They could use something to cheer about right now."

"Yes, I expect it will. But so soon. How will we get everything done?"

"It's all in motion. You don't have to worry about a thing."

Stella clapped her hands, excitement sparkling in her eyes. "Let me help plan it. I can work with the palace staff and help Sofía with all the protocol and rigmarole."

Nik lifted a brow. "*You* teach Sofía protocol? She'll have an adviser."

Stella scowled at her brother. "I'll be the *perfect* teacher. She'll know what's old-school nonsense and what she has to pay attention to."

And with that Sofía learned that Stella always got what she wanted.

Nik was still fuming as he sat down beside his father at the dinner table in the smaller, less formal dining room. He had been inexcusably rude to his fiancée. It would not continue, but it would have to be addressed later at a more appropriate time.

His attempt to steer the conversation to innocuous ground was circumvented by the sensational news coverage of his meeting with Idas today and his father's ire. "Your stance was called aggressive," his father pointed out. "International opinion doesn't like it, Nikandros, and neither does the council."

Nik's blood boiled a degree hotter. What was wrong with his father talking politics at the dinner table? His mind hadn't been right since Athamos's death. "Idas was the inflammatory one," he said curtly. "I was merely responding to him, an error, I know. It would not have been necessary had the council representatives with me had the *facts* at hand."

"What will you do?" his mother interjected. "Idas doesn't seem to be backing down. This seems like more than rhetoric."

"I have a meeting with Aristos Nicolades tomorrow."

"Aristos?" Stella frowned. "Why are you meeting with him?"

"To discuss an economic alliance to replace the Agieros."

Nik's sister looked horrified. "But he's the *devil.*"

"He is *necessary* now that Nikandros has eliminated the Agieros from the equation." King Gregorios scowled. "Now we will see the scourge of humanity his casinos will bring to Akathinia."

Nik threw his father a hard-edged look. "I don't think this is the right time or place to be discussing this. I will meet with Aristos tomorrow and we will move forward from there. Akathinia must be protected. That is the priority."

His father shook his head. "We will live to regret this. If Athamos were in charge, we would have had a deal with the Agieros. *This* would not be happening."

"Yes, well, unfortunately, Athamos was off fighting over his lover when his car plunged into the ocean and he is *dead.*" All eyes flew to Nik as he trained his gaze on his father. "*I* am the one making the decisions. I say we meet with Aristos."

His father muttered something under his breath, picked up his fork and started eating. The table was so silent, the clink of the king's fork against the china was the only sound in the room.

His mother, ever the peacekeeper, asked Sofía about her dress for the engagement party. Nik mentally checked out as the conversation flowed around him, his anger too great to corral.

When coffee and dessert were offered, Sofía thankfully declined, likely no more enamored with the idea of staying at the table than he was. They said their good-nights,

his fiancée promising to meet with Stella over breakfast
the next morning to discuss the party.

And then, mercifully, it was over.

If the dining room had been quiet, their suite was deadly
so. Nik poured a whiskey, took it out on the terrace and
stood in the moonlight looking out at the gardens. The
rigid set of his shoulders, his ramrod-straight spine, the
explosive intensity that had wrapped itself around him
all day warned her to stay away.

They didn't need any more tension between them.
She should go have a bath. But her concern for him out-
weighed her common sense.

She slipped off her shoes and joined him on the terrace, her elbows resting on the top of the railing beside
him as she considered the moon, a luminous crescent-
shaped sliver that sat high in the sky.

"I'm sorry my father was so rude to you," he said. "It
was unacceptable. My brother's death has hit him hard."

"You and he lock horns."

He lifted the glass in a mock salute. "A brilliant de-
duction."

She let that slide. "I'm sorry about the Agieros," she
said quietly. "I'm sorry this is such a mess."

He flicked her a sideways glance. "What's done is
done."

A wave of antagonism shot through her at the jaded
glint in his eyes but she tamped it down because now was
not the time. "What happened today, Nik?"

He turned to face her, a closed look on his face. "Why
don't we choose another topic? This one is getting a little old."

She looked at him silently, waiting him out.

He lifted a shoulder. "He was inflammatory, as I said. Half of what he was saying wasn't true, and yet I couldn't counter it properly because my advisers didn't have the information. Weren't prepared."

"And you blew up?"

"You watched the media coverage?"

"Yes."

He looked back out at the gardens. "It was unfortunate. He pushed the right buttons."

Silence fell between them. She studied the play of the moonlight across the hard lines of his face.

"I don't think your father is the only one who hasn't processed your brother's death," she said quietly. "It's been a huge shock. You need to give yourself time, Nik. Time to grieve."

He shot her a hard look. "I don't need a counselor, Sofía."

"Well you need something. You are like a powder keg today, ready to blow at the slightest provocation."

His jaw hardened. "I'm fairly sure I've had more than my fair share of it today. It was a mistake. We all make them."

"Yes," she agreed. "We do." She laced her hands together on the railing. "Where does the antagonism between you and your father come from?"

"We've never seen eye to eye."

"And your brother and he did?"

He turned to her, his gaze firing. "I said I was *done* with this topic."

She gave him an even look. "You can dish it out but you can't take it?"

"Signomi?"

"You picked me apart that night in New York, Nik. You pointed out things about me I hadn't necessarily had the courage to address. So I could see myself clearly. Are you too afraid to do the same?"

"I see myself just fine," he growled. "I let my temper get in the way today. Forgive me if it's a bit much to have what my brother would have done thrown in my face one too many times."

She cocked her head to the side. "Did your brother's philosophies differ from yours?"

His mouth flattened. "My ideas on how to run this country, on life, are pragmatic, progressive. I have a more international view. My father and Athamos preferred to remain mired in the past. Enamored of traditions and ideals that no longer make sense. Athamos did not always recognize the need to forge his own path."

And how difficult must that have been? For his brother and father to have been on the same page and Nik on another entirely? To be on the outside of that bond?

And now, she thought, studying the deeply etched lines on his face, the dark circles beneath his eyes, him as the new king, with the weight of a nation on his shoulders, still gaining his sea legs in a role she suspected he wouldn't have chosen. A father mired in grief and of no help to him. A man in the middle of a storm.

"You called me philosophical that night in New York," she said, "about my father. I was angry, too, Nik. For a long time. I didn't understand why he was taken from me. Couldn't stop thinking *what if.* I didn't get there overnight. You won't, either."

"Your father's death was a tragic accident, Sofía. Athamos's was senseless. Selfish. He got in that car and threw his life away over a *woman*."

"And the airline could have properly serviced my father's plane. If I had carried that around with me my entire life, kept assigning blame, I would have ended up bitter and angry. Don't do that to yourself."

"This isn't the same thing."

"Why?"

"Because he played with something that wasn't his to give." His voice rose until he was nearly shouting at her. "He was the heir to the throne. He threw my country into crisis without thinking of the consequences."

"And he put you in this position."

A stillness enveloped him. The icy anger in his blue eyes morphed into a white-hot fury that made her heart race. "I do *not* begrudge the role I have been given, Sofía."

She drew in a breath, her heart pounding. "I wasn't suggesting that. I was merely saying it would be understandable for you to feel resentment for having your life turned upside down. For having all of *this* thrust upon you."

He stepped closer, the smoky scent of whiskey filling her senses as he set his glittering blue gaze on hers. "I don't *need* your understanding. What I need from you is *less complication*."

Her chin came up. "It took two of us to produce *this* particular complication."

His eyes moved over her in a hot, deliberate appraisal that melted her insides. "And it was a hell of a good time doing it, wasn't it? *That* kind of comfort I can take. Otherwise, go to bed."

Her mouth dropped open. Nails biting into her palms she stood there staring at him. He was hurting, no doubt about it. Had ghosts she'd barely scratched the surface of. But *that* wasn't going to happen.

Spinning on her heel, she stalked inside.

* * *

Nik took a deep breath and exhaled slowly, his hands gripping the railing as he leaned back and flexed his arms. Sofía telling him how to feel, how to manage the maelstrom of emotions storming his head after the day he'd just had was too much. Much too much.

You need to give yourself time to grieve. When was there time to grieve when he spent every waking hour trying to find his way out of this hell he'd been bequeathed? Of course he was angry with Athamos. *Furious* with his brother for playing not only with his own life but with his, as well. For landing him back in an arena where his father had made it clear he didn't belong. *Athamos's domain. Athamos the born diplomat.*

And maybe his father had been right. Hadn't he walked right into Idas's trap today? Done exactly what he'd expected him to? What *everyone* had expected him to—the reckless, rebel prince turned king? Proved them all right about him?

He would rectify his mistake, he knew he would. He was mostly furious with himself for allowing his emotions to get the best of him. His weakness. What his father called his Achilles' heel.

He brought the tumbler to his mouth and downed the rest of the whiskey. But it wasn't having its usual dulling effect. He was too tense, too on edge. When he was like this, when a shot of something strong couldn't block out the furor in his head there was only one thing that could relax him, and that one thing had just turned on her heel and walked away from him. Had made it clear there would be no sex until they reached an *understanding* of each other.

Well, she had that wrong. This marriage might have been thrust upon him, along with everything else he'd acquired over the past month, but he'd be damned if he was going to sacrifice the physical aspect of his relationship with Sofía when it was the part they did so spectacularly well.

He turned on his heel and strode inside. Sofía was standing in front of the mirror, brushing her hair. It fell down her back like a dark silk curtain, contrasting with her honey-colored skin bestowed upon her by her Chilean heritage.

Heat moved through him. She was so beautiful, so desirable, what she had done to him, manufacturing a pregnancy, had no impact on his lust. It only made him want to have her more.

He deposited his glass on the coffee table with a deliberate movement. Sofía's wary gaze met his in the mirror as he walked up behind her and rested his hands on her hips. "This looks fantastic on you, *glykeia mou.*"

She kept the brush strokes going, rhythmically over and over. "I put the nightie on because the maid took my T-shirt. I haven't changed my mind, Nik. Get your hands off me."

"No." He lowered his mouth to her bare shoulder, scraping his teeth across her delicate skin. Her involuntary shudder made him smile. "Your body says yes."

"And I'm saying no." Her gaze speared his in the mirror. "You accused me of trapping you into marriage, Nik. You threatened to take my child away. As if you don't *know me.* Until we regain our trust in each other, this isn't happening."

Fire heated his gaze. "So you fell into the trap of wanting more. I'm past it, Sofía. I'm moving on. You should, too. Why drag this out?"

She threw the brush on the dresser and spun around. "The only thing I'm guilty of is wanting to be closer to you that night, Nik. There was no risk in my mind. If you really want me to come around, then start wrapping your head around a real relationship where we actually communicate. We're going to need it to get through this."

His gaze darkened. "And what would you like out of that *real* relationship now that you have it, Sofía? Let's get all our cards on the table. Would you like to *talk* like we did tonight? Are you looking for *love* perhaps? Or does your inability to make yourself vulnerable rule that out?"

"As much as it does for you," she bit out. "A relationship is about respecting and appreciating each other. *Knowing* each other so we can support one another. And clearly you don't know me at all right now. So we're each going to have to *learn* how to drop our guards, to let each other in, to *be* in a relationship or this isn't going to work."

His lashes lowered. "Sex is a vital part of a relationship. Sex *is* intimacy."

"It's one level of intimacy," she countered. "If I give in to you now, if I let you use sex as a weapon between us, as a way to avoid the issues we have, we are never going to confront them."

His gaze darkened. "Love is a *fantasy* people like to believe in. It has no place in the real world. We'd all be better off if we acknowledged that and viewed relationships as the mutually beneficial transactions they are."

"Transactions?" She lifted a brow. "I am certainly no expert here, given my poor track record, but my parents were in love, Nik. It was my mother's love for my father that sent her into the spiral she went into. She loved him *that* much."

"And *that* type of dependency we are to aspire to?"

"I don't know," she said. "I honestly don't know. What

I do know is that this is not working. Will not work. So figure out if you want this to succeed. And how you plan to do it."

He muttered an oath. Out of words. Out of *everything*.

She lifted her chin, her gaze on his. "What you said, in New York, about finding out what happens when winning isn't enough anymore… I think this is your chance to get to the heart of that. To confront the demons you obviously have and figure out what drives you. Otherwise, you're going to detonate like the bomb you are right now and I don't think anyone, yourself included, wants that to happen."

Turning on her heel, she stalked into the bathroom. He watched her go, clenching his hands by his sides. Why wouldn't she just admit what she'd done? Why wouldn't she just move on? He was willing to. He was being more than fair.

Diavole. He needed this thing with her sorted. *Done.* He could not fight battles on multiple fronts.

CHAPTER SIX

IN THE DAYS that followed Nik's confrontation with King Idas, tensions continued to mount. The Carnelian king responded to Nik's challenge to back off by mounting a series of military exercises off the coast of Carnelia, leaving the people of both Akathinia and Carnelia to watch in alarm as the two countries slid closer toward a confrontation.

It was the wake-up call Nik had needed. Sofía had been right. His grief was ruling him. He had been allowing his emotions to dominate his thinking, gut reaction to rule, something that might have worked in the eat-or-be-eaten world he'd inhabited in Manhattan, but couldn't be allowed free rein as king of his country.

It didn't matter if he hadn't wanted it, if he was still railing against the unfairness of having his life in New York ripped away from him, he had a nation depending on him to make the right choices at perhaps the most crucial period in its history. He could no longer be the one-man show he'd been in New York where risk taking had been the oxygen he'd breathed, he had to rule by consensus. He had to listen to *all* the voices.

He had a choice to make. He could accept the role he'd been given and everything that came with it, *truly* accept it and move forward, or he could continue to fight it. There was no question which way it had to go. He needed his peace of mind back.

An alliance with Aristos Nicolades in place in exchange for Nik's support of a casino license for the billionaire, Nik had come to Carnelia, his enemy's turf, to give diplomacy a shot, a council-approved plan in his hand. Although he was convinced the council was wrong in its estimation Idas was bluffing at future aggression, he would give the plan a shot, knowing a more robust armed forces was on the way as insurance.

He stood, looking out at a picture-perfect view of the mountainous Carnelian countryside, a host of emotions running through him as he waited for the king to arrive.

Athamos had perished in those mountains from which Akathinia had once been ruled, his car plunging to the rocky shore below in a death too horrific to imagine. His great-grandfather Damokles had fought for and achieved Akathinia's independence over a century ago on the Ionian Sea he could see sparkling from the king's personal salon, winning his nation's right to self-determination.

It could not be allowed to be taken away.

A door opened behind him. He swiveled to face the king, who entered the room alone. His surprise must have shown on his face for Idas shot him a pointed look, his hawkish face amused. "You came by yourself, Nikandros. I am assuming you are interested in having a frank discussion."

"Yes."

Idas waved him into a chair and sat down. "Allow me to express my condolences once again for your brother's death. It was difficult to do so with so many others in our last meeting."

Nik lifted a brow. "Kostas couldn't have said that to me personally?"

The king's eyes flickered. "My son has taken Athamos's death badly. They were rivals, yes, but their history is long, filled with a mutual respect that went very deep as you know."

"Was it a woman that provoked their disagreement?" He couldn't prevent himself from asking the question that wouldn't leave his head.

Idas shook his head. "I'm afraid I can't answer that question. Perhaps in time, we will both learn the answer."

He got the sense the old man was telling the truth. Idas rested a speculative gaze on Nik. "Congratulations on your match to the beautiful American. The star-studded engagement party is tonight, is it not? A message to the world, perhaps, Nikandros? That you have the international community behind you?"

"But we do," Nik said smoothly. "The world will not sit by and watch you do this."

The king sat back in his chair and folded his arms across his chest. "The international community seems to have a different opinion on territories with historic ties to one other. Particularly when segments of the population would prefer a return to the old boundaries. It tends to view them as local issues. Problem spots they don't want to get their hands dirty with."

"Not Akathinia. It is a former colonial jewel. Internationally loved. It would be seen as outrageous."

"Outrageous is something I'm comfortable with."

Nik's fingers bit into his thighs. "We don't need the world's help, Idas. We have the strength to make this a very bloody and costly war should you choose to take a wrong step."

"How?" the king derided. "Your military forces are nothing compared to ours."

"You have old information. Your spies should do better reconnaissance."

The king regarded him skeptically. Nik sat forward. "It's common knowledge Carnelia is struggling. Thus your need for Akathinia's rich tourism and resource base. That will never happen, but we are open to the idea of expanding trade talks with you. Lending you some of our natural resource expertise so you can further develop your own base. But this," he stressed, "is contingent on your ceasing your rhetoric in the media. On your agreement to respect Akathinia's sovereignty as we pursue discussions."

A play of emotion crossed the king's face. Greed, another hefty dose of skepticism and...*interest.* "It's an intriguing proposition."

"New sources of income are the answer, Idas." Nik drilled his point home. "Not an unpopular war."

A silence followed. "We will need some time to consider it."

"You will have it. If you give me your word you will not act militarily upon Akathinia during the time of these negotiations."

The king stood up and walked to the French doors. When he turned around after a lengthy silence, Nik knew he had won.

They shook hands. Nik walked out of the palace into the bright sunshine and on to the waiting helicopter. He wasn't stupid enough to think the threat of Idas had been neutralized. But it was a start. A very real success he could take to his critics, to the people, and move forward with.

He drew in a breath as the sleek black bird rose straight into the air. For the first time in weeks he felt as if he *could* breathe.

   The palace, surrounded by the mountainous Carnelian countryside, faded to a mere blip on the ground as the helicopter rose high in the sky. He sat back in his seat and turned his thoughts to his fiancée. His other persistent problem he couldn't seem to fix. She should have been neutralized as an issue when she'd agreed to marry him. When his heir had been secured. Instead her insistence she hadn't planned her pregnancy, her demand he trust her was an impasse they couldn't seem to get past.

   He agreed it was out of character for her to have done it. For the vastly independent Sofía he'd known in New York to get pregnant to keep a man. Nor was she acting like a woman who'd gotten everything she'd wanted. She was acting the opposite—as if *she* was the trapped one. Which made him wonder if it had simply been an error in judgment on her part. An impulse she regretted. Sofía reaching for the money and security she'd never had. Perhaps she hadn't even realized what she'd been doing?

   Or he could be wrong. Sofía could be telling the truth. The medication may have affected the efficacy of her birth control pills. But allowing himself to believe that, that she was that honest, *different* woman he hadn't been quite ready to let go of in New York wasn't an alternative he could allow himself to consider. He wouldn't be made a fool of a second time. Not when his last mistake with a woman had produced a scandal that had rocked his family. Not when now, of all times, his head had to be clear, something it evidently hadn't been up until now.

   What they needed, he decided, was a fresh start. With neither of them bearing any axes to grind. Which, he conceded, involved developing a healthy relationship between them as Sofía had said. Which he could do. He *liked* her. He admired her strength—the survivor in her. He appreciated her vulnerability—her soft underside that would make her a great mother. They had been good together in New York. If they could both move on from this, they could make a great team.

Tonight, he decided grimly, he was solving this impasse.

The helicopter banked and followed the coast, bound for Akathinia. An impulse took hold. He leaned forward and shouted an instruction to the pilot. The pilot nodded and changed direction. Fifteen minutes later, they landed on a flat patch of green halfway up the southern Carnelian mountain range.

Nik stepped out of the helicopter, walked across the field and hiked the half mile down to the treacherous, winding road that dropped away to the pounding rocks and surf below.

The site of his brother's accident was marked by the masses of flowers that lay at the side of the road, once a vibrant burst of color, now withering and dying.

Soon they would disintegrate into nothing.

For the first time since he'd been informed of the accident in that mind-numbing conversation with Abram, he acknowledged his brother wasn't coming back. Wasn't ever coming back. That this all hadn't been the horrific nightmare he'd wanted it to be. Just because they hadn't managed to find his brother's body when they'd pulled the car from the sea didn't mean he wasn't gone.

Hot tears slipped down his cheeks, scalding in the whip of the wind. *You need to give yourself permission to grieve.* He hadn't done that. Just as he'd suspected, it was a dark tunnel he had no desire to travel through.

Athamos smiling that wicked grin of his at him as they'd cut the sails in the America's Cup and declared victory for Akathinia. His brother's fierce countenance when they'd fought tooth and nail over their beliefs. His big grin when they'd made their peace with one another.

It was lost to him now. There wasn't any time left to tell him how he'd truly felt. To mend the fences that had risen between them. To ask his brother what the hell he'd been doing in that car racing Kostas that night. Answers he would never have. Answers he would have given anything to have.

In that moment, as he stared into the gray, stormy surf below, he had to believe all of this had happened for a reason. That there was some sense in this.

As the minutes ticked closer to Sofía and Nik's first official appearance together, Sofía's general demeanor vacillated from a numbness that shielded her from it all to a stubborn defiance that this media frenzy wouldn't get to her.

"It doesn't matter what I wear," she told Stella, who was putting the finishing touches on her hair. "They wanted a countess. They're going to crucify me regardless of what I show up in."

"Give them time," Stella soothed, wrapping a wayward strand of Sofía's hair into the sophisticated updo she'd engineered. "Once they get to know you, they're going to love you."

She already *had* that in New York. Her friends appreciated her. Her clients appreciated her. And yet in her first public appearance here, a visit to a youth charity with Stella, she'd been pegged as lacking in charisma. *Stiff.*

What did they expect? They had spoken of her as a foreigner from day one, incapable of understanding the nuances of Akathinian society. Nik's scandalous acquisition rumored to be pregnant. A far cry from the countess they'd been teased with, and the influence the Agieros exercised across Europe.

Was she supposed to have walked into that charity event and shone under that criticism? Under the barrage of it that seemed to come daily—when all she really wanted was to be back at the boutique, where business was booming as her face became a household name. The only upside that seemed to be coming from all this!

Stella eyed her in the mirror. "I was skeptical about you in the beginning, you know, like everyone else. Women have treated Nik as a prize to be won for so long we're all a bit jaded about it. But I can see that you care about him. That you are true, Sofía, in everything that you do. And that's exactly what Nik needs after that piece of work he was with."

Sofía frowned. "What do you mean?"

"A woman, of course. A nasty piece of work he could have done without." Stella made a face. "Rather than risk Nik's ire at divulging his secrets, I won't get into the whole sordid story. Suffice it to say he has reasons to be as cynical as he is. Give him some time, some latitude. He's worth it."

She closed her eyes as Stella engulfed her in a cloud of hair spray. If only she could confide in her future sister-in-law as to the lows her and Nik's relationship had hit. How they were hardly talking. How his mistrust of her was killing them. But as warm as her and Stella's relationship had gotten, Stella was still Nik's sister and she wasn't about to go there.

With Katharine busy running the boutique, she would have only her mother and Benetio, her fiancé, by her side tonight.

"Stop frowning," Stella murmured, fussing with one

last wayward curl. "Don't you know frown lines never go away?"

Frown lines didn't happen to be her biggest concern at the moment. Faking she and Nik were supremely happy in front of the world was. The only thing that kept her from a full-on pity party was the knowledge that Nik had placed himself on enemy territory today in an attempt to find a diplomatic solution with Carnelia. It made her stomach churn every time she thought of him meeting with that madman.

What if Idas tried something? Surely he wouldn't do anything provocative, the rational side of her brain proclaimed. The pulse pounding at the base of her neck suggested she'd be fine once he was back here all in one piece. Which was really rather traitorous behavior on her part because she *hated* him for thinking the worst of her. Hated he thought she could be so duplicitous as to trap him into marriage.

Stella made an approving sound and stepped back. "*Oriste.* You look spectacular."

"Indeed she does."

Both of them whirled around at the sound of Nik's deep, resonant voice. Sofía's pulse took off at a dead run. Not only was he in one heart-stoppingly gorgeous suit, there was a triumphant glitter in his eyes, an aura of power about him that did something crazy to her insides.

"What happened?" Stella demanded.

Nik shrugged off his jacket and tossed it on a chair. "Idas has agreed to back off while we discuss an economic renewal plan for Carnelia that Akathinia will help facilitate."

"You're kidding."

"I hope not," he said drily. "I was looking forward to giving the council some good news."

"And so you shall." Stella flew toward him and gave him a hug. "I wish I could have been a fly on the wall for that meeting."

Nik loosened his tie. "It doesn't mean the threat is gone. Idas is dangerous. But this gives us some time to build up our forces in case negotiations fall through."

Stella nodded. Glanced at her watch. "Good heavens, it's almost six. I need to get dressed."

Nik's sister whipped out of the room, promising to meet them downstairs in an hour. Sofía got to her feet, her knees a bit weak with relief. "Congratulations. I'm sure that must take a weight off your shoulders."

"For now." He crossed over to her until he stood mere inches from her. It was the closest they'd been to each other since the night of their big blowout and it set her heart thrumming in her chest. "Thank you for what you said to me that night on the terrace," he said quietly. "I needed to hear it. I needed the perspective."

Her heart skipped a beat. "If we're a team, that's what we should be doing for each other."

His gaze held hers. "Yes, we should. I want us to have a fresh start, Sofía. We need to end this impasse between us. We need to make this relationship work, for our sake and for our child's. Things may not have begun under the most ideal of circumstances, but *we* decide where our relationship goes from here. I want it to be a good one."

She pursed her lips. "But you still don't believe me about the pregnancy?"

"Sofía," he growled. "Let it go. The point is we need to move on. You said you want me to open up to you, to learn how to be in a relationship. I'm willing to do that. I'm willing to open up to you and learn to trust each other."

"To a point," she bit out. "That one thing will always

sit there between us festering." She crossed her arms over her chest and eyed him. "What's your ulterior motive here, Nik? Do you want to *fix us* so you can move on with more important things?"

His face tightened. "I'm offering an olive branch here. It would be nice if you would accept it."

"Why the sudden change in heart?"

"My parents' marriage was a political one. Amicable enough in the beginning out of the respect they had for each other. My mother came from an aristocratic family—she knew her role. But the one thing she couldn't handle were my father's affairs. Not unusual for a sovereign, but my mother has a great deal of pride. It was her one stipulation and he broke it.

"Their marriage became a war zone," he continued. "Our *home* became a war zone. I will not have that for my child. *Our* child."

"But can you trust me? *Truly* trust me?" She fixed her gaze on his. "We need that above all else if this is going to work, Nik."

His lashes lowered. "I will work on it."

Her heart dropped. She had the feeling he might never trust her. Never let go of what he thought she'd done. But what choice did she have but to try to make it work?

She spun away toward the wardrobe in search of her shoes. "You need to get ready."

"Sofía—"

"Not now, Nik." She turned around and faced him, hands on hips. "Every reporter in Akathinia is waiting for me to step into that ballroom so they can analyze me from every angle. So that they can further expose my deficiencies and label me not up to snuff. So let's just get it over with, shall we?"

His eyes widened, then narrowed. "The press will

come around. *You* need to be patient and stop worrying so much about what people think. I saw the coverage of the charity event. You didn't look like yourself at all. Stop hiding under that shell of yours and let people see *you*."

"So they can dig their claws in deeper?" She rolled her eyes. "No, thank you."

"I wouldn't do that again if I were you."

"Do what?"

"Roll your eyes."

"Why? Because you're a *king*?

"Because it's disrespectful." He stalked toward her. "What's really bothering you?"

Her chin dipped. "I just told you."

"How did the designing go today?"

"Not well. Nothing's working. I threw them all out."

He shook his head. "You can't force it. You're pushing too hard with everything. Give yourself some space. Take a day off."

"It's my sanity," she growled.

"Good thing, then, I've set aside some downtime for us."

"*Downtime?* Isn't that an oxymoron for you?"

He ignored the gibe. "Things are in control for the moment. Idas will sign. Which means you and I are going away for the weekend where we are addressing all of this, Sofía. *All of it.* I can't be fighting battles on multiple fronts."

And there was the *real* issue. Not him caring about her. She was taking up his precious brain space.

She lifted her chin. "*I* don't have time. I have a wedding to plan."

"To supervise," he corrected, stripping off his tie and starting on the buttons of his shirt. "And we aren't going far. Just to the summerhouse."

The one on the private island off the shore of Akathinia Stella had pointed out on their tour? Her stomach curled in on itself. "It's not necessary. We can work things out here."

"Like we've been doing?" He lifted a brow as he shrugged out of his shirt. "We are good together, Sofía. We will make a great team together if we can iron out this discord."

"If that's even possible."

"Oh, it's *possible*." He threw his shirt on the chair and breezed past her on his way to the bathroom. "The only variable is how long it takes for you to give in to what you know is the truth. And *how* I make you do it."

Her breath caught in her throat. "Did I actually *like* you once?"

He paused in midstride, his mouth tugging up at the corners in one of those rare devilish smiles that made her heart go pitter-patter. "You adored me once, *glykeia mou*. I'm sure you can get that loving feeling back."

"Oof." She stared at him as he walked into the bathroom. Her engagement ring shimmered in the light as she made a rude hand gesture at his back. The *cursed* ring.

"Haven't you already *doomed* us with this ring?"

He turned around, the smile fading from his face. "I bought you that ring because you loved it. Because we don't need luck. We can do this, Sofía. You just have to make the call."

She stood there, shoes in hand as he disappeared into the bathroom, the sound of the shower starting up. *Damn him.* This was not the way she needed to face the most intimidating night of her life. Off balance and suddenly unsure of *everything*.

CHAPTER SEVEN

SOFÍA HAD ATTENDED a seemingly endless amount of events in New York to promote her business to the fashionable women who frequented them. Hospital fund-raisers, art galas, gallery openings, society events, all at stunning venues with the crème de la crème of society in attendance. But not one of those occasions could have prepared her for the near frenetic energy that surrounded the palace as car after car of dignitaries and upper-crust Akathinians arrived under the furious shutters of the paparazzi cameras.

Lit this evening in the gold and blue national colors of Akathinia, the palace looked straight out of a fairy tale with its square turrets and gold-accented glory. Sofía and Nik stood at the center of it all at the head of the receiving line with Nik's family, Sofía in a bloodred gown by her favorite Italian designer and Nik in ceremonial military dress that made him look lethally handsome.

Her mother and her fiancé, Benetio, already inside, Sofía turned a smile on the King and Queen of Sweden, her lips feeling as if they were painted on by this point. "So lovely to meet you," she murmured to the queen.

On and on it went, for another thirty minutes, names and faces blurring into one another. Ambassadors, European royalty, upper-crust Akathinians and the filthy rich who spent their life moving from one party to the next.

She lifted her head to offer one of the final arrivals a smile. *Almost done.* And lost it immediately. Stunning in an ice-blue gown, the simplicity of which only enhanced her elegant, reed-thin figure, Sofía would have recognized the countess anywhere. She was so perfect she almost didn't look real with her coiffed, ethereal beauty.

Her own defiant choice of red suddenly screamed *overdone.*

"Countess," she murmured, inclining her head.

The countess's gaze slid over her in the same unabashed study as Sofía had given her. Sofía stood, back ramrod straight, head tossed back under the scrutiny.

"What a…sensational choice of dress," the countess finally responded, leaning forward to blow air-kisses to both of Sofía's cheeks. "It makes quite a statement. Congratulations to you and Nikandros."

Sofía drew back. *The scarlet woman*, she might as well have said. Nik's pregnant lover who'd reeled him in. She could just imagine all the labels running through the countess's head.

Frosty Maurizio and the rest of the Agieros were next, then the American ambassador to Akathinia, who, at least, finished off the endless precession on a pleasant note.

Nik curved his fingers around hers. "Now you can relax."

Relax? Was that a joke?

The paparazzi chanted their names from the bottom of the steps, the refrain growing louder with every second. Nik tugged on her hand to turn her around. "They've been patient," he said, "let's give them a good shot."

She didn't have a smile left in her as they walked down the steps toward the crowd of photographers. Not a single one. Nik slid an arm around her waist and pulled her close. "You're stiff as a board," he murmured in her ear. "You're supposed to be in love with me. Fairy-tale engagement and all that."

She pasted one last fake smile on her face. "I'm a terrible actor."

"Then don't act." He turned her toward him, his fingers curving around her jaw as he brought his mouth down on hers in a hard, possessive kiss. No avenue of escape existed with camera flashbulbs exploding all around them, Nik's less than PG-rated kiss passionate, demonstrative, demanding a response from her. Knocked completely off balance, Sofía curved her fingers around his lapel to steady herself.

The paparazzi loved it, catcalls and whistles filling the air as their flashes went mad. Sofía surrendered helplessly, for what else could she do, her lips clinging to Nik's, her body poised on tiptoe as she absorbed the magic of what it was like to be kissed by him.

A dangerous occupation.

Nik lifted his mouth from hers, eyes glittering. "Much better."

She fought for composure, heart pounding, lips stinging. "You have your reaction," she came back tartly. "We're needed inside."

His low laughter taunted her. "That wasn't even close to the reaction I'm looking for from you, Sofía. We save that for later."

Flashbulbs continued to explode in her face. She ignored him, or attempted to with her insides a hot mess of confusion.

"Sofía," a paparazzi called. "Who are you wearing?"

A genuine smile curved her lips. "Francesco Villa. He's a genius. He's making my wedding dress."

They answered a handful of other questions, then turned to make their way up the steps.

"Sofía. It's rumored you're carrying the royal heir. Care to comment?"

She froze, desperately grateful her back was to the cameras. She would have given it away in a shutter click. Nik's hand tightened around hers as they turned back to the cameras.

"I'm working on it," he drawled. "Isn't that supposed to be the enjoyable part?"

Laughter rang out. The photographer held up his camera in a wry gesture that said "I had to ask."

She and Nik resumed their path up the steps. "Better you took that one," she murmured. "Although I'm not sure that's the way I would have answered it."

They made their way into the palace and up to the second-story ballroom. The service staff scurried to ensure the guests had a glass of champagne in their hands before they made their entrance.

She stood beside Nik underneath the massive, twenty-foot-high double doors to the ballroom, her stomach spinning circles. The room looked magical cast in its blue-and-gold glow, its ten-foot-wide chandeliers dripping with crystal rivaling the jewels that adorned the exquisitely clad guests.

It was like walking into a fairy tale. *Except this was real. She was about to marry a king.*

A fleeting wish that this *was* real instead of being the pretend, practical union it was flashed through her head. She extinguished it as quickly as it came because believing in fairy tales had never been a luxury for her. That had all ended far too early in life.

A booming voice announced them. She took Nik's arm as they moved to the front of the room to give the welcome toast. The glare of the spotlight, the sensation of hundreds of eyes on her made her hand tremble as she took the glass of sparkling juice a waiter handed her. She kept her eyes on Nik to ground herself.

Nik lifted his glass. "Tonight is a joyous occasion for Akathinia. A time for us to celebrate this stunning nation we are fortunate enough to call our own, and my beautiful bride-to-be, Sofía." He turned to face her, his brilliant blue gaze resting on her face. "Sofía reminds me so much of our great country. Vibrant and proud. *Strong*. I know Akathinia will benefit from her warmth, wisdom and perspective."

Heat flooded her cheeks. It was a message, she knew, for the press and Akathinians gathered, but it did something funny to her insides.

His attention switched back to the crowd. "Let this also be a night for healing. A time for us all to move on. My brother was taken from us far too soon," he said, a rough edge inflecting his tone, "in far too unjust a way, but I know tonight, he would have wanted us to celebrate. To let him go.

"Thank you for coming," he said huskily, lifting his glass. "We look forward to sharing this special evening with you."

Sofía lifted her glass, a deep throb in her chest. It was as if he had finally let himself feel. To digest the pain that was clearly tearing him apart. She thought perhaps the message of renewal had been meant for her, too. That *they* needed to move on.

She and Nik circulated. They sought out her mother and Benetio first, who had arrived that afternoon. Sofía had never seen her mother so radiant and happy. It was bittersweet to watch with the turmoil going on inside of her. With how far apart they were emotionally. Her mother had never been able to give, only take. And yet, watching her with Benetio, their relationship looked reciprocal. Her fiancé had managed to draw her mother out of herself, something she had never been able to do.

But maybe someday that would change, she told herself, kissing Benetio on the cheek and hugging her mother. Maybe Nik was right. Maybe this was a time for renewal.

"It's all so exciting," her mother exclaimed, looking up at Sofía's fiancé. "A real king. How lucky is my daughter?"

A smile tugged at Nik's mouth. "She says that all the time. She just said it to me earlier actually. How fortunate she was to have met me."

"So true," Sofía drawled. "I could spend all day detailing your attributes. They are so...*compelling*."

Nik looked only more amused. Her mother rattled on about her own wedding plans until they were forced to move on, promising to find them later.

"Perhaps you'll catch some of your mother's enthusiasm for the wedding planning," Nik murmured as he guided her toward the next group, which he'd informed her included the devil himself, Aristos Nicolades.

"Perhaps I would," she conceded, "if I didn't have a million and one protocols to follow."

"Which are what the wedding planner is for." He pressed a palm to her back as the loosely arranged grouping that was their target parted to admit them. A tall, extremely well-built male who looked to be in his early thirties stepped forward. "Your Highness."

His designer dark stubble and piercing, black-as-sin eyes were a bit breathtaking. The dangerous, edgy vibe the stranger exuded suggested this might be Aristos Nicolades.

Nik stepped forward to shake his hand. "Aristos Nicolades, meet my fiancée, Sofía Ramirez."

Aristos's eyes moved over her in an appreciative slide that somehow managed to be proper and not so proper all at the same time. Instead of shaking the hand she offered, he brought it to his mouth, brushing a kiss across her knuckles. Nik stiffened beside her at the lapse in propriety.

"The king is a lucky man," Aristos murmured. "Congratulations."

As beautiful as he was, as fascinating as his predatory vibe undoubtedly manifested itself for just about any woman on the planet, Aristos's touch generated none of the electricity she felt when Nik put his hands on her. The magnetic realization that she had been wired for him and him alone.

The thought was more than a little disconcerting.

She retrieved her hand. "So lovely to meet you, Mr. Nicolades, after hearing so much about you."

Aristos's mouth curved. "I can imagine the king's opinion of me could prove quite fascinating. You must enlighten me."

Nik's fingers tightened around her elbow. "I am looking forward to us being on the same side, Nicolades. It should prove refreshing."

"Undoubtedly."

Nik flicked a glance over the group. "You came with someone?"

Aristos nodded toward a tall blonde immersed in conversation with another woman. "No need to introduce. It's dying a slow death."

Nik's mouth twisted. Sofía absorbed the nonchalant look on Aristos's face, then glanced over at the vivacious-looking, stunningly beautiful blonde, a response tumbling out of her mouth before she could stop it. "Does *she* know that yet?"

Aristos lifted a shoulder. "Considering the blowout we had before we came, I am fairly sure she does."

Sofía blinked. Regarded Nik's lethal rival as the two men embarked on a conversation about meeting the next week. "He's outrageous," she murmured to Nik when he wrapped the conversation and propelled her forward into the crowd. "Poor woman."

He guided her through a traffic jam. "His women are well aware of the score. I'm sure she's cognizant of the fact her expiration date is almost up."

"As was mine until the unexpected happened."

Nik leaned down and brought his mouth to her ear. "You know you and I were more complex than Aristos's careless liaisons. I hardly think they can be put in the same category."

Complex? What did that even mean? That the desire they'd had for each other had simply been more consuming than most? That it had been harder to walk away? What *would* happen when Nik's lust for her died? Would his attitude be just as apathetic and cynical as Aristos's? After all, they seemed to be two birds of a feather when it came to women despite what Nik said.

They attempted to greet everyone, but with hundreds in attendance it was almost impossible. Some of the Akathinians were gracious and welcoming to her, many more were cold and unfriendly to the outsider she clearly was. It was unnerving and depressing to put herself out there time and time again only to have her overtures thrown back in her face. By the time she and Nik moved to the center of the room to kick off the dancing, she wasn't sure if she was furious or utterly deflated.

He drew her into his arms, camera flashes extinguishing as she laced her fingers through his and set her hand on his shoulder. His gaze scoured hers. "If you let them get to you, they win."

"Easy for you to say. You haven't been the subject of a hundred snubs."

"Who cares what they think? You are *my* choice."

Because she was carrying his child. Because it was his *duty*. The humiliation that had been building inside her all evening spun itself into a fury, heating every inch of her skin. Clamping her mouth shut, she stared sightlessly over his shoulder.

"Sofía—"

"Leave it," she advised. "I'm fine."

She was anything but, but he did, likely as aware as she was that if they kept this up, the official photograph was going to be of them having a fight.

She danced with his father after that, which did nothing for her demeanor, Harry, Nik's best friend from New York, then with a succession of partners, following Akathinian tradition that the bride and groom-to-be began and ended the evening in the arms of their betrothed, but in between were encouraged to enjoy the charms of as many eligible guests as they could. To celebrate their last days of freedom as it were.

When Aristos Nicolades approached her to dance, his blonde goddess Lord knew where, she almost refused him, not sure she was up to it. Then the defiant part of her that had been kicking up its heels all evening took over.

"I would love to," she accepted, taking the hand he offered. He was wickedly tall and solid as he took her into his arms on the dance floor, moving with a smooth, commanding precision. He flirted with her with that irreverent carelessness that seemed to be so much a part of him and it was exactly what Sofía needed in her current mood. When she laughed at a particularly outrageous anecdote he recounted, Nik trained his gaze on her from across the dance floor.

Good, she thought. Let him watch.

She looked up at her dance partner. "Why don't you end it cleanly if you know your relationship is over?"

His black-as-night eyes glimmered. "Are you reprimanding me, Ms. Ramirez?"

"I think maybe I am."

He threw his head back and laughed. "Nikandros is going to have his hands full with you. No doubt about it. And yes, you are right. If I was anything but, what would the old-fashioned term be? A *cad*? I would have done so a few weeks ago."

"A woman would far more appreciate your honesty than to be treated as an expendable commodity."

An amused smile played about his lips. "Some of the women I date would prefer to bury their head in the sand when it's time to call it quits. Perhaps it is my bank account that gives them pause."

"Then you, Mr. Nicolades," she said tartly, "are dating the wrong women."

"Maybe so." He gave her a considering look. "I would wish your husband-to-be good luck taming such a fiery personality, but I have the distinct feeling he is up to the challenge. And that he will enjoy it very much."

She blushed and lifted a brow. "You think so?"

"Undoubtedly. Everyone talked about Athamos's cool negotiating skills, yet I would far rather face him across a boardroom table than Nik. Nik may be passionate, but he is the iciest, most formidable negotiator I have ever encountered when he sits down at a table. He is willing to take it to the limit, to the very edge of a deal to win. A much more worthy adversary."

Aristos's assessment of her fiancé only underscored

the sinking feeling in her stomach. She had given her life up to become queen in a country that didn't want her, for a man who thought she was a liar, who was only marrying her because she carried his heir. A man who would do what it took to have her fall in line so he could move on and rule his country. Her happiness was inconsequential.

Thinking she could ever belong to this world had been madness.

Her head reeling, a panicky feeling lingering just around the edges of her consciousness, she finished her dance with Aristos, grabbed a glass of sparkling water from a waiter's tray and sought refuge on one of the smaller, more intimate balconies, desperately needing air. Relieved to find it empty, she rested her elbows on the railing, the still warm, fragrant air drifting across her bare shoulders in a featherlight caress. It was too late to change her mind. Too late to put a halt to the chain of events she'd set in place when she'd agreed to become Nik's wife. But oh, how she wished she could in this moment. She would give anything to be back in New York, handling a busy rush at the boutique, her busy, ordinary life pulsing ahead. Instead she had descended into a version of hell she had no idea how she was going to manage.

"A bit overwhelming, is it not?"

She turned at the sound of the smooth, lightly accented voice. The countess. *Dammit.* She had done her best to avoid the woman all evening, yet here she was as if she'd specifically hunted her down.

"I needed some air," she acknowledged, turning back to look at the formal gardens, breathtaking in their color and symmetry.

The countess joined her at the railing, balancing her champagne glass on the ledge. "Akathinians are not the most welcoming to outsiders. Oh, we appreciate the influx of foreigners and the money they spend here, but when it comes down to it, they are not Akathinians. They will never achieve the same station, the same acceptance as a native with the right bloodlines."

Sofía's eyes widened. The countess held up a hand. "I'm not trying to be cruel. One could say I have, what do you Americans call it? Spoiled *grapes*? But in actuality, I'm telling you the truth. It will not be an easy ride for you."

Hot color filled Sofía's cheeks. "It seems that's the case. But since Nik has made his choice, I think the point is irrelevant, don't you?"

The countess shrugged. "Maybe so. It's unfortunate, however, that he has been forced into this course of action. It would have been easier for him to have had the Agieros on his side. A wife who understands the intricacies of what he is facing instead of one who will detract from his popularity."

Her breath caught in her throat. The countess shrugged. "The king will, at some point, realize his mistake."

"And you, Countess?" she challenged, her control rapidly dwindling. "Would you have been happy being married off for political expediency? Knowing a man was only sharing your bed because he *had* to? I would find that rather hard to swallow."

The countess's head snapped back. "It's preferable, then, to be the woman who trapped him into marriage with a baby? What else would have prompted him to break an alliance with my family?" She shook her head. "Relationships burn brightly, then they extinguish. I've had enough experience in my life to learn that. So yes, Sofía, I would have been fine with a political match. It would serve you well to lose some of your starry-eyed perspective if I can give you one piece of advice. To recognize the reality of what you are walking into."

Starry-eyed? She would have laughed at how far that was from the truth of her and Nik if it wouldn't have hurt too damn much.

Turning on her heel she stalked inside. Had she stayed she would certainly have ensured herself a position on Akathinia's persona non grata list. If she wasn't there already.

CHAPTER EIGHT

IT WAS THE early hours of the next morning before Nik and Sofía bid farewell to their final guests on the front steps of the palace. Sofía stood by Nik's side, so tightly strung underneath the hand he had placed at her waist he knew he had another battle left to fight tonight. It was in every veiled look of hostility she'd thrown at him for the past couple of hours. She'd only done it, of course, in those rare moments when it wouldn't be recorded by the cameras or hundreds of sets of eyes, but the message had come through loud and clear.

His fiancée was unhappy. Desperately so. And while he couldn't blame her given the reception the Akathinians had supplied, he had expected her to be tougher about it. Sofía had always been tough. It had been one of the things that had drawn him to her.

The senior event staffer nodded at him that they could quietly melt away. He guided Sofía into the palace and up the stairs toward their rooms. She shrugged his hand off and continued up the stairs, cheeks rosy, hair slipping from the knot atop her head, the enticing curve of her back arched above her delectable bottom as she charged on ahead of him. She was the most stunning female on the face of the planet in that moment, a curvaceous red flame any man would be wild to possess.

Including Aristos Nicolades. He had clearly been besotted with his fiancée.

Sofía threw open the doors to their suite and stalked in, headed toward the bedroom. Sitting down on the bed, she yanked her shoes off and flung them toward the closet.

Nik followed, shrugging out of his jacket and losing his tie. "So they gave you a hard ride. You knew from the press that was going to happen. We prepared you for that. Why let them get to you so?"

Her eyes darkened. "*That* was not a hard ride. That was a bloodbath. They chewed me up and spit me out, Nik. I am humiliated. No," she said, waving her hand at him, "that's not a strong enough word. I feel...*annihilated.*"

He narrowed his gaze on her. "I think you're exaggerating."

"*Exaggerating?* I made an attempt with every single one of them, *despite* their condescension. I laughed at their elitist jokes, made an attempt to *look* like I cared about cricket and the dying art of a good afternoon tea, and all I got back was a brick wall. *Nothing.* As if I might as well not even have tried. It isn't *me* that needs an attitude adjustment, it's *them.*"

"You need to calm down," he said quietly, eyeing her heaving chest. Worrying she was going to work herself into a panic attack. "Not everyone was unwelcoming. Some of the most powerful members of Akathinian society were *very* welcoming."

"I can count them on a hand." She started pulling pins out of her hair and tossing them on the bed.

"Enough of this, Sofía," he growled. "They'll get over it."

She fixed her gaze on him, twin ebony pools of fire that singed him with her contempt. "Do you know what she said to me, your countess? She told me that I will never be accepted by Akathinian society because I am just not one of you. That you should have chosen a woman who understands the intricacies of what you are facing instead of one who will detract from your popularity."

He frowned. "She said that?"

"That wasn't even the best of it. She told me it was unfortunate I wasn't taking your best interests to heart by trapping you into marriage with a baby. That you would realize your mistake of attaching yourself to a nobody like me."

He clenched his jaw. "*Thee mou*, Sofía, those are the words of a woman who has suffered her own humiliation. The Agieros have a name to protect. I don't condone her for attacking you like that, but she can be forgiven for slipping."

"*Slipping?* She came *after me*. I'd been avoiding her all evening."

That surprised him. He sighed, running a hand through his hair. "I'm sorry. I am. I wish it could have been different tonight. But it will get easier, I promise you."

She pulled the last of the pins out of her hair, the long silken tresses floating around her shoulders. Turned that volatile dark stare on him. "What do you want from me, Nik? I have agreed to this marriage. I have given up my life. And still you keep asking for more."

"I want you to stop fighting what you can't change. You're only making it more difficult for yourself."

"While you want *everything*." She glared at him, her cheeks firing a deep red. "Do you know how hard I've tried to put my past behind me? How much I'd like to forget I was the girl who lived in the apartment building none of my friends were allowed to go to because so many bad things happened there? I *had* put that behind me until the press dredged up my *meager* beginnings. Then they go and quote one of the women I *hated* from my fashion design class, who called me Scholarship Girl, who never let me forget I didn't belong in her high society circles, who refused to acknowledge the talent that got me there. Now *she*," she rasped, "was smart. She made it sound as if we were fast friends, so she could attach her name to mine for her own advantage."

He stared at her for a long moment, the misery she must have felt as a child hitting him square in the chest. He took a deep breath. "It's unfortunate, Sofía, how they have portrayed you. But if you let them destroy you over this, it's they who have the power, not you. You can't let them do that to you."

She lifted her chin. "I am *better* than that."

"Yes, you are," he agreed, sitting down on the bed beside her. "You blow me away with your strength. What it must have taken for you to survive as a young girl. So use it now. Design the best clothing line that silences them all. *Be* that designer you've always wanted to be. The people's respect will come if *you* show them who you are.

She stared mutely at him. "That's easy for you to say," she finally said. "I'm scared. I feel *lost* Nik. Hopelessly adrift. Way out of my depth. I don't know if I can do this. And that's *before* we add a child to the mix."

"Did you ever stop to think how I feel? This is new for me, too, Sofía. I am finding *my* way. Amid the press who make constant comparisons of me to my brother and father, who record my mistakes one by one. *I* have to believe in myself in this situation. Believe I can run this country, that I can set this nation on the right path. There is no room for doubt or constant second-guessing."

Her chin dipped. "Is it too much to ask for a little support along the way?"

He shook his head. "You need to do that. But you also need to tell me when you're scared. When you're feeling overwhelmed. I'm not a mind reader."

Her eyes fired. "All well and good for you to say. But since you made that promise to me a couple of weeks ago, Nik, I've seen you a total of about an hour a day, most of that time during dinner with your family. Should I book an appointment with you? Slot myself in?"

"Now you're being ridiculous."

"Am I?" She gave him a scathing look. "Aristos thought I was well in hand with you, you know. That you would enjoy *handling* me. Putting me in my place."

"You were discussing me with *Aristos*?"

"He brought it up, not me. He finds it impressive how you will take a deal to the very edge to win. Is that what you were doing earlier, Nik? *Now?* Telling me what I want to hear to solve your problem before it blows up in your face?"

"I *meant* what I said." He raked his gaze over her. "You were attracted to him."

"I wish I was. At least Aristos is an open book. What you see is what you get. God only knows with you."

Blood pounded his temples, frustration and jealousy mixing in a volatile combination. He'd had enough. *Quite enough.* He snared his fingers around her waist and dragged her onto his lap. His gaze speared hers as her lush bottom made intimate contact with his hard thighs. "You would be wise," he bit out, "to never discuss me with Aristos again. Or," he added deliberately, "to flirt with him as blatantly as you did tonight."

She didn't heed the warning. Instead her eyes went even blacker. "I thought that was the point of the Akathinian tradition… To enjoy the free members of the opposite sex before you are tied down for all eternity."

A surge of adrenaline picked him up and carried him past the point of no return. "Yes," he agreed. "It is also tradition that the bride-to-be ends up in the groom-to-be's bed. *Pleasuring him.*"

She caught her lip between her teeth. "Not this bride-to-be."

The flare of excitement in her eyes convinced him otherwise. Bending his head he tugged her lip between his teeth, taking over the job. She pushed her palms against his chest in a halfhearted shove, but her breath was coming too rapidly for him to put any stock in her protest, her luscious body in the sensational red dress plastered against him too great a temptation to resist.

His teeth sank deeper into her lip, punishing her. "You should know better than to bait me, *Sofía mou*. Or maybe that was the point?"

"As if I—" He cut off her sputter, taking her mouth in an aggressive possession designed to get to the heart of the matter. Her underneath him where she should have been for the past two weeks.

Her nails dug into his biceps in a punishment of her own. A soft sound emerged from the back of her throat, her mouth opening under his. He took advantage of it, burying his fingers in a chunk of her hair while he slid his tongue inside her mouth to taste her, stroke her. Another low moan as her fingers relinquished their death grip on his flesh reached right inside of him.

A push of his palm sent her back on the bed, her sexy red dress riding up her thighs. His hands pushed it up farther, his only intention to be inside of her. Her eyes were molten dark fire as they met his. But there was also indecision there. It made him curse low in his throat.

"There isn't one inch of you that doesn't want me to

take you right now," he rasped. "Allow us what we both want."

"I need time to think.

"About *what*?"

She pushed herself into a sitting position. "About whether I give you that power over me."

His brutally aroused body protested loudly. "I have made a promise to you, Sofía. I am committed to making this work."

"Then prove it." She shimmied to the side of the bed and slid off, the silky red dress covering up her delectable thighs. A dark brow winged upward as she turned to him. "We have all weekend, don't we?"

CHAPTER NINE

SOFÍA SPENT TWO DAYS with her mother and Benetio before they flew home to New York. They toured Akathinia, went for a cruise to the neighboring islands and spent considerable amounts of time in the jewelry shops in the Akathinian capital, where her mother fell in love with a local designer.

It was with mixed feelings that she walked her mother and Benetio down to the helicopter pad on the palace lawn for their trip to Athens. She had made an effort to connect with her mother, not an easy thing for her to ask of herself, but something in Nik's speech the night of their engagement party had resonated with her. She could either keep the shell she had built around herself intact, or put herself out there, make herself vulnerable, with the hopes of restoring her relationship with her mother. She had realized she couldn't not try.

She had told her mother about the baby. It had made her mother cry, as if breaking through some of her mother's own walls. It had been a step in the right direction for them and she'd invited her mother to come back by herself to spend some time together before the wedding.

"Thank you," her mother said, catching her up in a hug as the helicopter blades started to whir. "It's lovely to see you so happy, sweetheart." She drew back and for the first time seemed to see the conflict in her daughter's eyes. "You are happy, right? Nik is wonderful."

She bit her lip. She didn't want to worry her mother with her own wedding so close at hand. "Yes, *Mama*," she assured her, giving her mother a last tight hug. "I am happy. Call me when you're home so I know you're safe."

Her mother nodded and climbed aboard the helicopter with Benetio. It had been Nik's idea to organize the helicopter ride so the couple could enjoy the spectacular views before flying from Athens to New York. A thoughtful gesture on her fiancé's part that had Claudia Ramirez over the moon and terrified at the same time.

It seemed, Sofía thought wryly, as if her fiancé was intent on making all the Ramirez women face their fears.

Nik wrapped up his outstanding business and the next morning they flew by helicopter to the island of Evangelina, a few miles off the coast of Akathinia, to the summerhouse King Damokles had built for his wife, Evangeline. Aware of her nerves in the dipping and swaying helicopter that seemed so fragile to Sofía, Nik wrapped his fingers around hers and kept them there the entire short ride to the island.

His description of them as complex came to mind. It felt very accurate at the moment with a dozen different emotions swirling through her head. Would they be able to come to an understanding of each other? Could Nik really let her in? Trust her? Let go of his suspicions of her? Realize she was that same woman he'd met in New York? Or would their defensive barriers prove too thick for either to pierce?

Set on a pristine private island with glorious white sand beaches and surrounded by a brilliant azure sea, *summerhouse* seemed an amusing term to Sofía for the palatial villa that had been Nik's great-grandfather's hideaway, a place where he and his family could enjoy time away from the pressures of ruling.

Nik showed her around the eighteen-room villa built by a renowned Italian architect of the time, complete with fifteen bedrooms, an art gallery, a chapel and formal gardens.

"It's magnificent," she said as they finished their tour in the grand foyer with its spectacular staircase and priceless Renaissance paintings.

Nik took his sunglasses off. "It's cooling off now. I thought we might enjoy a walk and a swim before dinner."

She eyed him. "You really aren't going to work?"

"On us? Yes. On official business? No."

Her stomach rolled. The banked intensity that had swirled around her fiancé ever since she'd rejected him for the second time the night of their engagement party was an ever-present force that sat between them like a living entity. Unsure of what would happen when they unleashed the passion between them, the only thing she did know for certain was that it would change the rules of the game yet again. To what, she had no idea.

But really, she conceded, they had no choice. They had to make this work.

"I'll go change, then," she said huskily. "Will you show me to our room?"

He led her up to the ethereal, beautiful blue bedroom that overlooked a strip of white sand beach and an endless vista of blue. Dark, hand-carved furniture contrasted with the airy feel of the room, a massive canopied four-poster bed perfectly positioned to drink in the spectacular view.

A lazy morning sunrise or an evening sunset would be incredible from that vantage point, she determined, then steadfastly ignored the thought. She needed to see more evidence from Nik that he was willing to let her in before they went there.

Her clothes had been magically hung up while they had toured the villa, her bathing suits nestled in one of the ornate drawers along the wall. She slipped on a white bikini and some sunscreen, then pulled a short sundress overtop. By the time she was finished dressing, Nik had finished his call and was waiting in the bedroom for her clad only in low-slung black swim trunks.

Heavens. Her eyes drank him in. It was one thing not lusting after him when he was fully clothed, another thing entirely when so much of his tanned olive skin was on display. When the matching Vs that defined the top of his pecs and the bottom of his abs were cut deep into his rock-hard flesh in a work of perfection that begged to be drooled over. *Touched.* Paid homage to as he held himself over her and took her to heaven.

"You want to skip the walk, *glykeia mou*?" His gaze speared hers, all leashed testosterone. "I am all about a morning *nap*."

A flush heated her chest, working its way up to her face. "A walk sounds perfect." She picked up her hat and swished by him out the door. He cursed under his breath and followed. A smile curved her lips. She liked having the power for once. It was a heady feeling.

They walked along the pristine, blindingly white sand beach, cooled by a perfect light breeze that came off the sea. Nik reached for her hand and laced his fingers through hers. She didn't protest this simple intimacy because it felt so familiar, so right, it was impossible to.

She turned her gaze to the sea. It was the most perfect shade of blue she'd ever seen. Not turquoise, not the gray blue of the New York harbor, but a pure, vibrant cerulean blue that took her breath away.

Her thoughts turned to Athamos, whose body might still be out there somewhere, *was* still out there. "Do you think they'll ever find him?"

Nik looked down at her, his eyes shaded by the dark glasses he wore. "Athamos?"

"Yes."

He shook his head. "The currents are too strong. The divers spent weeks combing the waters. There was only so long we could ask them to be out there in a fruitless pursuit."

"That was the hardest part," she said. "Not ever being able to say goodbye to my father. We were fortunate they found his body. Some families were not so lucky."

He moved his gaze back to the water. "I went to the crash site after I met with Idas. It wasn't until then that I realized I was holding out some crazy hope by not finding his body with the car that perhaps it was all a big mistake, that he was alive out there somewhere. Some fisherman had picked him up, he was concussed and couldn't remember who he was. Or he'd ended up on one of the many deserted islands and we just hadn't found him yet." The grim lines around his mouth deepened. "That was, of course, wishful thinking. He would have been recognized if he was alive. And it never would have happened in the first place because no one would ever have survived that drop."

Her heart throbbing, she squeezed her fingers tight around his. "Was Idas able to shed any more light on what happened?"

"Nothing more than it was a personal dispute between the two of them. Which I believe now it was. He said that Kostas was struggling with it."

"I'm sure he must be. To be the one to survive, regardless of the dispute between them, it must be difficult."

"If guilt is *what* he is feeling, yes,"

She let that sit, the lap of the waves and the cry of the gulls the only sounds in the air.

"They had a complex relationship, Athamos and Kostas," he said after a moment. "They were rivals with a fierce respect for one other. They went to military school together. God only knows what happened between them."

She thought back to his father's cutting words that night at dinner. *If Athamos had been here, this wouldn't have happened. We would have had a deal with the Agieros.*

"Has it always been like this between you and your father? The differences you have?"

"Always."

"That must have been difficult," she said carefully, knowing she was treading dangerous waters but equally sure this was key to understanding her soon-to-be husband. "For your father and brother to be so close. For you to have such different leadership styles."

He turned his aviator sunglasses–protected gaze on her. "Confession time, Sofía?"

She lifted her chin. "I thought we were just having a conversation."

He bent, picked up a shell, examined it and tossed it back into the sea. "I have deep internal wounds because of it. It's shaped me into the closed, guarded man that I am. Is that what you want to hear me say? That my brother having my father's ear has driven a painful wedge between him and I?"

Her mouth compressed. "Only if it's the truth."

He stared at her, whatever was going on behind those dark glasses a mystery to her. "I graduated top of my class at Harvard. Summa cum laude. I was the valedictorian. And yet my father did not see fit to attend. It was not of enough importance to him. Whereas my brother's graduation from Oxford was. Where he did *not* graduate with honors. Where he was *not* valedictorian. That pretty much sums up the family dynamic."

A lump formed in her chest. "What about your mother? Are you closer to her?"

He shook his head. "My mother doesn't possess a strong maternal instinct. She left the child-rearing to our nannies. Particularly after my father's infidelities. She spent more and more time away working on her charitable endeavors."

And clearly she couldn't have divorced her husband. Leaving Nik with no anchor at home except nannies who would never be able to fully emulate a mother-son bond. It was little more than she'd had.

She frowned. "How did you handle all of that growing up? Where did you find your strength?"

"Athamos and I were close despite our differences. As were Stella and I." He lifted a shoulder. "I made my own way. Proved my worth through my own successes."

But not to his father. He could be labeled the Wizard of Wall Street ten times over and it would never attack the core of his pain.

She studied his hard, unyielding profile. Knew now that was what was at the core of Nik's demons… A father impossible to please, who had been more interested in the heir to the throne. Building success after success and never having it be enough…

"Did you want to be king? Ever, I mean?"

A frown furrowed his brow. "It was never a possibility."

"But you must have had some thoughts on the subject."

"No," he said evenly. "I didn't. I loved my life in New York. Some days I felt more American than Akathinian. It was the last thing I wanted."

"But you were restless. You needed a challenge, Nik. I'm not saying anyone would have asked for this to happen. I'm saying perhaps this happened for a reason. *You* were meant to rule Akathinia, not Athamos."

He was silent, the late-afternoon sun warming their skin as they rounded a curve and headed around the other side of the island. "I wish I'd had time to clear up some things between him and me," he said, a faraway look in his eyes. "That is my biggest regret."

Her heart contracted. "I am sure he knew. Whatever it was you needed to tell him... I felt that way about my father. I had so much I wanted him to know, but I had to believe he knew all of it. That our bond was that strong."

His inscrutable expression remained. They walked the entire circle around the island. When they returned almost an hour later, perspiration slid down Sofía's back, her skin like an oven. She stripped off her sundress, took the hand Nik offered her and waded into the stunningly warm water.

It was just cool enough to be heavenly. Slid across her senses like the most heady of caresses as they waded to deeper water and Nik drew her close. She clasped her arms around his neck, her legs around his waist, allowing him to anchor her in the bobbing waves. His eyes were an intense, brilliant blue as he held her, his palms pressed flat against her back.

"Is that open enough for you, Sofía? Have I *earned* the right to have you, then?"

Her heart tightened; poised on the edge of making a decision she knew would change everything. It *would* give him a power over her she was afraid of. And yet he was opening up to her. She had a feeling the things he'd just told her were thoughts he might not have shared with anyone else. It made her hopeful, willing to believe he was right, that they had to move on and put their trust in one other and the bond they shared. That, in time, that trust would fully repair itself.

"Was it that hard?" she asked quietly, her gaze fixed on his. "You're teaching me to take risks, Nik. That terrifies me. My *whole life* terrifies me right now."

His dark lashes lowered. "Expressing my feelings isn't easy. I wasn't brought up to do that. I was brought up to *suppress* my emotions. But I promise what I said the night of our engagement party is true. I am going to do my best to let you in."

He kissed her then. The most soulful, thorough slide of his mouth against hers. She clasped his jaw in her hands and angled her head to find a deeper contact. When it was like this, when she could feel the depth of the connection they shared, stronger than anything she'd experienced in her life, she believed they could do anything together.

They traded kiss for kiss, sensuous slides of their mouths against each other. She could have sworn the water around them heated to a higher temperature. He was hard, ready, his erection insistent against her stomach. She was putty in his hands as the sun beat down on them, her body melting into his. But he lifted his head, his lust-infused gaze tangling with hers.

"I want a bed underneath us, *kardia mou*. Do not expect to sleep."

The sun was scheduled to set just after six. Nik instructed the chef to leave dinner for them to have later, then waved the Paris-trained cook off to spend the night with her family. He did the same with the turndown staff who hovered to see to their needs.

He was craving his fiancée. He wanted no interruptions.

He waited for Sofía outside on the checkerboard marble terrace that overlooked the sea, resplendent with its stunning statues of Achilles in various poses and battles. Queen Evangeline had been a lover of Greek mythology, her obsession with the stories she'd adored apparent not only here, but in the frescos that covered the ceilings of the villa and the magnificent artwork on the walls.

The sun began its slow descent into the horizon, a golden-orange ball of fire sinking toward an endless horizon of blue. He wondered, as he drank in the spectacular sight only an Akathinian sunset could provide, about what Sofía had said earlier. About his wanting to become king. What made him so restless it was hard to be in his own skin at times…? What *drove* him?

He knew the answer lay *here*, in the heritage he had tried so ineffectively to distance himself from in New York. How every time he was in his father's presence, that interaction seemed to strip away every success he'd racked up until he was no more than the black sheep he'd always been.

Had he really loved his life in New York that much? Or had he convinced himself he didn't want to be king because that had been easier to swallow than being second best? It had been simple to tell himself his adrenaline-inducing life in Manhattan had given him the freedom and power he'd craved. Honest to a degree. He'd had the ability to determine his own destiny, what more could a man want? But now he wondered if he'd been running away from the one thing he'd needed to address. To conquer. The need to prove he was not second best. That his father had been wrong about him.

Was that why he'd felt unfulfilled in New York of late? Unsure where to go next? Because until he wrestled this particular demon to the ground he would never find peace?

He had outmaneuvered a tricky player in Idas and found a solution that benefited both countries, one which would hopefully keep his people out of a prolonged and bloody war. He had put what his father thought behind him and focused on what the country needed now. It wasn't about winning, defeating Idas, it was about *leading*.

"No thinking about work."

Sofía's husky, sensual voice slid over his senses. He turned slowly, drinking her in. Her dark wavy hair was loose around her shoulders, her olive green dress simple, her feet bare.

The connection they shared enveloped him; drew him in. He had never wanted her more.

"I wasn't thinking about work," he drawled. "I had a far more compelling subject on my mind."

She swallowed, the muscles at the base of her slim throat convulsing. He held out a hand. She walked to him and slid her palm in his. "Would you like to share?"

"I would like to *show*. But first we should drink a toast. And eat before you pass out on me."

"A toast?" she queried.

He handed her a glass of the nonalcoholic champagne he'd had chilled. "To us. To a new beginning."

She lifted her dark gaze to his and raised her glass. "To new beginnings."

They drank as they watched the sun sink into the horizon, a hazy pink lancing blue as it made its fiery descent. When it took its final dip into the ocean, bidding adieu to the spectacular show, Nik turned to Sofía. "We should eat."

She stood on tiptoe, brought her mouth to his ear and told him, very explicitly, what she *was* hungry for. And it wasn't food.

His blood fired. "You won't pass out on me?"

"Depends on what you do to me."

He picked her up in his arms and headed for the villa, his heart pounding with anticipation. Heading for the wide set of stairs, he carried her up to their room, set her down on the floor and flicked on a light.

He reached for the buttons of his shirt while Sofía walked to the window to look at the pink sky the sunset had left behind.

"I can't imagine a more spectacular view than this."

"I can," he growled, his frustration bubbling over as he ditched his shirt.

She turned, an amused smile twisting her mouth. "I've kept you waiting long enough, King Nikandros?"

He collected her from the window by way of response, picked her up and carried her to the bed. Depositing her on the silk coverlet, his hands moved to the zipper of her dress, yanking it down to expose the creamy skin he coveted.

He stripped the dress off her shoulders and pushed it down to her waist. Her breasts had swelled, bursting from the lacy cups of her bra. The blatant reminder of the child they had conceived together stopped him in his tracks. Stole his breath. The heir to this country, yes, but also *their* baby. The product of that mind-numbingly sensual night they had spent together.

He hadn't stopped long enough during the insanity of the past few weeks to even think about *this*. To come face-to-face with the evidence that he would be a father in short order was earthshakingly real. *Mind-bending*.

He splayed his fingers across her abdomen, where her flat stomach was just beginning to turn convex. "You are so beautiful," he said huskily, bending to bring his mouth to hers. "I only want you more."

He consumed her then with a kiss that plundered

every inch of her beautiful lips. She arched her neck back, giving him full access to the heat of her mouth. The sweetness he craved.

His palms cupped her engorged breasts, the skate of his thumbs across her nipples pulling a hiss from her throat.

"Sensitive?"

She nodded, ebony eyes drunk with a heavy dark desire. He bent his head and took a lace-covered nipple into his mouth, her low moan kicking him in the gut. Determined to master the insatiable urge to possess her *now* without waiting, he brushed his thumb over her other nipple as he sucked hard; laved her with his teeth and tongue until her fingers were buried in his hair, tugging. *Demanding.* He transferred his attention to her other nipple, bringing it to the same erect attention as its twin.

Sofía uttered his name on a low, sweet moan. He pulled free, surveying her complete surrender with satisfaction. "What do you want?" he asked roughly. "Tell me."

Her fingers traced a provocative path down his chest to capture his hand and bring it to her inner thigh. He closed his fingers around her soft, silky flesh. *"Tell me."*

"I want your hands on me. Here."

His inner beast liked that. A lot. Because he loved to touch her there. To feel how much she desired him. To *taste* it.

He sank his knee down on the bed between her thighs and moved his hand up, pushing her dress higher until his fingers came into contact with the edge of her silk panties. Her breath hissed through her teeth. "Here?" he asked, sliding his finger along the edge of the silk.

"Yes."

He pushed the silk aside with one hand, tracing his

thumb along her cleft with the other. She jerked against him, her highly sensitized reaction heating his blood. He dipped deeper, probing her wet, hot flesh. His sex throbbed to life at such an overt display of her desire for him.

He took her lips in an erotic, openmouthed kiss as he sank his fingers into her. He had big hands, powerful hands, and she moaned into his mouth as he filled her. He wanted her crazy, his inner beast dictated. As desperate as he'd been for her for weeks.

"Nik—please—"

He thrust his fingers deeper into her. "Tell me, *glykeia mou*."

"More," she begged. "More, please…"

He caught her lip in his teeth. "You want my mouth on you?"

"Yes."

He pushed her back on the bed and dragged her dress up to her waist. The need to taste her, to claim her, swept over him in the basest of urges. Lying there, her gorgeous hair fanned out on the bed, her dark eyes hot with desire, she was everything he'd ever coveted. The only woman who could destroy his control with her exotic, sensual beauty.

"Give yourself to me," he commanded, his mouth taking hers in a hot, breathy kiss.

She knew the command, spread her legs for him in that half-uninhibited, half-shy way that made him crazy. Her eyes burned into his as he worked his way down her body, watching him the whole time. And then his brain went a hazy gray as her scent blurred the thoughts in his head until there was nothing but the soft, sweet flesh between her legs under his mouth, the rounded globes of her bottom he cupped to hold her where he wanted her and her soft cries as he raked her with his tongue. Again and again until she was squirming beneath him, begging for him to make her come.

He flicked his tongue against the hooded center of her, featherlight movements at first, then when her fingers curled in his hair and pulled, urging him on, he laved her in purposeful circles, applying a deliberate pressure to take her where he wanted her. *She was close, so close.* He plunged his fingers back inside of her and her scream rang out in the night.

"Oh, God." She pressed her hands to her face, her body supine beneath his, her chest rising and falling rapidly. He crawled his way up her body, stripped her hands from her face and kissed her until she tasted his dominance.

He lifted his mouth long moments later and surveyed her hazy gaze. "You still need to soothe the beast."

Her delicious mouth parted. "How might I do that?"

He ran a finger down her cheek. "I want you on top of me, riding me, until there's nothing left in me. And then," he added deliberately, "you can do it again."

Sofía had never been so turned on in her life. Nik was like a cat who'd escaped his pen tonight, desperate to possess her, single-minded in his intent. It made her feel delicate and feminine and oh, so hunted.

She ran her finger along his bottom lip. He closed his teeth around it and tugged, pulling a smile from her lips. "That would require great stamina. Is the king up to it?"

He took her hand and brought it to his groin, closing her fingers around his thick erection. "What do you think?"

Electricity rocketed through her. He was so big, so

rampantly male. The thought of having him inside her after all these weeks was unbearably exciting.

She pushed a hand against his chest. He moved obediently off her, his gaze tracking her as she slid off the bed and shrugged her shoulders to send her dress slithering to the floor. The expression on Nik's face made her tremble. He looked as if he wanted to devour her whole.

Nik joined her, stripping off his pants and boxers. He sprawled on the bed, spreading himself out like an olive-skinned feast for her personal consumption. His impressive erection was impossible to ignore, skimming the taut, defined wall of his abdomen. *He looked as if he might last forever...*

She climbed on the bed and straddled him, her hair sliding against his muscular chest as she brought her mouth down to his. She kissed him, feasted on him until he captured a chunk of her hair in his fingers and lifted her mouth from his.

His eyes were a hot, feverish blue, burning with intent. He fisted himself and brought the wide tip of his erection to her hot, damp flesh. Just the touch of him sent an excited shiver through her. She lifted her hips to take him inside her; gasped as he palmed her buttock and arched his hips, filling her with his thick, hard length in one savage thrust.

She rested her palms on his abdomen, eyes closed as she absorbed the sensation of being impaled on him. When the world righted itself, she opened her eyes.

"You are an animal tonight."

"Too long," he growled. "It's been too long."

His fingers gripped her hips. He lifted her off him, then back down, filling her with his hard, hot possession. Blinding her to anything but what it was to be taken by him, body and soul. Because that's what this was, no matter what either of them said, wanted to admit to each other, this was far beyond sex.

A moan escaped her. He gave her no reprieve, pulling her down on him again and again, his rough commands to take him deeper, harder, more animalistic than they'd ever been before.

Her body stirred back to life at the feel of him everywhere. He was that big, that powerful in this position. *Indescribable.*

He wrapped a hand around her jaw, his eyes blazing a path right through her as he brought her mouth down to his. There was a fierce need for possession in his eyes, but there was also a hunger. A hunger so deep she felt it down to her toes.

He wanted her. He needed her. But there was more. A depth of emotion he couldn't hide.

Witnessing it evoked dangerous thoughts. The thought that maybe, someday, he could get past his lack of trust. Be able to *love* her. Because she was afraid that's what she was beginning to want.

His tongue raked her bottom lip, demanding entry. She opened for him as he thrust it inside, mimicking the hard drives of his body. Her flesh softened, melted around him, giving him everything he asked for. He continued his merciless assault until his breath came in harsh pulls and his big body tensed, poised on release.

He slid his hand between them then, the rough pad of his thumb finding her core. He circled against her, his breath hot on her cheek as they came up for air. Sofía moaned, low and desperate.

"That's it, *agapimeni*," he urged, "come with me."

His expert touch, his hard driving body pushing her closer with every stroke tumbled her into a sweet, deep release that washed over her like a powerful tide, radiating outward from where his thumb played her. She uttered a strangled groan as it racked every nerve ending.

Nik growled, took her mouth and ground against her as he sought his release, the friction pulling her orgasm out in an extended, exquisite shudder.

The hot clench of her body pushed him over the edge. He drove harder, his essence spilling into her in a sweet, hot rush. She wrapped her legs tighter around him, savoring him.

When their breathing slowed, Nik pulled her down to nestle against his chest. She rested her head against the hard thud of his heart as he stroked her hair. It slowed gradually to an even, regular beat beneath her ear.

The connection they shared, the perfection of it, brought a question tumbling from her mouth.

"Who was she, Nikandros?"

CHAPTER TEN

NIK'S HAND STILLED on her hair. "Who are you talking about?"

She pushed herself up on her forearms to look at him. "The woman who's made you so gun-shy. So mistrustful. Stella told me about her, but she wouldn't give me details."

A flat, self-contained expression moved across his face. "She was nothing."

"If she was nothing, then you can tell me."

"Why?" Antagonism invaded that cool composure. "Why dredge up old history?"

"Because it goes to the heart of your mistrust of women. And I need to know."

He lifted her off him and set her on the bed. Sitting up, he raked a hand through his hair. "There isn't much to say. I dated a woman in my early twenties. I was less guarded back then. I shared things with her I shouldn't have. Near the end, when our relationship was coming to its natural conclusion, she could sense it and used some of the things I'd told her against me and my family."

She frowned. "What do you mean 'used them' against your family?"

"She sold a tell-all story to the press about our relationship. In it she revealed intimate details about my family."

"What details?"

"About my father's indiscretions."

Her heart sank. *Oh, Lord.* No wonder Nik held such a severe mistrust toward women. No wonder he'd accused her of doing anything she could to hang on to their relationship when a woman had done *that* to him.

She shook her head. "She is one woman, Nik. *One* woman out of the greater majority who would never be so vengeful, so spiteful as to do something like that to you. Surely you understand most people are more trustworthy than that?"

"Are they?" A dark brow winged its way upward. "I have never been with a woman who didn't want me for something, Sofía. Some are simply power hungry. To walk into a room on the arm of a prince holds great appeal. To enjoy my personal fortune in a city like New York does as well. Their intentions might not all have been as vengeful as Charlotte's, but they all wanted something from me. That's the way women work."

Her shoulders stiffened, her gaze raking over his face. "*I* didn't."

He said nothing.

Blood pounded her head. He was never going to believe her. He was always going to paint her with that brush.

She slid off the bed before her anger consumed her. "I'm going to shower."

"Sofía—"

She waved a hand at him, continuing her headlong flight toward the bathroom. She was almost there when he caught up with her, his fingers digging into her biceps to spin her around. "*Thee mou,* but you are a recalcitrant creature."

"Recalcitrant? Are all women children to you, too, Nik?"

He cupped the back of her head, his eyes blazing. "What do you want me to say?"

"I want you to say you know I am different. That you know I could not have planned that pregnancy. That that isn't me." She lifted her chin. "Did I *ever* at any point in our relationship lead you to believe I wanted to hang on to you past our *due date*? That I wasn't playing by the rules?"

"That last night," he said in a clipped tone. "You were different. I think you were getting emotionally attached. You were ending it because you were afraid you were going to get hurt."

She stared at him. Caught red-handed because it was true.

"You know what, Nik, you're right," she agreed, knowing one of them had to end this game of chicken they were playing. "I was ending it that night because I was falling for you. Even though I told myself it was unwise, that I knew the rules, I thought somewhere in us, in that *complexity* you threw around the other night, we had something special. That it was beyond sex. That we were *different*. There was no planning. No *scheming* to make a baby. And *that* is the truth."

He said nothing for a long moment, clearly caught off guard. She studied the emotion darkening his eyes. "What's the matter?" she taunted. "Does it unnerve you that I care? That I think we have the potential to be more?"

"No," he said, after a long moment. "I think we need *more* to have a good relationship."

"Then what?"

He rubbed his palms against his temples. "I think maybe I've been wrong."

"About what?"

"About you. About you engineering this pregnancy. I made that accusation based on experiences, situations I've faced which have taught me that people can't be trusted, Sofía. That I can't *afford* to trust people. When I found out you were pregnant, it was a natural assumption for me to think it had been planned, considering how careful we had been never to let that happen. Perhaps not a *right* one, but the *one* way I've become conditioned to think."

She crossed her arms over her chest and gave him a mutinous look. "Contraception is not foolproof, Nik. I had no idea the medication I was on would have interfered with it or I would certainly never have suggested what I did."

"It was my responsibility, too," he admitted. "I could have used a condom. I didn't."

She bit her lip. "Why this sudden change of face? Why now?"

He shook his head. "Because it isn't you, Sofía. My head's been a mess from my brother's death. From everything that's been thrown at me. I wasn't thinking straight. When I did start thinking clearly again, it just didn't seem like you. You are so fiercely independent and honest. It seemed like you were fighting it too hard to have wanted it. But I didn't have the head space to process those thoughts. I didn't want to be wrong again and trust someone when I shouldn't."

She pursed her lips. "And now you've had time to process it?"

"Yes."

Suspicion warred with a desperate need to know he

believed her. She shook her head. "You *have* to trust me, Nik. You have to let me in. You have to know that I *am* different."

His mouth thinned. "I just shared with you an incident that nearly broke my family apart. I told you about my father earlier. We are *talking*, Sofía. I can't promise it's always going to be easy for me or I'm always going to be perfect at it, but I am giving it my best shot."

Her heart softened. He *had* been trying. Had been opening up slowly, piece by piece. She knew in her heart they could make it together if he'd just continue to let her in. If *she* could continue to let him in. They had so much to build on.

She stepped closer to him. "You promise I'm not going to wake up tomorrow with you doubting me again?"

"I promise." He slid an arm around her waist and pulled her close. "*Lypamai.* I'm sorry. I'm sorry my suspicions have made this so difficult for us."

She held his gaze with hers. "*Everything* for me right now is based on me trusting you. On taking a leap of faith that petrifies me, Nik. I need to know I can rely on you. That you will be there for me."

He brought his mouth down on hers in a whisper-soft caress that drained any remaining anger from her. "You can jump," he murmured. "I will catch you. You are right, Sofía. We are *more*. We can be a good team. I promise you."

Team. It was a vivid reminder of who she was marrying. A man who might have just promised to build a relationship with her, who liked and desired her, but who would never love her. Nothing had changed there. He had married her to secure his heir.

She vowed to remember that as her lips clung to his and the kiss moved deeper. This time their coming together wasn't about urgency or release, it was about leisurely exploring each other, about sealing a promise they were making. To do this together.

She sighed and sank back into the wall, her palms coming up to cup his face. He inserted a knee between her thighs and moved in closer, deepening the kiss. He had never really lost his erection. It lengthened, thickened against her now. Pulsed with his desire for her.

He wrapped his fingers around her thigh and hooked it around his waist. She pulled in a breath as he nudged the tender flesh between her legs with his shaft. "Sore?" he asked.

"Yes."

He buried his mouth in the hollow of her throat. "I'll be gentle."

"Yes."

He eased himself inside of her. Her body drew him in. He rocked against her, his eyes holding hers as he fused them together. Slowly, with heart-stopping tenderness, he took her. Higher, deeper until her sensitized body stirred back to life.

The struggle she saw in his eyes gave her hope. He didn't want to want her this much. He was fighting the connection they had. Fighting what they had always had that had seemed to be bigger than both of them. Out of their control.

It scared her too, *terrified* her. But she needed him to be her anchor in this. Knew that he would be even if he never loved her. And that had to be enough.

He surged inside of her again and again with deliberate precision, the friction of his body against her flesh almost painfully good. She came apart on a long, delicious surge of pleasure, her fingernails digging into his biceps. Nik groaned, clasped her hips tighter and came inside of her, the skin of his beautiful face pulling taught as the pleasure consumed him.

Their breathing slowed. Her legs slipped to the floor. The haze of passion enveloping her lasted throughout the hot shower Nik set her under and until he tucked her into the big, luxurious bed. As she drifted off to sleep she curled against his chest.

She didn't want to think about the jump she'd just taken. The stakes that had been raised, just as she'd known they would be tonight. The fact that if she crashed this time, it would be a far bigger fall than the last.

Two sun-soaked days passed, and with it Sofía's hope for her and Nik grew. They ate delicious food, played in the sea and indulged in an endless amount of lovemaking that had her convinced her fiancé had the stamina of four men.

It was the time they'd needed to be able to focus on one another away from all the pressure. It had made all the difference in the world. Slowly, Nik was opening up to her. He was still guarded. He would likely always be guarded given his past, but less defensive when she probed, as if he was learning the rules of a game he'd never played. But then again, so was she. In that way, they were perfect for each other.

What worried her, she thought pensively as she watched Nik return from a sail on their final day in Evangelina, his lithe, beautiful body as he secured the boat a major distraction from the sketch pad in front of her, was when they returned to their stressful life tomorrow where Nik literally carried the weight of a nation on his shoulders. Where she was going to have to face the forces that awaited her and somehow not let them destroy her. She feared their progress would be sorely tested.

And that wasn't even counting the part of her that knew she was falling in love with Nik, something that made her feel like crawling out of her skin. So vulnerable she felt raw and exposed. But she'd promised herself she was going to see this journey through. She was stronger than this as Nik had reminded her the night of their engagement party. She could do this for the sake of her child. And maybe, just maybe, she would end up with far more than she'd bargained for with Nik.

She looked down at her sketch pad rather than let that thought fester. Examined her latest drawing. *Still not right.* Yet again. Grimacing, she tore the sheet off, crumpled it into a ball and added it to the growing pile beside her lounge chair.

Dammit. Why wasn't it coming? All those ideas she'd had in her head weren't translating to the page. She picked up her cool lime drink and attempted to channel some Zen.

Boat secured, Nik loped up the beach and dropped down on the chair beside her. Plucking the glass out of her hand, he drained its contents and set it on the concrete. Her mouth curved. "Is there anything you think is *not* yours?"

His eyes glittered in the sunshine. "No. Did I not prove that last night? Do you need a reminder?"

Her chin dipped, a wave of heat descending over her that had nothing to do with the sun. "What I *need* is for one of these designs to work."

He picked up one of the balls of paper. "May I?"

"Will you be honest?"

He lifted a brow as if to say when hadn't he been?

"Go ahead, then. I'm working on a maternity line."

He unballed one of the drawings, then another. Until he'd looked at them all. Twice. A frown of concentration creased his brow. "Well," she said, teeth buried in her lip. "What do you think?'

He looked up. "Qualifying this with the caveat I know nothing about fashion, I agree they're missing something."

"Inspiration," she murmured. "Nothing's hitting me."

He sat back in the chair, sprawling his long limbs out in front of him. "I think you're doing a typical Sofía. You're going for the safe choices—what you think people will like, *approve of,* instead of giving your imagination free rein. You're not fully committing."

"I am," she protested. "I've been killing myself over these."

He gave her a look as if to say that was exactly her problem. "Draw something for yourself. Draw something crazy, way over the top to get your creative juices flowing. You can always pull it back."

She eyed him. "Where do you get all this creativity expertise?"

"You'd be surprised at the amount of creativity it takes to put a ten-million-dollar deal together, *agapi mou.*" He lifted himself off the chair. "Try it."

She chewed on her pencil as he went off to shower. Considered her surroundings and how the lush beauty of the island, the intensity of the colors, the smells inspired her. She started drawing and didn't stop until Nik came to get her for dinner.

"Any success?"

"Yes," she said, snapping the sketch pad closed.

"You going to share?"

"Not yet. They still need lots of work. But I'm happy with them. I think this is the direction I want to go."

"Good." He pointed her toward the villa. "Then I can have your undivided attention over dinner."

Nik's undivided attention proved as heady and fascinating a thing as always. But her head kept skipping forward to what lay ahead, distracting her.

Nik pointed his wineglass at her as their entrée plates were removed. "Where is your head?"

"I don't want to go back," she admitted. "I wish we could just stay here. Away from all the pressure."

"You aren't marrying a normal man, Sofía. You're marrying a king."

She sighed. "I know. Just wishful thinking."

"Come show me your drawings."

She gave him a pointed look. "I told you they aren't ready."

"I'll make it worth your while."

She pretended to think about it. But the temptation was too great. Pushing her chair back, she grabbed her sketch pad and walked around the table. Nik pulled her onto his lap, settling her against his chest.

"I want the truth," she reminded him, then flicked open the sketch pad and showed him the series of ten drawings she'd decided on, which still needed to be filled out and perfected, but they were a start. She talked him through each one, why she'd done what she'd done, what she liked about them. Nik studied them, then set the sketch pad down.

"I like them. They're elegant. Different."

She chewed on her lip. "You really like them? You're not just being nice?"

"You're a sure thing," he murmured. "Why would I be nice?"

Her mouth fell open. She was about to give him a knock across the head when she saw the sparkle in his eyes. "You are *terrible*."

"Sometimes you need to lighten up." He nuzzled her

cheek, the stubble on his jaw razing her skin. "I think they're great."

She rested her head against his chest, absorbing his warmth. He ran a hand over her hair. "Things are going to get crazy, Sofía. They always do. When it happens, when it feels as if we are surrounded by a force far greater than us, remember we can do this."

A sense of foreboding slid through her. "You make it sound so easy."

"It won't be. But you are up to the challenge, *agapi-meni*. I have no doubt."

She hoped she was. Thought she might be. Guessed she was about to find out.

CHAPTER ELEVEN

NIK SLID INTO his car on a bright, sunny afternoon in Akathinia, a peace treaty with Carnelia in hand. A series of meetings between the two countries in the weeks following his return from Evangelina had finally borne fruit as he and Idas had signed the treaty and begun to map out plans for an economic alliance.

Because he didn't fully trust the Carnelian king, Nik had also pushed the development of an enhanced military force forward, but it would take months to see real progress on that initiative given the scale and coordination involved. Meanwhile, he would continue to push the alliance forward with his neighbor by putting a framework in place.

Bringing the Jaguar rumbling to life, his favorite toy to taunt his detail with on the windy, coastal roads, he took the scenic route home to the palace. The sense of well-being that settled over him was profound. His press conference to announce the peace treaty had inspired a feeling of relief and celebration among Akathinians. He could now get on with the business of running this country and looking toward the future rather than the perpetual crisis control mode he'd been in since he'd become king.

The sparkling Ionian Sea to his right, the spectacular

peaks of the Akathinian hills to his left, it was hard not to appreciate what destiny had handed him in that moment. He felt content. It felt *right*, as if what Sofía had said was true. That perhaps it was his destiny to lead Akathinia at this stage of its history.

Part of that had come with letting go of his life in New York. *Truly* letting go of it. He couldn't live with his head in both places. He'd had to choose. It didn't mean he would never grieve his former life. It wouldn't be human for him not to. But as he got more comfortable in his role as king, the affinity he'd always felt toward his homeland had taken over. He *knew* he could take this country where it needed to go. Knew he had the global perspective his father and Athamos had not.

If he was content, his fiancée was another reason for it. Having her back in his bed, having that intimate bond to look forward to every evening made the long, complex days bearable. They'd taken to having dinner together in their suite a couple of nights a week so they could spend quality time with each other. He'd found himself sharing more and more of his thoughts and plans with Sofía as the days went on. Her sharp, objective perspective on things always gave him excellent food for thought.

Thankfully, his soon-to-be wife also seemed to have found a peace of her own. When she wasn't doing a public appearance with his mother or sister, she was caught up in her designing with a ravenous enthusiasm that made him smile.

They'd given a joint interview to Akathinian TV last week, their first broadcast interview together. Sofía's inner happiness had shone through this time, her innate wit and charm capturing the host's heart and earning her good reviews. The image-conscious press had also picked up on her fashion sense, grudgingly conceding she was a bit of a shining star.

It was the boost of confidence Sofía had needed. She was acting more like her charismatic self, the woman he'd known in New York. And if that took him dangerously close to exploring uncharted feelings for his soon-to-be wife, he had deliberately held a part of himself back for just that reason. Now was not the time to be clouding his head with emotions he wasn't capable of fully expressing. Feeling.

He had promised Sofía a partnership. To protect her, to be by her side. For a man who didn't do commitment this was one promise he could keep.

They were done. Sofía stood back and surveyed the ten prototypes she'd created for the maternity line she would launch at the boutique, pride swelling her heart. It wasn't a whole line, but it was ten solid pieces to start the fall/ winter collection with next year. Ten pieces Katharine had raved about and couldn't wait to sell.

A rather ridiculous number of customers had come in to the boutique asking for the dresses Sofía had worn in her public appearances. The press coverage she had once considered a suffocating fishbowl was paying dividends. The sooner she got these prototypes off to the manufacturer so they could source material for them and produce samples for approval, the better to take advantage of the current buzz surrounding her and Nik's engagement.

Satisfaction at a job complete filling her, she leaned back against a table and drank in the late-afternoon sunshine pouring through the windows of the studio. She felt remarkably content. She'd given up her obsession with what the people thought of her because she really couldn't control that and focused instead on her design work and the creative outlet it provided.

The restlessness that had consumed her since coming to Akathinia had faded as she'd gained a sense of purpose. When she was using her role for good as she had when she'd visited Stella's youth group and shared her experiences in business, when she helped Queen Amara with one of her charitable endeavors, she could see a vision for her life here.

It helped that she and Stella had become fast friends. Although Queen Amara had taken Sofía under her wing and guided her in her role, she had the sense the queen would always have a certain distance about her, just as Nik had said. As if she held part of herself back. Perhaps it was her way of protecting herself against the storms and humiliations she had endured with her husband?

And then there was Nik. Her insides warmed as they always did when she thought about him. Her cynical, hard fiancé was evolving into a more knowable, approachable version of himself as they continued to deepen their bond. It made her decision to gamble on them, to gamble on the fact he might develop deeper feelings for her someday seem as if it hadn't quite been the foolish thought it had seemed at the time. That capturing his heart was within the realm of possibility.

Heavy footsteps sounded in the hallway. Her heartbeat picked up in anticipation. *Nik home already?*

Her suspicion was confirmed as her fiancé walked in, a dark suit complementing his swarthy good looks, a sexy aura of satisfaction surrounding him. She smiled a greeting. "I saw the announcement. Congratulations."

He crossed the room and gave her a kiss. "*Efharisto. It feels good.*" He waved a hand at the prototypes as he released her. "What's this?"

"My first ten designs," she said proudly. "I'm about to ship them off to a manufacturer to get samples made."

"That's exciting."

"It is. I think we should celebrate."

He subjected her to a lazy inspection that bumped her pulse up a notch. "A personal celebration in our rooms later, to be sure, *agapimeni*, plus I thought I'd take you out to dinner. I have something I want to show you."

She *loved* that idea. "Give me a few minutes to change."

They dined at a tiny local seafood restaurant along the coast that was known to serve the best food on the island. Then they got back into Nik's car and drove another few miles to the rugged, most scenic east coast of the island, where the highest peaks of Akathinia dropped in a sheer cliff to the rocky shore below.

Sofía stepped from the car, her eyes widening as she took in the dramatic view and the remnants of the old fortress scattered along the edge of the cliff.

"What is this?"

Nik took her hand by way of answer and led her through the disintegrating ruins out to the edge of the cliff. "Carnelia," he said, pointing to a dark mass in the distance, lit by the dying rays of the sun. "This is where my great-grandfather King Damokles defeated the Catharian navy to secure Akathinia's independence. When they attacked us, the Catharians sent a smaller contingent to the harbor as a decoy knowing we would expect them to strike there, then massed most of their troops here. They bet on the fact my great-grandfather would mass his forces at the harbor to defend it, but Damokles was too smart to fall for that. He sent his best troops here, defeated the Catharians, and they retreated, never to come back."

Sofía stood there quietly, taking it in. The significance of where they were standing, what it meant to Nik slid over her, giving her goose bumps.

Nik pointed at the big cannons still guarding the cliff face. "Thousands of men lost their lives defending Akathinia that day. My great-grandfather said it was the bloodiest battle he'd ever been in."

She turned to him. "And you will never put your people through that again."

"If I can help it, no."

She studied the clear blue of his eyes. The strain seemed to have eased from his face with today's announcement. "I am so proud of you, Nik. You have been carrying the weight of a nation on your shoulders. Not an easy task in normal times. I hope you can relax a bit now. Give yourself some space to breathe."

He nodded. "It will be good to have that time. It's been difficult to process it all. To forge a plan for the future."

"And the responsibility that's been handed to you? Are you feeling more at peace with it?"

"Yes." He caught her hand in his and drew her close. "I need to thank you," he said quietly, "for being here for me. For telling me the things I needed to hear. For taking the risks you have. You inspire me, Sofía, your grit and determination to survive—to succeed."

A rush of warmth flowed through her. Her heart felt too big for her chest as she lifted a hand to his jaw. "You pushed *me* when I needed to be pushed. You made me realize I was living in fear. *I* should be thanking you for that, Nik. *I* of all people should know life is finite. I can't spend my days waiting for the penny to drop. For that bolt of lightning that might never come."

He inclined his head, his gaze softening. "We make a great team. I told you we would."

Team. She flinched at the word. They were more than a team, *dammit.* He *felt* things for her. Things he wouldn't address.

Nik's gaze sharpened on her face. "I care about you, Sofía. You know I do."

How much? The words vibrated from her across the crisp night air to him. They stayed there, hanging between them as both refused to break the standoff.

Was she completely deluding herself about how he felt? Would the wounds he carried only ever allow her so close?

She realized with a sickening feeling, in that moment, that she wasn't *falling* in love with him. She was *in love* with him. Had been ever since their weekend in Evangelina. Her heart lurching, she wondered how she had ever let that happen.

Sure she had to stop living in fear, but making herself that vulnerable to Nik of all people? A man who didn't even know what love was because he'd never been shown it? She had been bound and determined that night in New York to end it between them because she'd known this would happen. And now it had.

A grim look on his face, Nik snaked an arm around her waist and brought her to him. Her eyes fluttered closed as he kissed her. His usual tactic for fixing things between them. She remained unresponsive beneath the pressure of his mouth, too terrified to give him any more than she already had. When he finally let her go, she could feel the frustration emanating from him, an overwhelming force it would be all too easy to give in to. Instead she walked away, his muffled curse following her back to the car.

It had been bad enough when she hadn't loved him, these leaps he was asking her to make. This, *this* was just too much.

CHAPTER TWELVE

THE WHITE MALTESE stone Akathinian palace glittered in the sunlight as the helicopter dipped down over the sea and headed toward home. A strong headwind had been at their nose all the way back from Athens, increasing Nik's impatience, fueled by the news Sofía had given him on the phone last night.

She'd felt their baby kick for the first time. Hearing the wonder in her voice had turned his head into a hot mess.

Piero, his pilot, brought the helicopter in to land safely on the pad. Grabbing his briefcase, Nik stepped from beneath still-whirring blades and headed across the lawn toward the front steps to the palace he took two by two. Abram emerged as he reached the top step, his aide wearing that same frozen look he had the night he'd told him Athamos had died.

"What is it?"

"Idas has seized a ship in the Strait of Evandor."

His blood ran cold. "An Akathinian ship?"

"Yes. A warship doing exercises."

"It can't be Idas." His mind sped a mile a minute. "We have a peace treaty."

"The ship that took our vessel had Carnelian flags, Your Highness."

Thee mou. "Have there been any other reports of aggression?"

"Not that we've been able to ascertain."

It afforded him little comfort. His heart pounded as his brain funneled through procedure. "Call an emergency meeting of the Council, including the Joint Chiefs of Staff."

Abram nodded.

"I'll go by helicopter. Tell Piero to hold off."

He found his father and appraised him of the situation. Next he found Sofía in the salon with Stella, the two of them looking through magazines. She smiled when she saw him, but it faded when she saw the look on his face.

"Idas has taken an Akathinian ship in the Strait of Evandor," he said without preamble. "I'm on my way to meet with the Executive Council."

Sofía's eyes widened. "But you have a peace agreement in place."

Which meant nothing apparently. Idas had made a fool out of him.

Sofía got to her feet. "Maybe it's misinformation."

"The attacking ship bore a Carnelian flag." He pinned his gaze on his fiancée, a red mist descending over his vision. "Neither of you are to leave the palace until this situation is resolved."

"Have there been other attacks?" Stella asked.

"Not that we know of." Nik swung his gaze to his sister. "You still don't leave."

She nodded. He stalked to the door, so angry, *furious* with himself for being duped, he could barely see.

Sofía intercepted him at the door, her hand on his arm. "You don't have all the facts. It would be easy to jump to conclusions in this situation."

"Like Idas is a snake? That he broke his word?"

She blinked as he shouted the words at her. "Nik—"

He picked her up and moved her aside. She followed him into the hallway. "Do not let Idas drag you into a war you know is wrong. Listen to your instincts, now of all times."

He kept walking. *Listen to his instincts?* His instincts had been right all along.

The siege over the Akathinian warship taken in the Strait of Evandor lasted for forty-eight hours. Forty-eight nail-biting hours in which Sofía, Stella and Queen Amara paced the floors of the palace salon while Nik and a team of negotiators attended meetings in Geneva to free the ship and its crew, currently being forcibly held in Carnelian waters.

King Gregorios was ordered to bed when his blood pressure skyrocketed, something Sofía was inordinately grateful for. The elder king's vitriolic diatribe against Idas was only making a difficult scenario much, much worse.

Abram briefed them as he could. Nik was in the midst of a storm, with his Council divided on whether to provide a military response to retrieve the ship. Some felt enough was enough, Idas needed to be confronted. Nik was on the side of diplomacy, aware Akathinia's military was still heavily outmatched by its aggressors. He had refused to send negotiators to Geneva, insisting, instead, on being there himself and was doing his best to manage both sides of the equation.

The situation was not made easier by the reaction of the Akathinian people. Such an act of provocation on the heels of the crown prince's death could not be tolerated was the majority opinion. Get our men back.

Deep into the third day of the crisis, Abram appeared

in the salon to say it was done. Sofía's heart pounded as he announced the negotiations had been successful and the ship had been returned to Akathinian hands, but that five men had been killed in the taking of the ship.

When Nik walked into the palace hours later, dark circles ringing his eyes, Sofía, who had not slept for three days except for a couple of hours here and there, got to her feet, along with Stella and Queen Amara.

"Why did the Carnelians take the ship?" Queen Amara asked. "Why did Idas break his promise?"

Nik rubbed a hand across his brow. "They accused the ship of provocation toward one of its own. Clearly a fabrication, as our vessel was in neutral waters at the time, doing routine exercises."

His mother's gaze softened. "You must eat, Nikandros. Get some rest."

"I need to brief Father first." He flicked a glance at Sofía. "Go and eat. Don't wait for me."

She did, but the anxiety seizing her insides hardly inspired an appetite. Nik didn't join her in their rooms until well after eleven as she sat trying to read a book, but failing miserably.

"Did you eat?" she asked.

"I'm not hungry."

"Nik, you have to eat. Let me—"

"Don't." He held up a hand. "I'm fine."

He started undoing the buttons of his shirt, cursed as his fingers fumbled over them, then pulled the material apart with a hard yank, buttons scattering and rolling across the floor. Her stomach knotted. She put the book down, got to her feet and crossed to him. Ignoring her, he yanked his belt buckle open, freed the button on his trousers and shoved them down his hips.

"Nik." She moved closer as he stepped out of them. "Stop for a second. *Breathe.*"

He looked down at her, eyes blazing. "If I do, I will explode."

"It's not your fault. You can't blame yourself for this. You had every reason to believe Idas would keep his word."

"Did I?" He hurled the words at her. "Because in hindsight I feel like a fool. In hindsight he played me masterfully. He never intended on keeping that peace treaty."

She swallowed hard. "How did he think he would get away with that explanation? Surely it was clear the ship was in neutral waters."

"It's his claim a commander on the scene who considered the ship a threat made the call."

"Maybe that's the truth."

The curse he uttered snapped her head back. "We have a peace treaty, Sofía. He played me. Five men are dead because of my decisions. *My* naïveté."

Her insides twisted. "You were trying to avoid a war, Nik. You are doing everything you can to protect this country, but it can only happen so fast. No one can fault you for that."

"I could have been more *vigilant*. If I had listened to my instincts, I could have anticipated he'd do something like this. Instead I listened to everyone around me."

"You had to do that. You have a council and advisers for a reason."

He gave her a scathing look as if to say look where that'd gotten him. Then turned on his heel and headed for the bathroom.

She sat on a chair in the bedroom and waited for him. He was hurting. He felt he had to take responsibility for those men's deaths. He was the head of the armed forces.

The king of this country. It must be humiliating to be betrayed by Idas like that. But it didn't mean anything he'd done had been wrong. It had all been right.

Nik walked into the bedroom after his shower and pulled on a pair of boxers, barely sparing her a glance. "Go to bed, Sofía. You need sleep."

She stared at him, waiting, wondering what to do. He moved past her into the salon. The sound of the whiskey decanter being opened, the clink of ice hitting crystal and whiskey being poured filled the silence. The terrace doors clicked open, then shut. He needed time to process. To decompress. She should leave him alone. And for once she did. She was too exhausted not to.

She woke sometime later, something instinctively telling her Nik was not in bed. A look at the clock told her it was 2:00 a.m. Rubbing her eyes, she let them adjust to the darkness, then she slipped out of bed and went to find Nik. He was reclined in a chair on the terrace, the near-empty bottle of whiskey now sitting on the table beside him.

His eyes were glazed as she knelt down beside him.

"You need to sleep, Nik."

"I can't."

Her chest tightened at the haunted look on his face. She took his hands in hers. "I know you consider this your responsibility. I know you are angry at yourself for letting Idas make a fool of you. But you negotiated the release of those men. You sent them home to their families, Nik. Now you need to get some rest so you can deal with this tomorrow."

"Five men died today," he rasped. "More will follow if I don't handle this correctly."

"*Many more* will follow if you don't get some rest and get your head on straight." She shook her head. "I know it's painful to lose those men. But this is what you do. You make the tough decisions so the rest of us don't have to. But you can't do that if you're beating yourself up over a mistake, if you're too tired to think."

He turned his gaze back to the floodlit gardens. She knew what he wanted, but she wasn't leaving him alone.

She slid onto his lap. His face tightened. "Sofía—" She pressed her fingers to his mouth, took his hand and guided it to her stomach. To what had woken her. She thought maybe the baby had gone back to sleep when there was no movement beneath their fingers for a good five seconds. Then the kick came, fast and powerful.

Nik's eyes widened. The baby kicked again.

"This," she said to him, "is what you are doing this for. For your child. So that he or she will know the freedom your great-grandfather fought for. Stay the course, Nik."

His gaze lost its glassy look, dark emotion filtering through it as another kick came. "Sofía—"

She cupped his face in her hands and kissed him. Deep and slow and soulfully to banish the demons. He lifted a palm to cup the back of her head, returning the kiss with a hot fervor that told her she'd broken through.

She kissed him until they were all each other could see. Then he picked her up, wrapped her legs around him and carried her inside.

He laid her on their bed, stripped off his boxers and followed her down. Her heart pounded as he positioned himself between her legs, his heavy thighs parting hers. She closed her eyes, bracing herself for the explosive power of him because she was ready for him, always ready for him. Instead he worked his way down her body, lingering over the tiny swell of her stomach, waiting for another kick to come. Absorbing it with a reverent press of his lips, he moved farther down, between the heat of her thighs. His mouth found her most sensitive skin, laved her, licked her until she was crying out his name, begging for him.

Covering her with his heavy body, he sheathed himself inside of her in one powerful movement that stole her breath. The need to forget, the need to cleanse himself of what had happened chased their coupling. She wrapped her thighs around him and brought his mouth down to hers with fingers that cupped his head. He murmured her name hoarsely into her mouth as he plunged inside her again and again until there was only them, as deeply connected as two human beings could be.

Nik clasped her hips in his hands, angled himself deeper and took her hard and fast until his big body tensed and he came in a violent explosion of pleasure that rocked them both, Sofía's release coming quick on its heels.

Cradling her to his chest, Nik rolled onto his side, his palm on her belly. She curled into the heat of his body. Then there was only the sound of his deep, even breathing.

I need you to remember that when things get crazy. When it feels like we are surrounded by a force far greater than us. We can do this.

The promise Nik had made to her in Evangelina filled her head. They were in the center of the storm now, just as he'd predicted. Now they had to find their way out.

CHAPTER THIRTEEN

NIK ROSE EARLY the next morning, his meetings with the Executive Council on the Carnelian situation slated to start at eight and go late into the day. In the dim light slanting its way through the windows, he pulled on a pair of trousers and a shirt.

His head throbbed from the whiskey he'd consumed; his body ached from far too little sleep. He'd hoped by shutting his eyes for a few hours, the images of the five dead crewmen being carried off the rescued ship would stop torturing him, but they had been burned into his brain. He might be only the figurehead leader of the military, but he had done the training, knew the classic tenet that had been drilled into their heads as soldiers: sacrifice for the greater good. But the thought of returning those men home to their families in a box wasn't an emotion he'd been trained to process.

A fist formed in his chest. He buttoned his shirt up over it and swung a tie around his neck. His gaze drifted to Sofía asleep in their bed as his fingers fumbled over the knot. To feel their baby kicking last night had knocked some sense into him. Sofía had knocked some sense into him.

He needed to protect her and his child. He needed to protect Akathinia. Everything hinged on what he did next.

While he had been playing in the sun with Sofía, convincing himself he was smarter than Idas, convincing himself he could have it all, his enemy had been plotting his next move. Outsmarting him. Five men were dead because of it.

Perhaps his father had been right. Maybe there was no middle ground for a leader. Either you had complete focus on the job as his father had, to hell with the people in your life, or your distractions ruined you.

He yanked a jacket from the closet and slid it on. His emotions were too close to the surface right now. Too all over the place. He needed some distance between him and Sofía while he navigated this crisis. From emotions that were too strong to process.

It wasn't difficult. His meeting went late into the night as expected. When he returned home Sofía was asleep. The pattern went on for two weeks as he debated the question of Carnelia at Council. Those who wanted to deal Carnelia a warning blow to show Idas Akathinia wasn't available to take were numerous. Those who, like him, knew diplomacy was the only answer, a minority. There was no middle ground, he argued to the proponents of a warning blow. It would drag Akathinia into a war it didn't want and they would lose without its enhanced military force in place.

On the fifteenth morning of bitterly fought debate, he used his veto power at Council to dismiss military action and announced an international peace summit would be held in Akathinia in two weeks' time to discuss the Carnelian situation. Idas would be invited, but it would proceed regardless of whether he attended. Nik was banking on the fact the international community would have his back, particularly those powerful nations with whom Akathinia had colonial ties.

His veto in place, he dissolved the council and went home. Enough talk had happened. It was time to end this.

Dinner with Nik's family was a painful affair. Another day of negotiations about the Carnelian situation had meant another day without Nik, and with Stella out on a date, it had been just her and the king and queen at the table. As soon as dessert was served, she excused herself and climbed the stairs to bed, exhausted and miserable.

She knew she should try to sleep. She needed the rest. But she knew she wouldn't, so she headed instead to her studio to work.

The dress she'd been working on, a chic blue silk knee-length design, cut on the bias and forgiving for her thickening middle, beckoned from the table, pieces cut out and ready to be assembled. But the excitement she'd felt earlier for the dress didn't spark her usual creative urge.

How could she feel inspired when her relationship with Nik was falling apart? When he had spent the past two weeks avoiding her, saying no more than a handful of words to her before he resumed working or passed out, exhausted. Only one night had he woken her to make love to her. Once he had assuaged his frustration, he had slept again, leaving her emotionally and physically distanced.

Which was what he was doing. Distancing himself from her, shutting her out. She understood he was stressed, under immense pressure, but the unraveling of all the work they'd done broke her heart. What kind of a *partnership*, as he liked to call it, did they have when he wouldn't turn to her when he needed her the most? When he wasn't there for *her*?

Her vision clouded over. She blinked as hot liquid stung the backs of her eyes. Outside in the glittering harbor, lit up at night, the expensive yachts hosted million-dollar parties even as Nik struggled to prevent a conflict with Carnelia. She could tell herself he was leading Akathinia through its toughest times. That she couldn't expect them to be perfect right now. But she knew even when he figured this out, which he would, there would be another issue to take its place. And another. And he would continue to shut her out every time. Compartmentalize her.

It wasn't enough anymore, she realized. She couldn't settle for a partnership. She wanted more. She wanted all of him. She couldn't spend her days waiting for him to decide he cared. She'd done that her whole life with her mother. She wouldn't do it with him.

Desperate for a familiar voice, she picked up her cell phone and called Katharine. The call went to voice mail. She tossed the phone on the table and looked back out at the night.

"You should be in bed."

She spun around at Nik's deep baritone. He stood just inside the door, his jacket draped over his shoulder, leaning against the frame.

"It's not midnight," she noted, hating the bitter tone in her voice. "Was everyone passing out at the table?"

He eased away from the wall, tossed his jacket on a table and walked toward her. "I've called a summit of international leaders for two weeks' time in Akathinia. There will be no military action."

"You used your veto power?"

"Yes."

"Good." She twisted a chunk of her hair around her finger as he stopped in front of her. "I am sure the international community will band behind you."

"That is the hope."

Silence fell. He reached out and ran his thumb across

her cheek. She flinched away from his touch, her chin coming up.

A blaze of fire sparked in his eyes, but he banked it down. "You look exhausted, *agapi mou*. Is it the baby?"

A surge of fury bubbled up inside of her. She shook her head, attempting to contain it. Nik narrowed his gaze on her. "What?"

She yanked in a breath in an attempt to find calm, but it all came tumbling out. "You shut me out as if I don't exist for two weeks, while I *worry* about you, while I worry about what's going to happen, then you waltz in here and ask me why I look tired? Why I'm not myself? Did you ever stop to think at any point in this crusade of yours what this is doing to me, Nik? Did you even *care*?"

His jaw hardened. "I told you this was going to be all consuming. That I wouldn't be home much."

"*All consuming?* You haven't said ten sentences to me. You've tuned me out like the unnecessary complication you like to view me as instead of that *partnership* you offered."

"Would you prefer I woke you at midnight to give you an update?"

"*Yes.* At least I'd know you were okay. Instead I've relied on Abram to tell me how my fiancé is holding up."

Something she couldn't read flickered in his eyes.

"Unless," she amended, "it had been the two or three nuggets you chose to enlighten me with before you used me to assuage your frustration."

The glitter in his eyes sparked into a dangerous blue flame. "You were wholly into that, Sofía."

"*Yes, I was.* I wanted to comfort you, to connect with you so desperately, Nik, I would have done anything to make you feel better. Including letting you use me for sex."

He stepped closer, clenching his hands by his sides. "I did not *use* you for sex."

"Then what was it? Me comforting you the way I *do it best*?"

His lashes lowered. "I told you there would be difficult times. Times we had to get through together."

"*Together* being the operative word. Since then, you have demonstrated how that will work for us. How you will let me in when it pleases you to, then shut me out when you decide I'm getting too close." She lifted her chin. "It was never a real offer of intimacy, was it? I was just too stupid to figure it out."

"I *have* let you in."

"You *think* you've let me in. I'm sure you'd call it a superstar effort. But your fixation on proving yourself, on demonstrating to your father how wrong he is about you, how you have this all *under control*, leaves you with nothing left over for me or anything else."

His face tightened. "I am *focused* on preserving this country's freedom. My father has nothing to do with it."

"Really?" She shook her head. "I suggest you think long and hard on that. Because to me you're becoming more like him every day. You're becoming just as dictatorial, just as obsessed about the end goal. And to hell with everyone and everything in between."

His face tightened. "I could question your own selfishness, Sofía. Now is the time for you to be supporting me, when this country is in the biggest crisis of its history. And what are you doing? Giving me grief about *paying attention to you*."

A strangled sound left her throat. She threw her hands up in the air. "And what happens when the next crisis comes? And the next? Life is never going to be simple for us. You said that yourself. You asked me to stand beside you, to do this together. I have done that, Nik. I am play-ing queen-to-be to the very limits of my ability. But if you can't let me in, if I'm doing this by myself, it isn't going to work. I will not commit myself to a marriage, to a *life* with a man who isn't willing to share himself."

"You cannot *claim* these are ordinary circumstances, Sofía. The other things will be manageable."

"Not with you. You will compartmentalize me every time you need to. Bring me out to play when you so desire."

He blew out a breath. Turned to look out the window. When he looked back at her, his eyes were glazed with exhaustion. "You're being unreasonable. Get some sleep and we'll talk in the morning."

She bit her lip, desperately resisting the hot tears that blanketed her eyes. "I've spent enough of my life alone, Nik. Craving the love I never got. I won't do it with you. I won't put our child through a marriage, a life where I am miserable. You can't even manage a relationship with me, let alone a child."

His mouth flattened. A tear rolled down her cheek. He cursed and reached up to brush it away, confusion, wariness, darkening his eyes. "Sofía—"

"Yes, that's right," she interrupted. "I'm in love with you, Nik. I realized I was in love with you in Evangelina. And you knew it. You have cleverly leveraged it to get what you want and I have played right into your hands."

His gaze dropped away from hers. Her heart broke apart at the unspoken admission. He *had* known. And somehow that made it so much worse.

"Make up your mind," she said quietly. "Figure out whether you actually have a heart, Nik, and you can share it with me. Or let me go. It's your choice."

The damaged look in his eyes as he raised his gaze to hers tested her resolve. "I know you're damaged, Nik.

So am I. But I've stopped using that as an excuse to run away from how I feel."

She left him there and went to bed. It felt good to put an end to the misery. To know it wouldn't continue. If he rejected her now, at least she'd know. At least she'd save herself a lifetime of pain. And really, how much more could it hurt?

A whole hell of a lot more, her bruised insides told her. It was just beginning.

His confrontation with Sofía raging in his head, Nik avoided the whiskey bottle that had been calling to him a little too much lately and sought out fresh air instead. The palace gardens were quiet and peaceful, the night air crisp and clean. Unlike the frantic activity of the day with gardeners and machines buzzing relentlessly to keep the showpiece intact, the carefully manicured slice of heaven that covered ten acres was silent now, except for the breeze that came off the sea and rustled the leaves on the trees.

There was a place on the outskirts of the gardens, a lone bench that faced the sea, where he and Stella used to come when they were kids to escape their father's wrath. He headed toward it, found it unoccupied as it always was and lowered himself onto the worn wood, splaying his long legs out in front of him.

He rested his head against the back of the bench and closed his eyes. But the usual peace did not come. He couldn't deny every word Sofía had said was true. That he had known she was in love with him; that he had leveraged it for his own purposes. He had compartmentalized her to fit into his life because that was the only way he could operate. It wasn't something he was proud of, but he had accepted that particular transgression weeks ago. Forgiven himself for it.

But tonight, watching how miserable she was, when for a few weeks in time she had been so happy, tore him apart inside. He wanted her to be happy. *Needed* her to be happy after everything she'd gone through. He had promised he would be here for her, promised he would ensure that happiness, and then the Carnelian crisis had blown everything apart.

And that was a lie. He knew it as soon as the thought entered his head. Idas taking that ship, going back on their agreement, had made him question everything. Himself, the leader he'd become, whether he'd made the right choices, *whether he was cut out to be king.* But he'd made the decision to distance Sofía before that. When she'd gotten too close. When his feelings for her had become too strong.

Because making himself vulnerable, opening himself up fully to her, had meant abandoning his defenses, something he couldn't do because he wasn't actually sure he could function without them. Wasn't sure Sofía would even want what he had left inside. Wasn't even sure what was there anymore, he'd been closed off for so long.

He stared sightlessly out at the dark shadow of the water, the ironic truth of it all settling over him. *He* had been afraid. He had allowed fear to rule him while defiantly brave Sofía had taken every jump he'd asked her to. A woman he was afraid he'd been in love with for a long time.

He craved the peace she gave him. Knew she had the potential to heal the wounds inside of him. As she had done so again and again over the past few weeks, pulling him out of the darkness, steadying his path, convincing him to follow his heart. But he needed to pull his country back from the brink first. Solve this thing with Idas. Then he would address his relationship with Sofía.

The question was, did he have the capacity to offer her all of him? Or would he destroy her by making her stay?

CHAPTER FOURTEEN

"The first car will be here in thirty minutes, sir."

Nik turned to nod at Abram, who had appeared on the palace steps behind him. "Keep me posted."

With a dip of his head, his aide disappeared inside. Nik turned back to the sun-soaked harbor, bounded by the two Venetian fortifications that had once protected Akathinia from seagoing marauders. He was hoping today the international community would join forces to repel a very real and current threat to Akathinia's freedom in Carnelia.

Idas had, as expected, elected not to attend the peace talks, so the world would judge him in absentia.

He rubbed a hand to his pounding temple, operating on just about zero sleep after spending the past two weeks personally calling each and every one of the twenty-five world leaders in attendance today to persuade them to take the time out of their busy schedules to attend.

His gamble had paid off. A playground for the world's rich and famous, Akathinia was too bright a jewel of the Mediterranean, with too many colonial ties for its instability to be disregarded. All he had to do now was convince these powerful men to put their support on the table.

"They will be here soon?"

He turned to find his father making his way through the open front doors, moving slowly with his walking stick.

He nodded. "The first in thirty minutes."

His father stopped beside him, leaning heavily on the stick. "It is remarkable what you have done, Nikandros. I did not think this would happen."

What usually would have evoked bitterness, this inability of his father to believe in him, bounced off Nik without hitting its mark. He had been through too much these past few months, had endured too many highs and lows to continue to let it hurt. He knew what he was doing today was right. He was secure in his mind as the leader of this country. He only hoped it would wipe away the mistake he had made with Idas.

His father rested his gaze on him. "You have always been able to see the bigger picture. It is why you were successful in New York. In attracting the world to Akathinia. It's what you are building on today. Your connections, the relationships you have forged with these countries. It isn't something I nor Athamos could have done nearly as well."

"The world would not have abandoned Akathinia in its time of need."

"Perhaps not."

"It's not done yet. We could walk away from this with nothing."

"But you won't. The most powerful men in the world have not traveled here today to say they will not support you."

He surely hoped not.

His father fixed him with his steely blue gaze. "My grief has ruled me these past weeks. My anger. It is very easy to feel nothing but rage when your flesh and blood is taken from you. But I apologize if I have failed you, Nikandros. Not just now but in the past. You will learn, are *already* learning, that being a king is not easy. It will ask things of you you aren't prepared to give. Demand you make choices. Sometimes you will not always make the right ones."

How those words resonated in this moment. He fought the tightness in his chest at an apology issued decades far too late, resting his gaze on his father's. "I think I will make different choices. But I understand the complexity now perhaps much better than I did."

His father inclined his head. "I have always had equal respect for both my sons, but I fear I have not always shown it in the right way. Perhaps not much at all."

The fist in his chest grew. "That is in the past."

"Yes. Good luck today. I have every confidence you will be coming to me with good news."

Nik blew out a breath as his father leaned heavily on his stick and shuffled inside. Even when he'd told himself his father's opinion hadn't mattered, it had. It always had.

Sofía smoothed her hands over her hips as she surveyed her appearance in the mirror, a month's work staring her in the face.

Her dress. Her design. It was like exposing her insides to the world and hoping they loved her.

She turned to Stella. "What do you think?"

"Wow." The princess's gaze widened. "You look hot. Perfect, sophisticated, pregnant, queen-to-be hot."

Her stomach tightened. *If* she was to be queen. It had been two weeks since her and Nik's blowout. Two weeks since she had tossed her ultimatum in his face and her heart along with it. Two weeks in which he hadn't touched her, had spent all his time working on this summit while she worried they were done.

She bit her lip. "You're sure about the dress? If there's any doubt in your mind, I'll wear Francesco's."

Stella poked her in the shoulder. "There is no doubt in my mind. You are amazingly talented. Now grab your bag. We're late."

They were indeed late as they met the event liaison in the lobby of the palace for the photo op, to be followed by lunch with the wives of the foreign leaders. The buttoned-up, stern-looking woman frowned at them. "Everyone is gathered outside already."

"So we make a grand entrance," Stella came back mischievously, hooking her arm through Sofía's.

Sofía smiled through her misery as she and Stella stepped out into the bright Akathinian sunlight, the gods electing to greet their international guests with the country's usual golden splendor instead of the bizarre rain they'd had for the past week. Stella tugged her to a halt halfway down the steps. "Show off your dress."

The princess had a reputation for being a fashionista, too. The photographers swarmed to get a shot of her and Sofía, their flashes going off like mad.

"Stella. Is it true you are dating Aristos Nicolades?" a photographer yelled.

What? Sofía angled a look at Stella. "Tell me you're not."

The princess lifted a brow at the reporter. "Where do you *get* these ideas?"

Sofía's gaze flew to Nik, who stood at the bottom of the steps with the gathered contingent, his eyes fixed on his sister. His *furious* eyes. They glittered an electric blue in the sun, set off by his dark suit, crisp white shirt and ice-blue tie. When he turned them on her she went a bit weak at the knees at the banked intensity in them.

It took her right back to the night in New York at the Met when he had looked at her like that, the night that had set in motion a chain of events that had landed them here. And still she didn't know how it was going to end.

"Fabulous dress, Sofía," a photographer called out. "Who's it by?"

She lifted her chin, her heart swelling. "It's mine. I plan to launch a new line in my New York boutique next year."

"Would that be for a *maternity* line?"

She opened her mouth to fluff it off per usual, with the official announcement to come next week and who knew where she and Nik would be by then? Nik broke away from the crowd and climbed the steps to her side before she could find an appropriately evasive response.

"Yes," he said, slipping an arm around her waist. "Sofía and I are thrilled to say we are expecting our first child."

Stella choked out a sound beside her at the breach in protocol. The paparazzi went crazy with their cameras.

"What did you do that for?" Sofía demanded beneath her breath. "Now they're going to be a pack of wild animals."

"Because we *are* having a baby, *agapi mou*. It was getting painful watching you try to skirt the question."

She forced a smile to her lips as the flashes continued to go off. "Don't you think a press release is a better idea if we're not going to be together?"

He turned that ice-blue gaze on her. "I'm never letting you go, Sofía. *Ever*."

"You don't have a choice," she pointed out, maintaining her smile. "I told you I'm leaving after this if you don't let me in."

"That gives me twenty-four hours to change your mind."

She forgot about the cameras entirely, her heart tumbling to the concrete. "Nik—"

"Later," he growled, releasing her. "Unless you would like an audience for this."

No. No, she wouldn't.

They moved on to lunch. In the afternoon the leaders sat down once again to hash out a solution to the issue at hand. The palace PR person was called in to handle the communications crisis that erupted around the coming royal baby. By the evening news, the story was splashed across every news outlet on the planet with all kinds of sensational taglines attached to it. Jumping the Gun seemed to be a favorite, followed closely by Out of Wedlock Shock.

But the coming baby wasn't the only headline news. The fashion press went mad about Sofía's dress, calling it "ultrachic maternity wear" every design house would be duplicating by week's end.

After pouring through the masses of coverage the PR person gave her on her tablet, Sofía lifted her head, dazed. Finally she was a hit. Just in time for her and Nik's relationship to implode.

Nik walked out of the National Assembly as early evening fell, the political and military support of the international community behind him. If Carnelia acted against Akathinia, the world would respond. But Nik knew it wouldn't come to that. Not after the consensus of today made the news. Not after Idas realized his games were over.

He stopped to speak to the scrum of media waiting outside the Assembly. His PR person intercepted him on his way to the podium. "The news of the royal baby has gone viral. It's everywhere."

Tell him something he couldn't have predicted. He wasn't thrilled with himself for his impulsive move, aware his need to lay claim to Sofía could backfire badly on him if the media chose to focus on a royal baby rather than his country's political issues. But it was done now.

"Tell me some of the coverage has included the summit."

His PR person nodded, a smile curving her lips. "One of the big news channels was interviewing a pundit on the announcement. He joked Carnelia could hardly touch Akathinia now with a royal baby on the way. *Sacrilegious*, he called it. The clip was picked up everywhere."

His mouth slackened. "You're joking."

"I would not joke about something like that, Your Highness. Your fiancée is also being hailed as the next savior of fashion. They loved her dress."

That pulled a smile from him. Sofía had such high hopes for her maternity line but she wouldn't admit one of them.

He did the scrum alongside the superpower leaders, then headed back to the palace to change before the dinner and dance scheduled for that evening. The meeting had run long, which meant he had just enough time to change into formal wear before he and Sofía left for predinner cocktails in the palace ballroom.

His fiancée was standing in their dressing room putting a necklace on when he walked in. Her back was to him, her voluptuous body covered by a black, anklelength gown that hugged every delectable curve. It left her entire back bare, the drape of the dress swooping to almost her waist.

It was one of the dresses from her sketches. She looked devastating.

Sofía glanced over her shoulder, necklace in hand, a frustrated look on her face. "I can't get this. Can you?"

He walked toward her and took the necklace, draping it around her slim neck and fastening it easily. When he was done, she went to move away. He closed his fingers around her upper arms, holding her there. "The dress looks amazing."

She kept her gaze focused straight ahead. "Nik—"

He dropped his mouth to her smooth, bare shoulder, inhaling the heady scent of her spicy perfume. "I told you I wouldn't let you go today because I *can't* let you go, Sofía. I need you here by my side, helping me navigate my way through this. Only with you do I feel at peace."

She froze, so motionless, so still, he tightened his hands around her shoulders and turned her around. Her big, dark eyes were full of apprehension and a misery that kicked him in the chest.

She pressed her hands to her cheeks. "I can't—I need more, Nik. It's not enough for you to need me, to *want* me, because you can turn it off and on like a switch and it breaks my heart every time you retreat."

"I know. *Lypamai. I'm sorry.*" He shook his head. "You make me feel things that terrify me. That challenge everything I thought I knew about myself. About what I am capable of. And still I want you, because what I once was, I'm not anymore. I don't want that solitary existence. I want you."

Her eyes were glued to his. "What feelings are you referring to?"

He reached for her hand and curled his fingers around hers. "You were right when you said I knew you were in love with me and that I used it against you. I was scared of the emotion I had for you, afraid of what giving in to my feelings would do to my ability to make critical decisions.

So I told myself a partnership was better for us. So I could deliver on my promise to protect you, to take care of you. But then my feelings got involved and I hurt you. I didn't think I could offer you what you needed, so I backed off."

He shook his head. "I should have known it was never going to work. My feelings for you were too strong. It's why I hadn't broken things off with you in New York. Because I was beginning to care."

She frowned. "You told me you were going to cut it off."

"I hadn't given myself an end date, Sofía. That says something."

"Oh, it certainly does," she growled. "I was a possession you wanted to hang on to a bit longer. My expiration date hadn't come up. And now you want to do the same but this time because I'm carrying your child."

"No. Because I *love* you." He tightened his fingers around hers. "You asked me that night to figure out whether I have a heart, whether I could share it with you. I honestly didn't know. I've kept myself closed off for so long I didn't know what I had left in me. And then you threatened to walk away and I knew. I knew I didn't want to do this without you. That I loved you. *Yes*, I want our baby, but it's *you* I need, Sofía."

Her eyes darkened to almost black, a suspicious brightness forming in them. "What about the next crisis? And the next? I can't keep going through this vicious cycle with you."

"You won't have to. I exorcised some demons today. That need to prove myself to my father you pointed out? My need to live up to my brother's memory? Everything led to that, you were right." He shook his head. "I'm never going to be perfect, but I know now I can move on. I can focus on the present. *You*," he said huskily. "Our baby. A future I never thought I'd have."

A tear slid down her cheek. "I have been so miserable the past couple of weeks. I thought you were done with us. I thought we were over."

"We are never over," he growled. "I had to make sure my head was on straight before we had this conversation. I didn't want to make promises I couldn't keep."

"And you're sure now?"

He pulled her closer, his hands settling against her silky, bare back. "Sure. Take one more jump with me, Sofía. I promise you won't regret it."

She drifted closer to him, her dark eyes softening into that molten brown fire he loved to watch. "Is that an order, Your Highness?"

He shook his head. "No more orders. I just need you to love me."

She stood on tiptoe and brought her mouth to his. "I do, Nikandros Constantinides. More than I should."

He took her lips in a soft, seductive caress that promised her everything he had. When he lifted his mouth, she was breathless. "You still, however, need to be punished."

She frowned. "For?"

"Your Highness..."

She started to laugh, a sound he'd never been so happy to hear. "Later. We're late."

He picked her up by way of response and deposited her on the dresser. Kissed her again. This time their kiss was needy and hot, their mouths and fingers rediscovering sacred territory. He cupped her backside and pulled her to the edge of the dresser, needing to seal their pledge with the shattering intimacy only they could produce.

"Nik," she breathed, "we *can't*."

"Can't," he said, "is not a word in my vocabulary."

Her fingers found his belt buckle. Pulling it open, the button and zipper on his pants followed.

"I love you," she whispered as she arched her hips and took him deep.

He rested his forehead against hers and said those three words to her again and again until her body contracted around his and she took him to heaven.

He'd been given a second chance. He didn't intend to waste it.

Nik and his queen-to-be slipped into the cocktail hour with the other international leaders fifteen minutes late. Their absence and the blush on Sofía's cheeks were duly noted, as was her gown, which was another smash hit.

Nik stood back and watched his fiancée shine as the paparazzi flashes went mad. Her dazzling smile made his chest tighten. The king had found his heart and it was standing right in front of him.

EPILOGUE

SOFÍA RAMIREZ MARRIED Nikandros Alphaios Constantinides on a bright, sunny, perfect Akathinian day in October in the breathtakingly beautiful royal chapel that had blessed every set of royal nuptials since the monarchy's inception over two centuries ago.

Five months pregnant in her Francesco Villa strapless white satin wedding gown, featuring a three-tiered, hand-appliquéd lace overlay of different shades of ivory, HRH Queen Sofía, Duchess of Armendine, made her way down the chandelier-lit marble aisle to join her intensely handsome groom, dressed in full military regalia.

She walked down the aisle by herself behind Katharine and Stella, her two bridesmaids, dressed in elegant ice-blue gowns. It only seemed right to leave her father's place empty, because nothing could ever replace him. Her blossoming relationship with her mother, however, was something she had come to treasure as it grew with every day that passed. Sometimes things *did* change.

The Akathinian television commentators covering the royal nuptials continued to warm to their new queen as she exchanged vows with her king.

"Regal and stunningly beautiful, Sofía has blossomed in her role," they said. "Clearly she has captured the heart of our king and is well on her way to capturing the heart of the people. Although I think the real show today," the reporter added with a smile, "was watching Nikandros's face as his bride walked down the aisle."

The couple left the chapel hand in hand to the uplifting strains of Beethoven's *Ode to Joy*, retiring to the balcony of the palace to address the massive crowds. After providing a particularly passionate kiss for the photographers, something that was becoming their trademark, they were recognized with a twenty-one-gun salute.

It wasn't until they were seated at the head table in the palace ballroom, surrounded by every manner of global royalty and celebrity, that Sofía took her first real breath of the day. It had been a wonderful one, her happiness with Nik a living, breathing entity that seemed to grow stronger with every day. But she would be happy when it was just the two of them back in Evangelina on the weeklong honeymoon they had planned.

As the guests settled in, their champagne glasses full in the sparkling candlelight, Nik rose to give a toast. After thanking everyone for coming in both English and his native language, he expressed his gratitude to the Akathinian people for working through the past few trying months with him.

Following the peace summit, the international community had thrown its full support behind Akathinia and Idas had backed off his inflammatory rhetoric in the press. Should Carnelia elect to resume its opportunistic hostilities toward its smaller neighbor, Akathinia would not be alone. Nik worried the threat from the aggressive Carnelian king was not over, but a sense of calm and ordinary life had settled over the island. And for now, it was enough.

"To peace," Nik said, lifting his glass.

The guests raised their flutes and drank, a quiet gratefulness filling the air at the preservation of the independent, tranquil life they valued so deeply. Then Nik turned to his bride.

He was eloquent in his toast to her, as a man who had addressed the United Nations was wont to be, but it was his final words that drew Sofía's first tears of the day.

"I did not know how love could change a man," he said, his gaze on hers. "How much better it could make me be, until I met you, Sofía. You are my heart. *Always*."

They left the reception by helicopter in the wee hours while the guests still celebrated, the lights of Akathinia glowing beneath them as they rose high in the air. When they were close to landing on Evangelina, Nik held out his hand. "Ready?"

Nodding, she joined him at the open doorway, a bouquet of lilies in her hand that matched the bouquet Nik carried. One for her father, one for Athamos. They had not been here, but they had not been forgotten. Timing their throw, they sent the flowers scattering across the sea.

The tears came again for Sofía, silent and bittersweet. "Thank you," she murmured, wrapping her arms around Nik's neck. "That was perfect."

His eyes were as full of emotion as she'd seen them. "He knows," she whispered. "He knows."

He kissed her then as the helicopter swooped toward their hideaway. Clutching the lapel of his sexy military uniform, she held on to the moment as long as she could. These days she was living for the present, knowing with Nik by her side, no matter what arrived to test them, it would never fall apart.

Their time together in Evangelina was always perfect. She intended to make the most of every last magical second of it.

* * * * *

LET'S TALK
Romance

For exclusive extracts, competitions
and special offers, find us online:

📘 facebook.com/millsandboon

🐦 @MillsandBoon

📷 @MillsandBoonUK

Get in touch on 01413 063232

For all the latest titles coming soon, visit
millsandboon.co.uk/nextmonth